They Never DIE QUIETLY

D. M. Annechino

ISBN: 1-4392-1829-3
ISBN-13: 9781439218297

Visit www.booksurge.com to order additional copies.

To Jennifer
For your encouraging words and
unwavering support

PROLOGUE

I lie naked on the makeshift crucifix. Along the underside of my arms, down my spine, against the back of my thighs, I can feel splinters from the rough-sawn wood prickling my tender skin. My arms and ankles are bound to the crucifix with clothesline. I try to inhale a breath of the damp air, but my lungs feel oppressed, as if a heavy weight lay on my chest. My heart pounds against my ribs. He straddles my shivering body. My captor. A monster like no other. For an instant his wide-open eyes glance at my breasts. I cringe at the thought of him touching me. Then, he studies my face, searching for something; I don't know what. Perhaps he wishes to taste my fear, sip it like fine wine. I try to convince myself that this is a nightmare, that all I know about life and death and reality will exist when I awaken. But I will not awaken. I look into his eyes and see not a man, but my executioner. I no longer sob, or ask for mercy. My plea only serves to inspire and excite him. And I will not give him that satisfaction.

So this is how I will die.

I turn my head slightly and see my daughter lying on the bed. She sleeps peacefully, unaware that she will never see me again. He promises not to harm her if I do not resist, but I find little solace in his pledge. He is holding a hammer in one hand and a shinny spike in the other. I cannot imagine the level of pain I will experience when he drives the cold steel through my wrists and feet. If God is truly merciful, maybe He will lead me to a sanctuary of unconsciousness and spare me the agony.

Why does he hesitate? His pause only serves to further torment me. But yes, this is part of his game.

I fear death of course, the unknown, but the true terror lives in my still-alert mind. No one will recall my name. Linda Cassidy will be remembered as an obscure woman who made a poor choice when her car broke down. My life, all of my accomplishments and contributions to my family will fade to oblivion. I will no longer have an identity. I will be reduced to a statistic in the newspapers: Victim Number Two.

As I lie here, waiting for him to continue with his ritual, I think about the past, but more of the future, a future in which I will not participate. What will my husband tell Jennifer when she asks about her Mommy? Stephen will be devastated. I suspect it will take years for him to deal with the loss. The ointment of time may never heal his wounds. But in spite of his loss, life will go on. One day another woman will occupy my bed. She will hold him in her arms and make love to him like I did so many times. Jennifer will call *her* Mommy.

I now realize that the things most dear to me were those seemingly insignificant: reading a bedtime story to

Jennifer; cuddling next to Stephen and sharing a bowl of popcorn; picking roses from my garden; hearing red-breasted robins singing outside my bedroom window; the taste of fresh strawberries; taking my mom to her favorite buffet. Oh how I wish I had another chance to appreciate life.

"Are you ready, sinner?"

His words break the silence like a storm piercing the calm of night.

I will never be ready to die.

His eyes are different now. The corners twitch to a hideous smile. His face is beaming with purpose. In a moment of futile hope I imagine a hero, a John Wayne breaking down the door and rescuing me. I turn my head toward the door. Hoping. Praying. But this fantasy lives only in my imagination.

He presses the sharp spike against my wrist and holds the hammer in the ready position. "Are you prepared to atone for your sins?" He licks his lips as if preparing to enjoy an exquisite meal. "Do you accept Jesus as your Lord and Savior?"

This is it, Linda Cassidy. The beginning of the end.

Through blurry eyes, I quickly savor one last look at my beautiful daughter. I feel a lump grow in my throat and I can hardly suppress the tears.

Goodbye, my sweet child. I love you with all my heart.

I close my eyes and silently pray, hoping that God is indeed merciful.

ONE

Simon enjoyed this part of the hunt. His eyes were alert with the wild anticipation of another cleansing. Like a hungry alley cat stalking an injured bird, he had to wait for the perfect moment before striking.

He slumped low in the black F-150 Supercab Ford, seemingly unaware of the patrons dashing in and out of the local FoodMart. Anyone noticing him on this crisp November evening might guess that he was waiting for his wife to appear with a cart full of groceries. As he sat in the dark, enough of the bluish parking lot light spilled into the truck for him to read his favorite passage from the Bible, a passage his mother had read to him numerous times. *"He is a voice shouting in the wilderness: 'Prepare a pathway for the Lord's coming! Make a straight road for Him! Fill in the valleys, and level the mountains and hills! Straighten the curves, and smooth out the rough places! And then all people will see the salvation sent from God.'"*

Reading these words sent a chill up his spine.

As he waited impatiently, Simon felt a cramp in his lower back, a slight spasm from his intense afternoon workout. He believed in keeping his body fit as well as his soul. He adjusted his six-foot-six frame in the leather bucket seat and gently kneaded the tender muscles.

He'd been waiting for over an hour, but hadn't yet seen her. Her tardiness troubled him. A successful plan depended upon predictability.

Although he would not abduct the redhead today, he had studied her routine for over two weeks, observed her activities with the meticulous attention of a private investigator. Like clockwork, she'd race through the parking lot at seven-fifteen, squealing her tires and haphazardly maneuvering the gold BMW into two parking spaces. Always in a hurry, she'd grab her daughter from the back seat and sprint toward the supermarket.

About to abort today's surveillance, Simon looked up from the Bible and spotted the gold BMW racing toward a vacant parking spot. He glanced at his watch.

Fifteen minutes late.

As in the past, chosen ones made his heart pump fiercely. His face felt hot, ablaze, his breathing unsteady, labored. Watching her, knowing that soon she would be cleansed, overwhelmed him with a level of euphoria few people could understand. For just a moment, he closed his eyes and gently stroked the leather bucket seat, imagining that it was the woman's soft skin.

Simon loved touching people. As a physical therapist, he earned a living bending fingers and wrists and uncooperative joints. Inflicting pain through aggressive manipulation helped the healing process. Who would ever suspect anything unusual if he torqued a pinky a little too far, or bent a knee beyond its reasonable limit? How could anyone guess that his actions were anything but those prescribed by therapy? Pain, he'd been taught by his dear mother, cleansed the soul and purified one's heart. And Simon, appointed by his Creator and guided by the watchful eye of his mother, focused his efforts on the wretched women of the world. Yes, he was indeed a gifted therapist, but Simon prided himself more as a healer of souls than bodies.

She parked two rows over; close enough for him to observe her without obstruction. True to her nature, she again seemed to be racing the clock. After snatching her kid from the car seat, she half-jogged toward the twenty-four-hour FoodMart.

While studying her every movement, watching her through absorbing eyes, a new Infinity parked beside Simon's pickup. A short bald man eased out of the car with a great deal of effort, slowly stood upright, and slammed the door. From the passenger side, a young woman with a petite figure and long blond hair appeared. The man's daughter, Simon surmised. At first Simon couldn't see her face, and didn't really care what she looked like. Then, when she turned to close the door and the mercury vapor light illuminated her features, Simon's heart felt as though it had tumbled down a flight of stairs. The strikingly attractive teenager looked too much like Bonnie Jean not to be her twin.

Impossible.

Bonnie Jean would be over thirty by now, and the last he remembered she'd left Corpus Christi and relocated somewhere in the northeast. Although an uncanny likeness, he knew the resemblance was nothing more than a bizarre coincidence. Still, he felt uneasy.

As he watched the bald man grasp the young woman's hand and lead her into the FoodMart, Simon forced the haunting memory from his thoughts.

After waiting twenty minutes, he spotted the redhead hurrying a shopping cart toward her car. He snapped a mental picture.

"Not today," he whispered. "In time, chosen one."

Today, he watched and plotted. The redhead's cleansing would come soon enough.

Another sinner currently awaited salvation in Simon's Room of Redemption.

With flushed cheeks and knotted muscles along the top of his shoulders, Simon left San Diego, hopped onto Freeway 8, and headed for his home in Alpine. Plagued by an urgency to get home, an inexorable desire to cleanse another soul, he ignored the speed limit and drove in the passing lane. He slammed his clenched fist on the dashboard.

Sinners will have no place among the Godly.

Again, memories of Bonnie Jean Oliver flooded his mind.

He exited the freeway, turned left, drove seven miles along a narrow winding road dotted with farmhouses, dilapidated barns, and acres of open fields. Unlike near the coast, with ocean breezes, palm trees and knotted traffic, East County looked like any other rural community. He pulled into his long, gravel-covered driveway, pushed the button on the remote garage door opener, and sat in his truck for a moment.

Blood would flow tonight.

Fumbling with his keys, he got out of the pickup and walked toward the garage. A heavy fog hovered over the countryside; a smoky mist clung to the earth like smoldering embers. The damp air smelled of freshly cut timber. Samson, Simon's three-year-old chocolate Labrador retriever spotted his owner and his tail swatted the plastic trash barrel with a steady tempo. As predictable as San Diego sunshine, the anxious dog started moaning and doing his semi-circle-samba.

"How's my big boy?" Simon knelt on the garage floor and let Samson lick his face. "Ready for dinner?"

Simon tipped the forty-pound bag of food and filled Samson's stainless steel bowl. With the garden hose he gave the dog fresh water, then unlocked the kitchen door.

Except for updated fixtures in the two bathrooms, and a do-it-yourself kitchen the prior owner had put together with cheap materials, second hand cabinets, and a total lack of skill, Simon's modest home, built in nineteen-twenty-six, had never been completely remodeled. From the gaudy flowered wallpaper to the badly worn and yellowed linoleum, the interior of the house was in a state of disrepair. The poor condition of the home caused Simon great angst. For years he'd been a neat-freak, a man obsessed with impeccable surroundings. He enjoyed cooking gourmet meals and furnishing his home with tasteful décor; traits that would solicit his mother's approval. His mother would often quote the hackneyed proverb, "Cleanliness is next to Godliness," but always added, "There's no sweepin' your sins under the carpet in *my* house."

When he first moved to San Diego from Texas, he rented a condo near the ocean, close to Bayshore Hospital where he worked. But his daily jogs on the beach offered far too many opportunities for sinful thoughts. Scantily dressed, the young women parading up and down the boardwalk, their bodies barely covered, were too much of a temptation. By his own pathetic admission, he recognized his weaknesses, and had no desire to give Satan the advantage. Besides, he needed a remote dwelling, a sanctuary with plenty of acreage and wide-open spaces between houses. He moved to the country, where his closest neighbors lived over a mile away, far enough so they could never hear the helpless screams of the chosen ones.

They never die quietly.

Simon had not chosen this particular house for its beauty. Its full basement, an essential feature required for his holy work, distinguished it from most Southern California homes. With thoughtful construction and strategic soundproofing, Simon converted the musty, dank basement into the perfect Room of Redemption.

He reached in the refrigerator, grabbed a bottle of sparkling water and poured a tall glass. The door to the basement was off the kitchen, down the hallway. Carrying the glass of water, he flipped the light switch, and negotiated his way down the narrow stairway. The basement, higher than most, built with twelve courses of concrete blocks, allowed Simon to walk upright with at least eight inches between his head and the floor joists. Before unlocking the soundproof door, Simon peeked into the security lens he had installed so he could monitor the activities of his guests. About to turn the dead bolt lock, he stopped, closed his eyes, and could see a vision of the woman he'd just seen at FoodMart.

Bonnie Jean Oliver.

She'd been Simon's classmate and next door neighbor. He remembered her pigtails, dimples, eyes as green as jade, and the day she'd invited him to her house after school. Her parents were both working. They'd been listening to The Rolling Stones, munching potato chips, sipping Cokes, talking about school and homework.

Simon, on the threshold of puberty, could feel his hormones pumping vigorously. Curious about young blossoming girls—particularly Bonnie Jean, who had always been his favorite—Simon surrendered to temptation and ignored his mother's relentless warnings about sins of the flesh. He never intended to be so forward, but he could not stop his hand from caressing Bonnie Jean's tiny breast.

Her reaction both aroused and enraged Simon. Any self-respecting young woman should have been mortified at such a blatant act of wickedness. Instead of stopping Simon with a well-deserved smack in the nose, Bonnie Jean's lips curled to a smile. She clutched his hand, and guided it under her skirt, between her warm thighs.

Simon froze.

Bonnie Jean pressed her moist lips against Simon's mouth, and her tongue found its way past his teeth. Without warning, another self, one Simon had never known, took control. He pushed her away, knocking her backward. Bonnie Jean took one look at his grotesque expression and must have sensed that mortal danger loomed. She tried to flee, but Simon, his body hyped with sexual anxiety, grabbed a fistful of her long blond hair and viciously yanked her to the floor. What happened after that, Simon could not recall, not even today, twenty years later. He only remembered visiting Bonnie Jean in the hospital, watching in total puzzlement as she squirmed at the sight of him as if he were a poisonous snake. No one ever found out who had beaten her so brutally, stomped on her face, broken her nose. Only after Simon found bloody fragments of her left breast in his Levi's pocket did he realize he had been her assailant. In constant fear that Simon would disfigure her further, or even kill her, Bonnie Jean never told anyone what had happened.

Simon shook his head as if to erase his thoughts of Bonnie Jean. Visions of this incident often plagued him. He'd never been able to recreate the entire scene. But snapshots of the incident would assault his memory forever.

He turned the key in the dead bolt, unlocked the steel fire door and stepped into the room, closing and securing the door behind him. Molly sat on the bed with Benjamin on her lap. Reading aloud, she didn't look up from the book.

"Are we going home now, Mommy?" The three-year-old tugged on her sleeve.

"Soon, honey."

Simon had designed the Room of Redemption like a studio apartment. It had a full bath, a modestly appointed kitchen with a small refrigerator, a compact microwave, and well-stocked cupboards; a self-contained environment that could adequately support life for an indefinite period of time. He'd been careful choosing the utensils and other supplies. He didn't want an overly-heroic guest inventing a makeshift weapon.

From the half-filled glass Simon carried, he filled his mouth with water and swallowed hard. "Have you eaten anything?"

"Benjamin had mac and cheese," Molly said.

"And you?"

She gave him a cold stare. "No appetite."

In the corner of the studio Simon had equipped a recreation area with enough play things to amuse the most discriminating youngster: a television with an assortment of Nintendo games, coloring books with assorted crayons, building blocks, stuffed animals—all the essentials to keep a child occupied while Simon had serious conversations with their mommies.

"Benjamin," Simon said, "go into the play area."

"I wanna stay with Mommy." He hung his head and pouted.

Not wanting to antagonize her captor, Molly brushed the hair out of Benjamin's eyes and gave him a reassuring smile. "It's okay, honey. Do what he says." He moseyed over to the play area and turned on the television. Simon sat on the bed next to Molly.

"Why are you holding us prisoners?"

Simon sipped his water. "Do you love your son?"

"That's a ridiculous question."

"How much?"

"You expect me to measure my love?"

Simon grabbed her knee and firmly squeezed it. "Indeed."

The thirty-two-year-old blonde's voice was unsteady. "What do you want from us?"

"Would you do anything for your son?"

She glared at him with contempt. "What are you getting at?"

"I want Benjamin to go upstairs with me."

"You're out of your mind." *Of course he's out of his mind. Be careful, girl.*

"Don't test me."

"If you think for one minute . . ."

"You're making me angry, Molly." His voice remained calm "Do you want to feel the fury of God?"

She considered his threat. "Why upstairs?"

"I have my reasons."

"I'll bet you do."

Simon's eyes narrowed. "Would you rather I dragged him upstairs by his hair?"

She had no options. Perhaps if she cooperated . . .

❦

Simon reached into the refrigerator, removed a carton of milk, and poured it into a tall glass. "You like chocolate milk, Benjamin?"

"I love it!"

After pouring Hershey's Syrup into the milk-filled glass, Simon added a small quantity of powder. He stirred the mixture vigorously, making certain the mild sedative completely dissolved. He handed the glass to Benjamin. "Milk will make you grow tall."

Benjamin grabbed the glass. "Will it make me tall like you?"

"Only if you drink it all."

৵

Molly hopelessly pounded on the steel door with both fists. "Where *are* you, you son-of-a-*bitch*? Benjamin, can you hear me? Oh God, oh God, what have I done?" Simon had left with her son over an hour ago. How stupid of her to trust him. But did she really have a choice? She had to keep telling herself she didn't or else she'd lose her mind.

Screaming for over half an hour, her throat felt raw and on fire. Where could he have taken Benjamin? Why didn't anyone hear her screaming and come to her rescue? Feeling faint and out-of-her-mind frantic, she collapsed on the bed, sucking air in quivering gasps, tears streaming down her cheeks.

Three days ago, when the tire had gone flat and she pulled her Grand Cherokee to the side of the road, she tried calling her husband on his cell phone, but she'd been unable to reach him. She'd left him a message, but Robert had never been one to check his voice mail regularly. She'd never changed a flat in her life and had no idea what to do. When the guy in the black pickup stopped and offered help, he seemed to be a godsend. Acting like a perfect gentleman, handsome, refined, he looked like an athlete. How naive she'd been.

"Ma'am, I'm afraid your spare's flat too. There's a service station about a mile down the road. I'd be happy to give you a lift."

Over the last three days she'd had plenty of time to think. Had it not been for Benjamin, she would have completely lost her mind. Simon's conduct did not fit the mold of a madman. His quietness, his calm demeanor, almost schoolboy politeness puzzled Molly. Something wild brewed behind those ice-blue eyes. He had not behaved like a raving lunatic. Nonetheless, a demon lived inside him. Why would he kidnap them, lock them in this dungeon with all the basic amenities necessary to sustain life, and do *nothing*?

He hadn't tried to assault her, he'd been kind to Benjamin, and strangely seemed to be genuinely concerned with their comfort. He had, no doubt, a hidden agenda not yet revealed. He hadn't kidnapped them to treat them like guests. Then it occurred to her: a child molester.

She lay on the pillow, closed her eyes, and silently prayed. The thought was too much for her to bear.

∽

Half-asleep, Molly heard the key turn in the door. She stood up and felt a wave of dizziness. Wearing a carpenter's apron with a hammer hanging from his hip, Simon entered the Room of Redemption. Under his arm were two long four-by-fours, one twice as long as the other. He dropped them on the concrete floor.

"Where's my *fucking* son?"

"Watch your mouth."

"I want to see him, *now*!"

"He's fine."

"You're a liar!"

"And you are a sinner."

"Don't you dare judge me, you son-of-a-bitch!"

"Only God can judge you."

"Fuck you!"

Simon rushed toward her and Molly backpedaled, falling onto the bed. He stood over her and extended his hand. But she flinched, expecting him to strike her.

"It's time, Molly." His eyes were different. They glared at her with a penetrating intensity. It felt as if they were touching her skin. "Will you do anything to protect your son?"

Now she understood. She almost smiled. "That's what this charade is all about. You want to fuck me, don't you?"

He grabbed a fistful of her hair, his body trembling with rage. "Remove your clothes, sinner."

"You'll have to kill me first."

He turned and stomped toward the door. "Best that you cherish your memories of Benjamin." He turned the key in the lock. "You're never going to see him again."

"No! Please!" Molly clasped her hands as if in prayer. "I'll do whatever you ask."

Simon stopped just long enough to get a glimpse of the resignation in Molly's eyes. To surrender unconditionally, without resistance was the only way God would cleanse chosen ones' souls. "I know you will."

❧

Waiting alone in the dimly lit Room of Redemption, her eyes focused on the soon-to-be-built crucifix, Molly felt utter agony. Not knowing what the monster had planned for her son served only to heighten her torment. At this very moment, her captor could be doing the unspeakable to Benjamin. He'd always been such a fragile child. She began to sob, trying to suppress her emotions, fighting desperately to remove the vivid images from her mind, but she could not stop the visions or the flood of tears. For a breathless moment, Molly pressed her palms together and fell to her knees. She prayed to a God who had not been part of her life since childhood, a God who had taken her mother away when Molly was only seven years old. She had never been able to forgive her Creator for such a cruel misdeed. But now, at the threshold of death, an event grisly beyond anything she could imagine, she appealed to the only force in the universe with the power to rescue her.

"I don't care what he does to me, dear Lord. But please, I beg you, protect my son."

Strangely, a vision of Dorothy, from *The Wizard of Oz*, flashed through Molly's mind. She could see the young girl staring at the rapidly-draining hourglass, eyes wide with fear, waiting for the Wicked Witch to return. This was not a movie though. There were no Scarecrow, Tin-Man or Cowardly Lion to save her. Only a madman.

The metal door squeaked open. She looked into Simon's eyes and knew for certain that the hourglass had drained.

∽

Still sleepy from his sedative-induced nap, Benjamin asked, "Where we going?"

Simon smiled and buckled the seat belt around the three-year-old. "For a ride."

"Where's my mommy?"

"She's with God."

The boy thought for a moment. "You mean the God up in heaven?"

"He's the only God."

"When she comin' back?"

For a moment, Simon thought about lying. Under the circumstances, God would surely forgive him this one sin. But to preserve the innocent child's feelings was only a temporary solution. A lie would create false hope. "Never, Benjamin."

The young boy twisted his knuckles in his eyes and started to whimper. Simon opened the center console and pulled out a Tootsie Roll Pop. "You like cherry?"

Benjamin nodded. Simon removed the wrapping and handed it to the boy.

The boy grabbed the sucker, licked it several times, and then took it out of his mouth. "I wanna see my mommy."

"Some day you will."

He drove west on Freeway 8 and exited on Mission Center Road. At eight-forty, almost closing time, he pulled into the entrance leading to Grossman's Department Store. There were only a dozen cars in the parking lot. Simon stopped the truck in front of the main doors and turned on the emergency flashers. He adjusted his Padres baseball cap so the visor rested just above his eyes. He handed Benjamin a piece of paper.

"Do me a favor."

The little boy looked at him curiously.

Simon unfastened Benjamin's seat belt, and opened the passenger's door. "See that man standing inside the store." He pointed to a security guard leaning against a pillar. "It's very important that you give him that piece of paper. Your mommy wants you to. Can you do that?"

"For mommy?"

"Yes."

Benjamin balanced his unsteady legs on the aluminum running boards and struggled to the sidewalk.

Simon pulled the door shut. Before walking through the entrance, Benjamin stopped and looked over his shoulder. A young man wearing a baseball cap backwards, his jeans five sizes too big, held the door open for him. Benjamin shuffled inside. He jerked his head from side to side, as if looking for something unknown to Simon. Then, with his arms outstretched and the piece of paper between his tiny fingers, he made a beeline for the security guard as if he were the boy's favorite uncle. Simon watched the boy hand over the note. He stepped on the accelerator and sped toward the exit.

TWO

Homicide Investigator Sami Rizzo, the only woman to reach the rank of detective in the Major Offense Squad, marched over to her partner's desk, sat on the corner, and dropped a manila folder, almost knocking over his cup of coffee. Her black shoulder-length hair, with just a few strands of gray, was pulled back and held with a tortoise shell barrette. Her blue eyes were slightly bloodshot from her contact lenses.

"Take a look at these, Al. They'll really make you want to finish that jelly donut." She crossed her shapely legs and her skirt rode up just enough to catch her partner's always-wandering eyes. "Look at the pictures, Al. The *pictures*."

Alberto Diaz grinned and opened the folder. He took another bite of his half-eaten donut and examined the graphic photos of the woman's mutilated body. By his impassive reaction, Sami felt like she'd just handed him a feature article in *Food & Wine* magazine.

"Where'd they find her?"

"On the front steps of Holy Redeemer Church in La Mesa."

"Just like the other two?"

"This one was a blond, but she has the same wounds."

Diaz grabbed his lukewarm coffee and gulped it. Only thirty-two-years old, his attractive baby-face, always clean shaven, was almost pretty. Taller than most Mexican-Americans, Alberto Diaz maintained a lean and muscular body. He had a thick head of jet-black hair and his dark eyes were as slick as oil. "Has she been identified?"

Sami shook her head.

After spending ten years as a patrol officer, working out of the toughest precinct in South San Diego, earning three commendations for outstanding service, Sami Rizzo vied for a promotion. Ferocious competition raged among uniformed officers pursuing a detective appointment in San Diego. And of course sexism, rampant within the law enforcement community, made her quest even more formidable. But Sami aced the written test, proving that her knowledge of law, procedures, and the investigative process was unparalleled. Following the written test, a board of senior officers grilled Sami during what was called an interview, but more accurately was an intense interrogation. Their goal: to test her resolve under pressure. Sami thought she'd done poorly in front of the board. Two weeks later she'd gotten a call from Chief of Detectives Larson, welcoming her to the homicide squad.

Diaz opened the folder again and removed one of the photographs. He stared at it intently. "What do you suppose he does with their hearts?"

"I'd rather not think about it."

"Anything on the kid?"

"Not a word."

"He doesn't do the kids," Diaz offered. "Think he's changed his routine?"

"Let's hope not."

Captain Carl Davison, standing just outside his office, yelled across the room, "Diaz, Rizzo, in my office!"

The two homicide detectives hurried down the narrow isle between rows of messy desks. Their fellow detectives were huddled in groups, talking about cases and sharing the sordid details of last night's sexual escapades. As Sami negotiated her way past them, she could feel their eyes giving her the once-over. Normally, this wouldn't bother her, but today she felt a bit self-conscious. John Russell, a particularly obnoxious colleague, grinning like a crazed chimpanzee, held out his hand. "Nice knowing you, Rizzo."

"Wish I could say the same, asshole."

The Major Offense Squad comprised six sections: arson, burglary, homicide, robbery, sex crimes, and a special investigative squad responsible for extraordinary situations involving government officials, other officers, or investigations with high media coverage. Sami and Diaz had been warned by Captain Davison that if they did not apprehend the killer soon, he would be forced to turn the case over to the special investigative squad.

They entered the captain's office, and Sami noticed an unfamiliar woman seated opposite her boss. The woman eyeballed Sami curiously, as if to warn her that Diaz and she had better prepare themselves for a not-so-pleasant powwow.

Sami closed the door.

On occasion, Davison, a usually soft-spoken African-American, had the capacity to tear into the hides of overworked and under appreciated detectives. Sami studied his eyes and felt certain that today's little get together would not be pleasant.

Never caring much about state ordinances, particularly when his frazzled nerves needed a soothing blast of nicotine, Davison grabbed the burning cigarette resting in the over-full ashtray and deeply inhaled. The captain, two years from retirement, tipped the scales at two-thirty-five, forty pounds over his ideal weight. To look at him, he didn't appear to be over-stressed, and in spite of his usually calm demeanor, his blood pressure recently hit a level that forced his doctor to insist he take medication to control it. You'd never know it to look at him, but he was a walking time bomb.

"I'd like you two to meet Sally Whitman," Davison said. "She's a profiler with the FBI."

Sally stood up, pivoted gracefully, grasped Sami's hand and vigorously pumped the homicide detective's arm. The willowy, middle-aged profiler had a grip like Wonder Woman. She wore her dark brown hair severely short, almost buzz cut. High cheek bones and a pointed chin punctuated her narrow face. Wearing a trendy outfit, she could easily be mistaken for a punk-rock groupie. A couple of plates of her mother's lasagna,

Sami thought, and Sally could gain just enough weight to have a figure.

Ever so slowly, her fingers lingering a little longer than Sami thought reasonable, Whitman let go of Sami's hand. Something in Whitman's eyes troubled Sami. Whitman gave Diaz an acknowledging nod, but didn't offer her hand.

"Considering the lack of progress in apprehending this lunatic," Davison said, "I have enlisted the services of Ms. Whitman. Hopefully, she can offer some insights into the mind of a serial killer."

Serial Killer?

Although three women had been murdered—all presumably the same way—no one in the homicide squad dared to mouth the term serial killer. It was taboo, as if a curse would befall the first person to say the words. The possibility had been hinted in the *San Diego Chronicle*. And one television newscaster's overzealous commentary had caused widespread alarm among local residents, but no one had officially classified the three murders as a serial.

To use this term so matter-of-factly, struck a raw nerve in Sami. All her life she'd lived in San Diego, touted to be America's Finest City, and to the best of her recollection the area had not been terrorized by a serial killer since nineteen-thirty-two.

The captain crushed his cigarette in the ashtray. "Tell the detectives what we're dealing with, Ms. Whitman."

The FBI profiler sat, crossed her legs, and tucked her skirt under her thighs in a proper fashion, never taking her eyes off Sami. "The man we're looking for is a religious fanatic. They're the worst, because most of them believe that God has empowered them with absolute authority. When a murderer is driven by some perverse religious belief, his cruelty has no limits. With God's endorsement, each one believes he has his own set of twisted commandments. In this case we don't know if the perpetrator is doing God's work or Satan's. Sometimes there's a really fine line."

Whitman pointed to one of the victim's photographs. "There's little doubt the women were crucified. The pathologist's report indicates that tiny splinters of wood along with traces of metal were found in the wrist and foot wounds. The wood is white pine and the metal is alloy steel, probably from whatever kind of spikes or nails he used. My guess is he's either crucifying them as an offering to his God, emulating Jesus' death on the cross, or belittling the foundation of Christianity by performing mock crucifixions."

An air of silence descended upon the room. Diaz grabbed Sami's shoulder and gave it a reassuring squeeze.

"Could he be a women hater?" Diaz offered. "Maybe he's pissed off at his ex-wife and taking it out on other women."

"That's unlikely, detective," Whitman said. "Women haters typically de-feminize their victims by cutting off their breasts or sticking objects in their vaginas. Granted, he did have intercourse with each victim, but I'm thinking that the sex was part of some warped ritual."

"Any idea why he would cut out their hearts?" Diaz asked.

Whitman fixed her eyes on the detective. "He probably collects them. Keeps them as trophies."

"What about the children?" Sami asked. "Why weren't they harmed?"

"In his twisted mind they served some purpose," Whitman said, "but I can only speculate." She studied the photograph. "Maybe he used the children as pawns to get what he wanted."

"I'm not following you," Diaz said. "We've already established that the killer is a big man. Surely he could overpower these women. Why did he need the kids?"

Whitman adjusted her glasses. "Control. Maybe he doesn't want them to fight."

Ordinarily, Sami could manage her emotions, but as a single parent of a soon-to-be three-year-old daughter, she could not help but feeling great anguish. Careful not to expose her mental state to the captain, she tried not to make eye contact with him.

"What really bothers me," Whitman continued, "is that the killer is a sociopath."

Her eyes focused on something afar. "In some instances, victims are mutilated after death. But this is not the case with these women. They were alive, perhaps conscious when he crucified them."

With that statement, the room was as quiet as a mortuary. Davison lit another cigarette, and Diaz coughed into his hand. Sami wanted to be anywhere but in this office.

"Ms. Whitman, could you give me a moment with the detectives." Davison said.

Sally Whitman placed the folder in her brown leather briefcase, eyeballed Sami, and quietly left the office. Sami knew what came next. She'd seen this metamorphosis before.

The minute Whitman closed the door, Captain Davison stood up and wagged his finger at the two detectives. "You know how I hate to be a hard-ass, but the mayor is chewing on my nuts. You two will still lead the investigation, but I'm assigning a special task force to assist you." The captain swiped his hand across his moist forehead. "You've got to find this psycho."

"He's a shrewd one, Captain," Diaz said, "carefully covered his tracks."

The veins on Davison's neck were pulsing. His cheeks flushed. "Don't tell me that this fucking fanatic can crucify women, dump their bodies on the front steps of local churches, and drop their kids off at department stores without *somebody* seeing *something*."

Davison sucked on the cigarette and exhaled a cloud of blue smoke. "Get your butts to La Mesa and talk to the priest who found . . ."

The telephone rang. The captain snatched the receiver. "Davison. Yeah. When? Where?" He scribbled on a yellow pad. "Okay, thanks."

Sami could see the captain's face change. Like a violent storm, quelled by some mysterious wonder of nature, the captain lost his thunder.

"They found the kid." His voice softened. "The victim's name is . . ." he glanced at his notes. ". . . Molly Singer, thirty-two-year's-old."

"Did he hurt the kid?" Diaz asked.

"Just like the other two: not a scratch on him." The captain removed his glasses and massaged his temples. "Please find this fucking wacko."

ৎ৯

After cleansing a sinner, Simon had difficulty falling asleep. Neither guilt nor regret kept him awake. Why should he feel remorse after saving a soul from certain damnation? His restlessness resulted from a bitter reality: how could he possibly cleanse a world so infested with doomed women? One man, no matter how committed, could not tackle such a formidable task.

He sat up in bed and pulled his knees to his chest, wondering if his mother felt pride for her only son. Perhaps she sat beside God, watching down from the heavens, pleased with the path he followed. Had it not been for her stern hand, and love-driven discipline, Simon might himself be a hopeless sinner. How many hours had he spent punished in that dark, claustrophobic closet, atoning for his misdeeds?

As a child, Simon had often broken the commandments of God. His mother never scolded him. She pointed to the closet without uttering a word, and he knew exactly what to do. The cubbyhole had no light. He was allowed neither food nor water. Just plenty of time to reflect on his unholy behavior. He had to urinate and excrete in the corner of the cramped closet. The area, so confined, caused him to gag and vomit from the foul smell. Often his clothing would be soaked with his bodily discharge.

In the summer, when the Texas temperatures flirted with triple digits and the humidity felt unbearable, Simon sometimes believed he would suffocate in that closet, die a sinner, unredeemed and sentenced to eternal punishment. This inflicted greater torture than his physical pain. There were moments of sheer terror, a helpless belief that God would never absolve his sins. The period of time in which his mother incarcerated him depended upon the severity of his waywardness. There were sins that required only an hour's punishment. Others confined him to the closet for more than a day.

Once, shortly after celebrating his eleventh birthday, when his budding sexual awareness reached a new level, he'd borrowed a *Playboy* magazine from a schoolmate—the same young lad who introduced Simon to the joy of self-fulfillment. While sitting in bed one rainy afternoon, gawking at the blond centerfold with enormous breasts and neatly trimmed pubic hair, thinking his mother worked busily with her daily chores, Simon stimulated himself with unwavering enthusiasm. So preoccupied with his intended goal, he hadn't noticed his mother standing in the doorway.

"The lips of an immortal woman are as sweet as honey, and her mouth is smoother than oil. But the result is as bitter as poison, sharp as a double-edged sword."

That day, in mid-August, Simon felt certain he would surely die in the closet.

An eerie feeling of hollowness, a void of excruciating proportions crashed over Simon. He clutched his stomach with both hands, feeling as though he were impaled with a sword. The desperation emulated the same panic a drug addict might experience when the exhilaration from his chemical-induced euphoria plunges to the depths of despair and need, when all sense of reason disappears. Simon rocked back and forth on the bed, moaning, feeling the profound impact of withdrawal. The only medicine to ease his pain was to cleanse another soul. The redhead he'd been watching would soon occupy the Room of Redemption.

༄

At six-thirty, Detective Sami Rizzo swung by the precinct, dropped off Diaz, and headed for her mother's home in North Park. She wasn't in the mood to face Captain Davison. Their trip to Le Mesa hadn't yielded anything close to a lead; the priest offered little help, and the neighbors they'd interviewed hadn't witnessed anything worthwhile.

She pulled into the driveway and parked the Taurus next to her mother's worn out Buick. As soon as Sami stepped into the living room, Angelina came charging out of the kitchen with that awkward gait of a not-yet-nimble toddler, and gave Sami's knees a bear hug. "Mommy, mommy, me and grandma made brownies!"

Sami sniffed the air, but the smell of spaghetti sauce masked the scent of chocolate. She picked up her two-year-old and kissed her on the cheek. "I'll bet they're yummy. How many have you eaten?"

Angelina held up two fingers.

"You didn't spoil your dinner, did you?" Sami glanced at her mother who was leaning against the doorjamb leading to the kitchen, her arms folded across her chest

"She has her grandpa's hollow leg. Rest his soul. No need to worry about her appetite."

Josephine Rizzo, a portly woman with beefy arms and a round shiny face, stood barely five-foot-tall. Her mostly-gray hair, with a hint of black still surviving a trying life and decades of hard work, twisted into a neat bun. At night, just before bedtime, she'd let her hair hang freely to the small of her back and stroke it a hundred times.

"The sauce is almost done," Josephine said. "Want to stay for dinner? I made *gnocchi.*"

Sami wanted to go home and spend some time alone with Angelina, away from her mother and shopworn stories about how things might have been had Sami's father not died of lung cancer before his forty-fifth birthday. Besides, Sami had not been pleased with her figure of late—nothing new of course—and her mother's delicious *gnocchis,* packed with complex carbs were the last thing her body needed. In her father's charming way he had often reminded Sami of her less-than-Barbie-Doll-figure. Coming from anyone else, she would have been monumentally insulted. But she adored her dad. She had spent her life trying to be the son he never fostered.

Since surviving the awkward years of puberty, Sami had blossomed into a strikingly attractive woman, often catching the attention of an admiring eye. In spite of her in-home aerobics and three-times-a-week jog through Balboa Park, her nemesis had always been her hips. The bottom half of her hourglass figure was slightly disproportionate to her torso. She was probably the only one who noticed this. In fact, most men preferred woman with hips. At least that's what she'd heard. Still, Sami would have been much happier if God had been a little less generous in the hip area.

About to decline her mother's offer, Sami could see the neediness in Josephine Rizzo's eyes. "Sure, Mom, we'd love to join you."

Holding her soundly-sleeping daughter like a sack of flour, Sami struggled to turn the key in the front-door lock. She'd never been a fastidious housekeeper, but lately her house looked like a tribe of party-loving teenagers hung out there. With the exception of her mother, who had no reservations about condemning Sami's untidy domain, and Diaz, her true buddy, she rarely had company. The condition of the house didn't bother Angelina, so why live like the Vanderbilt's?

She dropped her briefcase on the cluttered coffee table, kicked her way past toys, magazines, and an assortment of obstacles, negotiated her way up the stairs, and set her daughter on the bed. Careful not to wake her, Sami undressed Angelina, tucked her in, kissed her on the forehead, and flipped on the Cookie Monster night-light. Before leaving, Sami stood over her daughter and watched her peacefully sleeping. That little face, lovely as it was, resembled Angelina's father. Asswipe Extraordinaire is what Sami called him. Not in front of Angelina of course. But she didn't mind sharing that pet name with the rest of the free world. Just thinking about the non-child-support-paying-bum infuriated her. So much for birth control pills and their ninety-nine percent effectiveness.

Sami went into the kitchen and snagged an ice-cold Corona from the almost-empty refrigerator. She could smell leftover Chinese food three days past its destiny with the garbage disposal. The only lime in the fridge had more fuzz growing on it than a baby chick, so she opted to enjoy the beer without its usual complement. She found a vacant spot on the sofa and plopped on the badly worn cushion. She kicked off her shoes and took a long swig of the beer. Sami had intended to preserve her much-needed quiet time and forget about the investigation, but her briefcase beckoned. She flipped it open and reluctantly removed the inch-thick file.

Each of the three brutally-murdered young women had been in their early-thirties. And they all had been abducted along with their young children. The children, interviewed under the careful supervision of a child psychologist, had not been visibly injured. This confused Sami. Why would a barbaric killer kidnap the kids and let them go unharmed? Not even Sally Whitman, a professional profiler could answer this question.

The children offered several significant details: one said that his mother and he stayed in the basement of a home in the country, and that a nice man let them play with all kinds of fun toys in this special room. One boy said the man stood a foot taller than his dad, and remembered that the man drove a big black truck. Another girl said he was white with blue eyes and light brown hair and that he was handsome.

Sami set down the file and cleared a space on the cocktail table. She placed the graphic photos of the three victims side by side and examined them carefully, observing the similarities. The women—at least based on several assumptions—had been murdered the same way. There were round holes, one-half inch in diameter through both wrists, just above the palms, and identical holes through both feet, right at the instep. The women's hearts had been cut out of their chest cavities with surgical precision, and did not look like the work of an unskilled hack. Obviously, the perp had some formal medical training.

Looking at the gaping wounds in the victims' ribs, overwhelmed Sami with a feeling of nausea. She set down the photos and guzzled the remaining beer. The gruesome photographs of three young mothers with hopes and dreams and children to nurture, savagely

murdered, walloped Sami with both profound anger
and fear. She'd witnessed her share of savagery, a part
of the human condition beyond her ability to understand, but these murders aroused a terror in her unlike
ever before. How she wished her father were still alive.
A firm hug from him could change her world.

Angelo Rizzo had been a policeman for eighteen
years, and for Sami to become a homicide detective was
her father's dying wish. "Sami," he'd whispered, lying in
a hospital bed, barely ninety pounds. "Do it for me, for
your *padre*."

He had dreamed of a promotion to detective status,
but never made it out of the blue uniform. Sami, an
only child, had aspired to the role of the son her father
desperately longed for. How could any daughter deny
her father's last request? At times, Sami believed she'd
been held accountable for her father's inability to follow Italian tradition by producing a son. He had never
accused her, but the undertone hung in the air every
time her mother reminded Sami that since her birth,
she simply could no longer conceive.

Not knowing how much pressure he had placed on
his only daughter to play the role as his son, Angelo
Rizzo shortened his daughter's name from Samantha
to Sami before her first birthday. Sami had no memories of dance lessons or trips to Peterson's Department
Store shopping for pretty Easter dresses. Instead she'd
been the neighborhood tomboy, her father's fishing
companion. When she'd announced that she wanted to
be a social worker, her father gave her "the look," and

she knew her aspiration would never come to pass. Her father's lofty expectations had been important to Sami. He wanted her to become a cop, ultimately a detective. She had honored his request, but to do so she had to suppress her own desires.

Samantha Rizzo's life had been neatly planned long before her birth. And although detective work did not truly suit her character, Sami found solace in the utopian belief that she could make a difference. She approached police work with an ironic blend of undaunted courage and naive expectation. Her efforts and performance as a detective were neither diluted nor compromised by the fact that her father's relentless crusade had forced her into a career she'd not chosen. In the wake of these feelings of displacement and the ever-present regret that she hadn't followed her heart's ambition, was a woman well respected by her male comrades. Teasing and sexual harassment aside, no one would argue that Samantha Rizzo was one hell of a cop.

At this particular moment, however, she was hypnotized by the bitter reality that these pictures represented a world beyond redemption. And this helpless desperation caused her to feel less effective than ever before. She turned over the photographs and forced herself to continue reading the written report.

There were no visible signs of throat or neck trauma, yet the victims died from asphyxiation, which is the cause of death with crucified victims who do not succumb from blood loss. Semen had been detected in their vaginas, but there was no physical evidence that any of the women had been raped. Normally, with forcible intercourse the tissue is bruised or noticeably damaged. It didn't seem possible that these women would have agreed to consensual sex with their assailant, but there existed no basis to prove otherwise.

Sami examined the photographs again.

Wrist wounds. Just above the palms.

Foot wounds. Right at the instep.

Sami glanced at the crucifix hanging on the wall across from her, an essential embellishment her mother insisted upon. A cold fist closed around her heart. Until now she had not clearly understood the magnitude of this investigation. Alone with her menacing thoughts, a million miles away from serenity, she understood why her feelings had been so fiercely roused. The mere thought of these women being crucified paralyzed her, assaulted her senses with unimaginable images. She'd been born and raised a Roman Catholic, familiar with the dynamics of the church and the teachings of the Bible. At this particular moment, she wished she were a heathen. The killer's motives were beyond the realm of human comprehension. And if Sami didn't find a way to stop him, soon, perhaps before the sun peeked over the eastern horizon, another innocent, unsuspecting woman would be nailed to a cross.

THREE

On Thanksgiving morning, a gloomy, chilly day by San Diego standards, Sami bundled up Angelina and drove to her mother's house. For the past five years, Sami had volunteered at Katie's Kitchen, where she served hearty Thanksgiving dinners to the less fortunate. It had been a tradition in her family to begin holiday dinners midday, so Sami's benevolence did not conflict with this practice. She had plenty of time to offer her services and then enjoy dinner with her mother and daughter.

"When are you coming back, Mommy?" Angelina sat securely in the car seat.

Sami pulled into her mother's driveway and turned off the ignition. "In a couple of hours, honey."

"Is Grandma cooking turkey and smashed potatoes and punkin pie?"

Sami nodded, unable to suppress the chuckle. "That's *MASH*ed potatoes and *PUMP*kin pie, sweetheart."

After greeting her mom, gulping a cup of coffee, kissing Angelina goodbye, and withstanding yet another query into why she should care about people who were lazy leaches of society, Sami drove to South San Diego, an area of modest homes and people of limited means.

Katie's Kitchen was in an old church that had been a vacant eyesore for over a decade. Katie O'Leary, a seventy-ish woman of limited financial reserves, an ailing back, and a lifetime of good deeds credited to her resume, began her crusade in a tiny home on Delta Street, three blocks away. With little assistance, she prepared huge pots of soup, chili, spaghetti sauce—anything she could afford—and go out into the streets searching for the homeless. It didn't take long for word of her kindhearted generosity to spread among the close-knit society of less fortunate souls. In less than a month, Katie found more empty stomachs than she could fill. Jake Stevens, a young reporter for *The San Diego Chronicle,* a veteran of the Peace Corps and other humanitarian organizations, heard about Katie's campaign. After interviewing Katie and writing a story about her contribution to the needy, a local philanthropist contacted the *Chronicle* and offered to fund Katie's operation. Two months later, a crew of volunteers gave the old, worn down church a major face lift, and named it Katie's Kitchen.

Sami could not find a parking place in the small lot adjacent to the building, so she parked on the street, two blocks away. As she briskly walked, gruesome thoughts lingered. If she weren't careful, this investigation would own her soul and spill into every facet of her life. She had never dealt with a serial killer, hadn't speculated how she'd react, and never fathomed encountering one as diabolical as this monster. To imagine the depths of evil swimming through the veins of a man so twisted that he could crucify three young mothers eluded Sami's ability to comprehend.

A group of raggedy-dressed people, mostly skinny, unshaven men, with a few unkempt women scattered among them, gathered in a haphazard line snaking out of the main entrance and down the steps. Smiling, Sami walked past them and into the building. A frantic buzz of activity hung in the air as mobs of people impatiently waited elbow-to-elbow to fill their usually-empty stomachs. On opposite sides of the filled-to-capacity room, two long tables, crowded with steaming chafing dishes of sliced turkey, dressing, mashed potatoes, sweet potatoes, and corn invited the hungry guests. At the back of the room, a table covered with an assortment of pies— apple, pumpkin, coconut cream—grew more popular by the minute.

Sami gently elbowed her way to the kitchen.

Katie O'Leary, hunched over, looking far too fragile to be participating in such demanding tasks, waved her hand at Sami. "Happy Thanksgiving, sweetie."

"Happy Thanksgiving to you." Sami said. "How can I help?"

"Sure could use a hand with these trays." Katie pointed to three recently replenished chafing dishes. "Would you please put these out on the table and bring back the empty ones."

"Be happy to."

෮෨

Two hours had passed, yet the crowds continued to pour into the dining room at a frenzied pace. It seemed to Sami that the homeless were spontaneously multiplying. Unaccustomed to bending and lifting, Sami's back vehemently protested. But determined to hang in until two p.m., she endured. Her white apron, decorated with various stains and an assortment of colors denoting the holiday feast, punctuated her earnest participation.

Assigned to various duties requiring their undivided attention, the volunteers had little time for idle chit-chat, and for the most part worked separately. At a point when Sami's back threatened to betray her, she tried to lift a tray full of turkey, but groaned out loud and set it down.

"Can I give you a hand?"

When Sami turned, she discovered that the soft mellow voice belonged to an extraordinarily handsome man. He grinned at her.

"You could really be my hero," Sami said.

"It seems that Katie must be a sexist," the man said. The corners of his mouth turned up. "I've been washing dishes for over two hours while you ladies have been struggling with these heavy trays. I'd be happy to trade assignments."

And she thought chivalry was a lost art? She wiped her hands on the apron and extended her arm. "Sami Rizzo."

He firmly grasped Sami's hand. His long narrow fingers felt as soft as a lambskin glove. "My name's Simon.

I'll skip the last name. It's one of those Polish handles with too many Z's and K's."

Amazing, she thought, tall, handsome, polite and a sense of humor? "I don't believe I've ever seen you here." She wouldn't have forgotten someone like him.

"It's my maiden voyage."

"I'm a veteran. Sixth year."

"Admirable." His blue eyes fixed on Sami's just long enough to make her feel uneasy. "Too bad there aren't more people like Katie. Sure would be a better world."

"No argument here." Sami wanted some vital statistics but wasn't sure how to ask. "So, when you're not washing dishes how do you occupy yourself?"

"I'm a physical therapist." He dug in his back pocket and handed her a business card. "I might be able to get that kink out of your back."

What woman in her right mind would object to having *his* hands on their body? "I might have guessed a professional athlete."

"Wasn't blessed with coordination or grace. Played a little basketball in junior college, but my trophy cabinet is pretty dusty."

A stocky woman charged into the tiny prep-room as if the building were on fire. For a moment she stood silent, hands parked on her hips, out of breath. Finally, she gulped enough air to speak. "Sorry to interrupt, hon, but we really need that tray of turkey. Never saw such a hungry bunch. 'Fraid there's gonna be a riot if we don't keep the food comin'."

Without saying another word, Simon effortlessly lifted the tray and disappeared.

After washing dishes until her hands were trembling, Sami decided that she fulfilled her Thanksgiving good deed. She wiped her hands, said goodbye to Katie, and waved to other volunteers as she walked toward the door. The crowds finally thinned and the onslaught of homeless people started to subside. She surveyed the room but could not locate Simon. She thought they had made a connection, but then again, she was often a victim of wishful thinking.

❧

On the Monday after Thanksgiving, Simon stood by the gold BMW and craned his neck to see if anyone was watching. Sure that he remained inconspicuous, he bent over, unscrewed the plastic cap on the tire valve stem and stuffed it in his jacket pocket. He removed the one-way safety valve with the special tool he'd purchased at Sears, and quickly—before too much air escaped— screwed on a plastic cap in which he had punched a tiny pinhole small enough for the air to leak slowly. In less than thirty seconds he completed the task. He stood and surveyed the parking lot again. People hustled in and out of the FoodMart and loaded groceries in their vehicles, but no one seemed overly curious with his activities.

Dinnertime, when people hurried home from work and needed to make a quick pit stop, proved an ideal time for Simon to remain unnoticed. San Diegans, or possibly all Californians, at least based on Simon's experience over the last ten years, pretty much kept to themselves. They weren't unfriendly, just aloof and self-absorbed, which suited Simon perfectly. He didn't need neighborly strangers jeopardizing his plans with gestures of goodwill and let's-get-to-know-each-other little chats.

Peggy McDonald, the big-breasted redhead he'd been observing for over two weeks, lived in La Jolla, about a twenty-minute drive from Pacific Beach. Her babysitter lived on Diamond Street—just around the corner—so every day, after picking up her daughter, Peggy would swing by the FoodMart before heading home.

While parked, very little air would escape from the tampered-with rear tire. But Simon knew from prior experience and meticulous testing that once driven the tire would go flat in fifteen to eighteen minutes. He'd driven the route a dozen times and felt certain she'd break down close to the top of Soledad Mountain Road—not the most remote area, but dark enough for a good Samaritan to help an unfortunate motorist without attracting much attention.

As in the past, Peggy hustled through the automatic doors and jogged toward her car, plastic FoodMart bag swinging from one arm, her daughter securely held with the other. She secured her daughter in the child safety seat, tossed the bag of groceries on the passenger side and positioned herself behind the wheel. Driving a little too fast for a busy parking lot, she raced toward the south exit.

Simon followed close behind.

She turned left on Garnet, headed east, and followed the road for five blocks until she stopped for a red light near the 24-hour Taco Bell. She continued east on Garnet, drove two blocks, and turned left on Soledad Mountain Road. Through a series of sharp curves, the scenic road wound upward past gated communities and pricey apartment complexes. Simon followed close behind, noticing that the BMW listed slightly to the right. The four-lane road narrowed to two, and Peggy's red brake lights warned Simon that she was slowing.

Just as Simon had estimated, Peggy's BMW limped to a stop three blocks from the Soledad Natural Park, just before Nautilus Street. Not wanting to raise suspicions about his timely rescue, he pulled to the curb a safe distance behind her and turned off his headlights. After waiting three minutes, he continued ahead, parked about two car lengths behind her, turned off the headlights, and let the engine idle. He could feel the fever building, but recognized that to be convincing and non-threatening he had to maintain a calm, even-tempered demeanor. He didn't want to spook her in any way. No doubt she had read about the other women, the common thread that each of their cars had been found abandoned with flat tires. If he sensed any unusual reaction, Simon prepared himself to abort the plan.

Peggy stepped out of her car and slammed the door with untamed anger. She perched her hands on her hips, vigorously shaking her head, gawking at the tire as if her cold stare could miraculously repair it. The dark surroundings, lit only by a half-moon struggling to burn through a misty haze, fit into Simon's plan perfectly.

As he sat quietly, a little anxious yet still in control, Simon could see the Soledad Mountain Monument, a pyramid-like brick structure built on a hill just off the road. On top of the structure stood a cross. A crucifix. There were no floodlights, but a silhouette of the cross stood out against the smoky-gray moonlit sky, creating an eerie image. How poignant, he thought, that he would capture this sinner only steps away from such a monument. He hadn't planned it this way, but truly felt as if it were a sacred message from God. For a moment, Simon transfixed his eyes on the cross, as if drawn by some divine magnet. Sitting alone in his truck, Simon felt serenity, blessed contentment only God could bestow upon a mortal. Of all the sinners walking the Earth, God had chosen Simon as His disciple.

Simon waited for her anger to subside before getting out of his truck. He watched her searching through what looked like an oversized purse. Not wanting to startle her, he called out as he ambled toward her. "Looks like you could use a hand."

She snapped her head toward him, obviously jarred by the strange voice piercing the quiet darkness of the night. "Geez, you scared the shit out of me." Her voice projected a feisty attitude, a biting growl of independence, an I-don't-take-shit-from-anyone tone. She would not be like the others.

"Sorry, miss. Didn't mean to frighten you." He stood several feet away, hands stuffed in his jeans, looking like a shy teenager. His eyes drifted to the faulty tire. "I'd be happy to change it for you."

"I just had the friggin' tires replaced two weeks ago. Eighty-thousand mile warranty, my ass." She kicked the tire. "Can I borrow your cell phone? I left mine at the office."

"Sorry, never had much need for one."

She looked at him in total awe, as if anyone on planet Earth without a cellular telephone had to be a complete moron. "You *don't* have a cell phone?"

"Only take me ten minutes to change the tire and you can be on your way."

She combed her fingers through her unruly hair, evaluating his offer. "Ten minutes?"

༄

While Peggy sat in the back seat trying to console her screaming daughter who was perturbed about the delayed dinner hour, Simon wiggled his fingers into cotton gloves—no need to leave fingerprints—opened the truck and went through his practiced routine. He removed the awl from his jacket pocket and carefully twisted the sharp point into the tread, puncturing the spare tire. Slowly, he eased the tool out. He leaned on the sidewall with both hands and could hear the air hissing out of the tire. In less than five minutes the tire deflated. He closed the trunk, and peeked in the open rear door, shaking his head. "I'm afraid your spare won't be much help, miss. It's flatter than a pancake."

"How can it be flat? The goddamn thing's never been used."

When Simon heard her curse, he had to control his anger. To use the Lord's name so blasphemously, infuriated him. But he had to focus on the more important objective.

As a vehicle leaned around a severe curve about a hundred feet away, headlights illuminated the landscape, casting long shadows on the highway. The Pathfinder slowed, and then stopped parallel to the BMW. Simon could feel the hair on the nape of his neck prickle. Some do-gooder, asking questions, meddling with his plan could prove risky. Quiet panic shuttered through Simon's body, the bitter realization that he might be forced to terminate his plan. He wished it were that simple.

Simon *needed* Peggy. Tonight. The decision to abduct her at this particular time was not a conscious objective. He had no choice. Driven by forces beyond his understanding, Simon could not easily postpone this epic event.

The passenger's window whined open and Simon stared at the pavement, not wanting the man to get a good look at his face.

"You guys need some assistance?" The young man looked like an attorney or accountant. His blond hair hung in his eyes. Without the business suit he could pass for a surfer.

"Got a cell phone I could use?" Peggy asked.

The man stuck his hand out the window and handed her his Nokia. "Help yourself."

She eyeballed Simon as if to say, "See, dip-shit, even the punk's got one."

Not wanting to get rear-ended, the man pulled the Nissan to the curb, in front of Peggy's BMW. Simon could feel perspiration dotting his upper lip. He licked it away. Simon expected the man to get out of the sport utility vehicle. To engage in idle conversation with a nosy stranger, one who might remember his face, didn't bode well with Simon. He couldn't let that happen. Leaving a witness would not be an option.

Quite to Simon's surprise, and relief, the young man seemed content to sit in the Pathfinder. He cranked up the volume on his radio, while his head swayed to the beat of the music. A minor victory, Simon thought, but his plan could still be jeopardized.

Peggy thumbed in a number and pressed the cellular to her ear. She paced while waiting for whomever she called to answer. Her daughter's temper tantrum had quieted to quivering sobs. After several seconds, Peggy said, "Come on, come on, where the *hell* are you?" She nervously tapped her foot on the pavement. "It's me, hon. I've got a flat tire."

Simon could feel the anger welling in his belly. Her husband would surely rescue her. He'd never considered a contingency plan, but now faced a serious wrinkle in his previously smooth operation.

" . . . if you get this message before . . ." she twisted her wrist toward the light and looked at her watch, ". . . seven-thirty, I'm stuck on Soledad Mountain Road, about three blocks south of Nautilus . . ." she looked at Simon as if she were appraising his character. "Forget it. I'll make other arrangements."

Without saying a word to Simon, she turned away and headed for the Pathfinder. Simon could see her handing the young man his cellular. They talked for several minutes, Peggy's arms waving like a traffic cop's.

"I knew it," Simon whispered. She was asking the blond for a ride. Anger washed over him, but disappointment dominated his thoughts. He glanced at the cross, black against the hazy night sky. What to do. He closed his eyes.

Are you going to let her get away, my son?

"Do I have a choice, Mother?"

Do whatever it takes.

Doubling up his fists, digging his nails into his flesh, Simon slowly moved toward the Pathfinder. He didn't have a plan, but knew he had to get rid of the blond. One way or the other. Just as he approached the sport utility vehicle, he saw the left rear signal blink red and the Pathfinder sped away.

Simon leaned against the BMW and folded his arms across his chest. He could feel his heart thumping against his ribs. Peggy hustled his way and stood in front of him, only two feet away. He could smell her floral perfume.

"How'd you like to earn a Good Merit Badge from the Boy Scouts?" Peggy said.

Simon cocked his head. "Excuse me?"

"Raise your right hand and promise that you're not some weirdo."

Simon raised his right hand and placed his left hand over his still-pounding heart. "Scouts honor."

Peggy pointed north. "I live about ten minutes away. Maybe you'd be kind enough to give April and me a lift?"

"What happened to the guy in the Pathfinder?"

"Something about him creeped me out."

FOUR

After wrestling with her pillow for more than two hours, Sami surrendered to the persuasive genius of name brand advertising and swallowed a Tylenol PM, a sample she'd gotten in the mail. Other than Excedrin, the only effective remedy for her frequent migraines, she never purchased medication. Except of course, that no household with an active two-year-old would be complete without St. Joseph Baby Aspirin, Vicks, and Dimetapp cough syrup. Wide-eyed and nowhere near sleep, she felt as if she'd drunk a pot of high-test espresso. In the ongoing battle between adrenalin and sedative, the stimulant kicked butt.

Explicit details of what the three murdered women might have experienced played in her mind's eye like a Saturday afternoon horror-film-marathon. Strangely, what she knew about the case didn't torment her; what she didn't know rubbed her nerves raw. Sami could see how the unimaginable pain must have twisted the victims' faces as their executioner drove spikes through their wrists and feet. She could hear the guttural screams, the breathless pleas falling on the ears of a man without pity or human compassion. Imagining how each woman endured while this maniac had his way with them, Sami could feel a throbbing ache deep in the pit of her stomach. What had they been thinking when he lay on top of them, penetrating their bodies, forcing his way inside them, his mouth pressed against theirs'?

In the final moments, when the certainty of death, so absolute, so imminent, coursed through their veins like lava, when their last heavy breath escaped from their lungs and the hopeless desperation that life for them would soon flicker away, what frantic thoughts burned through their minds?

Sami leaned on an elbow and turned on the light. Until she arrested the murderer, threw him behind bars, tried, convicted and sentenced him, sleepless nights and vivid images of the murders would plague her.

Sami had broken the first commandment of homicide investigating. She emotionally involved herself and connected with three women whom she'd never met. She had seen brutal murders before, viewed dismembered bodies, eviscerated corpses, people so savagely murdered that positive identification required dental examination. Of course they had affected her. Terrifying nightmares often awakened her, but this felt different.

Perhaps, she thought, a womanly connection, a visceral kinship deeper than flesh and blood existed between the women and her. Never before had she felt a victim's pain so profoundly. Then, as she tried to rationalize and discern her feelings, like a wild horse kicking her in the head, it hit her: the children. Each victim had young children, all about the same age as her daughter. No one clearly knew what these children witnessed, what heinous images might be securely locked in their subconscious. Yes, the children had been delicately interviewed with the assistance of a qualified child psychologist. And they *appeared* to be unharmed. But could anyone know for certain that repressed memories of unspeakable acts did not remain in the darkest corners of their minds? As a mother herself, a woman who would do anything to protect Angelina, Sami now understood the abominable torment these women had endured.

Amidst all the confusion and speculation, Detective Samantha Rizzo felt certain of one thing: if Captain Davison knew, even suspected that she lacked the ability to remain objective, he'd pull her off the case without the slightest consideration. No matter what her story, or how compelling her argument, the captain would act swiftly.

Sami couldn't let that happen.

The telephone rang.

"This is Al." Hearing her partner's voice eased her angst. "Did I wake you?"

"What makes you think I'd be sleeping at two a.m.?"

"Sorry."

"Don't be. I was counting sheep." She could hear Al breathing but he didn't say a word. "So, partner, is this an obscene phone call or are you just lonely?" At a young age, Sami learned that a little lightheartedness, even at times when stone-faced solemnness seemed more appropriate, tempered the tension and made it easier to cope with life. Or perhaps her attempt at humor represented hopeless self-preservation.

"A woman and her daughter have been reported missing."

Sami felt her stomach tighten.

"We found her BMW abandoned on Soledad Mountain Road . . . with a flat tire."

"Who filed the report?"

"Her husband claims that she'd left him a message on their answering machine."

"What time?"

"Around seven-thirty."

Sami stood and shuffled toward the bathroom. If she didn't know better, she'd swear that she just swallowed a cup of Drano. "Anything else?"

"Only that her husband guessed from her message that someone had stopped to help her."

If only she could say goodbye and crawl under the covers of her warm bed. Her voice was barely audible. "Thanks for sharing, Al."

"You okay, partner?"

"Just . . . fucking . . . duckie."

∽

Sami's clock radio clicked on at six-forty-five, and Tina Turner came screaming into the cranky detective's morning. Remarkably alert, Sami could see the middle-aged rock star strutting across the stage in an outfit only Turner dared to wear, singing: ". . . *What's love gotta do,*

gotta do with it. What's love but a secondhand emotion . . ."
She tapped the snooze button a little harder than she'd
intended and rolled onto her stomach. After the conversation with Al, she drank a generous glass of Chardonnay, hoping it might work in concert with the Tylenol
PM and knock her unconscious for a few hours. Instead,
the unlikely combo gave her a throbbing headache. She
needed Excedrin. *Now!*

When she sat up in bed, Sami felt a twinge in her
lower back, one of those stabbing pains with great potential for long term ferocity. One careless move and
she'd be lying on the floor, twisted like a pretzel. She'd
had back problems several years ago, spasms that could
bring Hercules to his knees. And what had her husband
Tommy done to help her? Not a thing. In fact, instead
of bringing her an ice pack and a pillow (no way she
could get off the floor), Tommy fetched a cold brew and
watched a basketball game. Thanks to Doctor Alvarez,
one of the few chiropractors willing to make house calls,
her back had been almost completely rehabilitated. Almost. Doctor Alvarez had a theory: if you have a back
and live long enough, eventually you'll have a problem
with it.

With painstaking precision, Sami swung her legs
and eased off the bed. She slowly stood. Tightness lingered in her lower back, convincingly reminding her
that the muscles were close to the edge. In addition to
dealing with her back, her temples were pounding furiously. She shuffled to the bathroom, listing slightly to
the right, opened the medicine cabinet, and took three

Excedrins. She looked up and saw her reflection in the mirror. "Too bad it's not Halloween."

Just to put her mind at ease, she decided to call Doctor Alvarez later that morning. A little preventive maintenance might stave off a relapse. Again the clock radio beckoned her. When she went into the bedroom to turn it off—moving like a rookie soldier in a mine field—she noticed the business card she'd left on her night stand. Simon Kwosokowski, Licensed Physical Therapist. He'd been right, it was quite a handle. She picked up the card and stared at it for a moment, fondling the raised letter printing. Something about this guy hypnotized her. A mysterious magnetism. In the past, she never considered making the first move. Sami liked to think of herself as a contemporary woman, but certain old-fashioned values were ingrained in her character. But if she *did* call him she wouldn't *really* be compromising her values. After all, she had a back problem and Simon *was* a physical therapist.

∾

Simon had just finished a hardy breakfast: eggs over easy, crispy home fried potatoes with a hint of onion, rye toast, and a tall glass of tomato juice. Just as he had suspected, Peggy McDonald proved to be a different breed of woman. Like a wild filly that had never been saddled, she hadn't taken kindly to being a guest in the Room of Redemption. Her foul mouth and bitter words served only to reinforce Simon's conviction that her soul desperately needed to be cleansed and her heart purified. Had it not been for Peggy's fear that Simon would manhandle her daughter, April, he might have had to abort his plan and take drastic measures right in his truck. But, as he had learned, mothers, even those as ornery as Peggy, would never place their children in harm's way.

Sitting at the kitchen table, he lifted the half-full glass of tomato juice and was about to finish it when a long-lost memory flashed through his mind.

Mother.

Simon closed his eyes and could see a clear image of his mother's face. It was Good Friday. Simon had just celebrated his tenth birthday. The Texas temperature was unseasonably cold; the young boy could see his own breath. His mother held a butcher knife that reflected light from the bare bulb above. In front of him was a lamb, hanging from the rafters in the garage, secured with twine around its hind legs. His eyes were glued to the squirming lamb. Its cry sounded almost human. At precisely three p.m., the time at which Jesus had died on the cross two millennia past, Ida Kwosokowski handed Simon the knife.

"You know what must be done."

Simon stood motionless, one hand stuffed in his corduroy pants, the other loosely held the butcher knife.

"I can't, Mother."

Her look was too familiar. Simon took a step toward the lamb. Its tongue hung out of its mouth as it labored to breathe. Saliva dripped to the floor. The animal's eyes were wide-open, almost pleading with Simon to show mercy.

Another step closer.

"Hold its head firmly, Simon. Cut swiftly. No need to make it suffer."

Simon wanted desperately to drop the knife, run in the house and lock himself in the closet. But there was no escaping his duty as a good Christian.

"He must be sacrificed, my dear boy. Just as Our Savior died on the cross to redeem our sins, this lamb must be offered to Jesus in remembrance."

Simon stood close enough to reach the lamb, but couldn't move. The garage smelled like oily rags. His mother grasped the animal's head and forced it back, exposing its neck. The animal let out a loud cry.

"Do it now, my son. Remember to cut the jugular, just like I showed you."

Simon reached up and gently rested the blade of the butcher knife against the lamb's shaved neck. He looked at his mother, then at the lamb. Closing his eyes, Simon pressed the blade against the lamb's neck, and with a swiping motion deeply cut across the flesh. Blood squirted across the garage, splattering on the wall. As the lamb gasped for air, its body violently wriggling, Simon could hear the animal's pathetic moans. Blood pumped from its neck and collected in the aluminum bowl sitting on the concrete floor. Simon watched in terror as life drained from the lamb's body.

When the animal stopped squirming, Ida Kwoso-kowski stood on a stepladder and cut the twine, allowing the sacrificed animal to fall to the floor. "On Easter Sunday we will feast on this fine lamb."

She lifted the aluminum bowl and carefully poured a good portion of blood into a gold-colored chalice. She handed it to Simon. "Drink, my son, so that your soul may be cleansed of mortal sins."

He had thought that his only duty was to sacrifice the animal. Not in his wildest dreams did he believe he'd have to drink the animal's blood. Simon grasped the cup, and with a trembling hand pressed his lips to the chalice and let the lamb's still-warm blood fill his mouth.

༄

Before entering the Room of Redemption, Simon needed a moment to regain his composure. Just thinking about having drunk lamb's blood made him nauseous. He peeked through the one-way lens. Peggy lay on the bed, perhaps sleeping. He could not see April, but guessed she occupied herself in the playroom. When he walked in the door, Peggy sprang to her feet.

Although terrified, Peggy's feisty nature could not be suppressed. The minute she saw his face, unbridled rage gushed through her body. Peggy had always been strong-willed. Often to a point beyond reason. "Well, if it isn't Mister Limp-Dick himself. Back from an afternoon of molesting sheep?"

Have I completely lost my mind? He's going to fucking kill me if I don't shut my mouth! That she could speak like this in front of her daughter mortified Simon. "You're making it difficult for me to be nice."

She let out a crazed laugh. "You call being locked up in this shit-hole by a fucking lunatic, nice?"

April sat quietly in front of the television, seemingly unaware of their conversation. "Why does your cursing persist, sinner?"

"Sinner? What gives you the right to judge anybody?"

"I do not wish to engage in harsh exchanges. All I ask is that you remain civil."

Peggy's wild eyes locked on Simon's face. She wagged her finger at him. "I know who you are. Should have known when you so conveniently showed up to rescue me. I read about you. You're not civil. You're nothing but a pussy. A sick fuck. A man without a dick. A fucking murderer!"

Peggy stood frozen. She studied his face and knew she'd gone too far.

Bonnie Jean Oliver.

A familiar storm welled in Simon's belly. When he looked at Peggy's face, he saw Bonnie Jean. He walked toward the bed, not like a deranged man, but reserved, in control. Peggy, apparently not threatened by him, didn't flinch. Before she could react to the impending danger, he doubled up his fist and punched her in the face. His knuckles collided with her left cheekbone and knocked her against the headboard. As if her body had no skeleton, she collapsed like a rag doll, unconscious.

❧

When Peggy awoke, she felt like she'd been kicked by a mule. Her left eye, swollen almost shut, ached like hell. Her face, severely bruised, pulsed with pain. At first she hadn't noticed, but now that the fogginess lifted from her thoughts, she realized that he had handcuffed her right wrist to the wooden bedpost. Where did the asshole expect her to go? Suddenly, Peggy McDonald felt the eerie sensation of being alone in her prison. "April, where are you?"

No answer.

Maybe she was in the bathroom?

A quiet panic shivered through her body.

"April, please come to mommy."

Nothing.

Chaotic thoughts raced through her mind, visions of unthinkable acts. "God in heaven, I beg you, please protect my daughter."

FIVE

After meeting with Captain Davison and surviving one of the rare occasions when he browbeat his subordinates, Sami Rizzo and Alberto Diaz drove to La Jolla to interview Andrew McDonald, the husband of the latest kidnapped victim. Situated high on a cliff overlooking the Pacific Ocean, the McDonald's two-million-dollar home sat among other jewels even more impressive. By San Diego standards, particularly in La Jolla, one of the more affluent communities, seven-figure properties were mainstream. In any suburb close enough to smell the ocean, starter homes—tiny matchboxes that in other parts of the country might sell for eighty-thousand-dollars—were priced at nearly a million.

Before the detectives made it to the top of the concrete stairway leading to the front entrance, Andrew McDonald opened the door. Wearing a Hard Rock Cafe T-shirt, khaki shorts, and sandals, an outfit unsuited to the sixty-degree day, he stood silent. His dirty-blond hair, cut short, looked unkempt. The puffy bags of flesh under his eyes seemed extreme for a man in his early thirties. Crow's feet punctuated the corners of his brown eyes.

Sami offered her hand. Her lower back, slightly improved, still felt tight and achy. "I'm Detective Rizzo, and this is my partner, Detective Diaz."

Declining a handshake, McDonald stepped to the side and motioned them in. They followed him to a small den decorated with southwestern furnishings. McDonald sat on a leather chair. Still silent, he pointed to a brown sofa.

To Sami, he appeared to be more composed than she expected. The other three husbands, men who'd been interviewed under similar circumstances, were frantic.

"Is she dead?"

The jaw-dropping question clobbered Sami. Diaz stared at his fingernails. "There's no evidence to support that possibility, Mr. McDonald," Sami said.

McDonald folded his hands as if in prayer. "He's murdered them all and he's going to kill Peggy."

"Not if we have anything to say about it," Diaz said.

"You don't know my wife," McDonald said. "She might be terrified, but she won't mince words with him. She's going to provoke him."

"We're doing everything in our power to rescue your wife and daughter," Sami said.

"Like you did for the other three butchered women?" McDonald's face flushed with blood.

Diaz sat forward and coughed into his hand. "I know this is difficult for you—"

"You two haven't a clue what I'm feeling right now."

"Mr. McDonald," Sami said, "you have a choice to make. We can sit here and listen to you berate us for

our incompetence and waste valuable time—precious
time—or you can cooperate and offer some information that may save your wife and daughter."

McDonald fixed his eyes on Sami's and sucked in
a quivering breath. "I'm sorry. You can't possibly imagine what it's like waiting for the telephone call or knock
at the door that's going to change your life forever. All
I can think about is how horribly she's going to . . ."
His eyes filled with tears. "Where do monsters like him
come from?"

Sami could say nothing.

"When did you last hear from your wife,
Mr. McDonald?" Al asked.

"Like I told the other detective when I reported her
missing, she left me a message last night. She got a flat
tire and was about to ask me to pick her up, but then
told me to forget about it."

"Have you erased the message?" Al asked.

He shook his head.

"May we listen to it?" Al said.

McDonald stood and pointed. "The answering machine's in there."

The detectives followed McDonald into a recently-
remodeled kitchen; it still smelled like cut wood and
fresh varnish. To Sami, it looked like it could easily make
the cover of House & Garden. Black and white marble
floors. Cherry cabinets. Commercial, stainless steel appliances. Sami noticed the remains of a partially eaten
frozen dinner sitting on the counter.

McDonald pushed the play button on the answering
machine.

"—if you get this message before—" a long pause "—seven-thirty, I'm stuck on Soledad Mountain Road, about three blocks south of Nautilus—"another pause. "Forget it. I'll make other arrangements." Her voice sounded anxious.

Other arrangements indeed, Sami thought.

McDonald folded his arms across this chest and leaned against the counter. "That's it."

There was, of course, the remote possibility that Peggy McDonald and her daughter, April, were not abducted by the suspected serial killer, which fostered a series of delicate questions.

"How long have Mrs. McDonald and you been married?" Sami asked.

"Our tenth anniversary is next month."

"Everything okay with the marriage?"

McDonald's eyes narrowed. "What the hell does that mean?

"You and the misses get along?"

"We have our moments."

"Ever have any major disagreements?"

"Nothing worth talking about."

Sami stroked her chin with her thumb and index finger. "How soon after you received the message from your wife did you become concerned?"

"I don't know . . . maybe an hour or so."

"You're about five or ten minutes from where your wife's car broke down, right Mr. McDonald?"

"And your point is?"

"I'm just a little surprised that you weren't tempted to hop in your car and check things out."

"Look, detective, I don't appreciate this interrogation. Maybe instead of breaking my balls you and your partner should be trying to save my family."

"That's exactly what we're trying to do, Mr. McDonald," Sami said. "Sometimes the slightest, seemingly insignificant detail can result in a clue. If I've offended you, I apologize."

McDonald combed his fingers through his hair. "He's going to butcher my wife, isn't he?"

Sami, her throat knotted up, couldn't answer.

༄

Sami and Al sat in the car, re-evaluating their conversation with Andrew McDonald. "So, what do you think, partner?" Sami asked.

"I think Mr. McDonald's going to be a widower."

Feeling a bit guilty badgering McDonald, Sami asked, "Was I too rough on him?"

He lifted a shoulder. "You're emotionally involved with this case, partner. You need to take a few deep breaths and regroup."

Sami's cell phone beeped.

"Sami Rizzo."

Captain Davison's voice thundered in her ear. "Just got a call from a young man who believes he saw Peggy McDonald and her daughter just before they were abducted. He claims that she borrowed his cell phone to make a call."

"When?"

"Last night. Around seven-thirty."

About the same time her husband had gotten a message from her, Sami thought. "Did he say where he saw her?"

"Exactly where we found her BMW."

"What else?"

"Said she refused his assistance—already had help."

"From whom?"

"A big guy—well over six-foot-tall."

The children of the victims had all claimed that the suspect was very tall. "Did he get a look at the guy?"

"Said it was too dark. All he could remember was that the suspect wore a Padres baseball cap."

Sami guessed that more than a quarter-million six-foot-plus men wore Padres' caps. "Did he see anything else, captain?"

"He spotted a black or dark blue, late model Ford Supercab pickup parked behind the BMW."

"Big surprise." This confirmed what one of the children had said. "Anything unusual about the truck? Roof rack, company logo, camper shell?"

"Couldn't remember a thing."

If the truck belonged to the killer, it could prove to be a significant lead. But more than two-million people lived in San Diego County. Thousands drove dark colored late model Supercabs.

"Did Mr. McDonald offer any clues?" Davison asked.

"Nada."

A long silence. "Everything okay, Rizzo?"

Not normally concerned with her state of mind, the captain's question alarmed Sami. Was he fishing for something? Perhaps he sensed her personal involvement in this case. "I want to nail this guy, captain. Really want to fry his ass."

"We all do, Rizzo. We all do."

∽

Forgetting the handcuffs, Peggy almost catapulted off the bed when she heard the door unlock. The bed moved six inches away from the wall before her body snapped back onto the mattress. The steel cuff cut into her wrist. "Goddamn it!"

The door creaked open and Simon walked in. Alone.

Her eyes were wild. "Where's my daughter, you sick bastard?"

"Safe."

"Where is she?"

He walked toward the bed and Peggy cowered, expecting him to strike her again. He reached in his shirt pocket and removed something colorfully wrapped in scarlet red paper with white hearts. A delicate bow sat on top. It looked about the same size as a deck of playing cards.

"I'm sorry I hit you. I'm not the raving maniac you think I am. Sometimes . . . I just get angry." He handed her the package. "Accept this as a peace offering? Please?"

How could she trust this lunatic? "What is it?"

"April picked it out."

His eyes looked sincere, but . . . "When can I see her?"

"Open the package and I promise to bring her back."

Her hands trembled as she tore off the paper and found a white cardboard box. Carefully, she removed the top. Inside the box she found the gift wrapped in tissue paper. She looked up at him. "April picked it out?"

He nodded.

She delicately separated the tissue paper.

Like a novice swimmer breaking the surface after a record-breaking free dive, Peggy McDonald gasped for air. With her free hand, she covered her gaping mouth. She could not find air to breathe, her lungs filled with terror. With out-of-focus eyes, she gawked at what lay in the bottom of the box. This must be a nightmare, she thought. This can't be happening. Her hands began to tremble and a wave of nausea gripped her. She could taste the bitter tang of bile in the back of her throat. She glanced at Simon and could see the look of satisfaction on his face.

With a glare of victory reflecting in his eyes, Simon grinned and walked out the door.

SIX

Simon lay naked in bed, staring at the colorless ceiling. The full moon, spilling through partially drawn blinds, provided the only light in the room. More than ever before he needed to hear his mother's soothing voice, to feel her loving authority in every reverent word. He had sinned. Pitifully broken God's word. Children were pure; God's most cherished creations. Yet, Simon, unable to control his fury, seduced by Satan, had used an innocent child as a weapon against her wretched mother.

It felt like his experience with Bonnie Jean all over again. The blind rage. The dark part of him that took control. The other self he feared so much. But unlike the incident with Bonnie Jean, Simon remembered every detail of his vile deed against the helpless child. Her eyes had been squeezed shut, tears dripped down her cheeks. Her slight body shivered like a puppy left out in the cold. He pressed his palms against his ears but could not quiet her screams. Locked in his head, they bounced around his conscious mind like ping pong balls in a vacuum.

"Please don't hurt me," she had mumbled. Bound to a kitchen chair with clothesline and duct tape, totally immobilized, the injection was starting to take effect. Her eyes were rolling and her head nodding to and fro. Simon grasped the straight razor and checked its sharpness by running his thumb across the blade. April watched him through terror-stricken eyes. When April appeared to be unconscious, he brushed her hair away from her ear. Before he began the operation, he snuggled his nose against her hair and inhaled her fresh, clean scent.

"It's your mother's fault," he whispered in her ear, "blame her, not me."

Believing that she was completely sedated, he held her head securely with one hand and began amputating her ear with the other. Halfway through the operation, April's body jerked and the razor slipped, cutting deeply into her flesh. Blood squirted everywhere. He pressed the absorbent towel against April's head to stop the bleeding, but the towel was quickly saturated with blood. Quite to Simon's alarm, April let out a horrifying scream. Her ear, half severed, hung grotesquely off her head. He had no choice but to finish what he'd started, but he hadn't planned on her being conscious. Simon placed duct tape over her mouth to muffle the screams he knew were coming. He twisted her long hair around his free hand to prevent her from moving. Holding her head secure with a not-so-steady hand, he finished the job, all the while wincing every time the little girl's smothered screams assaulted his ears. The bleeding was almost uncontrollable, so Simon quickly sutured the wound. By the time he'd finished, the sedative had taken hold, and April was unconscious.

Now, several hours later, lying in bed, thoughts of what he had done weighed heavy on his conscience.

"Can you hear me, Mother?"

I'm with you, Simon. Always watching over you.

"How shall I atone for my sin?"

A dark closet will not absolve this sin.

"What is God's word?"

An eye for an eye.

Simon rolled off the bed and stood tall. As if drawn by a powerful magnet, he marched toward the kitchen like a boot-camp recruit. His face felt as cold as stone, his eyes misty. The razor, still bloody, lay on the counter. He snatched it without a second thought and headed for the bathroom. His first inclination was to amputate his own ear. After all, he did wish to fulfill the eye-for-an-eye dictum. But by doing so he feared that it might interfere with his "work." He could, of course, grow his hair longer to conceal the missing ear, but the grain of rational thought that remained warned him not to cut it off. Studying his hand, he considered a finger, perhaps just the last joint of his pinky, but to do so would hinder his dexterity and potentially impair his ability to perform physical therapy. While evaluating other options, Simon turned on the hot water and rinsed the dried blood off the razor. He left it on the vanity and went back into the kitchen.

"Help me mother. I don't know what to do."

Perhaps you should consider something less obvious, son.

In the corner of the counter he spotted the rect-angular wooden block; knife handles sticking out. He grabbed the poultry shears, an absorbent dishcloth, and walked toward the table. He lifted his right leg and rested the heel of his foot on the chair. Then, he bent over as if he were going to trim his toenails. Gripping his first four toes, he curled them under, out of the way. The baby toe stood alone, pink and slightly crooked. He opened the shears and firmly pressed the sharp V against the base of his toe.

"Is this what you want, mother?"

It is not my will, dear boy. It is God's.

"Will he be pleased with my penance?"

His grace will fill your heart.

Simon tightened his grip on the shears. He placed the dishcloth under his foot, prepared for the gush of blood. Then, he closed his eyes and squeezed the shears with all his might.

ᖆ

On Saturday morning, the November sun rose over the eastern mountains, shimmering like a yellow disc. The cloudless sky looked as blue as Swan River daisies, and the crisp evening air quickly surrendered to the warmth of the solar awakening. Sami had just returned from a painful walk around Balboa Park. Her back would not have survived a jog. Angelina, still sleepy, hair tan-gled and unruly, thumb planted securely in her mouth, was sitting on her grandmother's lap when Sami walked in the front door. Usually Angelina charged toward her mother like a twenty-five-pound linebacker. Today she seemed content cuddling with grandma. Sami stood for a moment and snapped a mental picture of her daughter snuggled against grandma's warm bosom. As a child, Sami could never remember sitting on her mother's lap.

Carefully, Sami did a few side bends, then slowly tried to touch her toes. She winced from the pain.

"Did you call Doctor Alvarez?" Josephine Rizzo asked.

Sami sat on the sofa and unlaced her Nikes. "Not yet, Ma."

"You'll be flat on your back if you wait."

She'd not yet decided whether she had enough nerve to call Simon. "I'll call the doctor Monday morning." On one hand, having her mother live close enough to enlist her services on a moment's notice served Sami well. On the other hand . . .

Josephine huffed. "Got your father's head. Just like a rock."

How many times had Sami heard that cliché? In no mood to duel with her mother, Sami conceded. "Maybe I'll try to reach the doctor today." Oh, how she hated resignation!

Until her father died—almost eight years ago—Sami hadn't fully understood his vital role as peacekeeper and commander in chief of the household. Everything centered on him, and she adored her dad. He provided love, understanding, and a consoling shoulder whenever Sami needed support. This did not suggest that Sami escaped harsh discipline or punishment when she violated her father's strict commandments. After all, Angelo Rizzo, born in Palermo, Sicily, ruled his castle with a firm hand and European stubbornness. Nevertheless, Sami, no matter how disobedient, still remained his pride and joy.

Sami spent most of her life trying to please her dad, doing whatever she could to fulfill his lofty expectations, hoping to feel deserving of his love. Yet she believed that she never quite hit the mark. He never outwardly showed his disappointment, but Sami could see it reflected in his green eyes. Whether it was a substandard report card, a forgotten chore, or for serving him lukewarm espresso, his displeasure pierced her heart like a red-hot dagger. Had he lived another two years, he might have—for the first time in his life—shown pride in her appointment as a homicide detective. That he could never know his dying request for her to become a detective came true, punctuated Sami's forever-inability to please him.

Sami's mother, subservient to her husband, kept in check by her father's dominant character, suddenly, after his funeral, metamorphosed from a soft-spoken woman to a mean-spirited shrew. After his death, Josephine Rizzo couldn't meddle enough in Sami's life. It was as if she were making up for lost time. She criticized Sami's every move. Sami strongly suspected that for years her mother harbored repressed jealousy and ill feelings toward Sami and Angelo's unique father-daughter relationship.

Since her father died, Sami expended great energy trying to comply with her mother's wishes, often compromising herself in an effort to avoid conflict. But it seemed that Josephine Rizzo derived great pleasure undermining Sami; her daily agenda clearly focused on aggravating her only daughter. After repeated attempts to appease her, Sami gave up. Their relationship, fostered neither through love nor mutual respect, was impelled by obligation. To honor her mother could never be a conscious choice, but rather a commandment and accepted tradition. Freewill played no part in the "decision." Sami often wrestled with this paradox.

Honor and respect. Honor and respect.

This truth echoed the ultimate hypocrisy. How could she honor and respect her mother when she didn't even like her? How could Sami endure Josephine's harsh manipulation and constant criticism without suffering deep wounds of resentment?

With Angelina, Sami had read all the popular books on parenting, hoping to abandon her twisted notions. She tried, desperately, to approach parenthood with an open mind, to pave new pathways of understanding. But she had not anticipated rearing Angelina as a single parent. So when Tommy DiSalvo, Asswipe Extraordinaire, announced that "things weren't working out," Sami's meticulous plans and dreams of raising the perfect child, creating a household rooted by a strong family structure, were suddenly derailed. Facing the enormous task of raising Angelina on her own filled Sami with a profound feeling of inadequacy.

While Josephine watched Angelina, Sami tried to enjoy a long shower, allowing the hot water to pulse against the sore muscles in her lower back. For the last three weekends, her ex-husband had disappointed Angelina by calling at the last minute and announcing that he could not spend the weekend with his only daughter. Angelina didn't understand this, but Sami knew too well that Tommy, unreliable and rarely trustworthy, considered his daughter an inconvenience when other less noble activities presented themselves. Each week Sami had to invent excuses that Angelina might understand. Today, Tommy claimed that he had to help a friend move, but promised to "swing by" on Sunday. Did he actually think Sami would hang around for the entire day waiting for him to fulfill his empty promises?

Tommy DiSalvo hadn't wanted children, and had no desire to get married. Sami, regrettably, talked him into it, convinced him that it would help solidify their commitment to each other. She lied to herself and Tommy, pretending that marriage could fix their failing relationship. But marriage had not been powerful enough to heal their damaged love, if love even existed.

After toweling off, blow drying her hair, and coating her skin with raspberry moisturizing cream, Sami slipped into her favorite lounging shorts, threw on a baggy T-shirt, and joined her mother and daughter in the living room. Now wide awake, Angelina sat on the floor cross-legged, using the corner of the cocktail table to support her bowl of Cheerios.

"Want some coffee, Ma?"

"Gotta get moving." Josephine lifted her rotund body off the chair with a grunt. She looked around the messy room and shook her head. "Don't know how you live like this."

"Do we have to go through this every time you come over?"

"I don't have to come over, Sami." Josephine glared at her daughter. "Men like a clean house. You're never going to—"

"Thanks for watching Angelina, Ma." The last thing Sami needed from her mother was advice on how to find the perfect man.

Josephine struggled to bend over. "Give Grandma a kiss."

Angelina sprang up and kissed her grandmother's cheek, leaving a tattoo of milk on her face.

"Coming over for lasagna tomorrow?" Josephine asked.

"I'll call you."

After her mother left, Sami, feeling a moment of courage, decided to call Simon. She'd been thinking about it, but hadn't quite mustered the nerve. Not expecting him to be working on a Saturday, she could leave him a message and avoid talking to him. By doing this, she hoped he would return her call, and in an abstract way he'd be taking the initiative. A little twisted, but it worked for her.

She picked up the business card and dialed the direct number to physical therapy. It rang twice before Sami heard a young woman's voice.

"Bayview Hospital physical therapy, how may I direct your call?"

Unlikely that two Simons worked for the hospital, she didn't want to struggle with his last name. "May I speak to Simon, please?"

"One moment, I'll page him."

Page him? Sami expected to hear his voice mail. Unprepared to speak with him, she panicked.

"This is Simon."

Shit. She could see those ice-blue eyes. "You probably don't remember me—"

"Is this Sami?"

Her palms were moist. "You remember me?"

"How could I forget?"

A long silence.

"Is your back still giving you trouble?"

"It's slightly improved, but I thought maybe—"

"Your timing couldn't be better. I just finished with my last patient and . . . how quickly can you get here?"

This caught her completely off guard. How could she squirm her way out of this predicament? "I appreciate the offer, Simon, but I have a two-year-old daughter and my babysitter—"

"Bring her along. We've got a play area that'll keep her out of trouble for hours. Do you know how to get here?"

She felt like a trapped rat. "How about Tuesday or Wednesday?"

"Booked up solid, Sami. Besides, you don't want those back muscles to get more traumatized, do you?"

He certainly was tenacious. "I really can't, Simon."

"Look, Sami, I know a little bit about backs and they don't get better on their own."

Her cowardly plan had just been upended. "Um, I guess I can be there in about . . . an hour."

"Great. See you in a little while."

Her hair needed to be cut, her hips carried a few extra pounds, and the stressful investigation added new wrinkles to her face. But if her visit to the hospital was only therapy, why did she care how she looked?

ॐ

When Simon hung up the telephone, he thought he would surely pass out. Only through a divine miracle had he endured the racking pain. He bent forward, squatting slightly, and gripped the front of his thighs. His fingernails almost pierced his skin through the cotton fabric of the surgical scrubs. He closed his eyes and sucked in heavy breaths of air.

Carol, Simon's assistant, casually strolled past him and noticed him bending over. "You okay?"

He almost lost consciousness after amputating the baby toe. Suturing the wound without anesthesia had been even more excruciating. "Got up in the middle of the night and like a fool I jammed my baby toe into the bedpost. I think it's broken."

"Why don't you ask Doctor Martin for some Vicodin?"

Simon wanted no part of pain medication. How did he expect to atone for his sin without pain? "Already took some."

Carol flipped through the pages of her clipboard. "There aren't any more patients scheduled today. Maybe you should get an x-ray."

"Got it buddy-taped. Not much more you can do with a toe."

Carol shrugged and went into the office. Simon limped to the rest room. With each step the pain radiated through his entire foot. He could barely stand, let alone offer treatment, and Sami, at his request, would be there soon. What was he thinking? He had no idea how he would drive home. How would he work on Sami's back? When he'd driven to work, the simple act of stepping on the accelerator and brake pedal felt like a pit bull chewed on his foot. Had he given the situation more careful evaluation he would have taken a personal day.

He sat on the toilet and gently slipped the loosely laced sneaker off his right foot. A spot of dried blood the size of a plum stained his white cotton sock. It didn't look like fresh blood, but Simon thought it wise to examine it more closely. After removing his sock, he could see the dressing soaked with fresh blood. Had he not come to work this morning and stayed in bed, nursing his foot and keeping his leg elevated, the stitches might have held. But the stress from walking and driving had loosened the sutures. Besides, he wasn't a doctor. His stitch-job, adequate at best, barely served his purpose. How could he get his hands on a needle and sutures without someone noticing? After carefully pulling the sock back on, Simon slipped his foot into the sneaker. The Reebok running shoe felt as if it were two sizes too small.

Knowing that the physical therapy department closed at one p.m. on Saturday, Simon waited in the rest room until one-fifteen, hoping that his colleagues would be on their way home.

When Simon got back to the physical therapy department, he found the door locked. From his key ring, he located the brass key stamped with the words, "Do Not Duplicate," and let himself inside. Searching every shelf, opening boxes, moving rubber balls, building blocks, wrist braces, he rifled through the supply cabinet, and located a fresh supply of sutures. With his teeth, he tore open the sterile packaging and removed the contents. He gently removed the sneaker and bloody sock, and then propped up his foot on the chair. Finding the sutures was a windfall, searching for anesthesia, inventoried in a locked cabinet for controlled drugs would prove futile. No, Simon had to tough it out. He'd already sutured the wound once without lidocaine and had no choice but to endure the pain again. But this time he needed to prepare himself for even more torture. The wound throbbed intensely and the area surrounding the amputation was inflamed and super-sensitive. He threaded the curved needle with a shaky hand, drew a deep breath, then eased the needle into the tender flesh. He sucked air through his teeth as he pushed the needle through the wound and pulled the nylon thread tight. Beads of cold sweat dotted his forehead. He sighed deeply and proceeded. After each suture, he had to stop for a moment to catch his breath. Simon had never felt such agony. Almost finished, two stitches to go, he felt sick to his stomach. He closed his eyes and swallowed hard, choking down the taste of vomit. The agony from the last suture proved to be almost unbearable. He pulled the nylon tight and tied it off, feeling certain he'd lose consciousness. When he finished, Simon sat on the chair, and bent forward with his head between his legs. After several minutes, the wave of dizziness passed and the stinging pain eased up slightly. Simon then struggled to put on his sock and sneaker.

He heard a soft knock at the door. At first, he considered ignoring it, but could not imagine acting so insensitive. After all, he had invited her. Haphazardly, and most uncharacteristic, Simon crammed the therapy-related paraphernalia back into the cabinet with little regard for neatness. While slowly limping to the door, he imagined standing in front of Sami while blood soaked through his Reeboks. He opened the door and did his best to force a smile.

"Hi, Sami. It's great to see you again." He shifted his attention to Angelina. "And who's this lovely little princess?"

With her left hand clenched and partially stuffed in her mouth, Angelina clung to her mother's leg like Velcro.

"Angelina, say hello to Simon," Sami said. "She's always shy when she first meets people. When she gets to know you, watch out."

When Simon bent forward to offer his hand to Angelina, a gold cross on a thick chain slipped out of his shirt and dangled from his neck.

Certain his body would fold in half if he didn't sit soon, he gestured toward his desk. "Why don't you and Angelina have a seat?" He let them walk ahead of him so he could conceal his limp. As Simon eased into the chair opposite Sami and Angelina, he could not suppress a soft moan.

Sami's eyes searched his face. "Are you feeling okay?"

"Actually, I had a little mishap last night and broke my toe." He grimaced as he adjusted himself in the chair. "Hard to believe that a baby toe can bring a two-hundred-twenty-five pound man to his knees. I feel like an idiot."

Angelina hopped on Sami's lap. "Oh, Simon," Sami said, "you must be in a great deal of pain. I'm so sorry."

"I'll be all right. Just need to favor it for a couple of days."

She reached in her purse and handed Simon a business card. "Why don't you give me a call when you're feeling better?"

He held the card but didn't look at it. "I feel terrible that I made you drive all this way."

"It wasn't that far. Besides, I've got a good friend who lives a few blocks away. Haven't seen her in ages."

Simon looked at the card, glanced at Sami, and studied the card again. "I never would have guessed. So you catch the bad guys and lock 'em up?"

"I do my best."

Intrigued with the possibilities, he thought for a moment, trying to ignore the gripping pain. "Why don't you join me for dinner next Friday? I should be dancing the two-step by then. It's the least I can do to make up for my rudeness."

"That's sweet, Simon, but unnecessary."

"You like Italian food, right?"

"Simon, it's really not—"

"I'll call you Thursday to confirm." Without standing, Simon offered his hand. "I'm sorry about today, Sami."

After Sami and Angelina left, Simon leaned back in the chair and carefully swung his leg up on the desk. He examined the business card. "Sami Rizzo, Homicide Detective." Such a serendipitous encounter. For a moment, he forgot about the pain.

༺ஒ༻

After securing Angelina in the child car seat, Sami fastened her seat belt and headed for the hospital parking lot. Waiting for several cars ahead of her, bottle-necked where two lanes narrowed to one, Sami glanced to her left and noticed a black Ford Supercab in the employee's parking lot. Ordinarily, Sami might not have reacted. After all, thousands of trucks similar to the serial killer's cluttered the streets of San Diego County. If she paid attention to every one of them she'd spend the rest of her life running ID's on vehicle license plates. However, Simon's unusual behavior peaked her curiosity. And of course the cross around his neck added another dimension. Perhaps their meeting at Katie's Kitchen had not been a random event? She pawed through the glove box, found a crumpled napkin and pen, and scribbled the plate number on the napkin.

෴

Sami had just finished washing and drying two loads of laundry, so she grabbed a cold brew, sat on the couch, and turned on the Charger's game. They were an unpredictable football team, had been since losing the Super Bowl in ninety-four, but Sami, a diehard fan, stuck with them in spite of their heartbreaking seasons. They played the Detroit Lions today, a hapless team. But Head Coach Williams, ex-Charger coach, appeared to be leading the Lions to a shutout victory. Fourth quarter, three minutes to go. The score: twenty-four-zip. Not even Sami could stomach this thrashing.

She hit the off button on the remote and picked up the book she'd been reading: A Journey Through the Mind of the Serial Killer, by Brent Hartman, former FBI profiler. She turned to the bookmark. Hartman contended that all serial killers and repeat offenders of violent crimes were once victims themselves. Most were either abused as children or brought up in severely dysfunctional homes. Often the parents of future killers were alcoholics or drug addicts. "Loonies," as Hartman called them, unlike serial killers, were not difficult to catch. Driven by rage, uncontrollable behavior and irrational actions, loonies were usually one-victim killers who did not possess the presence of mind to cover their tracks or carefully "plan" the murders. On the other hand, the true serial killer, usually intelligent, cunning, and often charming, carefully orchestrated his murders. Textbook serial killers distinguished themselves from loonies because their actions were well planned, calculating, and their desire to kill was driven by a profound urge to inflict pain.

Sami's eyelids began to droop, so she set the book on the cocktail table, rested her head against the back of the sofa, and closed her eyes. She loved little naps on quiet afternoons.

Simon.

She'd been thinking about him. More than she wanted to. She could not ignore the attraction. The charming young man with his gentle voice and innocent politeness had stirred a hunger in her that she'd repressed for longer than she wished to admit. But now something troubled her. If the black Ford Supercab pickup did belong to him, she'd be forced to take the next step. But her suspicions stemmed from more than the truck. She couldn't ignore the gold cross, or the fact that Simon fit the serial killer's description. He stood well over six-foot-tall, had blue eyes and light brown hair. Another issue bothered her. Sami felt certain that Simon contrived the story about his broken toe. Why he would lie, she had no clue. To invite her, insist that she drive to the hospital immediately, and then fabricate a story about a broken toe didn't make sense. Simon's eyes had reflected something unsettling; a quiet storm. In Sami's heart she hoped that all her idle suspicions would prove unfounded because she felt wildly attracted to him. Friday seemed like decades away.

As Sami's thoughts faded to blackness, the door chime rang a familiar melody. She had drifted from consciousness just enough to give her a feeling of disorientation as she wobbled to the front door. She twisted the doorknob and Tommy DiSalvo stood on the porch, grinning like a little boy who'd just gotten everything he'd asked Santa for.

"Better late than never," Tommy mumbled. "Where's my little angel at?" As always, he was two-days-unshaven, and his eyes were severely bloodshot.

Not wanting him to come in, Sami didn't budge. "Get lost on your way to a poker game?"

"Ah, that's the Sami we all know and love." He puckered his lips. "Give us a kiss, sweetheart."

Sunday afternoon and already he was toasted. "What do you want, Tommy?"

"Would a blowjob be out of the question?"

"I don't have time to banter with you."

"Where's my daughter?" It was more a demand than a question.

Angelina loved Grandma Josephine's lasagna. So much so that she nagged for nearly an hour before Sami surrendered. "She's spending the afternoon with my mother."

"What, watching her when you're working isn't enough?"

Sami felt her stomach churn. "You've got exactly fifteen seconds to tell me what the hell you want or you'll be talking to the outside of an oak door."

He scratched his stubble. "Jesus, Sami, lighten up. When did you get so friggin' serious?"

Sami glared at Tommy. "Want to tickle my funny bone? Fork over some of the child support you owe me. Last I checked your tab was a buck short of five grand."

His eyes narrowed and he licked his lips. "That's what I wanted to talk about."

She didn't know what he really wanted, but doubted that he intended to give her money. She could have had the son-of-a-bitch locked up. Many times. And in a sense she would have been doing him a favor. But, he was Angelina's father, and once in a while he actually acted like a dad. Sami stepped to the side and he walked in the living room. He looked like a forlorn soul.

"Mind if I sit?" Tommy asked.

"Suit yourself."

He fell heavily into the armchair. Sami stood with her arms folded.

Tommy had introduced Sami to the once-uncharted world of intimacy, a world that had always been taboo, one in which the nuns at Saint Agnes Catholic Elementary School had conveniently edited from Sami's sex education class. Before meeting Tommy, Sami'd thought that sex consisted of guy-on-top, girl-on-bottom, over in a flash. Fun for the guy; obligation for the girl. But Tommy had overwhelmed her with passion she never knew existed. He taught her that sex had no limitations between consenting lovers. No one would argue that Tommy DiSalvo was for the most part a seedy reptile, but Sami, perhaps more than anyone, could not deny that on the rare occasion he actually maintained sobriety, Tommy made love like a champion.

"I'm in a bit of trouble, Sami."

"What kind of trouble?"

"Twenty-two-grand-trouble."

Again with the bookies. "And I should be surprised?"

"This is different."

"Look, Tommy, the last time you begged me for eight grand I cleaned out my savings. Remember? You promised to get help." His face looked pathetic, like he'd just been informed that every member of his family died in a plane crash. She wanted to tear into him, but suppressed her fury. "I'm living from paycheck to paycheck. There's nothing I can do."

Tommy combed his fingers through his greasy black hair. "If they don't get their money by Friday, I'm gonna be doing a triple gainer off the Coronado Bridge."

"Who are *they*?"

Tommy pulled a pack of Winston's out of his shirt pocket. "You mind?"

When they'd been married, Sami put up with his habits—all of them—but not in her house. Not anymore. "I'd rather you didn't."

He removed a cigarette from the pack and held it between his index and middle finger. "You know I can't tell you that, Sami."

"Maybe I can talk to them, buy you some time."

"Time? I take home four-fifty a week. Time ain't what I need."

"I can't wave a magic wand and make the money appear. Where am I supposed to get twenty-two-thousand-dollars?"

Tommy stood up, waving his arms. "There's a bunch of equity in this house. I heard that some banks can do a deal in forty-eight hours."

Sami could feel her face getting hot. "Better take some swimming lessons, Tommy, cause it'll be a cold day in hell before I tap the equity in this house to pay your gambling debts."

Tommy's face flushed red. "I don't think you under-stand what I'm dealing with here. These motherfuckers are gonna kill me!"

"If you want me to reason with these guys, I'll do what I can, but I'm not giving you any money."

Tommy stormed toward the door and yanked it open. "When they fish my dead ass out of the water, tell Angelina that you could have helped me, but instead told me to go fuck myself." He slammed the door.

SEVEN

Awkwardly using his left foot to accelerate and brake while he straddled his aching right leg across the seat, Simon survived a painful, nauseous drive home, one in which he was forced twice to park on the shoulder of the freeway and vomit on the pavement. Enduring punishing agony, he spent the rest of Saturday and all of Sunday in bed. He had no appetite but drank plenty of liquids. To reduce the swelling on his severely black and blue foot, he kept his leg elevated and used an ice pack. By late Sunday afternoon, the stabbing pain had lessened to a bearable throb. Still feeling guilty and not completely absolved of his sin, Simon decided to treat his guests to a special dinner.

Trying not to place undo pressure on his right foot, he hobbled around the kitchen and prepared roasted chicken, rosemary potatoes, grilled zucchini, and a fresh salad with walnut oil vinaigrette. He loaded the steaming dishes, garnished with mint leaves, onto the tray, and carefully negotiated his way downstairs. He peeked through the lens and saw Peggy and April lying on the bed, cuddled together. When he walked in with the tray, Peggy sat up, but didn't say a word. Simon set the tray on the table next to the bed.

"I thought April and you might enjoy a home cooked meal."

Peggy sniffed the air and licked her lips. April was still sleeping.

"I don't care what you do to me," Peggy whispered, "but please don't hurt my daughter again."

Her weak-willed tone pleased Simon. Maybe the wild filly had been tamed.

He sat on the bed. "I never intended to hurt her. Her fate was, and is in your hands." He pointed to the tray. "Why don't you wake April? I'm sure you both could use a good dinner."

Simon limped to the door, glancing at his wristwatch. He guessed that sixty minutes would be enough time for them to finish their meal. And for the doctored chocolate milk to take effect. "Bon appétit."

❧

For the sixth time since cleansing his first sinner, Simon went into the garage, grabbed the license plates hidden under the drop cloth, and switched them with the current plates on his truck. He was not a fool. No telling how many honest citizens may have jotted down his plate number while he was engaged in his holy work. When stealing plates, he'd been careful only to select vehicles identical to his own: same year, color and model. And he always replaced the plates with another set. Because most people didn't have a clue what their plate number was—unless of course they owned vanity plates, which he never stole—the plates were rarely reported missing. And even if they were reported stolen, he never kept them on his truck for more than a week.

Busy Southern Californian lifestyles were such that few people paid attention to their license plates. Driving around town with plates that did not match Simon's registration posed certain risks. However, most cops were looking for speeders, reckless drivers, vehicles with broken taillights or people driving around with one headlight. With a population of over two million people, many of whom drove like maniacs, the chances of Simon getting pulled over were minimal. As long as he observed the speed limit, he felt it was unlikely he'd ever be stopped.

Simon carefully sat on the garage floor and loosened the screws on the front license plate. He recalled how intensely Sami's eyes had focused on the cross around his neck when she came to the hospital. Her detective instincts, no doubt, were attempting to piece things together. He'd have to be extra cautious. Simon felt certain that meeting her had been a divine gift. He wasn't yet sure how the detective would fit into his plans, but knew for certain she would play a significant role.

ᕫ

Peggy sat upright with her back against the headboard. Her red hair looked ratty and uncombed, her skin ached like it did when she'd had the flu. How could this deranged monster cook them such a sumptuous meal? At first she'd been hesitant, thinking wild ' thoughts about what he might have hidden in the potatoes, or what Satanic ritual he'd used to slaughter the chicken. But having eaten only macaroni and cheese, canned soups, sandwiches, and snack foods for—had it been three or four days?—she couldn't resist. Carefully she examined the food and decided that the nut-case did not have a hidden agenda. At least not for the moment. The meal was nothing short of gourmet.

Curled beside Peggy in the fetal position, April fell asleep right after dinner. While she slept, Peggy gently replaced the dressing on her severed ear, cringing from the grotesque sight of it. The side of her head reminded Peggy of a species of monkey she'd seen at the San Diego Zoo. Revolting. Disfigured for life. Her little girl had been reduced to looking like a monkey. Peggy could not fathom anyone capable of hurting a child in such a way. As she stared at her peacefully-sleeping daughter, almost mesmerized by her missing ear, Peggy felt a wave of hopelessness wash over her. She'd read about her captor, how three other women had been raped and brutally murdered, their hearts cut out. Unless she devised a survival plan, soon her picture would be plastered on the front page of every newspaper in the country.

Quite to her dismay, Peggy McDonald did not feel terror from what most certainly would be an unimaginable and unavoidable death. Perhaps her motherly instincts, her will to protect April, diluted the impact of her impending appointment with the Grim Reaper. She knew that the children of the other three victims had not been injured, yet April had been maimed in a most gruesome manner. She could only blame herself for riling him.

Peggy heard the dead bolt unlock. Simon appeared in the doorway with two pieces of lumber under his arm. He wore some kind of leather apron with a hammer hanging from a metal ring. He closed the door and locked it.

"Is April sleeping?"

"Yes." Peggy looked into his cold eyes and knew: her time had come.

He set the wood on the floor and pointed to the chair up against the wall. "Move April to the chair." His voice chilled her to the core.

"I don't want to wake her."

"Do as I say, Peggy."

She knew not to disobey. Peggy carefully lifted April. Her daughter felt as limp as a dishrag. Gently, she lay her down, then stood at attention next to the chair, waiting for further instructions.

"Today is the most important day of your life," Simon said. "Are you prepared to cleanse your soul?"

Peggy's throat felt constricted. She couldn't form a word.

"Remove your clothing."

His words flipped a switch in her. A charge of bitter reality surged through her body. The thought of him inside her almost made her gag.

Keep your wits, girl.

At first she considered charging him like a mad bull. She'd noticed when he delivered their dinners that he favored his right foot. If she could catch him off-guard, jam her heel into his instep, maybe, just maybe she could incapacitate him long enough to snatch April and escape. But the son-of-a-bitch was big. Powerful. If she failed, what might he do to April? She forced the idea out of her mind; had no choice but to comply and wait for the ideal moment.

As Peggy undressed, she felt like a two-bit prostitute. She expected Simon to gawk at her with drool slobbering from his mouth like a rabid dog. But he paid no attention to her. This indifference puzzled her, and in a perverse sense humiliated her. Instead of enjoying the show like any self-respecting degenerate, he seemed content pounding nails into the lumber, making a T with the square beams. Peggy could not understand why the hammering did not awaken April. She hadn't even twitched.

Down to bra and panties, Peggy could not get herself to remove the last two pieces of clothing. It felt as though all her muscles suddenly atrophied.

I can't do this.

Simon glanced at her and set down the hammer. "What are you doing?"

"Nothing."

"I can see that."

"Simon . . . please don't make me—"

"You've got thirty seconds, Peggy."

Now he was facing her, his eyes penetrating. This is not what she wanted. Better for him to go about his business than watch. She reached behind her back and unsnapped her bra, all the while conscious of his stare. She could almost feel his eyes focused on her breasts. How horrifying. How totally degrading!

Enjoy the show, you son of a bitch!

After dropping her scarlet panties on the floor, the last piece of clothing to fall, goose flesh covered her skin. Peggy stood shivering, vulnerable. Her nakedness not only exposed her body, but her substance as a woman. Project completed, Simon stood up, almost losing his balance. Peggy watched him grimace when he put pressure on his right foot. She no longer had the advantage of wearing shoes, so digging her bare heel into his sneaker might prove fruitless. She had to inflict enough pain to be certain April and she could get away.

"Lie on the bed," he ordered.

If Peggy could tolerate his naked body on top of her just long enough, maybe she could distract him. She lay on her back, covering her breasts with her right forearm, while her left hand strategically concealed her pubic hair. The mere thought of him touching her sickened Peggy. Showing no interest in her nakedness, he stood over her and stared at the wall, hypnotized.

"Sinner, are you ready to give yourself to God, to cleanse your unclean soul and purify your impure heart?"

Now Peggy was mortified. She held her breath, terrified of what he would do next.

"You must give yourself to God without reservation and without remorse. If you do not offer yourself willingly, your sins cannot be absolved."

Peggy lay perfectly still, trying to make sense of his prayer-like riddle. Then, she looked at the hammer hanging from the leather apron, and thought about the beams he'd nailed together. He hadn't made a T, he'd made a cross.

A crucifix.

She remembered the headlines in the paper, the article about the last victim.

". . . wounds in her wrists and feet . . ."

Until this moment, Peggy hadn't believed that the other three victims had been crucified. She'd dismissed the evidence as media hype. Now, unfolding before her was the bitter truth.

Gripped with panic Peggy McDonald had never known, driven by raw animal instinct and an elemental will to survive, she leaped off the bed and tackled her captor with the force of a professional football player. Unprepared for the attack, Simon fell backwards and his body slammed against the floor. Peggy went wild. Before he could even begin to comprehend what had happened, or devise a way to defend himself, she doubled-up her fists and launched a barrage of punches to his midsection and groin. Somehow during the maniacal frenzy, a morsel of reason focused in her furious thoughts. Peggy remembered his limp. She turned her body and grasped his foot with both hands, twisting it and pounding his instep. What she didn't realize during this moment of delirium was that the foot she assaulted wasn't the injured one.

The first blow walloped her just below the solar plexus, his fist driving deeply, pounding the air from her lungs. She gasped desperately, but could not draw a breath. Now his hands were around her neck, his thumbs pressing against her windpipe, his body straddled over her. She could see a wild look of rage in his eyes. Gagging and choking, she grasped his thick wrists, but could not break free. Had he wanted to, she knew, his powerful hands could have snapped her neck like a twig. But there was a method to his technique. Of course, she thought, he doesn't want to strangle me. He wants to crucify me! At the moment before Peggy lost consciousness, Simon loosened his grip. It seemed that he had a sense of when she'd pass out. Peggy, frantic beyond rationale, grabbed Simon's groin and squeezed his testicles. Remarkably, he didn't even flinch. Instead, he grinned like a madman and yanked the hammer from the leather apron as if he were drawing a pistol. He cocked his arm and his eyes narrowed. This is it, she thought. This is how she would die. Time seemed to stop. He didn't strike her with the hammer, or utter a word. All she could hear was his heavy breathing. Then, just when she believed he might show mercy and not harm her, she felt the hammer ring in her ears when he whacked the side of her head. Her eyes went blurry and the only light in the corner of the room dimmed to blackness.

❦

At first, Peggy thought she awoke from a horrific dream, a moment she'd experienced dozens of times, when the terrifying world of make-believe surrendered to reality. But consciousness did not rescue Peggy today. She could not smell fresh brewed hazelnut coffee, only the musty odor of this prison-like basement. Andrew's soft cheeks would not be pressing against her inner thighs as he made love to her, as he did so often in the morning. April and she wouldn't bake chocolate chip cookies or watch The Cartoon Channel. When she awakened today, the violent throbbing in the back of her head reminded her that this nightmare was far from over.

Squinting, she opened her eyes. He stood over her, a hulking image gawking at her face with haunting penetration. Her body lay uncomfortably on a wooden cross, positioned on the concrete floor. Rope, tightly wound around her forearms and ankles, secured her arms and legs to the rough-sawn wood. He gripped a hammer with his right hand. In his left hand he held four silver-colored spikes, each six-inches long.

Peggy turned her aching head and could see April sleeping on the bed, still curled in a ball. She had no perception of time. She might have been unconscious for hours. What had he done to her during this period of time? What kind of twisted experiments had he performed? With a half-conscious brain and muted senses, Peggy inventoried her body. She sensed no discomfort in her lower abdomen, and it didn't feel like he had penetrated her, but how could she know for certain? The thought of this animal inside her assaulted her stomach with violent pain. She could taste vomit in the back of her throat.

He knelt on his left knee and positioned one of the sharp spikes gently against her wrist. He poised the hammer above his head.

"Sinner, do you offer your life to God as a sacrifice to cleanse your soul and purify your heart?"

Sweet Jesus, help me.

His lips tightened and his eyes narrowed. He pushed the spike firmly against her wrist, pricking the flesh. "Is it your will to die for your sins and redeem yourself?"

Peggy tried to speak but her throat was knotted.

"Sinner, I ask you: Are you prepared for everlasting life?"

In a mind of snarled thoughts, Peggy could only untangle one word. "April," she whispered.

"She will be spared if you willingly die for your sins." He tightened his grip around the handle of the hammer. "Are you ready to be cleansed?"

Peggy McDonald, thirty-five year old Irish Catholic, realized that her journey through life was about to abruptly end in a most diabolical way. Fate had intercepted her voyage and she would never see another sunset. Four-year-old April probably wouldn't remember her in adulthood. Andrew would mourn, go through a period of bitterness and solitude, but he'd marry again. Another woman would be lying beside him. Her entire life—summarized on the eleven o'clock news in less than five gory minutes—would be forgotten. Her total existence would forever be eclipsed by her role as the fourth victim of a crazed serial killer.

"Are you willing to die for your sins?" The hand holding the hammer trembled. Beads of sweat dripped down his face.

"What about my baby." It was not a question, but a breathless plea.

"She won't be harmed."

"No, you don't understand."

"I'm losing my patience, sinner. I told you that your daughter—"

"For God's sake, I'm pregnant!"

∽

As if Simon's hand had a will of its own, the hammer slipped from his trembling fingers and bounced on the concrete floor. He had never prepared himself for such an unmanageable possibility. Cleansing this sinner would also kill an innocent child, and Simon was acutely sensitive to the plight of unborn children. At an early age, he discovered the hypocrisy of our lawmakers; vile men who drafted laws supporting the butchers professing to be doctors. How conveniently Congress classified unborn children as embryos or fetuses. And for what purpose? Only to ensure the votes of pro-choicers. This sickened Simon. Often he fantasized about storming an abortion center and single-handedly executing each and every killer. Silently he applauded the holy crusaders, the brave soldiers so committed to their principles that they challenged the twisted system. He could never feel remorse for the murdered abortionists, for the death clinics burned to the ground or bombed to oblivion. It was the wrath of God.

But now Simon faced a most difficult dilemma. To release the sinner and preserve the unborn child's life would be just, yet not a feasible solution. How could he senselessly kill one of God's children? There was, of course, the possibility that she lied, pretending to be pregnant to preserve her life and derail Simon's Godly work. She had not deceived him though. Simon felt sure of this. When she lay naked on the bed, he'd noticed an unusual swelling in her lower abdomen, a bloating uncharacteristic of an otherwise physically fit woman.

He sat on the cold floor, pulled his knees to his chest and fixed his eyes on Peggy's face. Surely, if he let her go, she would promise not to betray him, assure him in a most convincing manner that she would never say a word to anyone. But in the end, when her anger swelled beyond the joy of having been set free, and her actions were driven by hatred and a profound sense of revenge, Peggy would tell the police everything.

If he ever needed his mother's advice, today was the day.

He closed his eyes and talked to her with words unspoken.

What shall I do, mother?

God has given you a bonus, my sweet son.

I don't understand.

The Earth is a wretched planet, overrun with violence, deception, fornication, and betrayal. It is a temporary stop, a momentary detour from our ultimate journey. You would be honoring this unborn child with a most holy gift if you gave its soul to the Lord.

Simon evaluated her words. He wanted to comply, but stood motionless.

Do it, my sweet boy. Do it now!

He hesitated for only a moment. Then, his body shivered and he could feel himself getting hard. Only his mother affected him so profoundly. As in the past, all he wanted in life was to please her.

"Sinner." Simon smiled at Peggy. "Today is truly a glorious day."

༄

Death for Peggy McDonald did not come mercifully. It had taken much longer than the others for her to draw her last breath. Simon, sitting on the floor beneath her, reading passages from the Bible, watched her wiggle and squirm for almost three hours. Her shoulders were torn from their sockets, and the wrist and foot wounds oozed blood. Her once rosy cheeks were ash-gray. Frequently, when the cold spikes piercing her wrists and feet rubbed raw against a nerve, she'd yelp from the pain. At several points her guttural screams were almost deafening. But knowing that pain was an integral part of redemption, her futile cries for help did not trouble Simon. In fact, he found solace in them. When she finally reached the defining moment, no longer able to lift her body enough to breathe, Simon stood and watched her transition with uncontrollable excitement. To think that he had delivered, not one, but two doomed souls to eternal splendor overwhelmed him with joy. With her lungs devoid of air, her cheeks purple-blue, it took four agonizing minutes for her heart to arrest. All the while, as life slipped from Peggy, the last vision in her cloudy eyes was April's little body curled on the bed.

Simon could see April beginning to stir. Before she awakened, he found a vein behind her left knee and injected the mild sedative, enough to ensure that she'd sleep through the night. He lifted the child off the bed and set her on the chair. Held upright, perpendicular to the floor, the base of the cross was securely fastened to heavy metal brackets anchored to the concrete. Carefully, he loosened the clamps and guided the crucifix to the floor. With a three-foot crowbar, he braced the round end against a wooden block for leverage, and slowly pulled out each of the four railroad spikes, much like removing nails from a two-by-four with a claw hammer. Blood still trickled from the wounds, but the flow did not surge as it did when her heart pumped. To absorb the blood, Simon wrapped cotton towels around her wrists and feet. Then, he lifted Peggy off the wooden cross, carried her limp body to the bed, and laid her on her back.

It was a moment he longed for.

The reunion.

He closed his eyes and cleared his brain of all thoughts, focusing on one image.

"Mother, are you with me?"

I've been calling for you, my sweet son.

"Shall I come to your bedroom?"

Yes, Simon, mother is waiting.

He opened his eyes and Peggy McDonald no longer existed. Instead, Simon's mother lay on the bed, her lovely eyes looked up at him and she smiled. Ah, how he remembered those soft breasts and long shapely legs. Just like he'd done so many times before when beckoned in the middle of the night, Simon removed his clothes and crawled into bed beside his beautiful mother. He lay holding her, stroking her silky hair, caressing her warm body. Then, gently, lovingly, he made love to the only woman he had ever intimately known.

EIGHT

Thursday was an unseasonably warm day when Sami left her home at nine a.m. The temperature was already at sixty-five. Ah, San Diego. Aside from the ever-growing population—by two-thousand-ten, forecasters predicted that America's Finest City would be more populous than Los Angeles—outrageous real estate prices, overcrowded freeways, the most discourteous drivers in the galaxy, and a culture driven by pure capitalism, it sure was a nice place to live. With the exception of a few stubborn clouds hovering over the shoreline—referred to by meteorologists as a marine layer—the sky looked clear and bright blue. She drove with her window rolled down, the invigorating air tousled her freshly trimmed hair.

Sami was not yet sure whether she felt disappointment or elation that the license plates on the black Supercab in the hospital parking lot did not belong to Simon. When she learned that the truck was registered to Alicia Chavez, fifty-five-year-old widow, a woman who'd never even gotten a parking ticket, Sami dismissed her original suspicions as foolhardy. Yes, Simon did fit the basic description of the serial killer, however, so did a few thousand other men. Perhaps, she thought, the lack of progress in this case was beginning to affect her ability to remain rational.

Normally, Sami worked Monday through Friday, eight-to-five, or at least those were the hours she turned in to payroll every week. To the outside world working a day shift seemed a bonus. Perhaps even unbelievable for a job in which the investigative process required that a detective be available whenever needed. Criminals didn't look at their watches before plunging a knife into a victim's chest. Therefore, Sami—and just about every other dedicated detective—invested plenty of off-duty time "working." If the San Diego Police Department compensated Samantha Rizzo commensurate to the actual time she spent performing police-related duties, everything from midnight surveillance, to early morning coffee with informants, to weekend research, to interrogating suspects, she could retire before her fortieth birthday. In spite of the craziness, she endured. Working a day shift was not a perk Sami earned. It just made sense. During the daytime hours, greater information resources were available, and detective support departments, such as the crime scene search unit, latent fingerprint unit, photography unit, police crime laboratory, and the document examination unit were more accessible.

Sami's concern with Captain Davison removing her from the case and turning it exclusively over to the Special Investigation Squad escalated with each moment she failed to produce a viable lead in the serial murders' investigation. Although the captain hadn't alluded to this possibility, Al and she had struggled through another unproductive week, and often, at least within the dynamics of police procedures, certain repercussions were understood without the benefit of spoken words. She did not expect a warning. One morning—perhaps even today—Al and she would be summoned to Davison's office and the bloodletting would be over swiftly. No debate. No begging for more time.

Unlike prior investigations, this case stymied Detective Sami Rizzo. Her acute investigative skills and inherent ability to unearth a clue from seemingly innocuous information had always been a topic of great amusement among fellow detectives. With playful respect she had been nicknamed Blood Hound. Not an image she aspired to, but Sami, a little appreciative, yet a bit insulted, reluctantly accepted the pet name in the facetious spirit in which it was intended.

Every once in a while, particularly after she'd uncovered a new piece of weighty evidence in a difficult case, a giant-size Milkbone dog biscuit would mysteriously appear on her desk, wrapped, of course, with a big red ribbon. She'd not received any doggie-treats on this investigation, and couldn't believe that she actually missed them. This case completely bewildered her. The killer was indeed stealthy. A cruel, crafty, calculating murderer.

She parked the Taurus in the underground garage, grabbed her briefcase and headed for the elevator. Just as she pushed the up-button, her cell phone beeped.

"Sami Rizzo."

"Are you prepared for a sumptuous feast of Italian cuisine?"

She'd forgotten about the tentative dinner. "Simon?"

"Just calling to confirm our dinner date for tomorrow evening." His voice sounded strange.

Date? Sami had always recognized the fine distinction between a date and enjoying dinner with a male companion. Did he really consider it a date, or was he merely playing the semantics game? The offer tempted her, but the week had been consuming, and as much as she needed and wanted a recreational break . . . "Can I ask for a rain check, Simon?"

"Do you really want to hear a grown man cry?"

"It's been a hellish week and I'm afraid I wouldn't be much company."

"All work and no play makes for a dull life."

"I really can't, Simon."

"Look, you have to eat dinner anyway, right? Why not with me?"

She thought about his logic for a moment. How terrible could it be eating dinner opposite a man she was attracted to? "What time would be good for you?"

"Seven-thirty okay?"

"Perfect."

"Would I be acting less than chivalrous if I asked you to meet me at the restaurant?"

Maybe this wasn't a date? In her little book of etiquette, an honorable man always picked up his date. "Where?"

"You're familiar with Pacific Beach, right?"

"Been there many times."

"How about Romano's Cafe, on the corner of Cass and Garnet?"

She'd never been there, but heard about the quaint and romantic setting. "I'll see you at seven-thirty."

"Great. I'm looking forward to it, Sami."

"Just in case something unexpected happens—you never know with police work—why don't you give me your home or cell number."

Silence. "How about I call you around seven, just to confirm."

"Sure."

He doesn't want me to have his number.

A pang of concern tweaked her subconscious.

∽

When Sami walked into the precinct, Alberto Diaz was sitting on the corner of her desk, talking to Captain Davison. Diaz did a double take. Sami and Al had developed an esoteric communication system. Certain looks or nods or facial expressions represented signals. Al gave her a quick glance and his eyebrows twitched, warning her to be prepared for something unpleasant.

Davison pointed to his watch. "Your alarm clock broken?"

She hadn't left the office until after seven yesterday, and thought she'd been entitled to a little slack this morning. By the agitated look on Davison's face, apparently not. "Worked late last night."

The captain, Sami thought, must have bought his brown suit long before the birth of his beer gut. His pants were so tight he had to wear them below his belly. The bottoms on his shirt pulled apart.

"I have some rather alarming news," Davison said.

At first, Sami panicked, immediately concluding that the captain had decided to yank the case. But then she realized such an unpleasant conversation would most certainly take place behind closed doors where the rest of the detective squad would be insulated from the bitter yelling. "Should I sit?" Sami asked.

The captain chewed on his lower lip and shook his head. "We found Peggy McDonald's body."

It felt as though Sami'd been punched in the stomach. "Where?"

"On the front steps of Saint Francis of Assisi's church in El Cajon."

"When?"

"Early this morning. Just before sunrise."

"And the little girl?"

Al stood up and stepped toward his partner. "Nothing on her. Yet."

A lot of questions whirled through Sami's mind, but suddenly she recognized that the captain hadn't followed protocol. "Captain, why wasn't I called?"

He folded his arms across his chest. "I didn't get the call myself until almost eight. Thought you were en route."

Sami felt that she needed to justify her tardy arrival. "The only reason I'm late—"

"Save it, Rizzo," Davison said, his voice edgy. "If you didn't bust your ass every day, you'd be wearing a blue uniform and walking a beat in South San Diego. Besides, we've got more important issues to discuss." He removed his glasses and rubbed his eyes. "Why don't you two step into my office?"

∽

The moment Captain Davison sat behind his desk, he lit a cigarette. After witnessing this phenomenon dozens of times, Sami concluded that Davison's habit was more reflexive than conscious. She wondered if he truly enjoyed smoking. Most of the time, halfway through a cigarette, he'd go through coughing episodes so severe that it sounded like he'd hack his lungs all over the desk.

As always, Al looked as passive as a man getting his fingernails manicured. Sami felt anxious. Davison leaned back in his squeaky armchair, sucked on the unfiltered Camel until his cheeks were concave, captured the smoke in his lungs for a few seconds, then exhaled a blue cloud of smoke. "You two got one week to find this guy. I'd take you off the investigation right now, but neither of you has ever let me down." Directing his words to Sami, the captain fixed his eyes on her. "I'm going to stick my neck out and assure the chief you'll make an arrest by next Friday. Don't make me a liar."

After digesting his words, Sami asked, "Tell me about Peggy McDonald's body."

The captain sat forward and rested his elbows on the desk. "Why don't you find out for yourself?" He glanced at his watch. "Her autopsy begins in an hour."

༄

Autopsies were an integral function of the investigative process; the gory part that Sami loathed. Thus far, forensic medicine had uncovered little information that offered a lead in this case. Sami never had the stomach for blood and guts. In fact, she didn't even like watching medical dramas on television. At times like this, when faced with an aspect of her job that she truly abhorred, Sami questioned why she'd kept her promise to her father. She'd been sucked into this career, seduced by the illusion of serving society. It felt like a one-way street with nowhere to turn around, no side streets to change directions.

Even if she'd decided to pursue another career, economics and her responsibility to Angelina made it impractical for her to consider furthering her education, which was the only possible way Sami could bid farewell to police work. Her mother, of course, was another issue. To rescind the promise she'd so thoughtlessly made to her dying father, a wish that bitterly portrayed her absolute love for her father, would surely give Josephine Rizzo yet another thorn with which to torture Sami.

But another, more compelling reason why Sami could not abandon the life of law enforcement loomed heavy: detective work was in her blood. It had nothing to do with earning a living, fringe benefits, prestige, or social status. Like a terminal illness that cannot be cured, one whose grip on Sami's conscience tightened with each new investigation, police work was an affliction from which Sami could never be healed.

The medical examiner's office was housed in the County Operations Center. The two-story structure, located in Kearny Mesa, a community of central San Diego, operated under county jurisdiction but still provided services to the city police department. Sami pulled the Taurus into the crowded parking lot and maneuvered the car toward an area reserved for law enforcement personnel. Al had just gobbled the last bite of his "breakfast" and a little confectionary sugar remained on his upper lip.

Sami eyeballed Al and let out a heavy sigh. "How can you eat donuts—jelly donuts no less—just before viewing a postmortem examination?"

Al licked his lips clean. "What's the big deal? Donuts are one of the five major food groups."

"Oh, really?"

"Never heard of them?"

"Not your version."

Al grinned boyishly. "Pizza, burgers, carne asada, donuts, and pussy."

Sami didn't flinch. Al amused her more than appalled her. Through their long relationship, she'd been conditioned to dismiss her horny partner's antics. "You're a pervert."

"Thank you."

Sami worked in a world dominated by men; crude, outspoken, self-absorbed men. Many still believed that women served only one useful purpose, and most men had few reservations exhibiting their chauvinism. Having been a minority in a vocation saturated with ego maniacs, Sami had learned how to survive: laugh at their obscene jokes, smile when they make indecent proposals, massage their delicate egos, but never, ever get romantically involved with a fellow detective.

In many ways, Al fit the sordid profile of the other male detectives, but his banter rang of an innocent teenager. He never treated Sami in a malicious manner, nor would he ever betray her. As partners, they were somehow able to shift through the sexism and establish a meaningful kinship. In many ways their relationship thrived because it could not be defined in traditional terms. Mutual respect created a strong foundation on which to build a solid friendship.

As they walked toward the building, Al draped his arm around Sami's shoulder. "You don't have to go in there, partner. Davison will never know."

"But I'll know."

"Why don't you let me observe while you wait in the car?"

"What would that accomplish?"

"It might help keep your Wheaties from decorating the autopsy room."

"You're in rare form this morning. Did you get handled last night?"

"Anticipation." He glanced at his watch. "Got a date with an angel."

Sami trusted Al implicitly. He had helped her through rough times. When Tommy DiSalvo abandoned her, Al behaved like a mother hen caring for an ailing chick. Three times a week Al spent his evenings with Sami, watching movies, playing backgammon, or just talking. Still pregnant when Tommy left, she'd considered asking Al to be her Lamaze coach, but when she realized that she might never be able to look into his eyes again, Sami decided to abandon the idea.

Sami had also fulfilled her role as an intimate friend to Al. Almost a year ago she'd discovered that he was drinking excessively. At first, she tried not to get involved, hoping it was only temporary. But when he started coming to work with excessive mint-breath, and his performance as a detective seemed impaired, Sami could no longer ignore Al's problem. A stubborn, proud man, it took a great deal of coaxing and even more patience to convince him to join AA. Sami had to bribe him, promising to attend the first five meetings right by his side. And she had. Sat next to him and held his hand.

"You'll never change, will you, Al?"

"I certainly hope not."

A certain hypocrisy existed in their relationship. Al's primary objective was to exploit the delicate feelings of vulnerable women who took one look at him and instantly fell in love. A rogue of sorts, a heartless manipulator, he would say and do anything to seduce a woman. Sami usually despised men like Al, yet he was her most intimate friend. Of course, much of what she knew about Al's sexual escapades was hearsay. In fact, of all the women Al supposedly dated, Sami had never met one. In spite of this, she believed that the sordid stories were mostly true.

Al, when he wasn't overtly conscious of his machoism, often conducted himself like a true gentleman. He opened the steel door and held it, allowing Sami to enter the facility first. They walked down a long corridor to the back of the building and entered the medical examiner's office. Immediately, Sami could smell that vile antiseptic odor. The air smelled clean, yet as offensive as concentrated chlorine bleach. Her stomach, having been filled only with black coffee, protested vehemently.

There were four postmortem examination rooms, brightly lit sterile environments where cadavers, bloodless ash-colored figures, once vital human beings— mothers, wives, brothers, friends—were systematically dismantled with stainless steel instruments and a matter-of-fact indifference that might lead an onlooker to conclude that medical examiners had Freon coursing through their veins.

To Sami, the whole business of postmortem examinations, a necessary evil in the art of homicide investigating, was an act of unthinkable disrespect. The environment in the confines of the autopsy rooms was neither solemn, nor mournful. It was almost like some bizarre recreation room where failed doctors got to work on patients they could no longer harm. Medical examiners approached autopsies with the casual insouciance one might exhibit while carving a Thanksgiving turkey.

Al tapped Sami's shoulder. "Should have asked you earlier in the week, but if you're free tomorrow evening, my neighbor, Rose, is having her annual before-Christmas-bash. Interested in joining me?"

"You mean Casanova himself doesn't have a date?"

"I don't date, Sami, I fornicate."

"Thank you for clarifying that." She hadn't planned to share this with Al. He often acted like an overprotective father. "Actually, I have to pass. Unlike you, my dear friend, I do have a date."

He looked at her with surprised eyes. "Anyone I know?"

"I doubt it. He's a gentleman."

"Aren't we the witty one." Al loosened his tie and unfastened his top button.

"With all due respect to you and your heritage, please tell me he's not a grease-ball."

"No, Al, he's not Mexican."

"Very funny. Is he the same breed as DiSalvo?

"He's Polish."

Al shook his head, giggling uncontrollably. "So when he takes it in the ass he thinks he's getting a prostate exam?"

"Did your mother wash your mouth out with soap when you were a kid?"

"When I was a kid, we didn't have any soap."

David Sherwood, sixty-two-year-old medical examiner, retired from the Navy, stepped out of his office and approached the detectives. The slight man—merely five-foot-five—had a severely receded hairline. What hair remained was unruly and pure silver. He wore reading glasses low on his nose, and looked over them when he spoke. He could easily pass for a mad professor.

"We have to stop meeting like this," Sherwood said. He smirked, obviously amused with his attempt at humor.

Sami had heard this line a dozen times. "Believe me, doctor, we'd rather be meeting you socially."

Without ceremony Sherwood turned his back on the detectives and led them to Autopsy Room #3.

Al elbowed Sami in the side. "Socially?"

The first thing Sami noticed as she trailed behind Al and followed him into the room was the cold air, almost frigid enough to see her breath. Her eyes surveyed the twenty-by-twenty room. Brightly illuminated, there were rows of fluorescent fixtures. Grey ceramic tiles covered the floors and the walls, up to the ceiling. In the center of the room sat a rectangular stainless steel table. A human-shaped figure lay on the table. Bluish-colored feet with painted toenails stuck out from under the white sheet covering the body. Attached to the cadaver's big toe was a pale yellow tag. Adjacent to the autopsy table was another smaller table abundant with instruments of the trade: scalpels, assorted saws of various lengths and shapes, strange-looking hammers, multipurpose tweezers, an electric rotary saw, and other incidentals. To look at many of these rather large surgical instruments, one might guess that this room was used to dissect elephants.

Sami gawked at what she knew was the lifeless body of Peggy McDonald and felt her knees buckle. She wasn't going to make it. She now knew that the moment Doctor Sherwood unveiled the woman's mutilated body, she would most certainly vomit. Regretting that she had not accepted Al's invitation to wait in the car, she grabbed his arm to help steady her unstable legs.

"You okay," Al asked.

"Never been better."

The room was like an echo chamber. Every sound—footsteps, spoken words, any noise whatsoever—bounced around and contributed to the already-spooky setting. Sherwood slipped on rubber gloves and stood beside the autopsy table. His arms were poised in a position ready to expose the body, to begin cutting, slicing and sawing. Al walked around to the other side of the table, facing Sherwood, and Sami stood in her partner's shadow, positioning her body behind him with her head peeking around his shoulder.

The medical examiner grasped the sheet covering her body. "Are we ready to begin?"

Such a melodramatic performance, Sami thought.

"Let's do it," Al said.

David Sherwood removed the sheet with the fluidity of a matador.

Sami stood stone still, hypnotized by a sickening image that punctuated a world in which the levels of human madness were infinite. Peggy's body was ash-colored with blotches of blue under her left eye, on both shoulders, under her left breast, and on the front of her right thigh. Sami's misty eyes quickly scanned the victim's body, then focused on her face.

"We will begin with a superficial examination," Sherwood said.

Sami took a deep breath, knowing that Sherwood wouldn't be using any of his shiny instruments. At least not for the moment.

"As you can see," Sherwood began, "unlike the other three victims, this woman's heart has not been excised."

So preoccupied with the grisly remains of a crucified body, Sami hadn't even noticed. She whispered in Al's ear, "His methods have changed."

Al pointed to the wrist and foot wounds. "Not all of them."

Sherwood examined her face. "There is a plum-size contusion under the victim's left eye, right at the temporal process, suggesting that her assailant struck her with his fist or maybe a blunt object."

Sami said, "None of the other victim's had injuries to their faces."

"Maybe she really pissed him off," Al said.

Sherwood lifted the woman's limp left arm and tilted his head back so he could view the bloodstained wrist with the benefit of his glasses. "The left wrist has been punctured with a sharp object between the ulna and radius bones of the forearm, just above the lunate bone in the proximal region. The wound is approximately one-and-one-half millimeters in diameter." He lifted her right arm. "This wound is almost identical in diameter and location."

Sherwood slipped his hand under the victim's right knee and slightly lifted the leg, so he could examine her foot. "The right foot has a wound approximately the same diameter as the wrist wounds. It is located at the transverse tarsal joint."

David Sherwood went through a series of observations, none of which resulted in findings dramatically different from those discovered during examination of the prior victims. Then, the medical examiner began a thorough examination of Peggy's genitalia. The total lack of compassion exhibited by Sherwood as he manipulated Peggy's body in a position compatible with his visual objectives seemed almost obscene to Sami. The woman lay dead. But did this give Sherwood, or anyone else the right to violate her in such a disrespectful manner? Surely, Sami thought, there must be a more dignified way to examine her.

As Sherwood poked and prodded, he kept mumbling under his breath, expletives that could not be interpreted. The emotionless medical examiner seemed perturbed.

"The assailant wasn't gentle with this one," Sherwood said. He swiped his arm across his sweaty forehead. "This woman has been savagely raped." He glanced at Sami. "And it appears that the rape was postmortem."

Sami squeezed Al's arm. "I'll be waiting in the car."

With his elbows planted on the kitchen table, Simon sat quietly with his chin perched on folded hands. His body shivered, dripping cold sweat. His mouth felt dry and tasted bitter. He wasn't sure how he managed such a lighthearted conversation with Detective Rizzo. Right after hanging up the telephone he almost passed out. He sat staring at the faded black and white picture of his mother. The years had colored the photograph with a magenta hue. In the background Christian music softly played on the radio. Simon's mind was submerged in a whirlpool of drowning thoughts. Unlike in the past, when all his actions were calculating and strategic, every move well planned and tactical, Simon lost his sense of self-preservation and had been careless. He had delivered April to Peterson's Department Store midday, amidst a flurry of holiday shoppers. What had he been thinking? His ability to make prudent decisions had been dangerously impaired.

The heavy fog had finally lifted.

All the excruciating details once securely hidden in Simon's subconscious, those cloistered memories protecting a powerful need in him to preserve an angelic image of his mother, were now jarred loose by Peggy McDonald. Everything, all the sordid episodes sequestered in his mind since childhood, had suddenly assaulted his conscious thoughts like a hungry beast awakening from long hibernation.

He lifted his mother's photograph. "Why, mother, why?"

He never knew his father. One day, before Simon was born, only weeks after his conception, Mikolai Kwosokowski—black lunch pail tucked under his arm and a sweat-stained baseball cap covering his curly brown hair—left for his job at the foundry and never returned. What little Simon had learned about his father had come from his Aunt Ana. His mother never spoke of Mikolai, and the one time Simon had been foolish enough to ask about his father, Ida Kwosokowski burned his tongue with a hot butter knife she'd heated over the gas flame of the kitchen stove.

Until last night, when Peggy McDonald unwittingly triggered a switch in Simon's mind, illuminating dark caverns filled with ugly secrets from his childhood, he had always believed, reveled in the false memory that his mother's actions epitomized her profound love for him. Wasn't it natural for a mother and son to touch each other? Didn't disobedient children, sinners who broke God's commandments deserve to be harshly punished? All of his perceptions suddenly changed.

Recalling how many times he had been summoned to her bedroom, he fixed his stare on his mother's seductive smile. He could still see her dimly lit bedroom, the white canopy bed, the blond-colored dresser, walls painted soft yellow, cold hardwood floors beneath his feet. How innocent he had been as a child. How totally naïve as a young adult. Oh how warm her body had been, pressed against his. The comfort. The security. Her skin so soft, like the satin fringe on an infant's blanket. The contours of her shapely body, her cream-colored skin, breasts so round and firm . . . his life was a lie.

He tried to suppress the memory, but the slow-motion video was already playing.

On the threshold of puberty, Simon had just celebrated his twelfth birthday. Still awake, lying in his bed, unable to fall asleep, his mother, wearing her powder-blue bathrobe, walked in the bedroom and sat on the edge of his bed.

"Give your mother a hug, sweet boy."

Simon sat up and she pulled him to her, squeezing him tightly, his face buried in her dirty-blond hair. Her perfume smelled sweet. She loosened her grip and placed her hands on his shoulders.

"You are a young man now, Simon. A beautiful young man."

She unfastened the top button of his pajama tops.

His mouth hung open but he couldn't speak.

She unfastened the second, then the third. Then, she gently stroked the smooth skin on his hairless chest, stopping for a moment to fondle his nipples.

"Mother. Please."

"Be silent, my son." She forced him to lie on the pillow and pulled the comforter down. "Do you trust me, Simon?"

"Yes, Mother."

"Then close your eyes my beautiful young man."

He had always feared his mother, but never quite like this. His body trembled and his mouth hung open in stunned surprise. When he felt her soft hand slip inside his pajama bottoms and gently caress his penis, he jumped. Then, as if under a spell, he lay motionless. With a steady rhythm, she softly stroked him. His mind raced with furious thoughts. At first he felt certain this was only a dream, that he'd awaken and it would be over. But as he felt himself getting hard, harder than he'd ever been before, more excited than he'd ever been before, he knew for certain this was real. Not even the photographs of the naked women in *Playboy* he'd gawked at while masturbating gave him such pleasure. That he could enjoy such an incestuous event sickened him to the point of nausea. But in spite of his disgust, he lay there, enjoying her skilled actions, gazing upon her beautiful face, desperately wanting to kiss her mouth.

She removed her hand, grasped his pajama bottoms by the elastic waistband, and slid them to his ankles. Then she stood, loosened the cloth belt holding the robe closed, slipped the robe off her shoulders, and let it fall to the floor. He had never seen her naked body, had never seen any woman's naked body. Not in real life. Her breasts were near perfect; symmetrical and full. Her nipples, the size of half-dollars, were almond-colored and erect. What shocked Simon most was her cleanly shaved vagina. He wanted so badly to hop off the bed and charge out of the room, but he felt hypnotized by her perfect body and lovely face.

Before he could even think about what she'd do next, she knelt on the bed and straddled his body. "Do you love me, Simon?"

He couldn't speak.

"Women are evil, my sweet boy. They will hurt you and deceive you. They will take your money and steal your love, and then they will leave you alone and miserable. One day soon, God will call upon you to be his special ambassador. You will have the honor of cleansing the doomed souls and impure hearts of unholy women. I will always be there for you, my wonderful son. My blood runs through your veins. Mother will guide you and nurture you and help you do God's work. I am the only woman in God's world who truly cares about you. Never forget that."

She grabbed his still-erect penis and carefully guided it inside her. "Happy birthday sweet boy." Slowly, she moved her body from side to side, strategically gyrating her hips. It didn't take more than thirty seconds for him to let out a yelp before he exploded inside her. She didn't stop moving. Instead she increased the rhythm, riding her son as if he were a wild stallion. Then, just when he thought she'd break him in half, she screamed and collapsed on top of him, her sweaty body stuck to his. After several minutes, she kissed him softly, hopped off the bed, put on her robe, and left the room without saying another word. Simon knew for certain that this was just the beginning of his journey into manhood.

Simon clenched his fists and pounded his mother's picture lying on the table. Rage welled in his gut. Repeatedly, he punched the photograph until his knuckles were swollen and bloody. How he wished his long-dead mother could feel the pain. He had always been a righteous man, had never been vengeful or vindictive. His lifelong goal was to carry out God's will, to purify the sinners of the world. Revenge was not in God's plan, yet the Bible, the written word of God proclaimed that an eye for an eye was just. Hadn't his mother quoted this exact proverb to him when he'd cut off April's ear? How then, would his mother atone for her sins? How could Simon cleanse her soul?

As if a suffocating weight were lifted from his chest, his soul purged of its suffering, Simon felt as if he could breathe again. What had happened in the past was God's will, and who was Simon to question his Creator's plan? After all, it was not uncommon for God to test his children. His mother would indeed be punished and he would participate in her cleansing. To dwell on the events of the past, to be riddled with regrets and ever-lasting analysis would only serve to sabotage Simon's appointment as a divine messenger. Continuing with Godly duties was the only thing that mattered.

Simon stood tall and took a deep breath. His commitment to carry out God's wishes was now fortified with a renewed resolve.

∽

More than an hour had passed since Simon had struggled with the memories of his twelfth birthday. Although still feeling unsettled, his emotions had calmed down. He sat at the kitchen table and glanced at the unread *San Diego Chronicle*. Under the front-page headline he read the story about the serial killer with great interest. The writer said that an undisclosed source claimed that the homicide department was close to an arrest. Nothing more than PR hype, he thought, a ploy to ease the public outcry. The article, of course, did not name the detectives, but Simon was reasonably sure that Sami Rizzo was one of the detectives assigned to the case. Her performance as a homicide detective was public record. No one in the department had a better history of arrests. Who else would they assign to such a high-profile case?

When he'd met her Thanksgiving Day, his interest in her had been merely that of a competent physical therapist and a servant of God. His offer to treat her back was motivated by a genuine desire to unselfishly help a sister in need. After all, weren't all of God's children brothers and sisters? Although he sensed that she was quite smitten by him, as were many women he encountered, he had never shared any of their romantic aspirations. Let the sinners play their foolish games. Detective Rizzo was a homicide detective. The homicide detective investigating the deaths of the women he had cleansed. He could no longer consider her a sister in need. She posed a serious threat to Simon's mission. He wasn't yet sure how things would progress, but would not allow Detective Rizzo to foil God's plan.

NINE

"Mr. McDonald," Sami said, "is this a convenient time for you to talk or should I call back?" Considering that his wife had recently been butchered and his daughter was missing an ear, Sami guessed that the last thing he wanted was to talk to a cop.

Silence.

"Mr. McDonald?"

"What do you want?"

Sami sat and rested her elbows on the desk. "Would it be possible for us to speak with April sometime this afternoon?"

"She just got out of the hospital, detective."

"I'm sorry, Mr. McDonald, but this is really important."

"Hasn't she been through enough?"

Indeed she had, Sami thought. "If there's any chance for us to apprehend the man who—"

"I'm not going to subject my daughter to an interrogation."

"I give you my word, she will be interviewed under the guidance of a certified child psychologist."

"And that's supposed to ease my mind?"

"Mr. McDonald, I know how difficult this is, but—"

"Tell me, detective, how do you presume to know what I'm feeling?"

"I can only imagine—"

"What can you imagine?" He paused for just a breath. "Do you have any children, detective?"

The question caught her by surprise. "I have . . . a two-year-old daughter."

"What's her name?"

"Angelina."

His voice softened. "Do you love her?"

At first Sami thought his question rhetorical, then realized he expected an answer. "With all my heart."

"How would you feel if some maniac chopped off one of her ears, if for the rest of her life she were disfigured?"

Sami'd been plagued by such a scenario many times. "It's inconceivable for me to fathom the horror I'd feel."

"Let me tell you what it's like, detective. First hand. My life is pretty much over. No, I'm not going to eat a bullet or OD on amphetamines. I'm grief-stricken, but not insane. No one—no matter how strong—bounces back from something like this. If Peggy had been killed in a car accident, or a plane crash, or even if she'd died of cancer, I could deal with that, digest it as the luck of the draw. I'm a fatalist, detective. I know that our lives are hanging by a thread. If she had died a normal death I would eventually heal and start over again." His voice was shaky and he kept sniffing. "That fucking monster cruci-fied my wife, hung her on a cross and tortured her. How do you recover from something like that?" He paused for a minute and sighed into the receiver. "I have a thriving law practice. I'm physically fit, and for the most part I've got the world at my fingertips. None of it means anything anymore. Every time I look at my daughter I'm going to be reminded. When I close my eyes I can see that bastard pounding nails through her wrists. I can see him raping her." Now he was sobbing. "Detective, when the medical examiner performed the autopsy . . . did he discover that Peggy was . . . pregnant?"

Sami felt her throat tighten. She swallowed with great difficulty. "We were aware of that, Mr. McDonald." Sami's palms were soaked with sweat. "Please help us catch this guy. April might have seen something that will give us a lead. You don't want him to kill again, do you?"

"What I want, Detective Rizzo, is to watch him roast in the electric chair."

"Then help us."

Again silence. "With all that's going on right now –" His voice was unsteady.

"—funeral arrangements and—" there was a long pause. "—I need some time."

Sami wanted to push him, but sensed it would be wiser to back off. "You have my number, Mr. McDonald. Call me anytime, day or night."

ॐ

Sami thought about canceling her dinner plans with Simon several times throughout the day. After all, if she had any hope of solving the case, she had no business going out on a date. On the other hand, as Simon so convincingly pointed out, she had to eat anyway. Maybe she'd meet him for a quick dinner and end the evening early. If that bothered him, then any possibility of an ongoing relationship would be impossible. As a homicide detective, working nine-to-five didn't solve cases. Besides, in the event of a sudden development, she could be reached on her cell phone or pager.

Sami couldn't decide what to wear. The look she searched for was casual-elegance, a term she'd first heard while watching a documentary on E! As of yet, she still hadn't quite figured out what it meant. Supposedly it was a California-thing. In choosing the right outfit, Sami had three goals: to appear fashionable, to camouflage her generous figure, and to look sexy without feeling slutty. A formidable challenge considering that her closets and dressers were full of clothes that would no doubt be rejected by The Salvation Army.

She rarely shopped for clothes and hated the thought of it. With the exception of the tailored business suits she purchased for work, most of her outfits were an accumulation of inappropriate birthday and Christmas gifts, presents from her mother that Sami truly should have returned, or at least donated to a charity for the visually impaired. Sami appreciated her mother's rare attempts to please her only daughter, but unfortunately, her Mother's flair for fashion was as lackluster as her zest for life. For years Sami'd pleaded with her mother, begged her not to buy gifts. But year after year the avalanche continued. Her closets were full of oversized blouses that could accommodate a nine-month pregnant woman, thick woolen sweaters designed to keep Eskimos warm, and an assortment of slacks and skirts in archaic styles, most of which were far too dull for Sami's taste. To further punctuate her bland wardrobe, on every occasion worthy of a gift, Tommy DiSalvo had given her, without fail, the world's most complete collection of tawdry jewelry. Much of the jewelry was so hideous, Sami wouldn't wear it to a Halloween party.

On this first, perhaps most important date, Sami wanted to impress Simon, maybe even entice him just a little, but she didn't want to give him the wrong idea. Sami had already paraded around the living room with five outfits at which her mother wrinkled her nose. She didn't really want to rely on the fashion sense of a fifty-six-year-old widow who'd been wearing the same sauce-stained apron and faded blue duster for over a decade, the same woman responsible for Sami's ghastly wardrobe, but she had no choice. Considering that much of what Sami had modeled were outfits her mother had purchased seemed to make Josephine's disfavor outrageously ironic. Maybe, in some demented way, Sami's mother had purposely bought her gaudy clothes?

Angelina—bless her dear heart—tried to offer support. Each time Sami did her runway strut around the coffee table, April had said, "You look sooo pretty, Mommy." She loved April's unwavering allegiance, but knew she'd get her daughter's endorsement even if she paraded around in her sweats.

It had been more than a year since Sami's last romantic misadventure. After being heckled by her partner, Al, who incessantly warned that she desperately needed to get laid before "the love canal closed for good," she foolishly placed a personal ad in the *San Diego Press,* a trendy periodical dedicated to food, theater, entertainment, cutting-edge cultural events, and a classified section jammed with single's ads. She'd placed it more to amuse Al than to feed some quixotic desire. She'd written what she thought was a clever ad. The headline read: Are You My Romeo? The body of the ad was poetically passionate, with a hint of Shakespearean wit.

Of the thirteen men responding to Sami's women-seeking-men ad, she'd eliminated nine of them via telephone conversations. Evidently, many of the eligible bachelors in Southern California needed a course in remedial reading. They responded to her ad with little consideration for what Sami was seeking in a mate, hoping, apparently, to charm her into compromising her standards. Two men admitted that they were married, and without the slightest hesitation proclaimed that they were looking for "something on the side." Neither had difficulty expressing exactly what they were seeking. Sami, amused by their outlandish proposal suggested that they visit Las Vegas, where prostitutes were abundant.

One elderly gentleman, soft-spoken and very polite, wanted to be Sami's Sugar Daddy. She'd never consider such a venal arrangement, of course, but when he announced that he was worth over a hundred-million dollars, Sami hesitated for just a minute before hanging up the telephone. Three men were struggling through gut-wrenching divorces, and Sami sensed each needed a therapist more than a soul mate. One of the men she met for coffee, who on the telephone spoke with the same charisma as a Kennedy, completely misrepresented himself. The supposed tall, fit, attractive, thirty-five-year-old attorney, was in actuality a squatty, nearly-bald, forty-five-ish librarian. Not that Sami was superficial. But she certainly wanted a partner who visually stimulated her, and she wasn't yet desperate enough to sleep with Mr. Magoo. Or a bold-faced liar.

To make it to Romano's Cafe on time—allowing for the usually-insane Friday evening freeway traffic—Sami had to leave her home in fifteen minutes.

Decision time.

As promised, Simon had called at precisely seven p.m. to confirm their dinner plans.

Wearing only pink panties and a matching bra, Sami stood in front of the full-length mirror mounted on the closet door and proceeded to torture herself. She turned from side to side, critically appraising her figure, wishing that the halogen lamp in the corner wasn't so bright. Her untanned skin looked pasty-white

How could she have lived in San Diego all her life, a community heralded to be the fittest city in the country, a virtual utopia of sun-rich landscape, and look like she should be milking cows in some Midwestern hick town? She folded her arms across her chest in disgust, and shifted her eyes to the more immediate problem: what to wear.

The black skirt, simple yet never out of style, slenderized her figure, and the slit in front was just naughty enough to expose a tasteful portion of her still-shapely legs. Okay, she thought, we're making some headway. She loved the feel of her powder-blue silk blouse against her skin. With the top two buttons left open, Simon might get a peek at her Wonder-Bra-cleavage, but not an eyeful. Now for the roadblock. Sami wished she could wear sheer, nude-colored pantyhose, but two varicose veins—gifts from Angelina's nine-month visit inside her womb—forced Sami to choose black, concealing hose, which defeated the whole purpose of the slit up the front of the skirt.

Go with it, girl, it's the best you've got.

After brushing her hair, Sami grabbed the almost-full bottle of Obsession perfume and dotted a few strategic locations on her body: both sides of her neck, just below her ears, in the bend of her elbows, and just above her cleavage. She finished her ensemble with a pearl choker and matching earrings. When she walked into the living room, she expected her mother to give her a disapproving scowl.

"You look very nice, Sami," her mother said. "This young man must be someone special."

Dumbfounded, Sami said, "We'll soon find out."

Angelina dragged her blanket across the room, struggling not to trip as she walked awkwardly toward her mother. "Mommy, you look sooo beautiful!"

"Thank you, sweetheart."

"Is Grandma Josephine gonna watch me tonight?"

"That okay, honey?"

"Um-hum. Will you read me a story before you go?"

"I'm sorry, baby, but I've got to leave in a couple of minutes. If you're a good girl—" Sami glanced at her mother. "—maybe grandma will read you a story."

"How about if we watch *Happy Feet?*" Josephine Rizzo said. "Would you like that, Angelina?"

She nodded her head vigorously.

Sami guessed that her mother had watched that movie at least fifty times with Angelina.

"What time is your gentleman friend picking you up?" Josephine asked.

"I'm meeting him at the restaurant, Ma."

Josephine fiddled with her apron. "Oh, a real gentleman, huh?"

"It's easier that way," Sami said.

"Easier for him."

Did she always have to meddle in her affairs? "Dating isn't what it used to be."

"I guess not."

Sami looked at the octagon-shaped clock above the television. "I've really got to go."

"You're gonna make him think you're some kind of cheap date."

Sami kissed Angelina on the forehead. "Maybe I am, Ma."

$\backsim$

Quite to Sami's pleasant surprise, the freeways were running smoothly. No ten-car-pile-ups or reduced-lane construction areas. Occasionally she encountered some nitwit so busy chatting on his cell phone that driving safely seemed to be an afterthought, but overall traffic cruised along without incident. When Sami exited Freeway 5 at Mission Bay Drive, twelve blocks from Romano's Cafe, her cellular rang.

She pawed through her purse, finding it just as she screeched to a stop for a red light at Grand Avenue. Ironic, she thought, that a detective would ignore the hands-free cell-phone law. She'd been meaning to buy a Blue Tooth, but hadn't gotten around to it. "Detective Rizzo."

"It's me, Sami." Al's voice was edged with tension. "Where are you?"

"Didn't take you long to forget about my dinner date."

"Sorry, partner, but you have to cancel."

"Unless you've got our favorite perp cuffed and ready to confess, you haven't a prayer."

"Sami . . . this . . . is . . . serious."

She couldn't remember the last time Al sounded so businesslike. "What the hell's going on?"

"Not over the telephone."

"Tell me."

"Get to the precinct as quickly as you can."

She wanted to argue, but the urgency in his voice begged for her to cooperate. "Give me twenty minutes."

"Drive carefully, partner."

Squealing a tire, Sami made an illegal U-turn and raced toward southbound Freeway 5. Other drivers, unaware that she was a cop, honked their horns. One woman waved an angry fist and gestured with her middle finger. Sami's thoughts were inundated with wild speculation. Maybe the killer had kidnapped another victim, perhaps even murdered her? But this didn't make sense. In the past, victims didn't end up in the morgue for at least three days after their abduction. The killer followed a pattern. Then Sami remembered Peggy McDonald's autopsy. Unlike the first three victims, Peggy had a bruise on her face, her heart had not been removed, and she'd been violently raped. The murderer's methods were changing, which could mean the time line of the murders might be more frequent. She remembered what Sally Whitman, the FBI profiler had said: " . . . when a murderer is driven by some perverse religious belief, he does not subscribe to conventional behavior . . ." With moist hands she tightly squeezed the steering wheel.

Sami eased her car across the flow of freeway traffic to the farthermost left lane. She paid no heed to speed limits. When she encountered a motorist unaware that the passing lane served no purpose for lazy Sunday afternoon sightseeing, she flashed her lights and engaged the siren. The intimidating power of that ear-piercing whine always amazed her. She could feel perspiration trickling between her breasts, and soon, her favorite silk blouse would have sweat-soaked stains under her arms. That Al would not openly talk via cellular heightened her angst.

As Sami raced toward downtown San Diego, re-evaluating Al's tense voice, she felt overwhelming alarm. Only a monumental event of a personal nature could force her partner into such an uncharacteristic tailspin. Al was a rock. Almost nothing rattled him. He knew something and couldn't muster the courage to share it with her.

Suddenly, Sami felt certain either her mother or Angelina had been injured. Perhaps both. Maybe there was a fire, or a household accident. Possibly her mother suffered a heart attack. But how could this be? She'd left the two of them only fifteen minutes before she'd gotten Al's daunting call. She reached for her cellular and thumbed in her home telephone number.

After four rings the answering machine picked up and she heard her own voice. Now panic-stricken thoughts raced through her mind.

She exited at Front Street, checked the cross traffic at Ash, then rolled through the red light. She peeked at her watch: seven-twenty-eight.

"Shit," she whispered. In her fury she'd forgotten about Simon. She had no way to reach him. She had only his work number.

As she pulled into the ramp garage, she flipped open her cellular and dialed four-one-one.

The operator spoke with a southern drawl. "What city, pa-lease?"

"San Diego."

"How may I help you?"

"The number for Romano's Cafe."

Sporting a charcoal Perry Ellis double-breasted suit, stark white shirt and amber tie, Simon, feeling rather dashing, sat at a corner table sipping kiwi-strawberry sparkling water, anticipating his impending date with great exhilaration. He enjoyed people-watching, an activity he found quite enlightening. Observing human behavior was an adventure. Studying their body chemistry and trying to read their thoughts through kinesiology was an art Simon had mastered.

The restaurant, crowded and noisy, buzzed with activity.

Next to Simon, snuggling together like Siamese twins was an intriguing couple. The gentleman—greying only at the temples, strong evidence he belonged to the Grecian Formula Club, looked about fifty, and appeared to be trim and fit. An executive going through an extended mid-life crisis, Simon concluded. The young brunette, giggling uncontrollably, barely in her twenties, pawing at him and burying her face in his neck like a kitten intoxicated with a sock full of catnip, was attractive, but obviously a trollop. Her skirt rode high on her bare thighs and her skimpy blouse offered an unobstructed view of manmade breasts. Simon never polluted his body or mind with alcohol. Nevertheless, he recognized the unique label on the champagne bottle the couple was drinking: Dom Perignon.

Sinners have no place among the Godly.

Just as Simon lost himself in thoughts of how he'd purify the souls of the couple he'd been observing, a tuxedoed blond waiter approached him.

"Excuse me, sir, is your name, Simon?"

Moderately concerned, Simon eyeballed him curiously. Why would a stranger ask such a question? No one except the homicide detective knew he was here. Simon's uneasiness heightened. His first inclination was to deny it. But to do so would serve no purpose.

"It is."

The waiter handed Simon the cordless telephone. "You have a call, sir."

Before speaking into the mouthpiece, Simon wiped it clean with his napkin. "Get caught in a traffic jam, detective?"

"How did you know it was me?"

"You're the only person walking the planet who knows I'm here."

"I've got some rather bad news."

"Let me guess. Some urgent police business has taken precedent over dinner."

"You must be clairvoyant."

Oh, how he wished he were. "And to think that I took my best suit out of mothballs just for you."

"How about a rain check?"

Only if you promise to bring your daughter. "Of course."

"I'll call you at the hospital early in the week."

"That would be fine." Feeling somewhat paranoid, Simon wondered if the urgent police business had anything to do with him. Perhaps his carelessness had given them a lead? "Does your change in plans have anything to do with the serial murder investigation?"

"Not really free to discuss that, Simon."

He curled his free hand into a fist. "I understand."

"Sorry about tonight." Sami said.

"Don't worry your pretty little head. You go catch the bad guys."

He dropped the telephone on the table and could feel that menacing rage churning inside him, the unharnessed passion to retaliate, a familiar need to release the stranglehold of a demon within.

Bonnie Jean Oliver.

He looked at the brunette, almost gawked at her ruby-painted lips. He knew that soon she would reward her Sugar Daddy for his self-serving generosity. Those pouty lips would do what they did best. Inside, a storm raged.

Slut. Harlot. Sinner.

He wanted to pick up a chair and smash it into her face until her flesh looked like a bowl of strawberry Jell-O. And her boyfriend? He drove the enticing vision from his thoughts. He motioned for the waiter. The young man hurried to the table.

Simon handed him a twenty-dollar bill. "I guess I'll be passing on dinner."

❧

When Sami walked into the almost-vacant precinct, she spotted Al in Captain Davison's office. Al's arms were flailing like a newborn eagle's wings. Considering how rarely anything affected him, his antics were not a good omen. Sami almost ran down the isle toward the office. Her lower back, which miraculously had healed without medical intervention, suddenly tightened. When she walked in the office out of breath, she took one look at Al's chalky-white face and knew that a devastating announcement loomed moments away.

"You'd better have a seat," Davison suggested.

She ignored him. "What's going on?"

Davison scratched the back of his head and eyed Alberto Diaz.

Al combed his fingers through his hair. "About an hour ago, the Scuba Squad fished Tommy DiSalvo's body out of the San Diego harbor."

Not having realized her deepest fear—hearing Angelina's or her mother's name—Sami felt a fleeting moment of relief. But when her mind processed Al's chilling announcement, the wink of deliverance was overpowered by devastating guilt.

She wobbled toward Davison's desk and fell into one of the chairs. "It's my fault," Sami whispered.

Al moved the other chair next to Sami, sat down and clutched her shoulder. "How could your ex-husband's murder be your fault?"

Murder?

Davison puffed his cigarette. "His body was in pretty bad shape."

"What do you mean?" Sami asked.

"Sami," Al said, "do you really want to hear the gory details?"

A valid question. Nonetheless Sami had to know everything. "Please stop treating me like a child."

"Cause of death has not been determined." Davison said. "He may have drowned, but our initial feeling is that he was murdered before they dumped him in the water."

Sami had little patience for their evasiveness. "Gunshot wound, stabbing, strangulation—how?"

Al let out a deep sigh and looked at Davison. The captain nodded. "His face was bludgeoned," Al said, "all of his fingers were fractured . . . and . . ."

Sami bolted upright and knocked over the chair. "Will you just . . . fucking . . . tell me!"

Al stared at the floor. "His testicles were cut off, stuffed down his throat, and his mouth was covered with duct tape."

Detective Samantha Rizzo suddenly felt detached from her colleagues. It felt as if she'd drifted into another dimension. Alone she sat in her guilt-riddled world. All she could see was Tommy's often-playful smile, a side of him she dearly missed. There were times when he could actually be charming, mischievous in an innocent, almost childlike manner. Struggling to maintain her composure, Sami told Al and Davison about Tommy DiSalvo's gambling debt and the threat on his life, that she had refused to help him.

"You can't blame yourself, Sami," Al said.

How she wished she could find solace in his words. "I have no illusions about Tommy DiSalvo." She paused for a moment, wiping her eyes. "But in spite of his shortcomings, he was still Angelina's dad."

TEN

Simon left the restaurant and stepped out into the cool dry evening. Only two blocks from the Pacific, a gentle breeze of salty ocean air filled his lungs. The cloudless sky looked crowded with stars and the sidewalks were jammed with Friday evening carousers hopping from bar to bar. Alcohol—one of Satan's most insidious servants—flowed freely tonight. By two a.m., when the local watering holes announced last call, Simon guessed that the area would be infested with drunken heathens tarnishing their souls through sins of the flesh.

Still reeling from his violent thoughts of the couple he'd seen at the restaurant, Simon decided that an invigorating walk on the beach would ease his tattered nerves. Episodes of stone-blind anger terrified Simon. He did not enjoy the disconcerting feeling of losing control. Periods of this unnerving condition plagued him more frequently of late, particularly since his first cleansing. He could not predict this eerie metamorphosis, nor could he manage it. The episode in the cafe had not been severe; he had dealt with his anger without incident. Simon feared that the momentary lapse of reason merely represented a dress rehearsal; that he stood on the threshold of something momentous. He didn't want to get careless; he needed clarity to continue with God's work. And a prudent man would heed this warning and remove himself from potential danger. But he felt drawn to the ocean by a powerful force, beckoned by some visceral connection to something.

As he weaved through groups of rowdy people, few he passed paid much attention to him. He brushed by them on the narrow sidewalk, favoring his throbbing right foot as he walked toward Crystal Pier. His dress shoes were much too tight for his ailing right foot. He passed outdoor cafes, coffee houses, secondhand clothing stores, souvenir shops, racks of post cards, T-shirt and sweat shirt kiosks, an ice cream parlor, a pastry shop, and of course an assortment of pubs and saloons.

The gate at the entrance to Crystal Pier locked at sundown, but the almost-endless concrete boardwalk following the coastline both north and south remained open and well lit, allowing crowds to wander at their leisure. Simon followed the path until he reached the stairway offering access to the beach. The moon, a sliver shy of full, illuminated the sand well enough for Simon to see that other than two clusters of party-loving law-breakers, gulping beer and slamming shots of tequila, the beach was relatively deserted.

In the distance he could hear the faint sound of a radio tuned to the local jazz station. Sade proclaimed that hers was no ordinary love. The low tide widened the sandy beach, and the ocean calmly slapped the shoreline. Moonlight danced on languid waves.

Before making his way down the sand-covered stairs, Simon, not wanting to lose his footing and risk tumbling to the bottom, removed his Valentino loafers and Gold Toe socks. The wound was still sore, but improving every day. Wrapped with gauze, it was protected from the sand. He rolled up his slacks to just below his knees. At the bottom of the stairway a forty-ish man, his full beard wiry and untrimmed, sat on the second last step, sipping something out of a brown paper bag. Sporting badly worn Army fatigues and a heavy camouflage-colored jacket, torn sneakers completed the tattered ensemble.

"Hey, bud, got any spare change?" His raspy voice typified alcohol-damaged vocal cords.

The sand felt cool under Simon's bare feet. "What exactly is spare change?"

The man gave Simon a cold stare. "You know. The coins jingling in the pockets of that fancy suit."

"Tell me something, my friend," Simon said. "If I were to give you some spare change, what would you do with it?"

The man cocked his head as if he were carefully considering Simon's question. "I ain't gonna bullshit you, bud." The man stood up and brushed the sand off his pants. "I'm about seventy-five cents short of a pint of Wild Turkey."

Simon guessed that the almost-six-foot man weighed barely a hundred-thirty pounds. "How long since you enjoyed a good meal?"

"Look, bud, if you got a few coins, I sure would appreciate it. But I ain't one for interviews."

"If you want me to give you money, the least you could do is answer a civil question."

The man pondered this for a minute. He licked his lips and took a swig from the paper-concealed bottle. "Lots of competition here in the beach area. Tourists are a little more generous than the locals. This time of the year, Christmas and all, it's tough. On a good day I can scrounge enough money to stay shit-faced, and keep me out of the morgue."

"What do you usually eat?"

The man smiled and shook his head. "Surf and turf."

Simon turned away from the man and headed for the water. "If you're going to insult me, I guess there's no need for us to continue with this conversation."

"Look, bud, what do you want from me? Wanna hear my hard-luck story? That I lost my job? That my wife left me? That I'm a victim of the system?"

"Just looking for honesty."

The man tipped back his head and poured the remaining alcohol into his mouth. Like a basketball player shooting a foul shot, he lofted the empty bottle into the nearby trashcan. "Mostly I chow down at Poncho's—a Mexican joint just down the street. They got five tacos for two-fifty. It ain't exactly the Ritz but it keeps me on the breathing side of the dirt."

"So all you eat are tacos?"

"A Big Mac now and then. I love Mickey-Dee's French fries."

"If you didn't buy liquor you'd be able to eat better meals, right?"

The man scratched his beard. "You some kinda social worker, or an AA member?"

"Just a servant of God."

The man stepped back, almost as if he were shoved. "Is that right? Well maybe you'd be kind enough to give your God a message from John T. Williamson." The man paused for a moment and fixed his eyes on Simon's face. "Tell him that the world he created in six days really sucks. And for some folks, living on this Earth ain't no Garden of Eden."

Surprised that the man's blasphemous accusation did not enrage him, Simon smiled. "Do you really believe that God should be held accountable for your chosen lifestyle?"

"Look, bud, all I asked for was some spare change, not a Sunday sermon."

Simon dropped his shoes and socks on the sand, reached in his pants pocket and removed a wad of cash folded neatly in half and held with a gold money clip. He moistened his fingers and peeled a fifty-dollar bill from the stack. "Are you a man of integrity, Mr. Williamson?"

The man squinted, as if he were trying to see the denomination of the bill Simon held between his thumb and index finger. "I don't rape, pillage or steal, if that's what you mean."

"Promise me three things—" Simon waved the fifty. "—and this fifty-dollar bill is yours."

The man studied Simon suspiciously. "You ain't one of those butt pirates, are you?"

Annoyed with the insinuation, Simon shook his head. "Interested or not?"

"As long as there ain't nothing kinky going on."

"On Christmas Day," Simon said, "I would like you to attend the ten o'clock services at Saint Michael's Church on Reed Street. It's right next to the library, only four blocks from here."

"My wardrobe ain't exactly fit for church."

"What you wear does not concern God."

He nodded. "Okay."

"After the services, assemble as many of your homeless friends as possible, catch the southbound bus on Grand Avenue, and take it to Katie's Kitchen in South San Diego. I want you and your buddies to enjoy a traditional Christmas dinner."

"I heard of the place but never been there." A strong wind blew in from the west. The man zipped up his jacket. "And what's the last thing?"

"From midnight Christmas Eve to midnight Christmas Day, promise me that you won't touch a drop of alcohol."

The man scratched his beard. "That's a mighty tall request, bud."

"I won't be looking over your shoulder, but if you agree I expect you to keep your word."

The man stepped toward Simon and held out his hand. "You got a deal, mister."

Simon handed him the fifty. He bent over and picked up his shoes and socks. "What size shoes do you wear?"

Williamson stuffed the fifty in his jacket pocket. "Eleven."

Simon handed him the two-hundred-dollar loafers. "You have a Merry Christmas, Mr. Williamson."

The man clutched the shoes to his breast as if they were a newborn baby. "You're a solid citizen, sir. God bless you."

Williamson watched Simon head north, noticing that the generous man walked with a limp.

෴

Only inches from the waves splashing the shoreline, Simon moseyed northward toward La Jolla. He had no particular destination in mind, only to benefit from the ocean's salutary peacefulness. The farther he strolled, the fewer people he encountered. When he reached a remote area of rock formations, a cape of sorts, Simon, his right foot now aching from negotiating his way over jagged stones, found a boulder with a flat surface, sat down and elevated his foot. The wind had picked up and the air felt much too cool for his lightweight suit. He pulled up the collar and closed the front of his jacket. In spite of the unfriendly air, a feeling of tranquility soothed Simon. His body warmed from within. He felt good about himself and his purpose in life. He had made some mistakes. Like all weak mortals Simon had broken God's laws. But in the Master's plan for mankind, He had provided divine forgiveness. Simon inhaled the salty air and felt his heart swell with excitement. One day soon he would be eternally rewarded for his intrepid crusade.

Simon had always felt an intrinsic connection to water. With its sophisticated ecosystem and innumerable species—many yet undiscovered, others having survived centuries of evolution—the vast oceans dramatically represented God's masterful and unlimited creative genius. Not that Simon needed proof to support God's all-good and all-knowing qualities, but the ocean offered countless examples of His wisdom.

Simon lived most of his life in Corpus Christi, Texas, a community situated only steps from the Gulf of Mexico, and his affinity for water began at an early age. As a child he would sit on the pier in the harbor and watch fishing boats for hours, imagining what it would be like if he could breathe underwater and swim with whales and dolphins and manta rays. He had become a certified open water scuba diver before his fifteenth birthday. By the time he turned eighteen, he had earned the status of dive master and had completed specialty courses in wreck diving, night diving, and underwater naturalist.

The wind whistled in his ears. The moon slipped behind one of the few clouds in the jet-black sky.

You have betrayed me, my impious son.

Her words exploded in his ears like a gunshot. "Leave me alone, mother. Haven't you hurt me enough?"

Such a naïve little boy Did you think that I would let you dismiss me like some cheap whore?

"You are a sinner, mother; a woman unworthy of a loving son."

Oh but you are so wrong, Simon. Remember those nights in my bed? Those long, lazy afternoons? Tell me that you did not enjoy the sweetness of my lips? Tell me that I did not taste like honey?

He pressed his palms against his ears but he could not silence her.

Prove to me that I am the only woman you will ever love.

"Please, mother, leave me be."

Know this, Simon: I will never leave you. You cannot wave your hand and banish me. I will be with you forever. I will live in your head till judgment day.

With his acute peripheral vision, Simon saw an indistinct figure approaching from the north. He quickly dismissed his mother's taunting words. Turning his head, he noticed a woman tiptoeing over unstable rocks, her arms held out like someone walking a tightrope. As she moved closer, only twenty feet away, he could see her youthful face. The gusty wind disheveled her long blond hair. Wearing blue jeans and a bulky sweater, the tall lean woman approached him. She stopped only feet away from Simon, staring at him in a peculiar way. The moon broke free from the cloud formation. The woman had the face and figure of a fashion model.

She smiled and stuffed her hands in her Levi's. "Thought I was the only one crazy enough to be out here tonight." Her voice was earmarked with a Scandinavian accent.

Watch out for this one, son. She will corrupt your pure heart.

"I don't think there's anything crazy about listening to the ocean."

"I'm Brigetta. Any room on that rock for another lonely soul?" Her soft words sounded pitifully desperate.

Simon moved over and she sat beside him. He immediately felt warmth radiating from her body pressed against his side. He thought it odd that a woman would be so forward on a dark deserted beach. "My name's Simon."

"Let me guess, your fiancée just jilted you."

"Why do you say that?"

"Only a deeply depressed man, lost in troubled thoughts would be sitting here alone, freezing his butt off, staring at the ocean."

Simon moved a few inches away from her. "I'm afraid that my story will not live up to your rather melodramatic premise."

For the second time, she adjusted her body against him. "So there's no heartbreaking story?"

He sensed her dissatisfaction with his inability to deliver a tale of woe. Maybe she herself felt melancholy and searched for comfort through another's damaged heart. "You sound disappointed that I'm not wallowing in sorrow."

She planted her elbows on her knees and rested her chin on folded hands. "Misery does love company." He noticed her staring at his bandaged foot.

"What happened to your foot?"

"Broke my toe." Simon felt a compulsion to put his arm around her, but fought off the instinct, believing it best not to give her the wrong idea. Especially after his mother's warning. "What's your story, Brigetta?"

She cocked her head and stared past Simon. A seagull gracefully landed on a rock to their left. The curious bird cautiously studied them. "The doctors tell me if I'm lucky, I'll live to see my nineteenth birthday."

At first Simon thought he hadn't heard her clearly. But when he looked into her eyes he could see only morbid blankness. "What do you mean?"

"Leukemia." She picked up a small stone and heaved it at the seagull. The bird let out a sequence of loud screeches, sounding more like faulty brakes on an old car than the protest of an angry bird. Clumsily it flapped its wings, and with graceless alarm the bird lifted off the rock and flew away. "The incurable kind that strangles your liver."

Simon felt an exigent impulse to harshly scold her for the blatant display of cruelness to one of God's creations. But considering her ill-fated future he sat quietly, without comment.

"If I had even an ounce of courage, I'd swallow a bottle of sleeping pills. But I'm too much of a wimp."

In spite of his common sense, Simon put his arm around her and pulled her closer. He could smell alcohol on her breath. "How much time do you have?"

"Six, maybe eight months."

Moved by her hopelessness, Simon squeezed her shoulder. "I don't wish to stick my nose where it doesn't belong, but I have to ask you, Brigetta, are you saved?"

"I don't think you get it." Her timid voice grew impatient. "I'm dy-ing."

"What I'm asking is if your soul is saved."

"You want to know if I believe in God?"

"Believing is not enough. Have you made peace with the Almighty?"

She didn't answer at first. Instead she stared at the ocean. "When I first heard the diagnosis, I spent most of my time—when I wasn't crying of course—praying to God, Saint Jude, and the Blessed Mother, asking all of them for a miracle." Her eyes welled with tears. "They didn't hear me."

Oh how Simon wanted to reassure her. Didn't she realize that God had indeed answered her prayers? He had sent her to him. "I can help you, Brigetta."

Her head snapped toward him. "Are you a physician with a miracle cure for leukemia?"

"I'm not talking about curing you physically."

Brigetta stood and steadied herself on the boulder. "You seem like a really nice guy, Simon, but what I need—"

"What have you got to lose?"

She pondered his words for a few moments. "Everything."

He stood and faced her, gripping her shoulders. "Trust me, Brigetta."

She gazed at him with haunted eyes. "Simon, I've got to cram a lifetime of fun into less than a year. If you really want to help me . . ."

Be careful, son.

"What do you want from me?" Simon asked.

She brushed the back of her hand against his cheek. Standing on her tiptoes, she leaned into him, cupped her hand around the back of his neck, and tried to kiss him, but Simon stepped back.

Told you, son. She's like all the rest.

Simon could feel his compassion for the young woman began to fade. His face felt warm. "I'm flattered, Brigetta, honestly, but I don't think this is a good idea."

"You don't find me attractive?"

"That's not it at all. You're a beautiful young—"

"Then why?"

Silence.

She shook her head and snickered, then pushed her hair out of her eyes. "What man in his right mind would turn down such a sure thing?"

"A man with integrity and moral fiber."

"Are you gay?"

His anger swelled. "Of course not."

"Then why are you being so difficult?"

"I can only help you spiritually."

Brigetta's face contorted. "Is it because I'm dying? Does that sicken you? Afraid you'll get infected or something?"

"Brigetta, please don't do this."

She didn't sense the danger. "Are you impotent?"

Simon took a deep breath and exhaled slowly. "Brigetta, please."

"I'm not asking for an engagement ring."

Are you going to let her humiliate you, son?

"I have a great deal of empathy for you, Brigetta, but I don't appreciate what you're trying to do."

"What I'm trying to do is have a little fun before I fucking die!"

"You picked the wrong guy. If I've misled you in some way—"

"You're really serious, aren't you?"

"I think it's time for me to go."

"I'll bet you're a fag, right?" Now she was almost screaming.

"You don't know what you're talking about?"

She taunted him with a mocking laugh. "You're not man enough for a woman like me."

"Please don't yell."

She loosened her belt and unzipped her jeans. "Let's get down and dirty right here on the sand."

He turned and moved away from her. She grasped his shirtsleeve, her long fingernails digging into his skin.

"Let go of me, Brigetta."

Without saying a word, she cocked her arm and slapped him hard. He shook it off, but his face was on fire.

As if standing in a dark tunnel, Simon's eyes went black for a moment. His heart thumped out of control. When he opened his eyes, Bonnie Jean Oliver stood in front of him.

Not all souls can be cleansed, my sweet boy.

ELEVEN

Saturday evening at eight-fifteen p.m., after reading Angelina a story from the Doctor Seuss collection, *Green Eggs and Ham*, struggling with every word as if English were Sami's second language, she tucked her daughter in bed. "Mommy, your voice sounds funny," Angelina had said. "Read it the good way." In spite of Sami's troubled state of mind, she couldn't help but laugh at Angelina's carefree innocence.

Sami flipped on the night-light, and just as she partially closed the bedroom door, she heard the doorbell chime. God, no. It had to be her mother. She had insulated herself from the world for the entire day—hadn't answered the telephone, ignored her pager, even turned off the cellular. And most remarkably she hadn't spoken to her mother. For all Sami knew, an asteroid could be hurling toward Earth, potentially ending all life. She seriously thought about ignoring the doorbell, but there were limits to her irresponsible hiatus from humankind.

She had spent the entire day with her daughter, but hadn't found the courage to tell her. Amidst a punishing feeling of guilt, Sami's anguish heightened to unbearable levels. At the mere thought of revealing to Angelina that her father had died, Sami broke out in a cold sweat. How could she explain to a two-year-old that she'd never see her dad again? How could she ever expect to compose a speech so delicately diplomatic that her daughter might be spared just an ounce of the misery associated with having to spend the rest of her life as a fatherless child? But making a morbid announcement to Angelina was only part of Sami's problem.

Sami walked by the mirror mounted on the wall in the foyer and reluctantly glanced at her unkind reflection. She hadn't showered today and her hair looked matted down and greasy. She wore an oversized terry robe that should have been cut into rags years ago. Without makeup she looked like she could play the lead in Night of the Living Dead.

The doorbell chimed again.

As Sami twisted the doorknob with one hand and unlocked the dead bolt with the other, she expected that her mother, annoyed and ready for a brawl, would be standing on the other side of the door with that agitated look she'd seen so often. When Sami saw her partner's friendly face, she let out a sigh of relief.

Alberto Diaz grinned. His ivory-white teeth were flawless. "Thought before we issued an APB, I'd knock on your front door."

"It's been a rough day."

"Is it safe to come in?"

"Enter at your own risk."

Sami sat on the sofa and Al seemed content pacing the floor.

"You look like shit," Al said.

"Thanks, Al, I can always rely on you to lift my spirits."

"It gets worse." Al shook his head. "Davison yanked us off the investigation."

"Son-of-a-bitch!"

"Guess Chief Larson crawled up the captain's ass." Al never minced words.

"He didn't have the courtesy to tell me himself?"

"Have you checked your messages? He's been trying to reach you all day."

Not only had she ignored incoming telephone calls, she'd turned down the volume on her answering machine. "But he said we had until next Friday before he'd pull the plug."

"There's been another young woman murdered. It doesn't fit the serial killer's M.O., but there are enough similarities to make Davison panic. He's yanking us and letting the special task force lead the investigation."

Sami wanted to scream, to pick up the crystal candy dish sitting on the corner of the cocktail table and heave it across the room. Oh how she wanted to break something! "I don't need this shit today, Al. And I don't want to hear the gory details."

"I'm sorry, partner." Al sat next to Sami and rubbed her back. "Hope you're not pissed with me."

"It's not your fault. You're just the courier."

They sat quietly for several minutes. Al's gentle hands massaged the taut muscles along the top of Sami's shoulders. His hands felt soothing, yet unsettling, reminding her of the tender moments she'd had with Tommy, moments in their early relationship that had faded so quickly.

"Davison wants us to investigate this most recent murder," Al said.

"And what happens if we find out that the woman was victim number five?"

Al lifted a shoulder. "Don't know."

Sami finally realized that Al had never seen her so slovenly. "So what do you think of my new hairdo?"

Al made a yummy sound. "If I were into alien refugees, you'd be first on my list."

"You are the charmer, aren't you?"

He smiled briefly, but then his lips tightened. "I thought you might want to know that Davison assigned Anderson and McNeil to Tommy's murder investigation."

Al's announcement, somewhat nonchalant, struck Sami in a peculiar way. Investigating Tommy's murder? It all seemed so unreal. "Tell them not to waste their time."

Al stopped rubbing her shoulders.

"Unless our extradition agreement with Mexico has improved," Sami said, "I doubt that they'll ever find the murderers."

"Why do you say that?"

"Tommy was a brainless gambler. A not-so-bright gambler. After burning every bookie from here to L.A., constantly hiding from those goons threatening to break his fingers, he found what he believed to be a windfall in Tijuana. He started placing bets with a group of Mexican hoodlums. Wanna be Mafiosos. These guys were a lot more liberal than American bookies. They let Tommy get into their knickers for thousands without hassling him."

"Something must have happened for them to murder him."

"Tommy had no sense of fair play. His motto was, 'You play ball with me, and I'll stick the bat up your ass.' When the Mexicans realized that Tommy had no intention of paying back the debt, they threatened to kill him."

Al grabbed Sami's hand.

Sami tried to swallow the lump in her throat. "I should have helped him."

"You weren't his keeper, Sami. Besides, the last time you bailed out his sorry ass he promised to seek help through Gambler's Anonymous. And what did he do?"

Sami didn't say a word.

"He blew you off, Sami. You can't blame yourself. Even if you'd been crazy enough to borrow against your home and save his hide, how long before he got himself into another life-threatening jam? Let it go, Sami. He's not worth it."

She didn't need to hear it from Al to know that Tommy was a hopeless, worthless liar. Still, she couldn't help but feel that in some indirect way she'd betrayed Angelina. "Think you could find it in your heart to give this not-so-lovely woman a hug?"

"You got it, partner."

Al's loyal friendship was much-needed therapy for Sami. It warmed her to feel affection. It had been such a long time since Sami had felt so safe and secure. She didn't want Al to let go.

"I hate to break up this party," Al whispered in Sami's ear, "but we've got a witness to interview."

"You mean tonight?"

Al glanced at his watch and nodded. "How fast can you shower and make yourself presentable?"

"It'd be easier if my plastic surgeon made house calls." Sami's mother was the only babysitter she could summon at a moment's notice. She dreaded calling her, but had no choice. "Why don't you brew a pot of coffee while I make arrangements for Angelina and get ready as quickly as I can?"

"Sure thing." He winked at her. "Welcome back, partner."

෨

Quite to Sami's surprise, her mother agreed to baby sit without comment or inquisition. Sami strongly suspected that her mother hadn't yet figured out how to approach her on the subject of Tommy's murder—a topic sure to be overanalyzed for decades to come. So instead of making small talk, Sami felt certain that her mother plotted quietly. In due time, Josephine Rizzo would launch a relentless attack, and Sami would pay a painful price for this momentary pardon from hell. Her mother would exhume any progress Sami might make to bury her guilt, which at this early juncture seemed incomprehensible. If any truth existed to the cliché, "you always hurt the one you love," her mother had indeed proved her love for Sami. Time and time again.

For the first time in months, Al drove and Sami navigated. Usually Sami took on both responsibilities, not by choice but necessity. On the many occasions Al had hopelessly tried to offer directions, he'd always found a way to get them lost. And Sami could never quite pass an opportunity to harass her partner, who for the most part enjoyed being the harass-er rather than harass-ee. "Al," she had said the last time they were lost somewhere in east San Diego County, "you couldn't find your ass with a detailed road map."

Bogged down in heavy Saturday evening traffic on the main strip of Pacific Beach, the detectives crawled along Garnet Avenue, neither having much to say, each of them caught up in private thoughts. Two blocks from Crystal Pier, they drove by Romano's Cafe, and Sami got an eerie feeling knowing that the murder had taken place only a short distance from where Simon and she had intended to have dinner. A meaningless coincidence, yet it added to her edginess.

Simon.

Since hearing about Tommy's murder, Sami had little time to think about Simon. In a twisted sense—

considering that Tommy's funeral hadn't even taken place yet—she actually felt guilty enjoying the little fantasies that often danced through her mind. But why should she feel guilty daydreaming about the charming man who had stirred her womanly emotions, feelings she'd given up for dead? Didn't she have a right to these visions? She now understood that guilt came easy to her. She embraced it like a treasured heirloom. Guilt, whether self-inflicted or induced by her mother's masterful insinuations, rendered Sami helpless. Time and again her mother used it so effectively, manipulating Sami throughout her childhood and now into her adult life.

Unable to find a legal parking space, Al pulled next to a red curb, a no standing zone, and flipped down the sun visor, displaying the Official Police Business sign in the windshield.

Al turned off the ignition. "Rank sure has its privileges."

"And you enjoy every one of them."

"Hey, for the paltry sum we get paid, we have to take full advantage of the fringe benefits."

About to get out of the car, Al grasped the door handle, but Sami grabbed his arm. "Tell me about the victim."

In the dim light Al studied her critically. "Sure you want to know?"

"No. But tell me anyway."

He hesitated for a moment. "She was young, Sami, born in Sweden, eighteen year's old. Her parents told me she had recently signed a contract with Models, Inc. Would have had a promising career as a fashion model. The ironic thing is, she had leukemia—had less than a year to live."

Sami thought about that for a minute. "Could it have been suicide?"

Al grasped the steering wheel and adjusted his body. "She died from repeated blows to the face with a rock the size of a cantaloupe."

Sorry she had asked for details, Sami took a breath. "What details of her death are similar to the serial murders?"

"The assailant cut a cross into her stomach. It might not be a connection, but then again, you never know."

"Are we interviewing a witness?" Sami asked.

He shook his head. "Not exactly. At the scene of the murder, the Crime Scene Unit found a Gold Toe sock. That information somehow ended up in a newspaper article. We got a call from some homeless guy." Al fished through his pockets and pulled out a crumpled piece of paper. "John Williamson. Last night he spoke with a tall man walking barefoot on the beach in a business suit. Said that the guy gave him fifty bucks and a pair of expensive loafers. In return, the guy asked Williamson to attend services on Christmas Day and to promise not to drink. While they were talking, our homeless guy noticed that the suspect was holding a pair of socks with gold toes."

Anyone could have carved a cross into the young woman's body. Perhaps to further incriminate the serial killer. But asking the homeless man to attend church on Christmas Day might suggest that the suspect was religious. That the man in question was tall, punctuated the premise.

"Where are we meeting Williamson?" Sami asked.

"Near the beach."

◌～◌

John T. Williamson, ex-marine, former father, husband, and taxpayer, waited under a bright mercury vapor light in front of the entrance to Crystal Pier, exactly where he'd agreed to meet the detectives. There were other people in the area—a few joggers, several rollerbladers, people casually strolling along the boardwalk—but Al recognized Williamson immediately from the description he'd given over the telephone. The homeless man looked fidgety. Headphones dangled around his neck and the wire disappeared in his jacket pocket. He held a backpack in one hand and a cigarette in the other, puffing on it nervously. He was pacing like a caged hyena when the detectives approached him. The man stood tall, skinny as a pencil, walked with a slight limp.

"Are you John Williamson?" Al asked.

"John T. Williamson, if you please."

"I'm Detective Diaz and this is my partner, Detective Rizzo."

Careful not to damage the half-smoked cigarette, he extinguished it and put it in his jacket pocket. "I'm not in any sort of trouble or anything, am I?" Williamson's voice cracked.

"Not unless you're an accomplice to the murder," Al said.

Williamson didn't connect with Al's twisted humor. "Well, God knows I'm not. What I meant was, being homeless and all . . . you know, panhandling. That sort of thing. It's not a crime is it?"

"Only if you're harassing people," Sami said.

The witness looked relieved. "Don't know that I can help you. Can't believe the guy I spoke to could hurt anybody. He was weird, but not the murdering type."

"Why don't you let us make that determination, Mr. Williamson," Al said.

Williamson pointed to a row of concrete benches lining the boardwalk. "Mind if we sit over there and talk?" He grimaced and rubbed his knee.

"Are you injured?" Sami asked.

"Got this trick knee that flares up in the cool weather."

Al and Sami followed the witness to a vacant bench sitting under a cluster of tall palm trees. From where they sat, they could hear the ocean washing the shoreline.

Sami removed a pad and pen from her jacket pocket. "Can you give us a detailed description of the man in question?"

"Well, you know, it was dark on the beach and I didn't really pay much attention to his face." He played with his grisly beard. "He was big, built like a brick shit-house. Broad shoulders. Looked like a linebacker."

"What color was his hair, eyes? Any distinguishing features?" Sami asked.

"Geez, I'm really sorry, but I can't remember." He licked his lips and twisted his neck as if his collar were over starched. "I was a little under the weather last night."

"You mean intoxicated?" Al asked.

"Not drop-dead-drunk. Just a little tipsy. It helps take the bite out of the chilly nights."

"If you saw him again," Sami asked, "do you think you could identify him?"

He did a thumbs-up. "Could pick him out of a lineup hands down."

"You told me on the telephone," Al said, "that you called because the man you spoke to was holding a pair of Gold Toe socks?"

"Yep. Every morning at sunrise, I get a cup of coffee at Johnnie's and read the *Chronicle*. Don't have to pay for the paper, cause there's a bunch of them for free. Johnnie's good about customer service and all. Mostly I read the sports, but I couldn't help but see the big headlines about the girl murdered on the beach. When something like that happens right in a guy's backyard, well, you pay close attention. Anyway, when I read that they found a sock with gold toes, I remembered that the guy I spoke to was holding a pair in his hand, so I made the call. Figured that's what I'm supposed to do."

"You mentioned that the man was weird," Sami said. "In what way?"

"He was one of those religious fanatics. Seemed awful interested in saving my soul. What kind of guy gives a total stranger fifty bucks and a pair of expensive shoes just to make him go to church on Christmas Day and promise not to booze it up? Seems strange to me."

"Do you still have the shoes?" Sami asked.

"You bet your life." His raspy voice bellowed with pride.

Williamson unzipped the backpack. As he gingerly removed the shoes, handling each one like a carton of eggs, this almost solemn ceremony struck Sami. It occurred to her that the man's total worldly belongings were stuffed in that tattered backpack. No home or furniture or cellular or big screen TV. Only the wares of utter necessity. The shoes, she guessed, represented a status beyond this man's grasp. He clung to them like a life preserver and linked him to prosperity and a lifestyle he might never know.

"May we see the shoes?" Al asked.

Williamson reached out and handed Al the black loafers. A profound look of concern painted Williamson's face. "You're not gonna . . . what's that word . . ."

"Confiscate?" Sami offered.

"Yeah, that's it. You ain't gonna confiscate them, are ya?"

Al eyed Sami. They both knew that the shoes, now contaminated, offered little information about the suspect. But to follow prescribed police procedures they were required to assume possession. "They're your property, Mr. Williamson, but we do need to borrow them."

Williamson shook his head. "For how long?"

"Just long enough for our lab to run a few tests," Al said.

"They ain't gonna ruin 'em are they? I mean cut them open looking for clues and that sort of thing?"

"Not to worry, Mr. Williamson," Sami said. "We'll return them to you as soon as we can."

Williamson sucked air through clenched teeth, shaking his head slightly. "I don't mean to be disrespectful, but can you give me some sort of receipt for the shoes?"

Sami smiled. "Sure, Mr. Williamson." She pawed through her purse and scribbled on the back of a bank deposit slip. "Here you go."

"Much obliged." He neatly folded it in half and stuffed in his jacket pocket.

Al carefully examined the shoes. The soles and heals were barely worn. Inside the soft leather loafers he noticed an insignia, a shield of sorts with the initials E. V. Under the shield, he spotted the name, Enrico Valentino

"Our suspect has expensive taste," Al said. "These are two-hundred-dollar shoes."

"I expected they were," Williamson said.

"Have you worn the shoes?" Al asked.

He shook his head. "I ain't exactly dressed proper enough for those shoes."

A rollerblader with purple hair came whizzing by, almost crashing into them.

"Ought to be a law against them damn skaters," Williamson said.

Not wanting to further contaminate the evidence, Al placed the shoes in a plastic evidence bag. "Tell me, Mr. Williamson, what did you and our generous mystery-man talk about?"

"He preached a bit, nagged me about my drinking and poor diet. Geez, you'd think the guy was my brother or something."

"When you finished talking to him," Sami asked, "in which direction did he walk?"

"North." Williamson pointed. "Toward those rocks where they found the girl's body."

"Anything else you can tell us?" Sami asked.

"Only that the guy walked with a slight limp."

An image of Simon flashed in Sami's mind. She recalled her visit to the hospital and Simon's story about the broken baby toe. "Can you remember which leg he favored?"

Williamson cocked his head to the side, considering her question. "It was his right leg."

"You're sure."

He nodded vigorously. "I'd make a wager on it."

Sami handed Williamson her business card. "If you think of anything else, please call me at once."

He angled the card toward the light and studied it. "Think he's the same sicko that's crucifying all those women?"

Sami shrugged. "It's hard to know at this point, Mr. Williamson."

"Seeing as we're all well acquainted now, there's no need for formal talk. Why don't you call me J. T.?"

Al shook his hand. "Thanks for your help, J. T."

Sami thought the conversation was over, but she caught a neediness in Williamson's eyes, a plea for her not to leave just yet. He looked like a child, about to say goodbye to his mother before stepping onto a school bus his very first day of kindergarten.

"Are you okay?" Sami asked.

"I just wanted you detectives to know that I appreciate you not treating me like some kind of misfit. It ain't no picnic having to beg for a livin'. I never hassle people. Whether they give me a little change or not, I always say, 'God bless you.' Even when they're rude. Not everyone living on the streets has a choice."

"We understand that." Sami said.

Al, apparently uninterested in hearing the man's life story, elbowed his partner, signaling that he wanted to leave, but Sami ignored him.

"How long have you been homeless?" Sami asked.

He counted on his fingers. "Six years. I'm not from these parts. Born and raised in North Dakota. When I lost my job at the sawmill, everything turned to shit. Lost my home, and then the wife took off with my kid . . ." he stared at his badly-worn sneakers.

". . . boy's name is Billy. Nine years, two months, and eighteen day's old." His eyes beamed with a cold intensity. "When I turned to the booze, I had no chance to find another job. Didn't want to. All I cared about was finding the kid. Only flesh and blood I got."

Al elbowed her again. Harder this time. She tightened her lips and gave Al a fierce look. "What brought you to San Diego, J.T.?"

"The Dakotas ain't the best geography for a man living under the sky. I figured if a guy like me's gotta live in the streets, why not where the sun shines and the snow ain't piled up to my butt? I found a job at this lumber mill. Stayed sober long enough to buy a one-way ticket to this fine community called San Diego."

Fascinated by his story, Sami said, "You said that some homeless people don't have a choice. It sounds to me like you have a lot of options. Have you looked for work?"

"Who's gonna hire a drunk with a bum knee and no legal address?"

"Alcoholism can be managed."

Al grabbed Sami's arm and gave her a hard stare. She had helped him through his drinking problem, and could read his mind. He wanted no part of counseling a homeless man. He let go of her and wandered to a vacant bench away from them.

"There are plenty of jobs that wouldn't require undue stress to your knee," Sami said. "Besides, maybe with proper treatment your knee can be healed."

"Yeah. I know. Heard all the success stories." Williamson stood up, groped through his inside jacket pocket, and pulled out a pack of Camel's. With his back to the ocean breeze, he cupped one hand around the cigarette and lit it with a match. "With all due respect, detective, the real world ain't much like the one you live in. For the kind of job I might be able to snag, there's a dozen men standing ahead of me with smarter brains and stronger bodies. Those Mexicans are hard working fools. I ain't got nothing against any of 'em, but they've made it tough for American-born people like me." He paused for a minute and looked out toward the ocean. "When I can't muster enough change to get by, I hang around the employment center, down off Mission Bay Drive. If I get there early, before sunrise, before me and a pint of Wild Turkey get reacquainted, usually I can get a few hour's work cleaning out a garage or doing some yard work for the uppity snobs living in La Jolla. The ones with the fancy German cars who have no ethical problem paying a man less than minimum wage." He sucked hard on the Camel. "Booze is all I got anyway. What good's a job when all a man thinks about is the son he's never gonna see again. It's better when my brain's numb."

His speech humbled Sami, helping her to recognize that she behaved like a self-righteous fool. For an instant, she thought about conceding, letting the man wallow in his misery. But for some unknown reason, perhaps in the spirit of Christmas, she felt drawn to the stranger's hopelessness. "There are a number of ways to find people. We have at our disposal sophisticated information resources and new technologies with global capabilities." Sami glanced at Al and watched him vigorously shaking his head. Her sanctimonious exhibition continued. She flipped the page on the notepad. "Would you like me to see if I can track down your wife and son?"

Williamson stood stone still. He smiled for the first time. "You would do that for me?"

That the mere suggestion of locating Williamson's wife and son could bring about such a dramatic transformation in a man who appeared to be aimlessly wandering through life without purpose or ambition, overwhelmed Sami. She felt a lump growing in her throat. For a fleeting moment all her worldly troubles and despair seemed to be eclipsed by the euphoric timbre in this stranger's voice. His eyes were alive with anticipation.

Sami's voice was a little shaky. "What is your wife's full name?"

"Mary Jane Williamson. Her former last name was Mitchell. I suspect that she's more than likely usin' her maiden name."

Sami scribbled on the notepad. "And how old is she?"

"Best as I can recall—" he used his fingers to count again. "—thirty-seven or there abouts."

"Your son's name is William?"

"Billy is what's on his birth certificate."

"What was their last known address?"

This question seemed to stump Williamson. "Lived on County Road 3, in a town called Mandan, about ten miles west of Bismarck."

Sami jotted down the information. "Can you give me a description of your wife?"

He didn't respond immediately. He licked his lips and his eyes blinked nervously. "She's a cute little thing." He extended his arm and held his hand palm side down. "Stood about five-foot-two. Long brown hair—the color of chestnuts." He paused for a minute, as if trapped in a memory. "Her eyes are big and brown, like a fawn's."

Noticeably upset, he swallowed hard. Sami gave him a minute to regain his composure. "Is there anything else you can tell us?"

"Would her social security number help?"

Stunned, Sami asked, "You can remember her SS number?"

"Funny thing is, I can hardly recall where I slept two nights ago, but for some reason, Mary Jane's number is stuck in my head. It's kinda like a tattoo on my brain. I suppose that part of my good memory is because the first three numbers are the same as mine. Five-o-one— like Levi blue jeans—seven-seven, one-two-five-four."

Sami closed the notepad and stuffed it and the pen in her jacket pocket. She extended her arm. "It's been a pleasure, J.T. Call me in about a week and hopefully I'll have some info on your wife and son."

Williamson's grip was vise-like. His dark eyes were glassy. "The pleasure was all mine. If I think of anything else about the guy with the fancy shoes, I'll be sure to give you a holler."

Sami turned, ready to join Al, but another question came to mind. "One more thing, J. T. You mentioned something about the suspect requesting that you have a special Christmas dinner? Did he ask that you go to any particular restaurant?"

"Ain't a restaurant at all. It's a place where homeless folks can get a hot meal for free. Katie's Kitchen. It's in South San Diego."

TWELVE

It wasn't until he read the chilling headlines in the morning newspaper that Simon felt the fallout of what he'd done. He felt dirty, as if a wave of toxic waste washed over him and contaminated his body and soul. For the entire day his mind had been crowded with malignant thoughts. He remembered the young woman. How could he forget such a stunning example of female beauty? He recalled their chance meeting on the beach. Talking to her under a moonlit sky. Hearing the waves gently slap against the rocks. Feeling empathy and compassion for the grim-fated teenager. He remembered every detail to the point that blackness filled his eyes, until his body no longer belonged to him, the moment it became possessed by an all-consuming force. Like in the past, his other self, a dark side of his character whose grip on Simon grew stronger every day, had overtaken him.

Still wearing his heavy cotton robe, he sat on his favorite leather wing chair. The newspaper lay on the ottoman. A cold cup of coffee sat on the end table. Next to the coffee was a plate of over-easy eggs, rye toast and home fried potatoes; a breakfast untouched. He glanced again at the front page article.

" . . . her face was so badly beaten she could not be visually identified . . ."

Simon's stomach turned sour with nausea. How could a man of God, a crusader with a mission to purify the world commit such a heinous act? To purify an unclean soul through crucifixion was a divine endeavor. But to murder an innocent woman while gripped with uncontrollable rage could only be the work of a demon.

"It is the work of Satan," he whispered. Who else could he blame, if not the architect of wickedness?

You are wrong, my son. It is the sacred work of God.

He had made peace with his mother, apologized for his unkind words, asked for her forgiveness. How foolish he had been to accuse his mother of such vile deeds. As in the past, she had been gracious and understanding. She'd explained that even God's most reliable servant can go astray.

"How can it be the work of God, dear mother?"

The world is infested with wanton women. Beware of their trickery, sweet boy. With deceiving words and seductive bodies they will corrupt you and lead you to a sinful path of faithlessness. Her punishment was just.

"But not all women are evil."

Oh, but they are, my naïve son. What did the young harlot on the beach want from you? Under the guise of a pitiful, dying woman, she stroked your compassion to get what she wanted. They are all serpents who speak with scheming tongues, pupils of the Prince of Darkness. Do you remember how Bonnie Jean tried to tarnish your pure soul? The world is infected with the likes of Bonnie Jean.

"Do you expect me to purify every woman walking the Earth?"

One at a time, sweet boy. One at a time.

Samson, the chocolate Labrador, waddled over to Simon, moaning and doing his dance, sniffing the uneaten breakfast. Simon leaned forward and scratched the sniveling dog's head. The grateful Lab licked his master's face.

"Need to go out, big boy?"

The dog reacted to his words with great excitement, his tail wagged furiously.

Simon went into the kitchen and opened the door. Samson dashed outside. He stood in the dark kitchen and closed his eyes.

"Is it time for another cleansing, mother?"

Indeed, my son.

"Then I will search for a sinner."

No need, my boy. You have one beckoning you.

"Who?"

The wretched detective.

∾

Her mind flooded with suspicious thoughts, Sami lay in bed and pieced together all the clues from the investigation. Now, more than ever, Simon was a prime suspect. She didn't want to believe it, but she could no longer ignore the evidence. Physically, Simon fit the serial murderer's description perfectly: Caucasian male, well over six feet tall, blue eyes, light brown hair. As a physical therapist, well trained and familiar with the anatomy, he might possess the knowledge to remove the victims' hearts with precision. The gold cross dangling around Simon's neck, his mysterious limp, and the fact that the suspect who murdered the woman on the beach mentioned Katie's Kitchen to J.T. Williamson could not be a coincidence. And it seemed rather convenient that the woman was murdered very close to where Sami had planned to meet Simon for dinner. Wanting to share her supposition with Al, she was tempted to call him. But at this juncture she felt as if she needed more hard facts. Besides, to this point, all the evidence was circumstantial, insufficient to issue a search warrant. And even if she could convince a judge to sign a search warrant, it seemed unlikely that Simon would be careless enough to murder his victims in his home. No, Sami would have to play this one out as a covert operation until she uncovered more compelling evidence. She turned off the light and rolled onto her stomach, knowing for certain that any chance of sleeping would be all but impossible.

༄

Because time was so critical and at any moment the serial murderer could kidnap his next victim, early Sunday morning, Sami drove to her mother's, dropped off Angelina, then went to the precinct to run Simon's name through the FBI database to determine if he had a prior history of felonies or misdemeanors. Her mother, of course, was not pleased with Sami's unannounced crack-of-dawn visit, but Sami didn't give her time to protest. Besides, her mother usually awakened at five a.m.

As was always the case, only a handful of detectives and support staff occupied the precinct on Sundays. Sami went into the computer room, closed the door, and entered Simon's name into the system. She pushed the appropriate keys that would initiate a thorough search of his name, and waited. After less than one minute, a flashing banner announced, "No Matches Found." Although significant, this information only confirmed that Simon had no prior record. It did not, however, remove him as a possible suspect. Now she would have to get close to him. Very close to him. She'd have to gently quiz him through dialogue rather than interrogation. As of yet, she hadn't a clue how to accomplish this objective. She only knew that time was critical.

❦

After picking up Angelina from her mother's home, Sami spent the rest of her Sunday morning curled on the sofa in her bathrobe, trying to imagine how she'd make it through the next two days. At ten-thirty, Al unexpectedly showed up with a carton of donuts under his arm. Sami brewed coffee and they sat side-by-side on the sofa. Al gobbled jelly donuts like a man recently released from a concentration camp, painting his face with powdered sugar, while Sami quietly sipped the Hazelnut coffee and Angelina watched cartoons. Sami was tempted to tell Al about Simon and her suspicions, but a little voice in her subconscious warned her not to. Not yet anyway. Al wiped his mouth with a paper napkin, flipped open the cover on the cardboard box, and studied the nine remaining donuts.

"You're not really going to stuff another donut in your face, are you?"

Al closed the lid and patted his stomach. "Maybe later." He slurped his coffee. "How about you? I bought your favorite: glazed buttermilk."

The thought of eating a donut made her ill. "Haven't you noticed? I'm trying to watch my weight."

He gave her a once-over. "I thought your butt looked a little trimmer."

Sami didn't wish to impose on their friendship, but she desperately needed a favor. "Doing anything exciting this afternoon?"

"Going rock climbing with my buddy, Louie."

"Sounds like fun."

Al clutched her hand. "Jesus, your hands are like ice."

"Cold hands, warm heart."

Al rubbed Sami's clammy hand, trying to warm it. "Your heart must be an inferno."

Al's hands were soft and his actions gentle. Since Tommy and she split up, Sami desperately missed human contact. Who could deny the inexplicable joy of sex? Certainly not Sami. But she longed for tenderness—a pleasure that Tommy ended the moment Sami announced she was pregnant. Al's touch punctuated how completely alone she felt.

"What time is the wake?" Al asked.

"Two o'clock."

"How about I pick you up at one-thirty?" He made the offer without missing a beat.

"You're going rock climbing."

"They'll be there next Sunday."

Sami turned and looked at Al. "You hated Tommy."

"Still do."

Sami's eyes filled with tears. "I appreciate your support."

"Support? Wait 'til you find out what I want in return."

Sami's eyes twitched to a smile.

Al excused himself and went to the bathroom. Angelina, bored with cartoons she'd already seen, turned the television off and found her mother's lap.

"Hi, mommy."

"Hello, sweetheart."

Angelina's hair stuck to her cheeks. Sami pushed it away from her eyes. "Are we going back to Grandma Rizzo's for dinner?"

It was a Sunday ritual. "Mommy has other things to do, but I'm going to take you to grandma's a little later."

"Where you going, Mommy?"

She had been preparing for this moment, but found herself almost paralyzed. "There's something I have to tell you, honey. About Daddy."

"Is he going to take me to Legoland?"

"No, sweetheart, he's not."

⁓

After painful deliberation, the DiSalvo family decided that a one-day wake was all they could endure. Had Tommy died of an illness, or even met his untimely fate in a car crash, the family might be able to withstand the pain and suffering of a longer wake. But the condition of his body, the utter brutality by which he was murdered, made even a one day wake intolerable. This decision did not serve to ease even a grain of Sami's angst. To walk into the Westwood Funeral Home required strength beyond her capacity. Although the DiSalvo family decided that Tommy's casket should be closed—not even the world's most gifted plastic surgeon could reconstruct his beaten face and make it presentable—Sami had decided not to expose Angelina to such a traumatic experience. Having had other babysitting options available—two dear neighbors who adored Angelina—she'd asked her mother to accompany her.

"He did not respect me when he was your husband, why should I respect him when he is dead?"

"I'm asking you to do it for me, not Tommy," Sami had pleaded.

Josephine wasn't budging. "Angelina needs her grandmother. I don't want you leaving her with some stranger." When Josephine Rizzo folded her arms across her chest and her face puckered to a stern frown, Sami knew that further debate would be futile.

Tommy DiSalvo was dead. The man who once swept Sami off her feet, introduced the chubby Catholic girl to her first breathless kiss, taught her that sex was an ongoing adventure, crawled underneath the sheets regularly and woke her in the early morning hours with a mouth so talented often Sami felt she would surely explode, a man who could be gentle one moment and unmercifully cruel the next, the father of her only child, a man she might have saved had she not been so selfish . . . was dead.

∽

Wearing the only black dress in her wardrobe appropriate for a wake, a wool knee-grazer slightly snug in the hips, Sami walked into the funeral parlor hanging onto Al's arm like a drowning woman clinging to a life preserver. She couldn't remember the last time she'd worn high heals, and her ankles wobbled in protest.

"Don't be nervous," Al said. He looked quite dashing wearing his two-button navy blue suit, accompanied with a crisp white shirt and blue paisley tie. With a generous amount of hair gel, Al had neatly combed and slicked-back his usually-messy hair.

"That's easy for you to say," Sami said. "I think I need to find the ladies room."

The Westwood Funeral Home, a white brick structure with four marble pillars supporting an expansive carport at the front entrance, was located on Genesee Street in Clairemont Mesa. The building, strategically designed to accommodate three wakes simultaneously, while still providing privacy for the bereaved visitors, stood among other commercial establishments. Today, only one body lie in state.

As Sami approached the East Room, fiercely gripping Al's left arm, she spotted Tommy DiSalvo's name displayed above the doorway. There were several people gathered outside the room, chatting, laughing, engaging in the camaraderie of a social ceremony lacking the fundamental solemnness of an event so tragic. Sami recognized none of them. What would she say to people when they paid their condolences? If she graciously accepted their gestures of sympathy for a man she intensely disliked, her actions would make her a hypocrite. There would be those who would look at her with judgmental eyes. After all, she was Tommy's ex-wife, a woman exiled from the family. Her participation in this event served neither to pay homage to her ex-husband, nor to offer her support to a family who never quite accepted her as "good enough." She attended this wake for Angelina. She felt, of course, a nagging pang of guilt, an indirect accountability for Tommy's murder that might always torment her.

Sami and Al walked into the East Room. The combination of flowers and women doused with cheap perfume, made the air smell sickly-sweet, reminiscent of Friday night bingo at Saint Michael's. Her mother hadn't persuaded Sami to accompany her in years, but the smell of the over-perfumed elderly women was hard to forget. A narrow isle in the center of the room led the way to the closed casket. On either side of the isle were rows of neatly arranged chairs. There were, perhaps, twenty people in the room, mostly familiar faces. Some were standing, others seated, and several huddled near the casket. To Sami, the room seemed too brightly lit. Twin crystal chandeliers hung from thick gold chains at either end of the ivory-painted ceiling. Sconces shaped like seashells were spaced evenly on the walls. The lush, garnet-colored carpeting looked brand new.

Sami and her noble escort waited patiently for a middle-aged man to say a prayer while kneeling in front of Tommy DiSalvo's eternal residence. Sami spotted Tommy's parents, Maria and Vincent DiSalvo, sitting in the front row. Maria glanced her way but didn't acknowledge Sami with the slightest nod. Sami wasn't sure if her former mother-in-law intentionally ignored her or felt so consumed with grief she didn't recognize her. After the divorce, Tommy's parents not only dissociated themselves with Sami, they unofficially disowned Angelina. To Sami, their behavior represented a classic exhibition of Italian stubbornness, and it served no purpose except to punish an innocent child. That Maria and Vincent DiSalvo could sever all contact with their flesh and blood granddaughter, forfeit the pleasure of participating in her evolution from child to adolescent to teenager to adult, all for the sake of foolish pride, was truly a tragedy.

Gestures of compassion were evidenced throughout the room: handshakes and kisses and hugs, people blowing their noses and weeping; the aerobics of a mournful congregation. The man kneeling on the padded bench suddenly disappeared, so Sami and Al knelt in front of the mahogany casket. There were vases of bright-colored flowers on both sides of the casket. Roses, Carnations. Calla Lilies. Birds of Paradise. Centered on the casket Sami spotted an arrangement of white and red roses. The words, BELOVED SON were embossed on the blue satin ribbon hanging from the bouquet. To the left of the flowers, propped on the coffin, stood an eight-by-ten picture of Tommy, a photograph Sami had never seen. By his youthful look, Sami guessed that the photo had been taken a decade ago. She couldn't help but wonder how things might have turned out if his character had been as wholesome as his looks.

Kneeling in front of the coffin, Sami faced the same dilemma she'd encountered in the past: what could she say to God? What words could she compose worthy of God's ear? It seemed so paltry and ordinary to simply ask the Creator to have mercy on Tommy's less-than-pure soul. Surely, a more compelling, less mainstream plea for his salvation might capture God's attention. She'd never quite figured out with any certainty or solid conviction what her religious beliefs really were. For most of her life she vacillated between devout Christian and agnostic. At times, the whole business of God, heaven and hell confused her to the point that Sami just didn't think about it.

On one hand, the doctrines of the Catholic faith had been etched into her impressionable young brain at an early age. The nuns at Saint Agnes Elementary School could have easily taught the Nazis a few lessons in the art of brainwashing. But in her adult life, when she often recalled some of these teachings, Sami couldn't help but question their validity, or the credibility of the Creator portrayed by the nuns. God, according to the nuns, was supposed to be flawlessly just and good. If this were true, why was the world He created such a hostile planet? Why didn't God intervene and stop the madness? Sami believed in a higher authority, a supreme power greater than humankind, that life on Earth served as a stepping stone to an existence more substantial and more permanent. She also felt certain that in the next life, mortals were rewarded for their goodwill and punished for their misdeeds.

Today, kneeling in front of Tommy's coffin, certain that Maria and Vincent DiSalvo were staring at her back, cursing the day she'd been born, Samantha Rizzo could not evoke appropriate words. She could not compose a prayer for the man who was once her husband and lover, the father of her child. She said a Hail Mary and Our Father, made the sign of the cross, and choked back the tears.

༄

Al stood and waited by her side, but Sami remained kneeling in front of the coffin. He touched her arm. "You okay?"

She took a deep breath and stood. "I'm fine."

She dreaded this moment most: paying her respects to Tommy's parents, searching their eyes for hatred. She turned and stepped toward the DiSalvo's. Vincent stood several feet away, talking to a bald, hunched-over elderly man. Maria sat quietly with her hands folded on her lap, clutching a wadded tissue, staring at the coffin with a mesmerized, almost possessed look.

Sami forced a smile and extended her hand. "I'm deeply sorry for your loss, Maria."

The slightly overweight, fifty-seven year old woman lifted her chin and blinked several times, as if trying to focus her squinting brown eyes. Then her eyes opened wide. With her right hand she grasped Sami's extended hand. With her left, she grabbed Sami's elbow and pulled Sami toward her. Maria's face was inches from Sami's ear.

"We couldn't help Tommy. You know how poor we are. But you could have saved my son, Sami. Instead, you let him die. God curse your soul."

The barely audible words assaulted Sami's ears like a gunshot. She had no retort. This was neither the time nor place for debate or rebuttal. What could she say in her own defense? Al stood in her shadow, waiting patiently, unaware of what the bitter woman had whispered in Sami's ear. Sami waited for Vincent to finish his conversation with the bent-forward man, so she could quickly offer her condolences. Vincent glanced at her several times, but seemed uninterested in ending his talk. Sami tugged on Al's sleeve and leaned toward him. "Let's get the hell out of here."

She held Al's hand and almost pulled him behind her as she marched for the exit. The crowd watched her hasty departure with searching curiosity. It seemed that everyone in the funeral home had been corrupted, convinced that Sami was responsible for Tommy's death. She felt like she was walking a gauntlet; their glares silent weapons. Sami could feel her temples throbbing. Her teeth were clenched and her jaw pulsing. If she weren't a civilized woman, a sworn servant of society, she'd stomp back in the room and tell the DiSalvo's a couple of choice stories about their beloved son. But doing such would only reduce her integrity to their level. Nothing she could say or do would temper the conspiracy. They believed what they believed, and no matter how poignant her defense she could never exonerate herself. At least not in their eyes.

During the ride back to Sami's house, Al knew that silence was the best medicine, that only time could moderate Sami's rage. He abhorred seeing her in so much pain, but other than offer his earnest support, what could he do? They'd been partners for over six years; friends from the moment they met. Al had heard all the details of Sami's troubled marriage, and was well acquainted with the likes of Tommy DiSalvo and his family of misfits. On countless evenings Al had sat by Sami's side and consoled her. On numerous occasions, Al's phone would ring in the middle of the night because Tommy had not been home for days, and Sami, frantic with alarm, needed to hear a friendly voice. He remembered the pitiful sobs, the anguish in her shaky voice. He had witnessed first hand the emotional damage Tommy had inflicted on a woman undeserving of such a fate. He had watched a vibrant, passionate woman reduced to a creature without enthusiasm. A woman once so positive and idealistic, a dynamic powerhouse, now turned cynical and uncertain of herself.

Tommy DiSalvo had left an indelible scar on Sami's heart. He had captured a woman with a profound zest for life, held her captive in his dark world, and when he finally released her, she no longer savored life with the same untamed spirit. Al had helplessly observed Sami's metamorphosis, the gradual dilution of her once potent personality. But like a man without arms, he did not have the means to rescue her from the quicksand.

Alberto Diaz had been there when Sami gave birth to Angelina. He stood beside Sami in the labor room, holding her hands, wiping the sweat from her brow, helping with her breathing exercises. Until the moment she disappeared through the doors of the operating room, Al had coached her through seven hours of labor. He had asked to accompany Sami during delivery, wanting desperately to witness the birth of Sami's child, but when she explained that she might never again be able to look in his eyes, he understood and respected her womanly pride without protest.

As the quiet ride continued, and Al's head flooded with memories, it occurred to him that there was something he could do for Sami. Al was born in Tijuana, a bustling city bordering San Diego, a community where the contrast between prosperity and poverty glared like sunshine on a foggy windshield. The city served as a haven for bargain hunters. Most of the daytime tourists patronized myriad retail stores and street vendors selling everything from hand-woven wool blankets to knock-off Rolex watches. But when the sun set, Tijuana's infamous reputation became immortalized by less traditional visitors, all searching for drugs, sex, and bars that never closed. On Friday and Saturday evenings, the streets of Tijuana were littered with California teenagers, all with the same goal: to get inebriated.

Three classes of people lived in Tijuana: those lucky enough to work for one of many businesses supported by American tourism, others with green cards who were legally employed in the United States but maintained residency in Mexico, and the less fortunate ones forced to beg for a living.

Al would never forget his poverty-stricken childhood. Only steps from the customs gate where the border patrol carefully screened an onslaught of Americans crossing the border into Mexico, Al camped on the sidewalk seven days a week. Many tourists parked their cars in designated lots and walked over the border into Tijuana. This created a great opportunity for enterprising children like Al. With ragged clothing, dirty faces, and pitiful frowns, Al stood among a group of children loitering on the busy pathway to Mexico, hoping to collect enough money to help his parents get through another difficult day.

Until his thirteenth birthday—when the competition from younger, more pathetic-looking children captured the soft hearts of Americans more effectively—Al sold Chiclets chewing gum to anyone kind enough to drop a nickel in his rusty coffee can. Al's teenage years were riddled with delinquent activities. He had never committed a consequential crime, but the local police knew him well and were always at his heels. Finally, at the age of nineteen, after repeated pleas from his mother, his Uncle Eduardo, a naturalized citizen living in National City, agreed to sponsor Al's immigration into the United States.

Al was well aware that the Mexican Mafia thrived in Tijuana. And although he had not shared this with Sami, he felt certain Tommy DiSalvo had not been murdered by the hands of this particular group of hoodlums. They were criminals in every sense of the word, heavily involved in drug trafficking, prostitution, and gambling. They had no reservations snapping a pinky or beating a freeloader to within an inch of his life. And occasionally, when they believed a "customer's" debt was substantial and uncollectible, one of their enforcers would press the serious end of a Colt .45 against the deadbeat's temple and end his life. They were an unscrupulous, corrupt pack of *bandejos,* but a peculiar code of ethics existed among them. They would never torture a man before murdering him. This was gospel. And they most certainly would not have castrated Tommy and stuffed his testicles down his throat. Al felt certain that Tommy DiSalvo had not been murdered by the Mexican Mafia, and he intended to prove it.

Al still had contacts in Tijuana, lifelong friends familiar with the dynamics of the underworld. He'd have to be careful with his covert investigation. If Captain Davison learned about his unauthorized detective work, the consequences would be grave. A few telephone calls, a trip to Tijuana, a handful of pesos to warm the palms of those connected to the action, and soon Al would solve the mystery and hopefully help quell Sami's feeling of guilt.

Not as her best friend, and not as her partner, Al reached across the seat and grabbed Sami's hand. She turned her head slightly and smiled at him. He stroked her fingers and could feel that familiar flutter in his upper chest, the tightness at the back of his throat. Oh how masterfully he had concealed the truth for so many years.

On the Wednesday afternoon they had met, at the exact moment Alberto Diaz had looked into Samantha Rizzo's beautiful blue eyes, he had fallen in love for the first time in his life. Al had heard all the utopian stories about love at first sight, but until the day his heart had swelled with a warmth he had never known, he had always believed that all the romantic tales were food for Gothic novels. How clever he had been: playing the part of a carefree rogue, a user of women. Making Sami believe that he lived the life of a playboy served as his only shelter.

Not a day passed without Al dreaming about making love to Sami. Now, sitting beside her in this car, Al came to the bitter realization that he could never reveal his love, that it would forever be exiled in a secret refuge in his heart. He was not good enough for Sami. Like a dagger twisting in his heart, this truth he could not deny. She deserved more than a Mexican-born maniac with reckless ambition. Sami needed stability in her life, and Angelina needed a father figure. It was not a role to which Al could ever aspire. His love for her was a romantic tragedy, and Sami would never know.

"Thanks for your support, partner," Sami said.

Drowning in his thoughts, the break in silence startled him. "Excuse me?"

"I'm sure you could have had more fun rock climbing with your friend than babysitting for me."

If only she knew. "What did the old witch say to set you off?"

"I don't remember her exact words, only the insinuation."

"And?"

"She blamed me for Tommy's murder."

Al's hands tightened around the steering wheel, committed more than ever to finding out who murdered Tommy DiSalvo. "Don't let her or anyone else lay that horseshit on you."

"I keep trying to convince myself that even if I had mortgaged my soul and given Tommy the money, eventually he'd run out of resources. It seemed inevitable."

"That's exactly right."

"But suppose this would have been the last straw? What if the threat on his life had been just the dose of reality he needed? You should have seen him, Al, he was terrified."

"There's never a last straw with losers like him. I don't mean to be disrespectful—I know he was once your husband—but you gotta call a spade a spade."

"I keep telling myself that I'm not my brother's keeper, but . . ."

Al turned into Sami's driveway and switched off the ignition. "I'll walk you to the door."

"It's broad daylight. I don't think I'm in any danger."

More selfish than chivalrous, Al hoped for a coffee invitation; any excuse to spend more time with Sami. "Hey, you never know."

At the door, Sami put her arms around Al and gave him a bear hug.

Like two puzzle pieces, the contours of Sami's body snugly fit against Al's. He thought his heart would leap out of his chest. "So what time tomorrow should I pick you up for the funeral services?" Her hair smelled like coconuts.

She let go of him and searched through her purse. "I'm not going to the funeral."

Her words relieved Al. "You sure about that?"

She found the ring of keys and slipped the brass-colored one in the deadbolt. "The only thing I know for sure is that I refuse to subject myself to more humiliation."

"Bravo. I admire your courage."

"Call it self-preservation." Sami glanced at her wrist-watch. "If you're not sick of hanging around a sniveling wench, we can probably catch the second half of the Charger's game."

"Promise not to blow your nose on my one and only dress shirt and you've got a deal."

"Be warned: when my mother drops off Angelina she'll probably hang around."

"You haven't scared me yet."

"Oh, yeah. Wait until she sits on your lap and asks you to read her a bedtime story."

"Angelina?"

"No, my mother."

Al grinned. "Now you're scarin' me."

Sami and Al walked into the cluttered living room.

"If you're really lucky," Sami said, "I might muster enough ambition to throw some leftover chili in the microwave. But no promises."

"And to think I could have been foolish enough to go home and grill that porterhouse steak defrosting in my fridge."

"When you taste my chili, you're gonna beg me for the recipe."

"Or, I can just read the ingredients on a can of Hormel's."

THIRTEEN

Not wanting to disturb Angelina, peacefully sleeping past her usual wake-up time on this cloudy Monday morning, Sami telephoned her mother.

"Would you mind driving over here, Ma?"

"Something wrong with your car?"

"I need to get to the precinct early and Angelina's still sleeping." Normally, Sami would drive Angelina to her mother's house at eight a.m. and choke down a quick cup of coffee, so Josephine would not accuse her of being too busy to spend a few minutes with "her only mother." Then, she'd fight her way through the snarled freeway traffic, and if she did not encounter gridlock, arrive at the precinct by nine a.m.

This morning, after a surprisingly restful night's sleep, Sami felt remarkably energetic. Considering the recent events, her good spirits seemed like a minor miracle. She had no illusions regarding the much-needed sleep, and attributed her windfall to fatigue and mental exhaustion. The body can withstand just so much pressure and then it shuts down.

Josephine Rizzo protested. "You know how much I hate rush-hour traffic."

"It's not like you're on the other side of the county. It's a ten minute ride."

"I haven't had my breakfast yet."

"Eat breakfast here."

"What, Pop Tarts?"

Why didn't I just wake Angelina? "Forget it, Ma. I'll be there in a few minutes."

"Sometimes I think you take advantage of me, Sami."

"And sometimes I think about moving to Tahiti."

"You're in a mood."

"Why does everything have to be a fight with you?"

Silence.

"Are you there, Ma?"

"I don't know what a mother's supposed to do anymore. I try to help and all you do is yell at me."

Josephine Rizzo could make the Pope feel guilty about the way he said mass. "I'm sorry, Ma. It's not you. It's me. I guess I'm having a hard time dealing with Tommy's murder. There's a lot of shit going on at work and I'm taking it out on you." Sami couldn't believe that she apologized. "I'll drop her off in a little while."

Josephine's voice rang in triumph. "I'll be waiting."

Sami tiptoed into Angelina's bedroom and sat on the bed. Rather than abruptly wake her, she gently stroked her hair. What a beautiful child.

Her rather flowery explanation of Tommy's death had not adversely affected Angelina. Or at least it appeared that way. When Sami had delicately made the announcement, the two-year-old chewed on her lower lip and rubbed her watery eyes, but did not shed a tear. That her dad now lived in heaven with God hadn't upset the child. In her callow mind, he embarked upon an exciting journey, and although she could no longer see him, or hear his voice, she could speak to him often and know that her words would be heard.

The carefree spirit of childhood can often be merciful, Sami thought. But an adult mind cannot find solace in the same safe harbor as a child's innocent heart. In due time, Angelina would come to grips with troubling questions. Losing her father at such an early age represented only a small portion of the issues with which Angelina would be faced. The real tragedy lay in Angelina's dim memory of an obscure man who did not participate in his daughter's life, a father who would tragically fade to oblivion.

In later years, Sami felt sure, Angelina's world would be rocked with a profound feeling of loss. For now, Sami found contentment knowing that Angelina sought refuge in the safe harbor of her youthful innocence.

Angelina yawned. Her eyes barely opened. "Time to go to Grandma's?"

"Yes, sweetheart."

"Can I wear my Winnie the Pooh shirt?"

"Of course."

For a moment Sami's thoughts shifted to her father's death. In an abstract way she felt as though she were no longer imprisoned by his expectations, or her inability to please him. Overwhelmed with culpability, she wrestled with this feeling for years. How could anyone benefit from a parent's death? It occurred to Sami that Angelina might be better off without her biological father. Perhaps she would be spared the bitter realization that Tommy DiSalvo would never aspire to her daughterly expectations.

Superficially, this presumption seemed cold-hearted and utterly callous. And Sami would never share these dark judgments with anyone. But the whole issue of parent-child relationships hovered as controversial a topic as politics or religion. Absolute truths did not exist. To Sami, nothing on Earth was clearly right or wrong. Each relationship delicately rested on a balance scale, the position of each side affected by the daily rituals of parent-child interactions.

Angelina sat up and reached for the ceiling with outstretched arms. "Am I gonna get another daddy?"

The jaw-dropping question shook Sami to her core. She had to think carefully before answering.

∾

Parked a block away from Sami's home in the rented Chevy Impala, slumped low and hyped with anticipation, Simon watched. Not knowing when she'd leave her home, he'd been waiting since six a.m. He swallowed the final mouthful of lukewarm coffee and set the stainless steel mug in the cup holder. At seven-forty-five, he saw her walk out the front door wearing a business suit, one a homicide detective would wear to work. The morning was cool, the sun hidden by stubborn clouds.

Sami held Angelina's hand, led her to the car, and secured her daughter in the child seat. Simon waited for Sami to back out of her driveway before starting the engine. He followed at a safe distance behind, wearing a Padres cap on his head. Afraid she'd lose him on the freeway, Simon felt relieved when Sami passed the on-ramp to Freeway 805 and continued through residential neighborhoods. She pulled into a driveway on 32nd Street. Simon parked at the curb and waited, snapping a mental picture of the address. He observed Sami leading Angelina to the front porch of the tiny, run-down home. They disappeared behind the front door. Sami emerged five minutes later. Alone.

～

Sami pushed through the double-doors leading to the Detective Division, walked by her desk, waved to three fellow detectives—Alberto Diaz wasn't in sight—marched into Captain Davison's office, and closed the door.

Davison peered at her over his reading glasses. "I thought you'd be at the funeral." The top button of his wrinkled shirt was undone and his black tie hung loosely around his neck.

"So did I," Sami said.

"You're not going?"

"It would appear that way."

Davison rubbed his chin. "So am I to assume you're officially back to work?"

"That depends." She sat in one of the two chairs opposite Davison. In the past, she always waited for an invitation.

The captain dropped a pen on the desk, removed his glasses, and rocked back in the chair. "Okay, Rizzo, what's on your mind?"

"I thought you were a man of your word, captain."

"What the hell does that mean?"

"You said we had until Friday before you pulled us off the case."

"So that's why your ass is chapped?" Davison folded his hands. "Diaz didn't fill you in?"

"I'd like to hear your version."

Davison reached for the pack of Camel's sitting on the corner of his desk. He stuck his index finger inside and fished around, but discovered an empty pack. He opened the squeaky center drawer and rummaged through an accumulation of rarely-used paraphernalia. Unable to find cigarettes, he stood up and frisked his pockets. "Shit." Davison fell into the chair. "I know you've been through a lot of shit, Rizzo, and you're a good cop, but this case is over your head."

Good cop? Apparently he had forgotten about her commendations. "And you think the boys in the Special Investigation Squad are going to bag the big one?"

"I had to do something."

Sami glared at Davison.

"You're emotionally involved, Rizzo. It's been obvious for weeks. There's no way for you to remain objective."

For a moment, Sami sat silent, thinking about what the captain said. His assessment of her was correct. But she wasn't going to give up her fight yet. "I know you're under a lot of pressure, captain, but—"

"I'm sorry, there's nothing to discuss. The decision's made."

"I'd like your permission to speak with Chief Carson." James Carson, recently appointed Chief of Detectives, supervised all six detective precincts in San Diego County. He had a reputation as a hard-nosed, inflexible tyrant, but Sami had nothing to lose but a little of her hide.

"I won't stop you from going over my head, Rizzo, but Carson is going to chew you up and spit you out."

"Wouldn't be the first time."

Like two chess players contemplating their opponent's next move, they sat quietly eyeballing each other.

Davison said, "Do you have one shred of evidence or even a lukewarm lead?"

"We've got a homeless man who can identify a likely suspect."

Davison's eyes narrowed. "You really believe the woman murdered on Crystal Pier was the work of the serial killer?"

"Absolutely."

"What proof do you have?"

She didn't yet want to tell the captain about Simon, so she couldn't offer tangible evidence or dazzle the captain with an argument that might strengthen her position. The only trump card she carried was her proven skills and sound reputation. "When you were a detective, captain, how often did you rely on your gut instincts?"

"I know where you're going with this, Rizzo, and it ain't gonna work."

"Indulge me. Please."

He let out a heavy sigh. "A cop without good instincts should look for a different occupation."

"How many times have my hunches resulted in an arrest?"

"No one is questioning your record, detective. The problem is—"

"Have I ever asked you for special consideration?"

He lost his thunder. "Not that I can recall."

"This investigation is a millimeter away from breaking wide open. I can feel it in my bones."

"Is Diaz as passionate as you with this investigation?"

She hadn't asked Al, and for all she knew he might be relieved that it had been reassigned, but she had the captain where she wanted him and had to keep pushing. "Al feels the same way I do, captain. I'm surprised he hasn't thrown a temper tantrum."

Davison set his elbows on the desk and steepled his fingers. "You do realize that my credibility as a commanding officer will be in the toilet if I reverse my decision."

"You're a big boy. You'll get over it."

"Even if I put Diaz and you back on the case, you'd still have to work with a task force."

"I realize that captain. Just give me another shot."

Davison shook his head and smiled. "Okay, Detective Rizzo, I'm gonna give you just enough rope to hang yourself." He leaned forward and slapped his palms on the desk. "If this asshole isn't behind bars by Friday at midnight, you'd better update your résumé."

She reached across the desk and extended her hand. "I won't let you down."

～

Normally, Sami disliked the enormous amount of paperwork associated with detective work, but today, this tedious task seemed like a godsend, helping divert her thoughts away from Tommy's funeral and Maria DiSalvo's cold-hearted accusation. It took almost two hours for her to complete her daily progress report. As a homicide detective, every detail—even those seemingly insignificant—loomed large. And a major part of her responsibility was to record every aspect of an investigation in writing. Not divulging her suspicions about Simon violated her code of ethics. But Sami's instincts, always reliable, urged her not to share her assumptions quite yet. She hadn't decided if convincing Captain Davison to reassign the serial murders to Al and her had been a good thing. By midnight Friday, she'd know for sure if her power play had been a wise decision or folly.

Sami left the precinct at ten-thirty a.m., and drove to the Police Crime Laboratory located on Broadway in downtown San Diego. Hopefully, the lab work would yield a significant piece of evidence from the Valentino shoes or the Gold Toe sock. The Crime Lab, officially named the Scientific Investigation Bureau, served as a crucial resource for homicide investigations, and offered much support to the detective squads. The SIB consisted of five sections: Biology was responsible for the identification, analysis, and differentiation of body fluids—blood, sperm, vaginal fluids, and saliva. It also performed tests on hair to determine origin (human, animal or synthetic), race, and in some cases DNA comparisons were done. Criminalistics provided chemical analysis of urine—to detect drug content—blood analysis for DWI, examination of alcoholic beverages, poisons, gunpowder and gunshot residue, paint scrapings, metals, glass fragments, fibers, soil, and identification of foot, heel and tire impressions. The Document Examination section performed tests to learn the age of documents; they restored charred or water-damaged papers, restored erasures, obliterations or alterations, and compared hand printing and handwriting. Firearms was responsible for firearm identification and determining their condition, examination of cartridge casings, neutron activation analyses of gunshot residue, restoration of obliterated serial numbers, identified pick marks on lock cylinders, determined distance between victim and firearm, and acted as liaison between law enforcement agencies, gun manufacturers and dealers. The last section—Controlled Substance Analysis—performed quantitative and qualitative analyses on all narcotics and drugs. Even with such a comprehensive resource, apprehending, arresting, and convicting a criminal was still an enormous undertaking.

Instead of waiting for an elevator, Sami took the stairs to the second floor Biology Lab. When she walked into the lab, Sami spotted Betsy, the technician assigned to analyze the Valentino shoes and Gold Toe sock. Standing only four-foot-eleven, barely ninety-five-pounds, the Vietnam-born woman had the spunk of a Norfolk terrier. Sami had grown particularly fond of her over the last three years.

Betsy sat on a stool in front of a Formica table. There were various size plastic containers scattered about, and a wooden rack filled with glass test tubes next to a sophisticated-looking microscope. Betsy looked up, her almond-shaped eyes as dark and shiny as chocolate frosting. "Long time no see, Sami." Having moved to America when only five-years-old, she spoke without an Asian accent.

Sami put her arm around Betsy and squeezed her shoulder. "How's my favorite tech doing?"

"I'd be better if I had major news for you."

"Please don't tell me it's a bust."

"Not exactly." Betsy held up a small plastic bag. "Found a couple of hairs in the sock. The guy's Caucasian—for all that's worth. Now all you have to do is ask every over-six-foot, athletic-type-white-dude in the county to shave his legs and drop a few hairs off at the lab, and with a little DNA magic you'll have your man."

"I'll start handing out the razors. Any luck with the shoes?"

"Well, I did find a little sand and clay, but they have little geographic significance." Betsy grinned. "On the bright side, though, I recovered a trace amount of blood inside the shoes. It may take a few days before we get the DNA results, but I think we've got enough for us to match his blood type."

"I'll keep my fingers crossed. And by the way, keep the shoes in a safe place, Betsy. I promised to return them to their owner."

Betsy had a look of total puzzlement. "You're going to return the shoes to the suspect?"

Sami shook her head. "It's a long story."

Betsy pointed to one of the shoes, cut in pieces and sealed inside a plastic bag. "Afraid it's a little late."

Betsy eased off the stool and looked up at Sami. "I was really sorry to hear about your former husband, Sami. Any progress in the investigation?"

"Not that I'm aware of."

"Must be tough on Angelina."

"She's okay for now, but only time will tell."

"Want to grab a beer sometime?"

"I'd love to, Betsy."

∽

Somewhat deflated, Sami returned to the precinct. About to sit, she noticed a lavender envelope sitting in the center of her cluttered desk with her name neatly printed on the face of it. She tore it open. The pure white greeting card had a purple tulip and the words, With Sympathy, on the front. She opened the card and read:

> *May the memories you cherish fill your heart with peace today and give you the strength and courage to sustain you on your way.*
> *Warm regards, Simon.*

FOURTEEN

Monday at six-thirty p.m., Sami's telephone rang. Angelina and she had just finished dinner—pizza from Vincenzo's—and Sami gulped the last mouthful of a Corona while clearing off the kitchen table. Angelina sat on the floor watching television. Takeout food had become mainstream at the Rizzo residence. So much so that one of Sami's many New Year's resolutions—quickly approaching—was to buy a half-dozen cookbooks and attempt to learn the craft of cooking. She made a fair spaghetti sauce, but as Josephine Rizzo often pointed out, "it tasted like the 'orange sauce' Americano's bought in a jar." On occasion, when Sami felt particularly adventurous, she'd stuff a chicken and roast it. But a culinary aficionado? Hardly.

By the volume of business-related calls she received every day, Sami was conditioned to answer formally. She picked up the receiver and without forethought said, "Sami Rizzo."

"Is this the devastatingly gorgeous Sami Rizzo, the female Sherlock Holmes of the western world?" Al sounded remarkably upbeat.

"Sorry, pal, but you've really got the wrong number."

"So I gather you made it through the day without your indispensable partner?" Al had spent most of the day interviewing homeless people and local residents close to the vicinity where Brigetta had been murdered on the beach.

"To be honest, Al, I didn't even notice you weren't around until I stumbled upon a box of uneaten jelly donuts."

"Did you save me any?"

"Not one." Sami eyed the last piece of pizza. "Any luck with the interviews?"

"J.T. is our only link."

An awkward silence ensued.

"How you holding up, Sami?"

She had to ponder his question for a moment. "Believe it or not, I actually feel guilty about not feeling guilty. It's as if Tommy's been gone for years."

"He has."

Tommy's only contribution to Sami's life was as tormentor. Should she feel guilty that in a sense his death liberated her?

"Is Angelina okay?" Al asked.

"So far, so good." The melted mozzarella beckoned Sami. "Will I see you in the morning?"

"Eight a.m. sharp."

"Got the lab test results on the shoes and sock this morning."

"Good news?"

"Betsy found a hair in the sock. Our perp's a white guy."

"That narrows the field to about a hundred-fifty-million suspects."

Temptation got the best of her and Sami folded the last piece of pizza in half and took a small bit. "Betsy also recovered a trace of blood in one of the shoes. We'll have the DNA results in a day or two."

"Anything else?"

"Captain Davison rescinded his decision to pull us off the serial murder investigation."

Al didn't speak for a few moments. "Let me alert the people at Ripley's Believe it or Not."

"Hard to grasp, huh?"

"What prompted that change?"

"A five-foot-seven Italian with her period."

"You sure that's what you want?"

Sami suddenly realized that she had made a headlong decision without having paid Al the courtesy of consulting him. "Are you okay with this, Al?" At this point, the question seemed rhetorical.

"Hey, you know me. I go with the flow. What I'm concerned about is you. Are you okay with this?"

That question she couldn't answer. "Ask me at midnight Friday."

∽

Perhaps because she had been numb for the last few days, brooding over Tommy's murder, wrestling with her conscience, it wasn't until her head touched the pillow Monday evening that Sami clearly understood the impact of her grandstand with Captain Davison. Without a substantial lead, how could she possibly crack this case and make an arrest by the end of the week? In a moment of wild-eyed idealism, Detective Sami Rizzo had placed herself—and her partner—in a hopeless situation.

To date, four, possibly five women had been murdered by the same man. What did she know about the perpetrator? He was a Caucasian with blue eyes and light brown hair, well over six-feet-tall, athletic build, drove a dark Supercab pickup, liked expensive footwear, and surely was a religious fanatic. That's it. Not a shred of substantial evidence. What was she trying to prove? Perhaps her reckless behavior suggested a repressed desire to self-destruct. She had not only placed herself in a potentially precarious situation, but her partner, Al, was also at risk. Other detectives were involved in the investigation. In fact, the last count was eight. But by lobbying with Captain Davison to reverse his decision, allowing Al and her to continue with the case, placed the onus on her. The captain had made it clear that Sami's hide was at risk, not her fellow detectives'. And to complicate the situation further, if Sami didn't make an arrest by Friday at midnight, Captain Davison would be professionally humiliated.

Sami peeled the covers off her sweaty body and switched on the lamp. She moved to the edge of the mattress and sat for a moment, squinting, letting her eyes adjust to the light. She reached for the lavender envelope, removed the sympathy card and read it for the third time since finding it on her desk.

Simon.

Now more than ever, the circumstantial evidence pointing to Simon seemed more concrete. Perhaps this was because Sami had nowhere else to turn. No viable leads. No other suspects. Or possibly Sami's usually-reliable instincts had kicked into gear. Whatever the case, Sami was ready to break all the rules—anything to crack this case.

Extraordinary circumstances sometimes called for extraordinary measures. And once in a while, a smart cop is forced to do something risky.

FIFTEEN

Ignoring vehement protests from her mother, a lengthy tirade that Sami would completely disrupt her morning, she left Angelina with Grandma Rizzo an hour earlier than usual, and walked into the precinct before eight a.m. Neither Al nor Captain Davison had arrived yet, which was exactly what Sami wanted. At her desk she opened the folder that contained all the documents associated with the serial murders. Page by page Sami examined every word, every photograph, studied transcripts of the sworn testimonies taken from the victims' husbands and children. There had to be something she'd overlooked. At eight-o-five, Al tapped her on the shoulder. So rapt with the file, he startled her. When she swiveled in the chair, she saw Al standing next to her desk holding a cup of Starbuck's coffee in one hand and the last bite of a jelly donut in the other.

"How'd you sleep last night?" Al asked.

"Remarkably well. It's amazing what an effective sedative mental exhaustion can be."

Al popped the last piece of donut in his mouth and slurped his coffee. "So what's on the agenda today?"

"I think we should contact the victims' spouses and ask permission to speak with the children again."

"Why?"

"Maybe in retrospect one of the kids might remember a minor detail that will point us in the right direction."

"Really think so, huh?"

"Got a better plan?"

Al sat on the corner of Sami's desk and gulped the coffee. "The fathers are going to give us a hard time."

"I expect them to be completely uncooperative." Sami leafed through the folder and handed Al two sheets of paper. "You contact Connelly and Singer. I'll call McDonald and Cassidy."

"Sure you can handle Mr. McDonald?"

"We'll soon find out."

Al studied the papers.

"I owe you an apology, partner," Sami said.

"Don't mention it. I didn't really expect you to save me any donuts."

Sami smiled. "I acted unprofessional and inconsiderate grandstanding Davison without first speaking to you. I'm sorry."

"Hey, partner, I want to collar this asshole as much as you. No need to apologize."

"We're going to be in a hell-of-a pickle if—"

"There is no, if. By midnight Friday we'll be celebrating."

Al's eyes betrayed him. Sami knew him too well. His words lacked the thrust to convince her that he believed what he proclaimed.

∽

Wanting privacy, all but impossible anywhere in the bustling precinct, Sami went into one of the interrogation rooms, closed the door, and sat on the rickety chair in front of the beat-up wooden table. She'd been in this room many times; grilling would-be perps; playing "good-cop-bad-cop." Many a cocksure suspect sat in this twelve-by-twelve room, while Al and Sami systematically reduced them to sniveling wimps. Sami searched through her purse until she found the mutilated business card. She flipped open her cell phone, and thumbed in the number.

"Bayshore Hospital, how may I direct your call?" The woman's voice sounded jaunty.

"May I please speak to Simon, in physical therapy."

"One moment."

While on hold, listening to Songbird by Kenny G, Sami seriously questioned her mental stability.

"This is Simon."

"Are you still speaking to me?"

"Sami? I'm so glad you called." He cleared his throat. "I'm deeply sorry for your loss."

"Thank you for the card. It was very thoughtful. How did you know that Tommy DiSalvo was . . ."

"The article in the newspaper mentioned that he was survived by his daughter, Angelina Rizzo."

Sami was surprised he remembered her name. Then again . . . "I appreciate your kindness."

"It must be difficult for Angelina."

"She's too young to really understand. I guess it's a blessing. For now anyway."

"How's that ornery back of yours?"

"Knock on wood, it's been fine."

"So you're not in need of my professional services?"

"Not at this time." She sensed an undertone, as if he were asking, "If your back's okay, why'd you call?"

His voice tightened. "Then I should assume that this is a social call?"

She decided to abort her plan. "I just wanted to thank you for the sympathy card."

"I was hoping you wanted to cash in that dinner-rain-check."

He caught her off-guard. "Um, well . . . "

"Are you adventurous, Sami?"

"I haven't been to this point in my life."

"Would I be acting inappropriately if I invited you to my home for dinner?"

His home?

"I hate to brag, but my lobster thermidor is divine. Do you like seafood?"

The last seafood she choked down was Mrs. Paul's fish sticks, Angelina's favorite. "I love seafood."

"How about Thursday evening?"

Her thoughts were racing. For any woman in her right mind to accept such an invitation was insane. Particularly from a man who could very well be a cold-blooded killer. But Detective Sami Rizzo wasn't any woman. She had a hunch and had to follow her instincts, even if she placed herself at risk. That he invited her to his home could prove to be a windfall. A wellspring of evidence might be waiting for her in Simon's home. No matter how clever, a murder's home more often than not revealed hard evidence. Sometimes Sami was required to be a cop first and prudent woman second. Such was the case with this situation. Besides, she could take care of herself. "Thursday's fine."

"How about I pick you up?"

"I don't want to inconvenience you."

"Sami, it would be my pleasure. You can keep Samson company while I prepare dinner."

"Samson?"

"My Labrador retriever. You'll get along famously."

"What time do you get out of work?"

"Around four, but I usually go to the gym for a couple of hours. I can pick you up at six-thirty-ish."

Sami had no intention of giving Simon her home address. She was bold but not crazy. "Tell you what. I've got a lot of running round to do. How about I meet you in the hospital parking lot at six-thirty."

"Um, yeah, I guess that would be okay."

"Great. Then we've got a date?"

"Absolutely."

"Anything you'd like me to bring?" *Other than my Smith & Wesson.*

"Not a thing."

"I'm looking forward to seeing you, Simon."

"Me too."

∽

At precisely four p.m., Simon left work and fought the snarled traffic on Freeway 5. When he reached the on-ramp for Freeway 8 east, traffic was at a standstill.

You are a smart boy, my son.

"Thank you, mother."

Dinner with the detective. Very clever.

"I thought you'd approve."

There's one little detail you've forgotten, dear boy.

"Oh?"

What if she makes the connection when she sees your truck?

He hadn't thought of that.

Through the slow-moving traffic, Simon inched his way to the right lane and exited the freeway at Taylor Street. He turned into the vacant Presidio Park parking lot and maneuvered his truck into the farthest corner of the dirt lot. He reached under the seat and removed a set of license plates, grabbed a Phillips head screwdriver from the center console compartment, and proceeded to replace the stolen plates with the valid ones. When finished, he tossed the plates in the aluminum trashcan.

Back on the freeway now, Simon crawled with heavy traffic for another thirty minutes, until finally Freeway 8 began to move. He exited at Auto Circle and passed one car dealer after another, until he found Benson Ford. He pulled his truck into the driveway and found a spot in the designated customer parking area. When he walked into the dealership, a salesman approached him almost immediately.

"Welcome to Benson Ford." The ungainly young blond offered his hand. "My name is Jason."

Simon pointed to his truck. "I'd like to trade my 2004 for a new model."

"Interested in making a deal today?"

"I'm not here for practice, Jason. Cut me a fair deal and I'll drive it off the lot."

ॶ

Feeling as though fifty pound bags of sand were strapped to their backs, Sami and Al lumbered into the precinct late Wednesday afternoon, defeated and dejected. Two of the four victims' husbands had agreed— reluctantly—to subject their motherless children to further interrogation, but neither offered new information.

"So much for my brilliant theory," Sami said. She sat at her desk and crossed her legs. "Any last minute requests before Captain Davison puts us in front of a firing squad?"

"How about a one-way plane ticket to Bora Bora."

"How about two."

Al toyed with his week-old mustache. Since Sami first met Al, he'd attempted to grow one several times, but it never survived more than two weeks.

"Again you're growing that fur on your upper lip?"

"Don't like it?"

Sami shook her head and giggled. "Now all you need is a horse and sombrero and you can change your name to Poncho Villa Junior."

"Are you mocking my heritage?"

"Blatantly."

"There are harsh penalties for ethnic harassment."

"I'll remember that the next time you call me grease-ball."

Al stuffed his hands in his jacket pockets. "Are we on for tomorrow evening?"

Every Thursday for the last three years, Al picked up pizza and chicken wings, arrived at Sami's house around seven-thirty, and they spent the evening munching finger-food, gulping a few beers, and watching their favorite sitcoms on NBC.

"I'm afraid I have other plans."

Al gave Sami a peculiar look.

She wasn't sure whether or not to tell him about her covert operation. That pesky little voice in the back of her mind told her not to. "Remember the dinner date that never happened? I'm collecting the rain check Thursday."

"I see." Detective Diaz rocked from side to side.

"You seem upset."

"Should I be?"

She studied his face. "What's wrong?"

"When were you going to tell me?"

Sami had never seen him act this way. "Al, you sound like my father."

He lifted a shoulder. "Tell me about this guy."

"There's not much to tell. I met him on Thanksgiving Day. We hit it off pretty well, talked on the telephone a few times, and he asked me to dinner."

"Where's he taking you?"

Under the circumstances and considering Al's unusual behavior, Sami didn't dare tell him that Simon was preparing dinner at his place, nor did she wish to share her suspicions with him. "I'm not sure." She could always justify harmless little lies when designed to spare someone's feelings.

"Hope you have a grand ole time." Al blazed a trail to his desk.

Sami's mouth hung half-open. It occurred to her that Al's friendship and companionship had been the closest thing to a "relationship" she'd had since divorcing Tommy. Partners enjoyed a special intimacy not easily defined. Al's sudden possessiveness wasn't unreasonable. But Sami sensed anger in his eyes, and this troubled her. It felt like she was cheating on him. In truth she was working, not really on a date, but she couldn't yet reveal this to him. For one fleeting moment she thought about approaching Al and discussing it further, but when she spotted Captain Davison goose-stepping toward her desk, she knew the captain had a more important agenda.

Captain Davison sat on the corner of Sami's desk and folded his arms across his chest. As he'd done so many times before, prior to delivering a verbal thrashing, he stared at her over his reading glasses. "What's the good word, Rizzo?"

"I'm working on a new lead."

"Indulge me."

"Not much to tell yet.

"In other words you've got squat, right?"

"I'm piecing things together right now."

"Don't bullshit me, detective."

"I'm going to break this case wide-open, captain. I promise." Her voice, lacking conviction, had no impact on the wary captain. Until this moment, she'd hoped that her suspicions about Simon were wrong, that the charming man she'd met at Katie's Kitchen was everything he represented himself to be. Now desperate to solve this case, facing professional suicide, she could only follow her instincts and hope that tonight would prove to be the break she'd been searching for.

"Okay, Rizzo. I'm going to leave you on a long leash. Be careful not to hang yourself."

༄

Thursday proved to be the most non-productive day of the investigation. Sami hadn't seen Al since their tense conversation Wednesday afternoon. All day he'd been working with the other six detectives assigned to the case. He hadn't called her or even walked by her desk one time. That his demeanor could change so suddenly puzzled her. She expected this kind of treatment from the others, but not from Al. Working with the task force rather than with Sami was almost an act of treason. Never before had she felt like such an outsider. She didn't want to jump to conclusions, particularly because Al and she had been through so much together, but now he seemed like the rest of them. Without Al, she stood alone. Now more than ever, Sami had to crack this case. She knew how insane it was to pursue Simon without backup, but at this particular moment whom could she truly rely on?

Screw all of you. I'm gonna nail this son-of-a-bitch myself and pucker up your no-account little asses!

⁓

Not wanting to deal with the painstaking task of deciding what to wear, Sami chose the same outfit she'd worn to the dinner date that never happened: the black skirt with the naughty slit, a powder-blue silk blouse, dark pantyhose, and cleavage-enhancing Wonder Bra. Although her objective tonight was as detective rather than seductress, she still had to dress the part. Angelina and Sami arrived at her mother's home a few minutes before five-thirty, allowing more than thirty minutes for Sami and Josephine Rizzo to engage in their usual mother-daughter joust before Sami had to leave for her rendezvous with Simon.

"Hi, Ma." Sami closed the door behind her and Angelina hugged Grandma Rizzo's knees.

Josephine studied Sami's ensemble with critical eyes. "Isn't that the same outfit you wore the last time?"

Sami set her purse on the sofa. "It is indeed."

"Why wouldn't you wear something different?"

"He never saw this outfit, Ma. Remember?"

Josephine thought for a moment, then nodded. "You should button your blouse. He might get the wrong idea."

To appease her, and to avoid a lengthy exchange, Sami complied.

Angelina tugged on Josephine's apron. "When we eatin' supper, Grandma?"

"In a little while, honey."

"What are we eatin'?"

"How about macaroni and cheese?"

The two-year-old nodded furiously. "It's yummy."

"Why don't you go into the playroom, Angelina. Grandma will call you when dinner is on the table."

Angelina toddled to the spare bedroom where Grandma Rizzo kept an assortment of toys.

"Where are you meeting him this time?" Josephine asked.

Sami would not give her the satisfaction. "He's picking me up in about thirty minutes at my place."

Josephine shook her head and sat on the sofa. "So he decided to be a gentleman?"

"I guess so, Ma."

"Is he going to come to your door or blow the horn?"

"Actually, Ma, he's going to drive by slowly enough for me to dive through the open passenger's window."

"Such a mouth on you."

Sami sat next to her mother and patted her hand. "You think that one of these days before I die you'll stop treating me like a child?"

"Is it wrong for a mother to care about her only daughter?"

"No, but it's wrong for you to coddle me like I'm a nitwit."

As always, Josephine sulked.

"Yes, Ma. The mystery man is going to knock on the door like a real gentleman."

"What does he do for a living?"

"He's a physical therapist."

Josephine nodded. "Ah, like Stella's daughter?" Stella was Josephine's lifelong friend.

"That's right, Ma."

They sat silently for almost five minutes.

"Do you think it's right for you to go on a date so soon?" Josephine asked.

"What do you mean?"

"Well, only three days ago, Tommy . . ."

"I don't think there are rules regarding acceptable periods of mourning over ex-husbands."

Josephine evaluated Sami's logic for a few seconds. "But what would people think if someone saw you?" Always the case with Josephine Rizzo, she never did anything without first weighing how it would be judged by society. Consequently, her life had been unremarkable and humdrum.

"To be honest, Ma, I couldn't care less what people think."

Josephine struggled off the sofa, and without saying another word disappeared into the kitchen. For the next ten minutes Sami sat quietly, thinking about Al's uncharacteristic behavior and Captain Davison's candid reminder that the hourglass was quickly draining. At six p.m., Sami said goodbye to her still-sulking mother, gave Angelina a hug and started toward the front door.

"How late will you be?" Josephine asked.

"Not sure."

"Want Angelina to sleep here?"

Sami hadn't asked for fear of yet another lecture. "I'd really appreciate it."

"Pick her up in the morning. I'll make breakfast."

"Thanks, Ma."

⁓

At six-twenty-two, Sami pulled into the Bayshore Hospital parking lot, parked facing the entrance so she could watch for Simon to pull in, and turned off the ignition. It occurred to her that she had no idea what kind of car Simon drove, but knew if he was indeed the serial murderer he'd be much too clever to drive the Supercab pickup. In the dark parking lot, lit only by scattered sodium vapor lights, he might be hard to spot. Sami was reasonably sure that Simon would find her. She barely had a moment to compose herself, check her weapon to be sure it was secure in her purse, when headlights flooded the inside of her car. A white Ford Explorer pulled next to her. Leaving the engine running, Simon got out of the sport utility vehicle, and limping slightly, approached Sami's car. She eased out of the car; careful not to twist her lower back, pushed the power door lock button, and watched Simon walk toward her. Razor-sharp creases punctuated his tan slacks, and he wore a jade-green V-neck sweater. His hair was wet and slicked back. Sami caught a whiff of his citrus-scented cologne.

"Well, Sami, we meet again." He extended his right arm.

When she grasped his hand, Simon sandwiched it between both of his and gently pumped her arm. His hands were as soft as satin. "It's good to see you, Simon." Her voice was a little unsteady.

"You look smashing, Sami. Ready to take a ride into the country?"

"Want me to drive?" Sami offered.

He shook his head. "I'd rather if you don't mind."

He opened the passenger's door on the shiny white Explorer, and carefully helped Sami step up into the sport utility vehicle. Conscious of her short skirt, Sami maneuvered into the passenger's seat in ladylike fashion. Dark stockings or not, she didn't want Simon to get an eyeful. The potential for awkward silence concerned Sami. During dinner, no doubt, they'd have plenty to talk about—she hoped—but how could she keep the dialogue moving during this long ride?

She noticed the "new-vehicle-smell." For lack of a more sophisticated opening, Sami said, "I like your Explorer."

"It's new. Finally decided to get rid of my rickety-old pickup. When you live in the country, a truck's pretty handy." Simon turned out of the parking lot and headed for Mission Bay Drive.

"So where exactly do you live, Simon?"

"On the outskirts of Alpine."

Of course. Where else would a murderer crucify his victims? "You like it out in the boonies?"

"When I first moved here from Texas, I figured that if you're going to live in Southern California it would be silly not to be near the ocean. I tried a beach community, but just couldn't deal with the traffic and the all-night-party-animals."

"Are you a native Texan?"

"Born in Corpus Christi."

"Did you move here when you were a child?"

He shook his head. "Ten years next month."

"How did you manage to lose the Texas accent?"

Simon put his foot into the accelerator and headed for the Freeway 5 on-ramp. "For some reason I never acquired that Texas twang. To be honest with you, I'd rather listen to fingernails dragging across a blackboard than a southern drawl."

Or, you could be lying through your teeth. "Y'all can't be serious."

Simon gave Sami a sidelong glance and grinned. "I reckon that's true just as sure as bacon comes from hogs. And that be the gosh-darn truth."

Sami leaned back and rested her head against the headrest. For a fleeting moment, she thought about

Al, and wondered if he decided to watch NBC's lineup alone. Considering his stable of women, he probably found a more stimulating way to enjoy Thursday evening.

"What's your story? Are you a surfer girl?"

Apparently he hadn't noticed her pale skin. "I'm a Native San Diegan, but I can count on one hand the number of times I've dipped my toes in the Pacific."

"Really? I would think a local would have gills."

"The weather here is to die for, but our ocean never gets warm enough for me. Seventy-five degrees max. And that's only in summer."

"Tell me about it." As they approached the on-ramp for Freeway 8, the traffic was almost at a standstill. "I love to scuba-dive and I'm accustomed to the warm Gulf waters. The first time I dove here I thought I was in Antarctica. Immediately bought a dry suit."

Simon turned on the radio and slid a CD into its slot. "You like Basia?"

"As a matter of fact I do."

൭

In spite of Simon's ability to conceal his true feelings, engaging in idle chitchat with a chosen one sickened him. Until he had her locked safely in his Room of Redemption, he'd have to pretend that their encounter was a "date," and play the role as a captivated suitor. If only she knew what he had in store for her. Detective Sami Rizzo would not be easy to overcome. With the others, it had been child's play. He had shown the frantic mothers his hunting knife and whispered in their ear that he'd fillet their kids like a fresh salmon if they even thought about fighting him. Without resistance, all the mothers complied with his wishes. With Detective Rizzo, he didn't have her daughter for leverage, and unlike his other guests, she was well trained in the art of self-defense. And more than likely that oversized purse concealed a firearm. Simon couldn't take anything for granted. He enjoyed a challenge, and choosing Detective Rizzo as an honored guest represented a dichotomy of exhilaration and concern.

He wondered about the investigation, curious if anyone in the homicide division had uncovered anything that might incriminate him. He knew she'd never answer direct questions. Perhaps he could find a back door?

"How long have you been a homicide detective, Sami?"

"For more than six years." She paused. "Sometimes it feels like a century."

"Don't take this the wrong way, but you don't look the part."

"Is that a compliment or otherwise?"

"Believe me, it's a compliment."

She thought about his observation for a minute.

"I could never deal with all the blood and guts. How do you sleep at night?"

Blood and guts? Interesting choice of words for a could-be-killer. "Mostly I don't."

"Then what drives you?"

"I often ask myself the same question, Simon. I never intended to become a homicide detective, it just happened." She thought it unwise to share a tale about her father's dying wish.

"Trying to track down a serial killer must be difficult."

"He'll make a mistake. They always do."

Her comment excited Simon, making him believe that he hadn't yet made a mistake and she had no viable leads. "According to the newspaper, there are no suspects as of yet."

"We'll, that's not entirely true."

Simon glanced at Sami with a peculiar look on his face.

∽

Tangled Freeway 8 finally started to move. Simon put on his signal, eased over to the left lane, and engaged the cruise control. "Are you going to arrest me if I exceed the speed limit?"

"As long as we get to your home in one piece, you can kick it into warp drive."

They sat quietly. Basia sang a tune called, *Time and Tide*.

Simon exited the freeway and turned left. "Who's babysitting Angelina?"

Sami dug her fingernails into the soft leather seat. *You got no shot at finding out, pal.* "She's sleeping at my partner's home."

∽

The bumpy country road was dark and winding, lit only by the moon and an occasional mercury vapor light mounted on a garage. It gave Sami the creeps. There were no palm trees in sight, a trademark synonymous with Southern California. So far from the ocean, Alpine looked like anything but part of the Golden State. For a moment, Sami felt panic-stricken. *What the hell am I doing?* If Simon was the serial murderer, she was on her way to his home. When she'd devised the plan, it had made sense. Now, sitting next to him, moments from turning into his driveway, she realized that pride and stubbornness had colored her thinking. How did she propose to search his home? If he offered a tour, surely he'd exclude any area that might incriminate him. Even if his home were abundant with evidence, he most certainly would have sterilized the interior to protect himself. Instead of acting so headstrong, she should have arranged for backup, organized a plan with Al and the task force. Unless she could find a way to contact her fellow detectives via cell phone, Detective Samantha Rizzo was on her own.

I must be out of my friggin' mind.

The Explorer slowed and Simon turned into a drive-way. Sami watched the garage door open. Light poured out onto the gravel surface.

"Home sweet home," Simon said.

In the garage a stocky brown dog went berserk. "Is that your watchdog?"

"More like a pussycat. If anyone ever broke in, Samson would lick them to death."

Still upholding his urbane stature, Simon got out of the Explorer and opened the door for Sami. "I must warn you," Simon said as he grasped her hand and led Sami toward the entrance, "my humble abode will never make the cover of Architectural Digest."

Simon stopped briefly to quiet Samson. They walked into the kitchen and Simon turned on the light. He secured the dead bolt, pushed in the lock button on the doorknob, and fastened the chain lock. He helped Sami remove her jacket and hung it in the closet. That he'd secured the door like Fort Knox troubled her.

"Are you hungry?" Simon asked.

"My bellybutton's playing tiddlywinks with my backbone."

He laughed. "We'll handle that problem right away." Simon opened the refrigerator, removed a plate of assorted cheeses and crackers, along with a bottle of *Robert Mondavi* chardonnay. He set the plate on the kitchen table and held up the chilled bottle of wine. "Do you like white or red?" He pointed to a wine rack in the corner.

Sami, of course, was terrified to eat or drink anything. She would have to watch Simon carefully to be certain he did not doctor what she consumed. If she observed him opening and pouring wine into a glass from a sealed bottle, he would be unable to contaminate it without her seeing him. As much as she needed to remain level-headed, a few sips of wine could help calm her frazzled nerves. She could feel perspiration dripping from her armpits. "I'm a red-wine-kind-of-gal."

"Cabernet, Merlot, or Malbec."

"Malbec, please."

Simon popped the cork on a 2004 bottle of *Catena* and half-filled two wine goblets. "Everything's prepped. All I have to do is add a few finishing touches, pop the main course in the oven, and we'll be eating in twenty minutes." He handed Sami a glass. "To serendipitous beginnings."

Sami gently clicked her glass against his, waiting for him to drink the wine before she filled her mouth with the berry-flavored Malbec.

As Simon wrestled with the plastic wrap covering the cheese and crackers, Sami noticed his shiny brown shoes. Except for the color, she'd recently seen loafers just like them. They were a popular men's style: low profile heels, little tassels, and slightly pointed toes. But what distinguished these particular shoes from most loafers was the rough-textured leather, looking like alligator or lizard skin. She took another sip of the wine, more convinced than ever that she was about to share an intimate dinner with a serial killer. A rush of warm blood filled her face. She suddenly felt flu-dizzy.

Calm down, girl.

"I'm afraid we're stuck with dining in the kitchen," Simon said. He sipped the wine. "This matchbox house doesn't have a formal dining room."

The rectangular oak table was set with a vase of fresh calla lilies, crystal candleholders, and a jade green linen tablecloth.

Is there no end to this masquerade? "How can I help?"

"You can set the table." He pointed to a lower cupboard. "You'll find placemats and napkins in the bottom drawer, silverware in the top drawer, and dishes in the upper cabinet."

Simon's china was exquisite: ivory dinner plates with gold trim; simple yet elegant. The silverware felt heavy and masculine. Sami wasn't surprised. Everything fit. Many serial killers were not only handsome and refined, they were regular Martha Stewart's around the house. When they sat for dinner, Simon dimmed the lights, lit candles, and delivered two plates of steamy cuisine that looked like presentations from the FoodTV network. She had carefully watched him spoon the lobster thermidor to the plates and felt certain he had not tampered with her portion.

Again he offered a toast. "Here's to good food, vintage wine, and a captivating lady."

Goose bumps covered Sami's skin. She held up her glass. "To an elegant host."

As they ate dinner and exchanged carefully edited biographies, each playing the role as would-be lovers, Sami felt profound sadness that the evening was a ruse. She could not suppress her primal attraction to Simon. Her life had been devoid of intimacy for so long, it was hard for her to insulate her heart from such a romantic setting. It was possible that all of the circumstantial evidence, no matter how convincing, existed only in Sami's vivid imagination. Perhaps her unrelenting drive to solve this case skewed her usually-rational thinking to the point of total make-believe. The possibility existed that Simon actually was as charming and well breed as he represented himself to be. When was the last time anyone prepared such an exquisite meal for her? The one time Tommy DiSalvo had even attempted to cook dinner, he tossed a plate of leftover meatloaf in the microwave and delivered the lukewarm food to the kitchen table as proud as a man who had just won the gold medal for best entree at a world-renowned culinary competition. She could not afford to get careless, but if the evening proved that Simon was not the serial killer, she surely would not be disappointed.

The lobster thermidor was a triumph; a dramatic departure from Sami's usual fare. She hadn't enjoyed wine in quite some time—beer was her usual choice of libation—and after only half a glass her head was reeling. Not wanting to numb her senses further, and potentially place herself in danger, she finished the lobster, but did not drink the rest of the wine.

"Well, do I have a shot at a feature recipe in Food & Wine?"

So preoccupied with her intense thoughts, Sami hadn't bothered to compliment him on the extraordinary meal. "Forgive my inability to comment earlier, Simon. I was too busy savoring your creation."

"Is that a thumbs up?" He gestured with his hand.

"You get the Nobel Prize for Culinary Excellence."

Simon stood. "Did you leave room for dessert?"

Her skirt—tight before she'd eaten—felt dangerously close to choking her mid-section. "You must be joking."

Simon cleared the table, set fresh wine glasses on the counter, and filled them with a slightly chilled French Sauternes dessert wine. From the refrigerator he removed a chocolate cake covered with whipped cream and raspberries.

With her mouth agape, Sami watched him deliver the impeccably designed mountain of decadence to the center of the table. "So that my feminine ego isn't forever-bruised, please tell me you bought that cake."

"Baked it myself." He held up his arms like a magician showing the audience that his hands were empty. "With my own two hands."

Simon set the half-filled wine glasses on the table. Condensation had already begun to form on the outside of the glasses. He cut two small wedges of the luscious cake and carefully served them to dessert plates. "Hate to leave you alone, but I need to use the little boy's room. You can sip your wine, but promise me you won't taste the cake until I return."

"Take your time, Simon." This was the opportunity she'd been hoping for.

As she watched him limp to the bathroom, she couldn't help but wonder what might happen tonight if Simon proved to be nothing more than a delightful man wanting to impress a woman he felt attracted to. If his intentions were truly honorable and his motivation sincere, how could she ever deal with the guilt of falsely suspecting that he was a diabolical serial killer?

Time to depart from her fantasy world and put on her detective badge. Sami guessed that she had about two minutes before Simon took care of business. If he caught her snooping around she would say that she decided to tour his home. A believable story, she thought. It didn't make sense to search open rooms or visible areas. After all, it seemed unlikely that Simon would have incriminating evidence lying on the cocktail table or his next victim gagged and bound to a bed. She didn't expect to find a crucifix erected in the living room either. No, somewhere in this house was a sanctuary, a room or closet or private area that told a chilling story.

As soon as she heard the bathroom door click shut, Sami tiptoed past the living room, down the hall. She noticed three rooms off the hallway, two with their doors wide-open, one closed. She didn't bother with the two that were open. But the room at the end of the hall with the door shut heightened her curiosity. Walking as softly as she could, the hardwood floors creaking with each step, she inched toward the farthest room.

She grasped the doorknob, hoping that the door was unlocked, and turned it clockwise. Click. Her face flushed warm with blood. Sami pushed the door open and stepped over the threshold into the dark room. Light from the kitchen poured down the hallway and spilled into the room. An unidentifiable object stood in the middle of the room, but there wasn't enough light to determine what it was. She caught a whiff of scented candles or flowers or perhaps one of those newfangled Glade deodorizers that plug into a wall socket. Something floral. She groped for a light switch on the wall next to the door molding. Nothing. Now the opposite side. Her fingers found the switch. For a moment, Sami hesitated. She had no idea what she'd see in this room. It might just be a spare bedroom, or a utility room, or maybe a catch-all for seldom-used possessions.

She flipped on the light.

For an instant that seemed like an eternity, Sami's eyes—not yet adjusted to the bright light—darted around the room in a frantic frenzy to absorb everything at once.

"*My God!*"

In that one sobering moment Sami Rizzo clearly understood how utterly foolish she'd been; how her ego had triumphed over reason. Everything she knew about logic and discretion proved to be a fairy tale. All she'd been taught about prudent detective work was now meaningless. She had made a horrendous tactical error and her poor judgment had placed her in a life-threatening situation with a madman. Her only hope was to dash out the door and call for help. She slipped her hand inside her purse, searching for her handgun.

The floor squeaked behind her.

One of Simon's powerful arms wrapped around her torso, chest-high, and restrained her arms. Before she could utter a sound or jam her heel into the instep of his injured right foot, he covered her face with a damp cloth and pressed it firmly against her mouth and nostrils, making it impossible for her to draw a breath of fresh air. As she fought to break free, unable to loosen his grip, the vapors from the ether-soaked cloth assaulted her lungs. The bleach-like odor immediately made her woozy. The room began to spin like a carousel, and Sami lost the strength to fight, her body feeling as if it were a rag doll. For one crazed moment, she clawed at his hand, digging her fingernails into his flesh. But his grip only tightened. At a point when Sami's legs could no longer support her weight, Simon let her go and she collapsed to the floor. Before her eyes blurred to blackness and consciousness yielded to the powerful anesthetic, Sami glanced at Simon and saw the face of the devil himself.

SIXTEEN

Certain Sami was out cold, Simon went back into the kitchen, finished the wedge of chocolate raspberry cake, and swallowed the last mouthful of wine. He cleared the table, rinsed the dishes and silverware, and neatly arranged them in the dishwasher. Then Simon lifted Sami off the floor, bent her limp body over his shoulder, and as if he were doing squats with a two-hundred pound barbell, balanced her weight, flexed his powerful legs, and stood upright. He negotiated his way down the stairs and laid her on the bed in the Room of Redemption. For several minutes, Simon stood over Sami and stared at her.

You will be my most cherished offering.

Suspecting that she might have an easy-to-conceal weapon on her person, he stripped her to bra and panties and carefully searched her clothing. He found nothing. He sat on the bed and gently pushed the wisps of hair away from her eyes. Simon could not deny that Detective Rizzo was a striking woman. Her skin felt like ivory; off-white and smooth to the touch. Her lips were full and inviting. But in spite of her pleasing external appearance, she was an infidel, a sinner, a detective trying to thwart God's work. Knowing that she'd been skillfully trained to defend herself, he considered handcuffing her to the bed. But when he'd done the same to Peggy McDonald, she'd rubbed her wrist raw. Simon didn't wish to treat his guests like animals, but to prevent her from attacking him he needed leverage.

He covered Sami with a blanket, locked the steel door, and went upstairs. On the floor next to where Sami sat for dinner, he spotted her handbag. Simon shook the contents onto the kitchen table and pawed through the pile of rubble: wallet, cell phone, pager, two makeup bags, pens, tissue, gum wrappers, business cards, snub-nosed revolver. Attached to a fob the size of a quarter, he found a metal ring with a dozen various keys. On one side of the fob was a balance scale; the astrological symbol for Libra. On the other side was a picture of Angelina.

You've done well, my sweet son. I'm proud of you.

"Thank you, Mother."

I must caution you, Simon.

He listened carefully.

You look at this one with lust in your eyes.

"That's not true, Mother."

You cannot hide your weakness of the flesh from me, dear boy.

"You are the only one, Mother."

Don't disappoint me, son.

"Never."

Simon wrapped the cell phone and pager in a dish-towel and set them on the floor. He searched through the drawer next to the sink and found the metal hammer he used to pound veal and chicken breasts. With repeated blows he smashed the cell phone and pager until they were reduced to tiny pieces. Then, he shook them out of the towel and into a plastic bag. Simon flipped the cylinder open on the .38 special, poured the hollow-point bullets into the palm of his hand, stuffed the revolver in the kitchen drawer, and tossed the bullets into the same bag with the remains of the pager and cell phone. He examined Sami's assortment of keys, focusing on Angelina's photograph.

Leverage.

৶৩

Alberto Diaz quite smoking over ten years ago, and with Sami's encouragement and the help of AA, he stopped drinking more than three years ago. On this particular evening, just before midnight, unable to sleep and as jumpy as an expectant father, Alberto Diaz ventured to the corner twenty-four-hour 7-Eleven. Buying a pack of Winston's did not prickle his conscious too severely. The adjacent isle with an endless assortment of booze, however, made his mouth water. Ah, California. Where else could a man buy a bottle of salvation from the neighborhood convenient store in the wee hours of the morning?

Al left the Winstons on the glass check-out counter and moved toward the display of alcohol. As if hypnotized, his eyes transfixed on an impressive variety of

Scotch whiskey. One particular brand caught his eye and immediately evoked bitter memories. He reached for the bottle of Dewar's White Label and held it like delicate crystal.

Need to take the edge off. Just a pint. Sixteen ounces. Can't possibly hurt.

He ran his thumb over the label as if he were stroking velvet.

One drink. Just one.

He remembered the throbbing hangovers, his stomach on fire, kneeling in front of the "porcelain throne" and puking his guts out. He'd never forget waking up in the middle of the night and hanging his foot off the bed onto the floor to stop the room from spinning. Was it worth it? He set the Dewar's on the counter next to the Winston's and dropped a twenty dollar bill in front of the clerk.

Fuck it.

When Al returned home, he poured the Scotch over ice, sat in his favorite Lazy Boy recliner, set the glass on the cocktail table, and lit a Winston. In the dark, he puffed away. Oh, how marvelous to fill his lungs with the soothing smoke. He'd forgotten that wonderful high. Sucking on the cigarette did not cause Al too much angst. But the booze on the other hand, jabbed at his conscience and sense of well-being like a hot poker. Several times, Al held the glass in his hand. He even sniffed the seductive aroma and licked his lips. He could not take a sip. Yet.

He'd picked up the telephone a dozen times in the last hour, but couldn't muster the courage to dial Sami's number. What if the answering machine picked up? That would mean she was still with him. How long did it take to have dinner? If she did answer, how would he justify calling so late?

His behavior was adolescent. Al knew this, but couldn't help himself. He'd known that one day Sami would start dating again. Until now, Sami felt uncomfortable with the whole concept of dating, even though she and Tommy were divorced. Al believed it had something to do with Angelina. But now everything had changed, and Sami was with another man, a man Al knew nothing about.

The Scotch beckoned again, and without further evaluation, Al emptied the glass with three long gulps. He could feel the warm alcohol slowly blaze a trail to his stomach. Almost immediately, his face felt aflame, and his head spun as if he were riding on a merry-go-round. After chugging a second drink, a strong dose of alcohol-courage overwhelmed Al, so he reached for the cordless telephone, pushed TALK, SPEED DIAL, then the number four. After three rings he heard Sami's recorded message.

"Shit!" He heaved the telephone across the room and it ricocheted off the wall.

❧

To ensure that Sami's mother was sound asleep, Simon waited outside her house until after two a.m. The house was dark, and except for an occasional car whizzing by, the street deserted. There were several assorted house keys on Sami's key ring, and Simon guessed that one fit her mother's door. He could easily break in, but that could be risky. Using keys made him less conspicuous. He got out of the Explorer and looked up and down the street. No one in sight. Walking swiftly, he crossed the street and hopped up the steps leading to the front entrance of Josephine Rizzo's house. The only glitch in his plan would be if Sami's mother secured the door with a chain lock. Not that he couldn't effortlessly snap a thin chain, but any unnecessary noise could attract attention.

The screen door squeaked when he opened it. He held his breath for a minute. The first two keys did not fit the dead bolt lock; the third one did. Simon turned it clockwise. He tried to turn the doorknob but it had also been locked. This time the first key he chose slid neatly into the slot. Click. He craned his neck and surveyed the landscape. Still no visible activity on the street. Perspiration dotted his upper lip. He twisted the doorknob and slowly opened the door, but as he suspected, the old woman had secured a chain lock. Simon owned two pairs of bolt cutters, one of which was in his Explorer. Just in case.

Leaning into the wooden door with his shoulder, Simon planted his left foot for leverage and pushed hard against it. The wood split with a cracking sound and the chain broke free easier than he'd expected. *Such a foolish deterrent.* A child could have broken the chain. A night-light spilled from the kitchen into the living room; just enough light for Simon to find the hallway leading to the bedrooms. He had no way of knowing in which bedroom Angelina slept. He stood in the hall and listened. From the door on the right he could hear Josephine Rizzo snoring loud enough to wake the dead. He eased past her open door. At the end of the hall a dim light shone through the partially opened door, casting a ceiling to floor rectangle of light on the wall. He tiptoed toward the bedroom. With each step the old wooden floor creaked in protest.

Simon poked his head into the bedroom. Angelina looked sound asleep. He knelt beside the little girl's bed. He didn't wish to harm or frighten her but if she didn't cooperate he'd have to restrain her. He removed a roll of duct tape from his pocket and set it on the floor. Just in case.

Gently, he grasped her shoulder and shook. Angelina's body twisted and she rubbed her nose with the palm of her hand. She yawned and her eyes opened just a slit.

Simon held his index finger to his lips. "Shh. We have to whisper so we don't wake your grandma."

Angelina didn't utter a sound.

"Your mommy has a present for you."

She leaned on an elbow. "She does?"

"Yep. She's waiting for you right now."

"Where is she?"

"At my house."

"Can we go there?"

"Only if you promise to be very quiet."

Angelina rolled her eyes and smiled. She cupped her hands around her mouth and whispered, "Is it a big present?"

Simon extended his arms. "It's this big."

Her eyes were like saucers.

Simon pawed through the chest of drawers and found an adorable pink dress. Then, he helped Angelina put it on, grasped her hand, and she followed him toward the door. Suddenly Angelina stopped.

"Mommy told me not to go with strangers."

Simon knelt down and gently grabbed her shoulders. "Do you remember when you and your mommy came to the hospital to visit me?"

She nodded.

"And remember when your mommy got all dressed up last night?"

"She went on a date."

"That's right, Angelina. Your mommy came over to my house for dinner. She wouldn't have dinner with a stranger, would she?"

She thought about that for a moment. "Can we bring grandma?"

"She's really tired, so we're going to let her sleep."

❧

At first, only a glimmer of disoriented consciousness interrupted Sami's stupor. She had no concept of time, no immediate recollection of what happened, and didn't know where she lay. The only thing she knew for sure was that at any moment she would throw up. Her head, feeling as if it were floating above her body, spun out of control. The damp room smelled musty, adding to her nausea. From a small adjoining kitchen-like area, dim light spilled into the room; barely enough for Sami to see. It looked like a studio apartment, equipped with all the essentials to live a modest life: TV, microwave, small refrigerator, and a large cardboard box overflowing with toys. Toys to occupy the children. Ah, yes, he had thought of everything.

She lay on the bed beneath a blanket, caressing her bare skin, trying to rub the chill away, searching her not-to-keen memory. Why was she wearing only a bra and panties? The obvious conclusion sickened her. Lucidity didn't come quickly; it took several minutes for Sami to reconstruct the foggy puzzle. When she did, a feeling of chaotic frenzy overwhelmed her.

Simon.

Her body shivered.

She did not need bright light to know that she lay in Simon's holding room, where Jessica and Linda and Molly and Peggy had lain before he crucified them. Now it was her turn. But not without a fight.

Sami swung her legs off the edge of the bed and tried to sit upright, but she could not find the strength. Whatever potent drug Simon had used to knock her out caused her muscles to feel like oatmeal. She hung her head over the side of the mattress and vomited on the floor. Her stomach felt ablaze.

How could I be so stupid?

All along, a cautionary voice had whispered in her ear, but Sami's desire to prove to Captain Davison and the other members of the task force that she could crack this case before the Friday midnight deadline pushed her to act irresponsibly. She could not fathom the level of reckless arrogance she'd employed to devise such a naïve plan. To have dinner at the home of a likely serial killer without backup proved to Sami that her once-reliable cop-instincts had vanished! She now realized that Simon had planned their meeting, and everything he did had been a means to an end. Now so obvious, she couldn't believe her gullibility.

Keep your wits, girl. Panic now and you're dead meat.

In spite of feeling dizzy and nauseous, she tried to ignore her ornery gut and forced herself to stand. She felt certain her stomach would betray her again. If she had any hope of surviving this ordeal, she had to assess the situation before he returned. And that could be at any moment. Who could possibly know how his twisted mind functioned? To protect her bare skin from the chilly air, she wrapped the bedspread around her body and wobbled her way toward the dim light. The concrete floor felt cold and hard against her bare feet. She couldn't help but wonder if the other four women had clung to this same bedspread. The thought sent a chill through her.

In the far corner, she found a halogen floor lamp and turned it on. She first noticed the steel door. Not a surprise. Next, she spotted a round hole in the floor filled with dirt, about the diameter of a beach ball. Why would he dig a hole in the concrete floor? Then Sami saw her clothes neatly folded, sitting on the corner of the bed. *Strange.*

Still hazy, Sami didn't need all her faculties to deduce that Simon had imprisoned her in his strategically-designed basement for only one reason. She suspected that such a calculating sociopath soundproofed the room as well, so screaming like a maniac or pounding on the door would be fruitless. Besides, she didn't want to rile him.

Standing near the light, surveying the room, Sami listened for any sign that he plotted somewhere in the house. She couldn't hear footsteps or faint music above her. For all she knew he could be standing outside the steel door with his ear pressed against it. Perhaps he slept peacefully, dreaming about his next crucifixion, grinning hideously. She noticed the play area, the assortment of children's toys and games . . .

Angelina.

At least her daughter was safe. Or was she? Sociopaths rarely changed their killing patterns. She remembered Peggy McDonald. Her wounds were the same as the other three victims, and Simon undoubtedly crucified her, but he had not cut out her heart. Patterns can change. Simon had proven that. But to what extent? With each victim Simon had kidnapped mother and child. Had this been planned or a coincidence of circumstance? Suddenly, a feeling of alarm settled in the back of Sami's throat, closing off her windpipe. All she could do was wait.

❧

Angelina slept the entire ride back to Alpine in the back seat of Simon's Explorer. Without waking her, Simon carefully lifted the child and carried her into the garage. A blustery wind blew from the west; thick clouds covered the stars. The air smelled damp. Southern California was near the threshold of its rainy season. As he searched for the key to unlock the door, Samson, overwhelmed with curiosity, stood on his hind legs and sniffed Angelina's sneakers. The Labrador's tail wagged furiously. Simon patted the dog's head, then unlocked the door. He laid her limp body on the living room sofa and covered her with a thick cotton blanket. She immediately rolled on her side, curled into a ball, and stuck her thumb in her mouth. For several minutes Simon stood over her, staring at the little girl, almost mesmerized by the child who looked nothing like her mother.

He felt an eerie hollowness, as if his body had no organs. Flesh stretched over bones. He'd experienced this emptiness before. He often wondered why God had chosen him. To serve his Creator unconditionally, Simon had to forgo many of life's mortal pleasures. To forfeit parenthood was a considerable sacrifice. Why couldn't he be a father? Would it really interfere with his divine duties? A part of him longed to be a father. Not in the traditional sense, but as a single parent. He looked at Angelina. Perhaps he could be a father and still carry on with God's work.

With the back of his hand, Simon gently stroked Angelina's soft cheeks. Such a precious child, he thought. Who would assume the role as Angelina's guardian after he purified Sami's heart and cleansed her soul? Her father had been murdered, and her grandmother? Too old and physically incapable of raising an energetic child, the old woman could never handle such a demanding responsibility. Besides, Josephine Rizzo was not qualified to direct Angelina in the Christian way. Simon would indeed rear a child under God's careful supervision. How would anyone know if he adopted Angelina? No doubt he would act as an exemplary father, read her the Bible every day; teach her about God and salvation and how to live in God's grace. Maybe meeting Sami would prove more bountiful than he had originally thought.

ᕦᕤ

Josephine Rizzo opened her eyes and tried to focus on the clock radio digital display. Without her glasses she could not clearly see the time. It made no difference. Her bladder was full. To disregard nature's warning would prove to be unwise. Especially at Josephine's age. Josephine knew better than to drink coffee after seven p.m., but last night she could not deprive herself of such a simple pleasure. Particularly when her home-made butter cookies tasted so much better with a strong cup of Columbian.

The sun hadn't risen yet, and she could hear a gar-bage truck roaring outside. She guessed it was early morning. If she went to the bathroom and did her business, she'd never fall back to sleep. Such were the challenges of old age. She closed her eyes for a minute, trying to ignore nature's call. No use. If she didn't hurry, she'd dribble a trail to the toilet.

After using the bathroom and washing her hands, Josephine tiptoed to the end of the hallway to look in on Angelina. The door was ajar, enough for her to peek inside. Usually, Angelina slept sideways with the covers twisted in a ball. Sometimes Josephine would find them on the floor. Such a restless sleeper. Quite to Josephine's surprise, the pink comforter neatly covered her entire body. Even her head. Josephine walked toward the bed and gently folded down the comforter to uncover Ange-lina's face. She read stories about young children suffo-cating. Never a quick-minded woman, Josephine stood with her hands perched on her hips, staring at two pil-lows neatly arranged under the covers. "Angelina?"

Josephine didn't panic. Of course, she thought, Sami's date had been a disaster, so she decided to pick her up last night instead of in the morning. Sami didn't wake her mother because she didn't want to hear Jose-phine say, "I told you so."

Suddenly, Josephine felt the pang of alarm. Why did Sami lay two pillows under the comforter? She pondered for a moment.

After considering all logical reasons—none of which made much sense—Josephine went into the kitchen and dialed Sami's number. The telephone rang four times, then Josephine heard Sami's recorded message. Why couldn't she hear the telephone ringing? Now she could feel her gut tightening; the quiet panic and cold sweat she once felt when Dr. Shepard announced that her husband, Angelo, had less than a week to live. She inhaled a quivering breath. Then, her eyes wandered to the broken chain on the front door and she fell to the floor paralyzed with fear.

∽

At five-twenty a.m., Alberto Diaz—dreaming of selling Chiclets at the San Diego-Tijuana border as a child—jumped when he heard a siren outside his bedroom window. Normally a light sleeper, the alcohol he consumed last night served as a strong sedative, making him dead to the world. He switched on the lamp and the light assaulted his eyes. Squinting, he looked at the empty pint of Dewar's White Label sitting on the nightstand. How he remembered the violent hangovers. That only a pint of booze could cause so much agony bewildered him. He took a moment and gently massaged his hammering temples. He always slept in the nude, so when he tossed the covers the cool December air turned his skin to goose flesh.

Considering that he wouldn't be able to look into Sami's eyes for fear she'd pick up on his still-bruised ego, today was the perfect day to proceed with his covert operation. Suffering from a hangover that Sami would surely recognize reinforced Al's decision. He knew that the serial murder investigation beckoned him, but didn't think a few hours would make much difference. Besides, he'd be back from Tijuana before noon, and seven of his fellow detectives, including Sami, were working feverishly on the case. No one would miss him.

He brushed his teeth in record time, threw on some clothes, and swallowed three Advil. Before bolting out the door, he called Captain Davison's private number and left him a message. Still groggy and lightheaded, Al secured his shoulder holster, put on his jacket, grabbed his cell phone, and bolted out the door, forgetting that he'd turned off the phone.

SEVENTEEN

Droopy-eyed and still groggy, Sami tried to organize
her thoughts. Whatever Simon used to drug her, packed
a wallop. Fully dressed now, she sat on the corner of the
bed, fidgety as a teenager waiting for the results of a
home pregnancy test. Butterflies fluttered in her stomach. Not ready to be victim number five, Sami searched
her disoriented thoughts for a way to outwit Simon. For
the last hour she enlisted every ounce of strength to
suppress her fear and concentrate on a survival plan.
She did not want her eulogy read by an eleven o'clock
newscaster.

No matter how calculating, all killers had a hot button. A weakness. Through her extensive training, she
had learned this fundamental concept. The battle would
not be won by the most skilled gladiator; but rather by
the more astute chess master. Sami had to outsmart
Simon, catch him off guard, infiltrate his vulnerability
just long enough for him to let down his guard.

Simon's past victims were crucified three days after
their abduction. If his time line didn't change, Sami
guessed that Sunday would be the day of reckoning;
less than seventy-two hours away. The mere thought of

Simon's diabolical plan filled Sami with dread. Unlike the other victims who might not have clearly understood the depths of evil in Simon's plot, Sami had examined detailed photographs of the crucified victims. She observed part of an autopsy. She knew that their deaths were grisly. She did not wish to share their fate. And of course, the thought of Angelina alone terrified her. How would she survive in such a hostile world without her biological parents?

For the first time since awakening in this prison, Sami heard footsteps above her. Heavy footsteps. Soft footsteps. The creaking floor of an old house. Wild images flashed through her mind. She sat quietly and listened, forcing her self-preservation instincts to foster a plan.

༄

Al left his apartment in Chula Vista, filled his gas tank at the local Shell station, bought a giant-size cup of black coffee, and hopped on southbound Freeway 5. When he thought about the message he'd left on Captain Davison's voice mail he couldn't help but grin. Using his most convincing "sick voice," which was not difficult considering his raspy-hangover-throat, he had said, "Sorry, boss, I'm getting a bad case of the flu (sniff, sniff, cough, cough), and don't think I'll be in today. Tell Sami I'll speak with her later." To avoid the captain's inquisition, Al had purposely telephoned Davison before the captain normally arrived in his office.

The international border was only a fifteen-minute ride from Al's apartment, but often the number of cars converging on the inspection booths created heavy congestion. As always in the morning, most of the border traffic headed northbound, entering the United States, so Al found the shortest line and inched his way toward the next available inspection booth.

"Good morning, sir." The short, stocky Mexican agent bent forward, removed his Ray Ban aviator sunglasses with Hollywood style, and his molasses-colored eyes scanned the interior of Al's old Chevy. The young man couldn't have been twenty-five.

To save time and avoid a lengthy exchange, Al pulled his police ID and detective shield out of his back pocket and held them out the window. "I've got official police business in Tijuana."

The Mexican eyeballed Al for a moment then waved him on.

৩০

To Alberto Diaz, leaving U.S. soil and entering Mexico felt like visiting an ancient civilization. The contrast between the opulent lifestyle of southern Californians, and the third-world poverty of our Latin neighbor startled even Al, a Mexican native. He saw this economic disparity everywhere he looked. While many west coast Americans drove pricey cars, lived in amenity-enriched environments, and enjoyed the opera, and exquisite cuisine, the majorities of Mexicans lived in ramshackle homes, survived on beans and rice dishes, and were sentenced to an impoverished, substandard existence. There were, of course, destitute Americans, but poverty was as much a trademark of Mexican lore as piñatas. And unlike living in the United States where opportunities to elevate yourself from pauperism to prosperity flourished, Mexicans could rarely improve the condition of their lives through hard work and ambition. Privation perpetuated itself as an axiom of Mexican culture.

Whenever Al returned home, the eye-opening transition—almost like going back in time—rubbed a raw nerve. He no longer had animate roots in Tijuana. Al's parents were dead and his only sister, Alita, married a wealthy Brazilian and moved to Rio de Janeiro. Although his sister telephoned every Christmas, and never forgot to send him a birthday card, Al hadn't seen her in five years. Al's life was now in the states, but there still existed a patriotic connection to this picturesque country. He struggled with an inherent love for a Mexico that evoked bittersweet memories.

The early morning traffic in downtown Tijuana was snarled with impatient drivers, most of whom were angry Mexicans blaring their horns and yelling Spanish expletives. Most Mexicans having enough money to own a broken-down car could easily secure a job as a New York City cab driver. Although most of downtown TJ had been revitalized with newly-constructed buildings to support tourism—boutiques, restaurants, designer shops, and a variety of specialty stores—just on the fringe of the central area existed a Tijuana unmolested and third-world, a poignant reminder that American intervention had its limitations.

Al drove south, about a mile from the pulse of the city, to a small tavern called Lorenzo's. The owner, a longtime friend of Al's, kept his eyes focused and ears tuned to the rhythm of criminal commerce, and occasionally dabbled in a particularly lucrative enterprise. He knew more about the dynamics of Tijuana than the mayor.

Memories from Al's upbringing flooded his mind.

Driving the familiar country roads, he drifted back to his childhood, reflecting on a Christmas past, the only time of the year when the oppression of poverty seemed diluted by the holiday magic.

Cesar and Lucita Diaz, Al's parents, struggled to provide for Alberto and his older sister, Alita. Although Cesar worked steady, seven days a week as a short-order cook in a small restaurant in the heart of Tijuana, he earned barely enough to survive. The family lived in a three-room home on the outskirts of the city. Lucita could no longer contribute financially to the family. She suffered from two herniated discs, the result of a life laden with strenuous work as a housekeeper for a local hotel. Twelve-hour days of backbreaking work, flipping mattresses, vacuuming miles of carpeting, scrubbing showers and toilets, had finally taken their toll. Mexican employment laws were much less stringent than in the United States: they virtually didn't exist. The few that did were not enforced.

In spite of their meager existence and often-insurmountable challenges, the Diaz family tried to live a spirited life. For the entire year, Cesar and Lucita deprived themselves of anything but the essentials for a simple existence. Each week they stashed away a small portion of Cesar's paycheck. At Christmastime, they used the savings to buy Alita and Alberto a wonderful Christmas gift.

The last December Al's mother was alive—Al had just become a teenager—he had gotten a Huffy ten-speed bicycle for Christmas. Considering their paltry lifestyle, to receive such a gift was an epic event. But Al, too angry to appreciate the significance of his parents' generosity and sacrifice, had not properly thanked them. They had scrimped all year to buy such an extravagant gift and Al did not receive their unselfish gesture in the same spirit in which it had been offered.

Al was pissed off at the world, fed up with poverty, tired of selling Chiclets to rude Americans at the international border. He could not find the words to thank his parents.

In later years, when Al fully understood the altruistic nature of his parents and the depth of their love, he wept for them often, regretting his lack of gracious approbation. Whenever he visited their graves, he cried. Memories of Christmas choked him up. While kneeling beside their graves, he asked them to forgive him for never appreciating how wonderful they were.

With blurry eyes, Al remembered. Bitterly. And painfully. He never got the chance to thank his parents for their devotion and uncompromising love. These were not the memories he wished to elicit. Not now.

Al pulled into the dirt parking lot and a cloud of dust whirled around his Chevy. He waited for the air to clear before stepping out of the car. The gloomy, overcast sky, pale as granite, threatened rain on this unusually humid day. The wind whirled out of the west, and Al inhaled the faint smell of cosmos. Al didn't expect the tavern to be open this early. Lorenzo, a nighthawk, never awakened till noon. He walked to the adobe structure set about fifty feet behind the saloon and knocked on the front door, hoping to awaken his old friend. If Lorenzo, known to empty a quart of tequila on occasion, suffered from a hangover, not even a fire siren could stir him.

Al waited a minute, and then with the side of his fist he pounded with more conviction.

About to knock a third time, the severely weathered door creaked open just enough for the barrel of a shotgun to poke out and greet Al's face.

"Lorenzo? It's Alberto." Al wanted to speak Spanish, but he no longer rolled his tongue with the precision of a native, and nothing insulted a Mexican more than desecrating his language.

The door squeaked open a little farther and Lorenzo's heavy-jowled face appeared. As always, his meaty cheeks were dotted with three-day stubble. His shaggy black hair, longer and more unruly than Al remembered, hung below his ears.

"Alberto?" Wearing only baggy tan shorts, so soiled they looked like he used them as a drop cloth, the two-hundred-seventy-five pound Mexican bulldog swung the door wide open and stepped out onto the landing. His naked barrel chest was covered with curly black hair. Even the tops of his broad shoulders were hairy.

"How are you, my friend?" Al said.

Like a sumo wrestler, Lorenzo wrapped his beefy arms around Al, and lifted him off the ground, almost crushing his ribs. "Have you forgotten your way back home, amigo?"

Al could hardly breathe let alone speak.

Lorenzo released Al and kissed him on both cheeks. He smelled like cigarettes.

"It's been a long time, Lorenzo."

"Too long, my friend. Come into mi casa."

Lorenzo's lack of personal grooming did not accurately represent the condition of his home. Although not spacious when compared to the average American home—barely eight hundred square feet—the modest two-bedroom structure, lavishly furnished and impeccably neat, impressed Al. The living room looked like a photograph out of a furniture store's autumn catalog.

Lorenzo pointed to a garnet Victorian sofa. "Make yourself at home and I will prepare breakfast."

Al didn't feel hungry, but to deny his friend the enormous pleasure he derived from his kindhearted hospitality would be rude. As Lorenzo worked busily in the kitchen—banging pans, chopping, rattling dishes, singing in Spanish—Al sank into the cushy sofa and tried to forget about everything in the universe except the tranquility of such a seldom-appreciated moment. He heard the stairs creak and turned his head. Tiptoeing down the stairway, Al saw a young woman wearing only a long T-shirt that barely covered her torso. She almost flowed down the stairs. She gave Al a sidelong glance, her eye muscles twitched to a smile. Her erect nipples looked like they were sculpted into the cotton. The woman was breathtakingly beautiful. Al didn't think Lorenzo had a daughter—he wasn't old enough to have fathered a woman in her late teens—but Al guessed there were many mysteries about his childhood friend that would surprise him.

She stood about five feet from Al and cocked her head to one side; her wavy black hair lay on her shoulder. Her skin looked the color of caramels. "*Me llamo Rita.*"

Al stood up. "*Es buen conocerlo. Soy Alberto.*"

"*Eres un amigo de Lorenzo?*"

He nodded. Certain he would embarrass himself if they continued speaking Spanish, Al asked, "*Habla ingles?*"

"*Un pocito.*"

"Is Lorenzo behaving himself?"

She grinned and shook her head. "He is bad boy."

From what Al remembered about Lorenzo's teenage years, he was indeed a bad boy.

Lorenzo stuck his head through the doorway. "You have met my Rita?"

My Rita?

"Is she not beautiful like a wildflower, my friend?"

"She's lovely, Lorenzo."

Like an embarrassed child, Rita, face flushed red, stared at the wood floor and nervously toyed with the bottom of her T-shirt.

Curious and somewhat dumbfounded by their relationship, Al wanted to learn more, but before he could ask a delicately composed question, Lorenzo disappeared again. Al didn't think it probable that something romantic existed between them, but Lorenzo, although not wealthy, was well-to-do by Mexican standards. And a Latino with money could have almost anything he wanted. Al couldn't take his eyes off the young woman's face.

"You live America?" Rita asked.

"San Diego."

"*Una ciudad bonita.*"

"It is beautiful. Have you been there?"

"Brother send pictures. Live San Ysidro."

A sudden look of bewilderment came over her face. Al guessed Rita searched for words she could not find in her limited English dictionary. Instead of speaking, she sat on the leather chair opposite Al and snugly tucked the T-shirt under her thighs. They sat silently, Rita studying Al, and Al admiring this pristine example of God's exquisite craftsmanship.

With steamy dishes piled on top of a serving tray, Lorenzo emerged and hustled past Al and Rita. He set the breakfasts on the dining room table. Out of breath, he motioned to Al. "*Vamos a comer.*"

Al sat opposite Lorenzo. Rita stayed on the sofa.

"Isn't Rita joining us?" Al asked.

"She will eat later."

Al didn't question Lorenzo, but felt uneasy.

Lorenzo had sautéed a variety of peppers, onions, garlic, cilantro, chorizo, and eggs, topped the mixture with fresh tomatillo salsa, and rolled the combo in giant tortilla shells.

Al took a bite. He loved spicy food, and was surprised Lorenzo could cook. "When did you go to cooking school?"

"You like?"

"Fantastico! If you weren't such an ugly *diablo*, I'd ask you to marry me."

Lorenzo stuffed almost half of the burrito in his mouth and chewed like he hadn't eaten in days. He swiped at his mouth with the back of his hand. "Why would I sleep with a gringo when Rita warms my bed?"

Al almost choked. "Right, Lorenzo. And I'm the Mexican president."

When they were kids, there had always been a rivalry between them, a fierce competition to outdo each other. The stocky Mexican must have sensed a challenge. He dropped the half-eaten burrito on his plate and yelled, "*Rita! Be pa ca!*"

Rita leaped off the chair as if it were on fire, charged over to Lorenzo, and stood by his side. She looked like a first-day boot camp recruit. Lorenzo pivoted forty-five degrees and faced Rita. With his thick arms, he reached around the young woman and rested his palms on the back of her knees; her breasts were pressed against his face. Slowly he slid his chubby hands up her thighs until they disappeared underneath the T-shirt and rested on her backside. For a minute, Lorenzo fondled Rita's butt as if he were molding clay.

Al sat stone-still.

With his mouth still covered with fragments of the breakfast burrito, Lorenzo kissed the young woman on the mouth. Lorenzo slapped her butt, waved his hand as if dismissing a servant, and Rita couldn't leave quickly enough. Al watched her almost float up the stairs and disappear.

"So, Presidente Diaz," Lorenzo said, "you were saying something?"

They finished breakfast with little conversation, left the dirty dishes on the table—Lorenzo yelled upstairs for Rita to clean the mess—and Lorenzo invited Al into his private den.

"Well, my friend," Lorenzo said, "what is troubling you?"

"Other than what I just witnessed in the dining room?"

"You are jealous, no?"

"No."

"You lie, Alberto. What man would not want to have my Rita?"

"How old is she, Lorenzo?"

"Fifteen. Sixteen. What is the difference?"

"It's not right, Lorenzo"

Lorenzo opened a wooden box on the corner of his desk. "You still like Cuban cigars?"

Al shook his head.

Lorenzo lit the thick cigar and puffed a cloud of blue smoke. "How quickly you have forgotten the ways of our country."

"I haven't forgotten anything."

"I have offended you?"

It wasn't his business, but Al couldn't let it go. "Why with a teenager? Mexico is full of adult women."

"I like the taste of fresh mango more than grapefruit"

"What the hell does that have to do with anything?"

"Mango is sweet. Grapefruit is sour."

"And?"

"Rita tastes like mango."

Al realized that he was attempting to impose his moral standards on Lorenzo. Was it an argument he could win? His business in Tijuana didn't include reforming his lifelong friend. Besides, did he really want to consider just how righteous he'd be if a teenager as lovely as Rita offered to be his concubine?

"I'm sorry, Lorenzo. You invite me into your home, cook me a lovely breakfast, and I repay your hospitality by attacking you."

"You would not be the friend I remember if you did not try to save my soul." Lorenzo sat next to Al and draped his arm around him. "You didn't come to Tijuana just to have breakfast with an old friend."

"I never could hide anything from you, Lorenzo."

"Tell me what I can do for you."

Al explained the details of Tommy DiSalvo's murder, the mutilated condition of his body, Tommy's history of gambling, and suspected involvement with the Mexican Mafia.

"Carlos and his *bandejos* are *animales*, but they do not like blood. One bullet. Behind the ear. Quick and easy."

"That's what I thought."

Lorenzo leaned into Al. "You are sure he was killed because of gambling?"

"Why do you ask?"

"The way this man was murdered sounds like the work of Flavio Ramirez. It is . . . how you say? His . . ."

"Trademark?"

Lorenzo nodded vigorously. "You fuck with Flavio and he cuts your *huevos* off."

"You know the guy?"

"He is a drug dealer. Big operation in L.A." Lorenzo looked confused. "Nobody owes Flavio money. All cash. No credit."

"If Tommy DiSalvo didn't owe Flavio money why would he murder him?"

"Maybe he wanted a piece of Flavio's drug business. He does not like . . ."

"Competition?"

Lorenzo nodded.

It was possible that Tommy had asked Sami for money to make a drug buy. Perhaps he'd given up gambling and decided to go into business for himself? "Do you have any connections in L.A.?"

Lorenzo smirked. "Alberto, why would you ask such a question?"

"Can you make a few calls?"
"Anything for my *amigo*."

౪

Al left his lifelong friend and headed for the border. He thought it a good idea to call Captain Davison, just to check in. He removed the cell phone from his belt and realized he'd turned it off. Shit! He thumbed in the captain's private line.

"This is Davison."

"Feeling a little better captain. I should be there in about—"

"Where the hell are you, Al?"

"Didn't you get my message?"

"I've been trying to reach you since early morning. If you're sick, why aren't you answering the telephone?"

"Sorry, captain, I guess my cell phone was turned off."

"And your home phone?"

Al remembered smashing it against the wall. "Guess it was turned off too."

"Well your timing was just . . . fucking . . . perfect."

"I'm sorry, captain, if I'd known—"

"Sami and her daughter are missing."

Al couldn't muster a word.

"We got a call from Sami's mother early this morning. Sami never made it home from her date Thursday evening, and Angelina mysteriously disappeared from Mrs. Rizzo's home sometime during the night."

Al could feel his pulse pounding in his temples. He tightened his grip on the steering wheel with sweaty hands. "Who's working on this, captain?" He could see the international border just ahead.

"Hicks and Robinson are en route to Mrs. Rizzo's house as we speak."

"Call them off. I'll be there in twenty minutes."

"You sure you can handle this, Al?"

"Positive."

ᏟᏉ

Quite to Al's dismay, the volume of cars converging on the inspection booths was heavy. In the shortest line at least thirty vehicles waited their turn to be carefully scrutinized by the Border Patrol agents. Feeling great anxiety and painfully aware that time was precious, Al planted the flashing beacon on the dashboard, engaged his siren and raced to the front of the shortest line. Sitting parallel to a beat-up Dodge pickup truck, waiting to be inspected next in lane six, Al glared at the driver and waved his arms, trying to make the obviously-confused Mexican understand what he was trying to do. The man backed up his truck, almost hitting the Lexus behind him, and Al wedged his Chevy in front of the truck. A symphony of horns protested Al's actions. Watching Al carefully, a noticeably upset agent waited to hear Al's story.

Border Patrol agents paid particular attention to foreigners—especially those even remotely appearing to be Latino. In spite of the Immigration and Naturalization Service's (INS) efforts, which included a campaign to recruit additional agents, over three-million illegal aliens lived in California. Since 9/11, various plans to control the influx of illegal aliens had been initiated. Nonetheless, the problem grew more chronic every year. Consequently, many INS agents took their jobs too seriously.

The tall agent with sun-bleached hair and a perfect Coppertone tan folded his arms across his chest and gawked at Al over his sunglasses. "What's your story, buddy?"

Al didn't waste a moment. He flashed his badge and ID. "Sorry, sir, but I'm a homicide detective and I just received an emergency call from my captain. Would you hurry me through, please?"

Unimpressed, the agent ignored Al's attempt to expedite the interview. "Are you a U.S. citizen?"

Didn't he know that only bona fide citizens are hired as law enforcement officials? "Yes I am."

"And how long were you visiting Mexico?"

Al felt like screaming at the agent, but forced himself to remain calm. "For a few hours."

The agent pondered Al's answer for a minute. "Are you carrying firearms, alcohol or controlled substances?"

Is this guy kidding? Al grabbed the lapel on his leather jacket and gave the agent a glimpse of his Glock 9 mm. "I'm a homicide detective, sir. I don't even go to Sunday mass without a weapon." Al huffed. "Would you please let me through?"

"Please pull your car over there." He pointed to an area to the right of the road where believed-to-be drug dealers and other suspicious characters watched in horror (some of them prayed) as specialized employees of the INS systematically disassembled their vehicles, searching for contraband.

"Maybe I didn't make myself clear. I've been called to a police emergency and you have to let me through. Now!"

"I don't have to do anything, detective. Now pull your car behind that van."

Not wanting to antagonize the agent further, Al extinguished his fury, kept quiet, and parked the Chevy behind a beat up, light blue cargo van. Al watched two agents tear through the old Ford like a couple of children wired on an overdose of Coco Puffs.

What a joke. No wonder California is overflowing with illegals.

From out of nowhere, a giant figure, a man over six feet tall and as brawny as a professional wrestler appeared outside Al's window. The freckle-faced redhead wore a standard-issue brown Border Patrol uniform. "Would you mind stepping out of the car, sir?"

Al pushed the door open hard, almost hitting the hulky man. Standing face to face with the agent, Al stood only a few inches shorter. The man's body language emanated hostility.

For the second time in less than ten minutes, Al flashed his ID and detective shield. "Why are you people detaining me?"

"Why are you trying to cross the border with a firearm?"

"I'm a cop."

"Then you should know that nobody is allowed over the border with a weapon."

Al, of course, knew this, but had never been hassled before. Professional courtesy had always existed between cops and agents. When Al had been in uniform, he often overlooked an agent driving a little too fast or one slightly intoxicated. Not recklessly, but as long as they hadn't been driving like a maniac or severely inebriated, he looked the other way.

The agent bent over and perused the interior of Al's car. "Tell me about your official business in Mexico."

"I'm investigating a homicide and met with one of our informants."

"In Tijuana?"

Al nodded.

"What's the guy's name?"

"I'm afraid that's confidential."

The agent rested his hand on his holstered pistol. "Don't get cute with me, detective."

Al took a deep breath.

"I'm gonna ask you again: who did you meet in TJ?"

He glanced at the man's nametag. "Listen Agent Sullivan, I can appreciate that you have a job to do, and I respect your attention to detail, but I'm sure you're aware that I have to follow strict security guidelines regarding informants. If I were to break the rules and reveal the identity of my source, it would seriously jeopardize our continued relationship."

The agent planted his hands on his hips. "Give me your superior officer's name and phone number. I need to verify your story."

Al had heard stories about Border Patrol agents caught up in the splendor of their authority, but this guy thought he was Genghis Khan. "Let me put it another way, Agent Sullivan. Can I appeal to your sense of self-preservation?"

"What's that supposed to mean?"

"Have you ever heard the term: obstruction of justice?"

"Of course."

"Do you read the newspaper or watch the eleven o'clock news?"

"Every day."

"Then you must be familiar with the nut-case crucifying young mothers, right?"

He nodded. "Guy should get the chair."

"You're absolutely right, Agent Sullivan. The only problem is this: I'm the detective heading this investigation, and by detaining me you are obstructing my ability to gather evidence that may help us roast this bastard's nuts. Mayor Stevens is personally involved in this investigation, and I can tell you first hand, she ain't a happy camper. If you don't stop breaking my balls and let me over the border immediately, I'm going to inform the mayor that some overzealous cowboy fucked me over, and I promise you, Agent Sullivan, Mayor Stevens will see to it that your shiny badge ends up in a recycling bin, and you, my friend will be picking strawberries for a living."

Sullivan's face turned so red his freckles almost disappeared. "I'm sorry for the delay, detective"—Sullivan spoke with a shaky voice—"the next time you make a trip to TJ, I'll see to it personally that you're moved through customs without a hitch. Um . . . I'm sorry for the misunderstanding."

ço

The rain started shortly after Al reached American soil. A heavy downpour pounded Al's windshield. The wipers—even on high speed—couldn't keep the glass clear. As usual, when it rained in San Diego the freeways looked like parking lots. Al could never quite understand why wet roads had such a profound impact on traffic. You'd think that ten inches of snow had fallen. While stopped on the gridlocked freeway, listening to the news on KTAK radio, Al closed his eyes for an instant and again tenderly massaged his temples.

The Advil was losing the battle.

He'd fallen again. Hungover and nauseous, he craved a morning beer. Big trouble loomed. Considering Sami and Angelina's disappearance, he had to enlist every ounce of willpower to remain sober. Oh, how he loathed himself right now.

Al's cell phone rang, but when he flipped it open, the line was dead. Suddenly, it occurred to him: why not call Sami's cellular and pager? Wherever she was—if not incapacitated, a realization he forced out of his thoughts—perhaps she'd respond. That Al hadn't thought of this earlier baffled him. The alcohol had diluted his ability to think clearly. First he called Sami's cell. A little from last night's binge, but more from fear, his hands were trembling.

After two rings: "The cellular customer you are trying to reach is unavailable. Please try again later, or wait for the tone and leave either a numeric or verbal message."

"Sami, this is Al. Please call me ASAP." He thought about a lengthier message, but to what avail?

Al now tried Sami's pager. After four rings: "After the beep you may leave a numeric message. When you are finished, please push the star key." He punched in his cell number. Now all he could do was wait.

Al didn't anticipate using the siren and red beacon, but without their help he'd never make it to Josephine Rizzo's house. Unfortunately, all four freeway lanes were jammed with bumper-to-bumper vehicles. If he turned on his siren and flashing red light, where would these cars go? They weren't helicopters. Al placed the flashing beacon on the dashboard, pulled to the right shoulder, and drove on the narrow apron.

For the entire ride, wild thoughts plagued Detective Diaz. He didn't want to overreact, but his cop instincts were screaming in his ear: Sami and Angelina are in a life-threatening situation. Having a reliable nose for trouble was not always an asset.

He squealed into Josephine's driveway, and then raced to the front porch through a torrential downpour. Only thirty paces from his car, Al stood in front of the door, dripping wet. Before he could knock, Josephine opened the door. She wore a navy terry cloth bathrobe. Her eyes were red and puffy.

Detective Diaz wiped his feet on the doormat, shook the rain off his head the best he could, and stepped into the living room. Josephine dabbed her eyes with a knotted tissue. He removed a notepad and pen from his pocket, and hung his windbreaker on the coat tree.

"I'm so glad they sent you, Alberto." Josephine was the only person north of the border who called him by his given name. "I'm worried sick."

They sat on the sofa.

"Tell me about the guy who picked up Sami."

She blew her nose. "I didn't see him, but his name begins with an "S". It's not a regular name."

Al scribbled on the pad. "Did Sami say what he looked like?"

"Handsome and tall. Really tall."

"Did Sami tell you anything about him?"

"He's a physical therapist."

"Do you know where he lives or works?"

"I don't, Alberto."

"Where did they go?"

"Out to dinner, but I don't know where."

Al asked Josephine a series of questions about Sami's date. He filled two pages with notes. Time to switch gears.

"What time did you first notice Angelina missing?"

"Must have been around four."

He didn't want to insult her but had to ask. "You've thoroughly checked the house—under the bed, in closets, anywhere she might hide?"

"She's not here, Alberto," Josephine's lips tightened to a thin line.

Al craned his neck and surveyed the room. He noticed the broken chain on the front door and the splintered wood. As soon as he finished interviewing Josephine, he'd contact Davison, fill him in, and ask the latent fingerprint department to thoroughly examine the premises.

"Don't touch anything until we have a chance to dust for fingerprints."

"Okay."

"Do you have keys to Sami's house?" Al asked.

"Why do you ask?"

"It would be a good idea if I went over there and checked things out."

Josephine went into the kitchen and returned with two keys attached to a panda bear key chain. She tossed them at Al.

Al stuffed the keys in his back pocket. "Anything else you can tell me, Josephine?"

Josephine spoke through grim eyes. "If I lose my Sami and my granddaughter . . ."

"Sami and Angelina are fine. I promise."

Now all Al needed was to buy into his own promise.

EIGHTEEN

Surprised Angelina slept most of the morning, Simon sat in the recliner beside the sofa, watching her sleep. He opened his Bible to a passage he'd read several times: Proverbs 22:6 "Teach your children to choose the right path, and when they are older, they will remain upon it." Intoxicated by this little girl, he fantasized about how wonderful it would be if he were her father. He didn't expect that he'd ever father a child; in order to do so he'd have to get married, and his mother would never approve. Besides, as a devoted servant of the Almighty, God had already set his destiny. The Creator had not planned for Simon to be married. But who would be more suited to raise a child than he? Surely God Himself would endorse this admirable ambition. And just like his mother had done, he could introduce Angelina to adulthood on her twelfth birthday. Oh how proud his mother would be, knowing that her only son followed in her footsteps.

He knelt by the sofa and gently stroked Angelina's hair, brushing it away from her face. Such a beautiful child. Did he really have to wait until she turned twelve to show her how much he adored her? Perhaps now, during the quiet hours of the morning would be the perfect time. At the mere thought of touching her, he could not help but get aroused. Maybe he could make love to her while she slept. He carefully removed the blanket covering her. Sleeping in the fetal position, her pink dress barely covered her legs. He brushed the back of his hand up and down her milk-white legs. She didn't move. Bending forward, he pressed his wet lips against her thigh.

Don't you dare touch that little girl!

"Mother?"

Just what do you think you're doing?

"I think you know."

She is merely a child, Simon.

"Does that really make a difference, Mother?"

It does in God's eyes. The time will come soon enough, sweet boy. You must be patient.

He thought for a moment, then covered Angelina with the blanket. "You may be right, Mother."

I'm always right, Simon.

∾

Before Angelina awoke, Simon prepared scrambled eggs, bacon, home fried potatoes, and buttered toast. He arranged the late-morning breakfast on a dish and set it on the kitchen table. He poured two glasses of milk. Angelina started to stir, so Simon knelt beside the sofa and gently shook her shoulder.

"Good morning, princess." He pushed the hair out of her eyes.

She sniffed the air. "I smell bacon."

"Are you hungry?"

"Really, really hungry." She sat up.

He grabbed her hand and led her to the kitchen. Her two-year-old body could not comfortably reach the table, so Simon piled some magazines on the chair to prop her up.

Angelina examined the plate. She wrinkled her nose. "Eggs are yucky!"

"They're good for you."

She shook her head. "I don't like 'em."

"My scrambled eggs are delicious. Please try just a taste."

"Can I eat the bacon with my hands?"

From a plate in the center of the table, Simon grabbed a piece of bacon and took a big bite. "If you try just a tiny bite of my eggs, you can even eat the potatoes with your hands."

She smiled, forked a small portion of the scrambled eggs, and wrinkled her nose. As if she were taking cough medicine, she slowly slipped the fork past her lips. She chewed slowly and rolled her eyes. "I like 'em better than Mommy's."

Simon sat next to Angelina and they quietly ate breakfast. Angelina finished the bacon and home fried potatoes, took two bites of the buttered toast, but she left most of the scrambled eggs.

She rubbed her belly in a circular motion. "That was really good."

"Would you like to see your mommy?"

Angelina nodded. Her eyes opened wide. "Does she got a present for me?"

"Finish your milk and we'll see."

∾

Sami heard the deadbolt turn and sprang off the bed. Without an agenda or reason, she unconsciously brushed the wrinkles out of her skirt and fussed with her hair. Her heart thumped against her rib cage. Trying to remain calm, she attempted to fill her lungs, but could only inhale a shallow breath. Step one of her survival plan was to hide her churning emotions from Simon. She felt as if she were unraveling.

Steady, girl. This is the moment of truth.

The door swung open. Before Sami even realized that her daughter lingered in the shadows just behind Simon—her eyes were transfixed on Simon's taunting sneer—Angelina spotted her mother and charged toward her like a three-foot-three sprinter. "Mommy, Mommy! Where's my big present?" Angelina wrapped her arms around Sami's knees and almost knocked her backwards on the bed.

Sami's eyes narrowed with contempt. She glared at Simon and silently mouthed the words, "You bastard!"

Simon grinned from ear-to-ear. "Thought you could use a little company."

Before Sami could respond, Simon did an about-face and slammed the steel door.

So much for hiding my emotions.

സ

On the way to Sami's house, Al telephoned Captain Davison and told him what he knew thus far.

"I've got every available detective on stand-by," Davison said. "Any progress?"

"Not really."

"Think Sami's disappearance has something to do with the serial killer?"

Al thought of this possibility. Her date fit the profile, but he refused to accept it as a valid supposition. What were the chances that Sami's mysterious suitor was the same man they were after? It seemed unlikely. "I think it's a bizarre coincidence, boss."

"After you check out Sami's house, give me a call."

"Even if I don't find anything?"

"I want to hear from you on-the-hour—even if you just breathe in my ear. Got it?"

"Yes, sir."

"And one more thing. If you need anything, call me immediately."

Al parked in front of Sami's house and frisked his jacket for cigarettes. There were only two left in the crumpled pack. In the past, when he'd fallen off the no-smoking-wagon, one pack had been enough to set him straight. He had a funny feeling that soon he'd be buying a carton. What worried him most was the lingering taste of Scotch, so convincingly whittling away his willpower.

The violent rainstorm surrendered to a light sprinkle. The ominous clouds were losing their grip and odd-shaped patches of blue randomly dotted the sky. Stubborn clouds gave way to California sunshine. Soon the sky would be the color of balloon flowers. Al heard on the radio that many streets in Mission Valley were flooded. The engineers who designed the San Diego sewer and drainage system must have believed the Mama's and Papa's song: "...*it never rains in Southern California*..." Bullshit. From March to November you couldn't fill a thimble with rain, but during the winter months, particularly January and February, it often poured with a vengeance.

Parked in Sami's driveway, Al sat in the car, sucking on a cigarette for almost ten minutes. To waste crucial time made no sense. In fact, minutes often made the difference between life and death. Yet Al lingered, feeling almost paralyzed, terrified by what he might find inside Sami's house. He could not dismiss the possibility that Sami was indeed inside. Perhaps unconscious. Maybe seriously injured. Or maybe she could be ...

He yanked on the handle and swung open the door. Al plodded toward the front door like a man trudging through mud. In his infinite optimism, he rang the doorbell and pounded the side of his fist against the door. No such luck. After steadying his shaky hands and unlocking the door, Al stepped into the living room and looked around, clinging to the quickly-vanishing hope that Sami and Angelina were safe and sound. Cupping both hands around his mouth, he yelled.

"Sami. Are you here? Angelina."

Other than the clock on the far wall ticking away, Al heard nothing. One more time.

"Sami, it's Al. Where are you?"

Al's eyes were misty, his throat tight.

The condition of the living room emulated classic-Sami-housekeeping. Untidy and cluttered with debris, Al observed two empty pizza boxes on the cocktail table, toys scattered about, empty coffee mugs and glasses, books, newspapers, magazines, and a half-filled Tic Tac container. He hadn't fallen in love with her because of her domestic flair. He loved just looking at Sami, smelling her hair, feeling her leg pressed against his when they stuffed pizza in their faces while watching a Chargers' game. Samantha Rizzo rocked Alberto Diaz's world.

He found his way to Angelina's bedroom and poked his head inside. Immediately, Al caught a whiff of baby powder and chocolate. Oh how Angelina loved chocolate, particularly Tootsie Rolls. He could almost see that exaggerated grin and her baby teeth covered with the sticky brown candy, her tiny fingers navigating the inside of her mouth to break it free. Without entering, he carefully flipped the light switch with his elbow and looked around. Nothing appeared out of the ordinary. Then again, he thought, how could a single man have a clue as to what was "ordinary" to a child? Reason took control and he stepped into the room. Hanging to the floor, a Mickey Mouse comforter covered the unmade bed. Pink pajamas lay on the corner of the mattress, and furry Oscar the Grouch slippers sat on the powder blue carpeting. Although Angelina had been abducted from Josephine Rizzo's home, he still proceeded cautiously, not wanting to contaminate anything until the latent fingerprint department dusted for prints. The top dresser drawer was slightly open, the closet door ajar, toys dotted the floor.

What the hell am I looking for!

Convinced that Angelina's bedroom offered no clues, he headed for Sami's room.

The bedroom door was closed. In a final attempt to cling to the last grain of hope, Al gently knocked. Using his sleeve, he twisted the doorknob and pushed open the door. He saw an assortment of clothes piled on top of the untidy bed. Several pairs of shoes sat on the floor. He couldn't help but feel like an intruder, an uninvited guest molesting Sami's privileged world, desecrating the sovereignty of her private domain. On the other hand, Al felt warm all over. This is the bed where she lay beneath the sheets every night. How many times had the full-length mirror reflected an image of her naked body?

Al sat on the bed and touched Sami's pillow. He picked it up and pressed it to his face. Ah. Sami's scent invaded his senses. He could never quite explain what she smelled like. Getting a whiff of Sami was like walking through a lemon grove. She had a fresh, citrus scent. Must be her shampoo, he guessed. For several minutes

Al sat in a trance-like state. Like a photo album of their six-year relationship, crisp images flashed through his mind. Every detail so clear. He closed his eyes for a moment and burned an image of her face into his memory bank.

Give it up, Al. Time to be a cop not a heartsick fool.

One by one, Al searched her dresser drawers, carefully examining everything with precision. He could not afford to take anything for granted. Somewhere in this room, Al felt certain, a clue waited to be discovered. The contents of the drawers yielded only a momentary departure from reality. In the third drawer he discovered Sami's lingerie. He imagined what she might look like in the black lace bra and matching panties. Granted, Sami didn't have a model's figure, at least not by today's standards. Sami's figure was more hourglass like Marilyn Monroe. But Al liked a woman with curves. And by God, Sami sure had plenty of curves!

Now the closet. Piece by piece, he rummaged through pockets: blazers, slacks, jeans, jackets—hunting for something. Anything. Again, a dead end. He sat on the bed and stared at the floor, angry, annoyed, helpless. Glancing at the nightstand, Al spotted what looked like a greeting card. Without touching it, he examined it carefully. He noticed Sami's name neatly printed on the face of the envelope. Below her name he saw the address of the precinct. A Pacific Beach postmark was imprinted next to the stamp. He used the corner of the sheet to lift the envelope. No return address, front or back. Touching just the edges of the card, Al strategically slid the card out of the envelope and read the inside greeting.

May the memories you cherish fill your heart with peace today and give you the strength and courage to sustain you on your way.

Warm regards, Simon.

Simon?

Josephine Rizzo thought that the name of Sami's Thursday evening date began with an "S." Could be a coincidence, but what else did he have? Josephine also remembered that he worked as a physical therapist. With a Pacific Beach postmark, Al guessed that Simon either lived or worked in the area. If he lived in PB, how could Al possibly find him without knowing his last name? Bayshore was the only hospital in the area, but several stand-alone facilities offered physical and occupational therapy.

For another thirty minutes Al ransacked Sami's bedroom, but to no avail. Having no other lead, he went with his gut and decided to pay the hospital a visit.

⌒

"Are we going to live here, Mommy?" Angelina sat in front of the television watching cartoons, munching Cheeze-Its. Sami paced the floor like a caged animal.

"Only for a few days, honey."

Since delivering Angelina early this morning, Simon had all but vanished. The sound of footsteps above was the only sign of his presence. Sami had no idea what activities occupied him; maybe constructing a crucifix? Can't just walk into your local lumberyard and buy one ready-made.

Although being in the same room with Simon would cause Sami unbearable anxiety, particularly with Angelina present, she hoped that he would spend time antagonizing them. Isn't that what killers lived for, to taunt and tease their victims, like a cat toying with a mouse? Didn't they derive just as much pleasure from psychological cruelty as physical torture?

To survive, Sami had to get into his head, find out what made him tick. He had to have a weakness. All nutcases did. How could she find his hot button if he remained upstairs?

After the shock of Angelina's kidnapping wore off, Sami felt immediate concern for her mother's welfare. Simon didn't merely knock on her mother's front door in the early morning hours and snatch Angelina without a struggle. Sami had to rely on what Angelina had told her, "we didn't wake grandma cause she was sleeping," and pray it was true.

While the television continued to hypnotize Angelina, Sami examined every square inch of the "living quarters." The forethought Simon employed to design this prison with such exacting detail further proved that he was a calculating sociopath. Only a man mentally deranged could have constructed an area so fastidiously. He thought of everything; the self-contained environment could support life indefinitely. Or for as long as he deemed it necessary. Replenishing the food inventory was Simon's only task. Sami didn't expect she'd be here long enough for the supply of bath towels, linens, and toilet paper to run out. No, by Sunday evening, she guessed, either she'd be dead or rescued.

By now, her mother had contacted the police; hopefully Al. Her partner had strong cop-instincts, and she couldn't think of anyone she'd rather have sniffing her trail than Al. If she hadn't been so headstrong and co-ordinated backup, Angelina and she would not be in such a predicament. But now was not the time to second-guess her poor decision. Sami needed to focus all her energies on more productive issues. Her mother, Sami felt certain, would be in a state of utter panic. That Sami could not contact her mother just to let her know that Angelina and she were fine caused her great distress. No doubt her mother was consumed with frantic desperation. Sami had never felt so helpless.

Sami heard the deadbolt unlock. She hurried to the bed and sat, facing the door.

Deep breaths, girl.

Hopefully, Angelina would continue watching television and not be distracted by their conversation—if he would even speak to her. The few times they'd spoken, Simon portrayed the image of a well-bred man. Now that the masquerade was over, she didn't know what to expect.

The door swung open and Simon stepped inside. He wore jeans, a white sweatshirt, and a Padres baseball cap. As much as she despised him, she could not deny that he was handsome. Remembering her serial-killer training, she knew that many infamous murderers—particularly those most diabolical—were charming and seductive. Simon certainly fit the M.O.

After securing the door, he stood with his arms folded, gawking at her like a zoo patron observing the behavior of a caged animal. "Just wanted to check on you ladies."

"Is my mother okay?"

"She's fine."

All she could do was hope. "How can I be sure?"

"You'll have to trust me."

"Fat chance."

"Need anything?"

"How about a pair of handcuffs and a Louisville Slugger?"

"Afraid not."

"Then an explanation would be a good start."

Simon smiled. "Come on, detective. Do I really have to fill in the blanks?"

"You owe me at least that, Simon."

He ambled toward her. "May I sit next to you?"

That a monster could be so polite bewildered her. His demeanor hadn't changed a bit. Not yet. She moved over and patted the mattress with her hand. He sat a foot to her left.

"You can cut to the chase, Simon. I don't need to hear the nitty-gritty details of your troubled childhood and love-deprived life. Just tell me why."

"Because the world is overrun with sinners."

"How does killing people change that?"

He glared at her. "I free them from everlasting damnation."

"Shouldn't that be their choice?"

"There is no choice. God has selected me to do His work."

She found the opening. "God has asked you to crucify women?"

"He talks to me."

"And he tells you to crucify them?"

"I save their souls. Death is a consequence."

"How do you choose who should be saved?" She checked Angelina to be sure she was still occupied.

"All people are sinners." He glared at her. "Especially women."

"Are you a sinner, Simon?"

His eyes twitched nervously. "Yes."

"Then why don't you save yourself?"

"I *am* saved!"

"Why me, Simon?"

He hesitated. "With you there are two benefits."

"Should I feel honored?"

"You will. I promise."

Don't lose control. Keep the pressure on.

"Why am I so special?"

"You're not only a sinner, you're trying to foil God's plan."

"And you think by kill . . ." she had to choose her words carefully ". . . by saving me, other detectives won't come after you?"

This question seemed to stump him. "I don't have time for this senseless banter."

"Simon, if you are truly doing God's work, wouldn't He want you to be honest with someone about to be saved?"

"You're trying to confuse me."

"No, Simon. I'm just trying to understand."

The tension slowly vanished from his face. His shoulders curled forward and he looked more relaxed.

Sally Whitman, the FBI profiler had been right, Sami thought. Simon was indeed a religious fanatic. But how could Sami use this information to save her hide? Maybe by massaging his religious sensitivity?

"Why did you take my clothes off?"

"I didn't touch you if that's what you're suggesting." His cheeks flushed pink.

"What else would I think?"

"I had to be sure you weren't concealing a weapon or some means of communication."

Amazing how easily he volunteered information, she thought. "You couldn't just frisk me?"

"I had to be sure."

"And how about the other women, Simon?"

His eyes locked on an object in the distance. "What are you talking about?"

"You're familiar with the sixth commandment aren't you?"

"I'm well acquainted with all of God's laws."

Her hands were shaking now, so she stuffed her palms under her thighs. She didn't know how far to push him, but had no idea if she'd get another chance.

"Did you rape them, or was it consensual sex?"

"Don't test me, sinner."

She had indeed found a raw nerve, but didn't dare continue. "Tell me about your family, Simon."

His head snapped toward her. "Are you trying to psychoanalyze me, detective?"

"I'd just like to hear about your family."

"Searching for a deep dark secret?" His voice was riled again.

Sami felt certain she'd hit another nerve. "Are your parents still alive?"

He sprang off the bed. "I don't have time for this chitchat."

Sami wanted to press on, but decided she needed a little time to develop a strategy. "When will you return?"

"Soon enough."

Just before he closed the door, Sami asked, "Would you be kind enough to bring me my purse. I left it on—"

"If you're looking for your cell phone, pager, or weapon, I'm afraid they've had an unfortunate accident."

"I'm not surprised."

"Still want your purse?"

"Please."

After he left, Sami sat on the bed and pondered their conversation. She had to learn more about his family, and provoke his obvious sensitivity to having raped these women. Somewhere there existed a link between his insanity, violent sex, and a parent or sibling.

She could only hope that the next time she saw him wouldn't be the last.

Sami eased off the bed and went into the "playroom." Angelina's eyes were glued to the television. Sami stood between her daughter and the TV and held out her arms. "Would you give Mommy a big hug?"

ↄ૭

When Simon closed the door behind him, he could barely contain himself. Grinning like a mad professor, suppressing a loud guffaw, he shook his head and eased out a huff of air.

She must think I'm an idiot.

Detective Rizzo's question and answer game both amused and disappointed Simon. He'd play her little game; let her think that she could get into his head. He'd thought the detective was clever. Evidently, he'd given her too much credit. He couldn't wait to return for round two.

NINETEEN

Just after one p.m., Detective Alberto Diaz, weary, cranky, unshaven, and slightly hung over, walked through the automatic doors of Bayshore Hospital sipping the last mouthful of 7-Eleven coffee. He passed the information desk and headed straight for the administrative offices. Although the pounding had subsided, his temples still throbbed unmercifully. The main door was locked, but Al found a teller-like window with a circular hole in the glass, allowing people to speak to a receptionist. A young, Hispanic-looking brunette with full lips, bronze skin and eyes as dark and shiny as obsidian glass, greeted him with a smile. Her teeth were pure white.

"Good morning, sir." Her cheery voice was earmarked with a thick accent. "How may I help you?"

"It's urgent that I speak with your human resources director."

"If you're seeking employment, I can assist you."

Al let out a heavy sigh. He pulled out his wallet and flashed the police ID. "I'm Detective Diaz, and I'm not looking for a job."

The woman stood. "I'm so sorry. Give me a moment, please." She did an about-face and dashed away, disappearing into a smaller room. Two minutes later, the young woman returned to the window. "I'll buzz you in, detective." She pointed to the door.

Al waited to hear the annoying buzz—a sound his ailing head didn't need right now—and entered the bustling office. There must have been a dozen people crammed into the twenty-by-twenty room, shuffling papers, talking on telephones, working on computers, and stuffing folders into metal filing cabinets. From a private office in the far corner a middle-aged woman appeared, marching toward Al with purpose. The rather rotund woman offered her hand.

"I'm Kathy O'Brien, Detective Diaz. Come with me, please."

Al followed the waddling woman to her office and sat in a chair that looked like it should have been donated to Goodwill a decade ago. And Al thought the hospital business was booming. They obviously weren't spending their profits on furnishings. When she closed the door on the closet-sized office, Al suddenly felt claustrophobic. His queasy stomach certainly didn't need a concentrated dose of her cheap perfume. It smelled so sickly-sweet it prickled Al's nose hairs.

Out of breath, O'Brien wedged her hips between the armrests of her dilapidated executive chair, and eased back. "How can I help you, detective?"

"Do you have a physical therapist named Simon working here?"

"Simon who?"

Christ, how many Simons can there be! "Don't have his last name."

"I know most of the employees on a first name basis, but Simon doesn't ring a bell."

He was in no mood for stupidity. "Perhaps you'd be kind enough to call physical therapy and ask?"

She rolled her eyes and thought about his comment as if she were trying to solve a calculus problem in her head. "May I ask what this is all about?"

"It's an urgent police matter," Al barked.

As if she were trying to stare him down, O'Brien glared at Al for a moment. Then, she picked up the telephone and pushed four numbers.

It occurred to Al that Simon could himself answer the telephone, and this nitwit might be dumb enough to tip him off. Al held up his hand. "Wait a minute."

O'Brien held the receiver away from her ear. She cocked her head to one side and peered at Al. "What?"

"Please hang up."

O'Brien dropped the phone in its cradle and sat quietly with her arms folded.

"Ms. O'Brien, this is a delicate matter. If you do have a Simon working here—the one I'm looking for—I don't want to spook him. Understand?" Al gave her enough of an explanation to stress the urgency and the need for confidentiality. Showing a little enthusiasm to help Al for the first time, O'Brien's chubby fingers banged on her computer keyboard.

While watching the blue computer screen reflect in O'Brien's oversized glasses, Al could not repress his growing concern that Sami's kidnapper and the serial killer were one in the same. No matter how hard he tried to dismiss this suspicion as ridiculous, the possibility seemed more than idle speculation. Furthermore, Al could not disregard the convenient timing of Angelina's abduction as mere coincidence.

After several minutes, O'Brien leaned on an elbow and half-smiled, glowing with an air of self-importance. "We have a Simon Kwosokowski employed by us."

Al rubbed his moist palms on his jeans. "He's a physical therapist?"

She nodded.

"Is he working today?"

She held up her finger as if to say, "wait a minute," and pressed a few more keys. She shook her head. "Nope. Used two vacation days. Today and Monday."

Of course, Al thought. How convenient. "Do you have a photograph of him, vital statistics, home address?"

"Give me a minute and I'll pull his personnel file."

While O'Brien searched the file cabinets in the main office, Al sucked in as much un-perfumed air as he could. If he didn't get out of this office quickly, he would surely decorate her desk with his coffee.

O'Brien returned with a manila folder. Again, she stuffed her portly body into the chair and opened the folder. Al's stomach felt like he'd just eaten a dozen jalapeños. For some reason, O'Brien still didn't grasp the exigent nature of the situation. She lollygagged like a woman thumbing through a photo album. Detective Diaz came dangerously close to snatching the folder and verbally abusing her. God how he hated pokey people!

She handed Al a copy of Simon's driver's license.

Al studied it carefully. Name: Simon Kwosokowski. Address: 850 Felspar, Apt. #3, San Diego, CA 92109. Sex: Male. Hair: Brown. Eyes: Blue. Height: 6' 6". Weight: 225. Date of Birth: June 10, 1975.

Al didn't want to panic, but Simon's profile closely fit the serial killer's. He tried to ignore the haunting voice jabbing the back of his mind, but now it screamed.

"Ms. O'Brien, do you know what kind of vehicle Simon drives?"

"Sure do." She leafed through the folder again. "Employees are issued parking permits and we require specific information on their vehicles." She found a copy of the parking permit application. "Here you go, detective."

At first, Al couldn't look at the paper. He felt light-headed, seconds away from vomiting. Then he glanced at the application, hoping that his worst fear would not become reality. With jaw-dropping fear, Al read the words but could not believe his eyes. Simon drove a black Ford Supercab. *God in heaven.* When he found his voice, he looked at O'Brien with misty eyes. "May I have copies of these documents?"

"Surely." She stepped out of the office and returned with the copies, placing them in front of Al. "Is there anything else you need, detective?"

Al could not be certain if O'Brien would call Simon and warn him. How could he control this? He had to rely on her integrity. And integrity—at least from Al's experience—was a lonely word. She seemed like a solid citizen, but Al had met one solid citizen who shook his three-week-old infant to death. He'd met another solid citizen, a well-adjusted sixteen-year-old girl, an honor student with troops of friends and teachers who were shocked when she shot her mother and father in the back of their heads while they slept. If a solid citizen was capable of murder, then one could also pick up the telephone and warn a fellow employee that the cops were hot on his trail.

"Only your promise that you'll keep the details of this meeting confidential."

"You have my word on it."

∽

Al left the hospital and walked out into the bright sunshine, feeling as if he were dreaming.

This has got to be a fucking nightmare!

Always clear-headed and methodical, Al didn't know how to proceed. Under the circumstances, how could he remain objective and repress his fear? When he got back to his car, he telephoned Captain Davison. Maybe the boss could offer some wisdom. He could only pray that Sami and Angelina were not yet harmed.

∽

Quite to Sami's surprise, Simon returned promptly with her purse. She felt uncomfortable wearing her short black skirt and silk blouse—the last thing she wanted was to look sexy—but what were her options? Having turned off the television, Angelina now prepared breakfast for one of the Beanie Babies, and seemed preoccupied enough for Sami to speak frankly without disturbing her.

"Can we talk?" Sami asked Simon. She sat on the edge of the bed facing him.

He set the purse on the floor. "Do you think I'm naïve?"

"You're anything but naïve, Simon."

"Then why do you continue to insult me with this pointless interrogation?"

"I'm quite clear what's going to happen soon. Doesn't it make sense that I would search for a little peace of mind?"

He scratched his stubble. "Okay, I'll concede that point."

"If you truly believe you're doing God's work, wouldn't it make sense for you to console me and help me to repent?" Her tactic a long shot, Sami had to keep him talking.

He kept his distance, and leaned against the door. "Okay, Sami, I'll play your foolish game."

"When will you actually . . ." she couldn't finish the sentence.

"Cleanse your soul?"

She nodded.

"Sunday at six p.m."

That he said it so casually, made her skin crawl. "Does that particular time hold religious significance?"

"No."

"Then why so specific?"

"I have my reasons."

"But you're not going to share them with me?"

"You get the door prize, detective."

Back to the drawing board. "Why do you involve the children? Are they part of the ritual?"

"They serve a purpose."

"Why expose innocent children to such a painful experience?"

"They are not harmed."

"April McDonald might strongly disagree."

His face tightened. "An unavoidable mishap."

"Did God tell you to cut off her ear?"

"Don't be ridiculous."

"Did she disobey you?"

"It was her mother's fault."

"So you don't feel responsible?"

"It was an unfortunate mistake. I've made my peace with God."

"How?"

Simon stared coldly at Sami. He inched toward the bed. Her heart pounded furiously. He unlaced his right sneaker, kicked it off, and pulled off his sock. He pointed to the still-black and blue skin near the missing baby toe. "I have paid my penance."

Sami could barely breathe. It felt like her lungs were full of lead. That he could disfigure himself further illustrated the depths of his insanity. "What must I do to ensure that Angelina is not hurt in any way?"

"Give me your unconditional cooperation."

"And what does that entail?"

"When the time comes, you'll be the first to know." Finality echoed in his voice.

He sat beside Sami and put on his sock and sneaker. "You're having all the fun, Sami. How about I ask a few questions?"

Fun?

She'd never been a violent woman, but Samantha Rizzo could, without guilt or remorse, strangle this bastard to death! For now she had to stay focused on her primary objective. But if she ever got the upper hand . . . "What do you want to know?"

"You're different from the others."

"How?"

"You don't seem frightened or angry."

"Is that what you want?"

"No. But I'd like to know why you're so calm."

"Maybe because of my deep religious beliefs." This, of course, was a total lie. But her answer got his attention.

"Are you a practicing Christian?" A sudden excitement exuded from his intonation.

"I attended both a Catholic grammar school and high school."

"That doesn't make you a Christian. Do you live by the word of the Bible, Sami?"

She couldn't figure out where he was going, but guessed that to portray herself as a God-fearing, Bible-touting woman couldn't hurt. "I believe in God and Jesus Christ and try to obey the Ten Commandments."

The corners of his mouth curled to a smile. "I think you're lying through your teeth."

Sami's Italian temper quickly diluted her sense of reason and self-preservation. "How dare you challenge my beliefs."

"Ah. So you do have a pulse. I was starting to think you were a robot."

Now her blood was boiling. "Is this how you get your thrills, Simon, by tormenting your victims?"

"Thought we were just having a conversation."

"What's next? You going to tear off my clothes and rape me like you did the other four women?"

His face twisted with anger. She struck a raw nerve. "I never touched those women—not in that way."

"That's a bold-faced lie and you know it."

He spoke through clenched teeth. "I said I never touched them!"

"Then explain to me how semen found its way into their vaginas?"

Angelina heard the commotion and ran to her mother's side. Sami held her close.

"That's impossible!" Simon's hands were trembling now.

Sami didn't know how far to push him. Things could get out of hand. Then again, facing certain crucifixion if she didn't take drastic measures would far exceed her current danger. How could she be sure he wouldn't retaliate by assaulting her—or worse—Angelina?

"You may not remember, Simon, but you did have sex with these women, and I can prove it."

His face flushed red and his eyes burned with fury. "You can't prove anything."

Sami had to keep the pressure on. "You're afraid to remember, aren't you, Simon? Terrified that your holier-than-thou crusade is a fraud."

"I fear only God's wrath."

"Do you think God is pleased that you raped these women?"

He charged toward the door. "This isn't over."

When he slammed the steel door, the entire room shook.

Angelina clung to Sami like Velcro. "He scared me, Mommy."

"I'm sorry, honey."

"When can we go home?"

"Soon, Angelina. Soon."

◦◦◦

Brooding over Sami's harsh words, Simon sat in the living room searching his cloudy memory, trying to recall if her accusation had a basis. Absurd as her indictment seemed, there were certain events he could not remember, periods of blackness and blank spaces in the continuity of his Godly work. There were times when one minute he'd be in the Room of Redemption, and the next sitting in the kitchen, without knowing how he got there. But a trigger, usually a confrontation, preceded these blackouts. What happened during the lapses? Could the detective be right? *Impossible!* Then again, maybe she was shrewder than he'd originally thought.

Simon poured a tall glass of milk and guzzled it.

She's getting to you, my son.

"Is it true, Mother?"

If it is, I would be truly disappointed, Simon.

"Tell me, Mother, please."

I cannot watch over you every minute.

"What should I do, Mother?"

Pray, dear boy, pray.

TWENTY

Al pulled the Chevy to the curb in front of eight-fifty Felspar Street, pushed the power button to roll down the window, and turned off the ignition. From a crumpled pack, he shook out the last cigarette and lit it. Sitting quietly, he puffed and observed, trying to unsnarl his tangled thoughts. From where he parked, he could see the Pacific Ocean. White caps rolled toward the shoreline; morning surfers fought for parking spaces close to the beach; traffic on Mission Boulevard—a quarter block away—whizzed by. The sun now dominated the once-overcast sky.

After speaking with Captain Davison, Al could no longer deny the compelling truth: Sami's captor, Simon Kwosokowski, was indeed the serial killer. Al's brain thundered with haunting premonitions, vivid visions of Sami's violent demise. But if Detective Diaz didn't suppress these thoughts, any hope of saving Sami and Angelina would be lost. Al didn't need morbid thoughts clouding his mind. He had to stuff these distracting emotions in a leak-proof vault and seal it shut.

The building Al observed had eight apartments. If Simon lived there, Al asked himself, how could he hold two people captive without neighbors hearing or seeing something unusual? How could he possibly crucify his victims, transport their bodies to east county churches, and drop off the children at local department stores four times without attracting attention?

The area, like most beach communities, throbbed with activity from early morning until the local pubs and restaurants closed. Surely someone would have seen something. If Simon did live in this apartment building, Al doubted that Sami and Angelina were inside. The killer, Al felt certain, performed his diabolical deeds somewhere remote and less populated.

Wearing old blue jeans and a flannel shirt, Al didn't look like a cop. In fact, with his unkempt hair and unshaven face, he looked exactly the way he wanted: inconspicuous and unremarkable. After carefully considering the possible risk, he decided to ring Simon's doorbell. Why not? What could happen? Al pulled the Glock 9mm from the glove box, ejected the clip to be sure it was fully loaded, cocked and locked it, stuffed it in front of his jeans, and covered it with his shirt.

Standing in front of the center entrance to Simon's apartment building, Al noticed eight doorbells to the right of the main door. Next to each doorbell, haphazardly scribbled on withered paper, barely legible, were the occupants' names. Curiously, Simon's name had not been posted next to the apartment #3 doorbell. Instead, Al read the name, Stella Anderson. To be certain his mind had not deceived him, he fished the copy of Simon's driver's license out of his shirt pocket and examined it carefully. Sure enough, Simon—at least in theory—lived in apartment #3.

Al rang the doorbell.

No answer.

He rang it again.

Through the dirty glass on the front door he could barely make out a silhouette erratically moving toward the entrance. He heard the lock click and the door swung wide open. The elderly woman, wearing a shabby lavender robe three sizes too big, couldn't have weighed more than ninety pounds. Her wild hair, pure white, looked as if it hadn't been brushed in days. Dark, puffy bags of flesh hung under her bloodshot eyes. Her total lack of caution struck Al more than her corpse-like appearance. She opened the door not knowing who waited outside. What if he were a thief? Or worse. As a homicide detective, he knew first hand how vulnerable elderly people were. He'd investigated more robbery-homicides than he wished to think about.

The hunched-over woman looked up at Al and squinted. "You got my medicine?"

"Pardon me, ma'am?"

"Medicine! Where's my pills?" The woman looked frail, but barked like a pit bull.

"I think you're mistaken."

She studied Al's face. "Ain't you the delivery guy from"—she paused and shook her head—"Grand Pharmacy?"

"Afraid not, ma'am."

"And stop calling me, ma'am. It's Mrs. William Anderson. If my William were still alive, next month would be our fiftieth anniversary. But after three heart attacks . . ." again she squinted at Al. "Who the hell are you?"

He held his police ID close to her face. "I'm Detective Diaz. May I speak with you for a moment?"

"Am I in trouble with the cops?"

"No, Mrs. Anderson. I'd just like to ask you a few questions."

"You're not here because of those parking tickets I never paid, are ya?"

If people like her were allowed to drive, Al thought, he would surely start taking the bus. "You have nothing to worry about."

"Wanna come in? My apartment ain't nothing fancy, you know." Without waiting for Al to answer, she turned around and shuffled away. Al followed close behind.

Her apartment was tiny, but impeccably tidy. No dishes in the sink, the worn out thick pile carpeting looked freshly vacuumed, and the kitchen floor glistened. A hint of Pine Sol hung in the air.

They sat at the kitchen table.

"I'd offer you coffee, but it gives me the jitters, so I don't buy it anymore. Really miss a good cup of coffee in the morning. Can I get you some herbal tea?"

"No thank you."

"How's about some butter cookies? They're not the store-bought kind. Got 'em at D'Angelo's bakery. They melt in your mouth. Gotta hide 'em from my daughter. She barely leaves me the crumbs."

Al found the old woman charming, but he didn't have the luxury of time. "No thank you. Would you be kind enough to answer a couple of questions?"

She folded her wrinkled hands and rested them on the table. "I'll do my best."

"How long have you lived here?"

"When William died in September of eighty-eight, I sold our paid-for home in La Jolla. Too much upkeep for an old crow like me. Lived near the ocean most of my life, so I got me this here apartment right after the deal closed. I about died when the home William and I paid fifty-thousand dollars for, sold for over a million dollars. Don't that beat all? Gave some of the money to my daughter, the rest I invested in mutual funds. Never live long enough to spend it. I suppose my daughter wouldn't at all mind if her mom died."

If she's the one eating all your butter cookies, Al thought, you're probably right. "Do you know a gentleman by the name of Simon Kwosokowski?"

"Are you a detective or postal inspector?"

"Why do you ask?"

"I warned Simon that someday he'd get in trouble."

"So you know Simon?"

"Such a sweet man. Lived here for a couple years. Treated me better than my own flesh and blood. A real gentleman."

"He doesn't live here anymore?"

"Been gone for a long time."

"Do you know where he lives?"

She shook her head. "I suppose in the country some-where."

"You warned him that he was going to get in trou-ble?"

"With the post office."

"Why?"

"I suppose it's okay to tell you cause you're a detec-tive." Stella Anderson drummed her crooked fingers on the table. "I used to live in unit number two, but when Simon moved out, he convinced me to take his unit. It was a little bigger than mine, had newer appliances, and a nice view of the ocean from the bedroom window. So I said, 'what the heck?' I didn't lift a finger. Simon moved everything for me."

"What did moving into his apartment have to do with upsetting the post office?"

"Simon asked me if it would be okay if all his mail was still sent here—to eight-fifty Felspar, apartment number three. I don't know why he would want to be inconvenienced, but I couldn't see no harm in what he was asking. Only thing is, I thought it was temporary. But seeing as how this little deal's been going on for-ever, I told Simon not too long ago that he better watch out for the postal inspectors. You can't pretend you live somewhere when you don't."

Bewildered, Al asked, "So what you're saying is that Simon's mail still comes to this address even though he hasn't lived here in years?"

"That's what I just said."

"So how does he get his mail?"

"Every Wednesday, after he gets out of work, he swings by and picks it up."

"Only on Wednesdays?"

"You can set your watch by him."

Al felt a twinge in the back of his neck. Today was Friday. The last four victims were murdered less than seventy-two hours after their abduction. By Wednesday, it would be too late. "Do you have a telephone number for Simon?"

"Only his number at the hospital, where he works."

Al pondered for a moment.

"Is Simon in trouble with the police?"

"Possibly, Mrs. Anderson."

"Can hardly believe that." The woman looked at Al, her eyes distant. "Every Wednesday, without fail, when Simon picks up his mail, he takes me to dinner. And I'm not talking about Denny's or a fast food place. Always someplace fancy. Never once did he let me pay." She was lost in her thoughts. "I don't know what you think this young man did, but sure as my name is Estella Abigail Anderson, that boy is as pure as mountain snow."

∽

Al's head was reeling with disjointed thoughts. He couldn't stop thinking about Mrs. Anderson's final words: "pure as mountain snow." If only she knew. It could be possible that he followed the wrong trail, but he didn't think so. In fact, Al felt even more convinced that Simon Kwosokowski and the serial murderer were one in the same. Al knew that most serial killers were schizophrenic, and often displayed split personalities. That Simon lived several distinctly different lives made sense. It explained how such an evil murderer could show kindness to an elderly woman, and possibly to J.T., the homeless man.

If I live to be a hundred, I'll never understand people.

The Pacific Beach post office stood only three blocks from Mrs. Anderson's, so Al decided to have a little chat with the supervisor. The parking lot was jammed, but Al found a spot on the street a block away. When he approached the main door, a line of people snaked outside. At first, he didn't understand why the post office would be so busy Friday afternoon. Then it hit him: he'd forgotten about Christmas. He brushed past a long line of people struggling with packages and bundles of envelopes, and he walked up to one of the clerks as if he had a special pass. He could feel the cold stares of the patiently-waiting patrons angrily accusing him of cutting in front of them. The clerk pointed to the end of the line, but before he could reprimand Al, Detective Diaz stuck his ID under the man's nose.

Al's mood grew more ornery by the minute. "I need to speak to your supervisor right away."

"Yes sir." The tall skinny man almost ran to the private office off to the side. The defiant-looking teenager standing next to Al, sporting trendy sunglasses, obviously unimpressed with Al's credentials, stared at Detective Diaz murderously. Al stared back. The bleach-blond punk wore a pair of jeans so oversized that the crotch hung to his knees. The waist of his pants rested below the young man's hips, exposing more of his festive red and green boxer shorts than any decent citizen cared to see. Wouldn't take much for Detective Diaz to grab the young punk by the nape of the neck and introduce his wise-ass face to the counter.

Al might be able to live with the lad's nonsensical attire, if he didn't exude such an air of antiestablishment arrogance. Al could ignore the ridiculous clothes. But not the attitude. The punk continued to stare at him.

"Excuse me, son, did you happen to read the sign posted on the front door regarding shirts and shoes?" He forced himself to be polite.

"I'm not your son, pal."

Wrong answer. Al grabbed the punk's biceps and squeezed. The man grimaced. "Excuse me asshole, did you read the fucking sign posted on the front door?"

The punk squirmed. The audience mumbled and gasped. "No, I didn't."

"Well the next time you come into the post office, don't forget your shoes and a pair of pants that fit you. Understand?" He let go of the punk's arm.

"Yes, sir."

The postal clerk returned with the supervisor, a forty-ish woman barely five-foot-tall. "My name is Mary Beacham, how may I help you, detective?"

Al didn't think it prudent to put on another exhibition. "Can we talk privately?"

She opened the security door and Al followed her to a small office adjacent to the main counter.

The office, cluttered with piles of legal-size envelopes and manila folders, had one-way, smoked glass, apparently so the supervisor could monitor the activity in the main lobby. The office smelled like a high school locker room.

"I'm trying to find out if you have any forwarding information on a man who once lived at eight-fifty Felspar, apartment three."

She scribbled on a yellow pad. "Can I have his name, please?"

Al spelled it. "Simon K-W-O-S-O-K-O-W-S-K-I."

"Wow, that's quite a handle."

"How quickly can you check?"

"It'll take me no more than ten minutes."

While Al waited for her to return, a wave of helplessness gripped him. Again his temples pounded and his stomach felt like an alien creature would explode through his flesh at any moment. Time burned away, and he hadn't a clue how to find Simon. Yes, he had a plan, and would facilitate it through a series of inquiries—more a process of elimination—but his effectiveness was hampered by an unpredictable timeline. Time was his enemy. At any moment, Simon could decide to make Sami his next sacrifice. The killer wasn't bound by a timetable. There were no rules. Only Simon controlled Sami's destiny. Al could only hope that Sami would find a way to outwit Simon and derail his plan. At least long enough for Al to rescue her.

Another issue gnawed at Al's subconscious: why had he spent the last six years hiding his love for Sami? Such grade-school foolishness. He had no delusions about Sami's love for him. Her feelings were driven purely by friendship. But even if she felt a sliver of what he felt, it could have been a start. He knew now, sitting in this smelly office, that fear had silenced him. Fear of rejection. Fear that their friendship would be jeopardized. Fear that she'd never act quite the same. By his own hand he had issued a verdict and sentenced himself to a loveless existence.

As he thought about his less-than-exciting life, Al bitterly realized that he lived the life of a lonely man. He didn't really participate in life; he stood on the sidelines as a spectator. Other than his sister, Alita, living in Brazil, traveling the world, fulfilling her dream to marry a man of means, Al had nobody. If he could turn back the clock, just for a moment, Al would look into Sami's beautiful blue eyes and tell her exactly how much he loved her.

Mary walked in the door and sat behind her desk. "According to my records, Simon Kwosokowski still lives on Felspar Street. The mail carrier responsible for that area told me that he's been delivering Mr. Kwosokowski's mail to eight-fifty Felspar for years."

"Thank you for your time, Mary."

∽

Deflated and panic-stricken, Al hopped in his car and called Captain Davison. After bringing the captain up to speed, Al said, "The Clairemont branch of the

DMV is only fifteen minutes from here. I'm gonna scoot over there and have them run his VIN and plate number. Hopefully, they'll have his real address."

"Why go to the DMV, Al? We can run the VIN and plates here in the office."

Although the police department had access to the Department of Motor Vehicles database, occasionally an unexplainable glitch in the system would result in inaccurate information. Al wasn't going to take any chances with Sami's life. "I'd rather go right to the source, boss. In the meantime, would you have someone contact Pacific Tel and South Coast Gas and Electric and see if this asshole has a phone or electric service?"

"I'm on it, Al. I'll call you back in thirty minutes."

The conversation was over but neither man hung up.

"She's going to be okay, Al. Sami's a tough cookie. She'll figure out a way to get the upper hand."

"I hope you're right, captain."

TWENTY-ONE

Not surprising, Sami had no appetite, but to absorb the acid eating away at her stomach she had to force something down her throat. As she stood with the refrigerator door wide open, staring at a well-stocked assortment of fruits, vegetables, cold cuts, bread, bagels, prepared salads, cheeses, various dressings, and condiments galore, it struck Sami that Simon's plan might be different than he claimed. If he truly intended to kill her Sunday at six p.m.—the mere thought made her shiver—why had he stocked the refrigerator full of food that would last for weeks? Granted, Simon was completely out of touch with reality. But he wasn't stupid. There was, of course, the grim possibility that he intended to immediately abduct another mother and daughter when his work with Sami was finished. She tried not to consider this scenario.

"Would you like something to eat, honey?"

Angelina was restless; tired of television; bored with the assortment of toys; cranky. She snapped her head from side to side. "I wanna go home, Mommy."

Sami postponed breakfast and sat next to Angelina. Her stomach growled. She combed her fingers through her daughter's hair. "Would you like to play a game, sweetheart?"

"No."

"How about I tell you a story?"

"No!"

Sami didn't know how to occupy her. How do you reason with a two-year-old locked in a cage? "Mommy loves you."

Angelina cocked her head and glanced at Sami. Her mouth twitched to a smile.

"Will you give mommy a hug?"

Eyes moist with tears, throat tightening, Sami held her daughter close.

What a nightmare.

❧

Thoughts of her mother drifted into Sami's mind. She wondered how she was coping with the situation. Foolish thought. How would any mother handle such a traumatic circumstance? If only she could send a message just to let her know that Angelina and she were okay. There was the possibility that Simon had lied, that her mother was . . . Sami pushed the thought out of her mind. She'd give anything to speak to her mom. Ironic, Sami thought. For most of her adult life, she avoided her mother as much as a daughter could, making their encounters as brief and perfunctory as possible. Sami maintained a self-serving kinship, wrestling with this hypocrisy for years. The guilt of daughterly obligation was forever dueling with her free will. She could not deny that she exploited the relationship with her mother, selfishly trading companionship for her mother's babysitting services.

Given over thirty years of vivid examples, no one could deny that Josephine Rizzo was a close-minded, meddlesome old woman. But the compelling question haunting Sami at this moment of self-recrimination was this: why hadn't Sami ever accepted her mother for who she was without judging or trying to change her? There were so many things Sami needed to say. She searched her memory, but could not remember the last time she hugged or kissed her mother. Their relationship had been lacking affection for as long as Sami could remember. Never willing to accept part of the responsibility, Sami now recognized that a good part of their tepid relationship rested on her shoulders.

Sami jumped when the steel door swung open. Lost in her thoughts, she hadn't heard the deadbolt unlock. "Would you go watch television for a while, honey?"

"Do I have to?"

"Please."

Sami waited until she heard the sound from the TV, then left Angelina and sat on the bed. Time for a different tactic. "I owe you an apology, Simon."

He stared at her suspiciously. "For what?"

"I said a lot of horrible things earlier, and I'm sorry."

"I don't expect you to understand all this, but it would be easier for both of us, and Angelina, if you remained civil."

She curled her hands into fists.

I'll show you civil, you fucking asshole! She wanted desperately to smash his face. *Easy, girl. Stay focused.*

"I'd like to learn more about the Bible and redemption. Will you teach me?"

He moved toward her. "You're playing with me."

"I swear, Simon, I'm not. If my life is going to end soon, I want to prepare myself emotionally and spiritually."

"Your life won't be over. It will begin."

"Help me to understand this."

"Would you like to read the Bible with me?" His face glowed.

"Very much so."

He turned and opened the door, his eyes sparkling with spirited anticipation. "I'll be right back."

∾

The line trailing out the front entrance of the DMV looked longer than the one Al encountered at the post office. He slid past the crowd and walked up to the man posted at the central information booth. A young brunette woman waved her arms, inquiring about registering her out of state Toyota. Al stepped in front of her.

He flashed his police ID. "Sorry to interrupt, but I need to run a VIN and plate number immediately."

The man's eyes narrowed. "Can't you do that at the police station?"

"I don't have time to play twenty questions. I need to speak to someone now!"

The man turned around to see which service representative was available. "Go to window four."

"Thank you." Al jogged to the window.

"How may I help you, sir?" The stunning African-American woman smiled.

Al handed her a piece of paper. "Would you check the VIN and plate number of this vehicle and give me the owner's current address?"

"And you are?"

Again he showed his ID. "Detective Diaz."

While she typed, Al admired her lovely face. He glanced at his watch: two-fifteen.

"Well, sir, it seems that the prior owner traded this vehicle in for a new one. Wait just one minute." She pushed a few keys. "Yep. We received the report of sale from the dealer yesterday."

"Can you give me the name and address on the report of sale?"

"Simon Kwos—"

"Kwosokowski?"

"Right."

"What's his address?"

"Eight-fifty Felspar, apartment number three."

Son-of-a-bitch!

"What kind of vehicle did he purchase?"

"A two-thousand-eight Ford Explorer."

"Where did he buy it?"

"Benson Ford in Mission Valley."

In California, license plates were not issued on new vehicles until six to eight weeks after they were sold. "Would you be kind enough to write down the VIN number and a description of the vehicle, please?"

Al dashed out the door without thanking her or saying goodbye. No time to win the Mr. Congeniality Award. Running toward his car, perspiration dripping off his forehead, his cellular rang.

"This is Diaz."

"The plot thickens." Captain Davison's voice had no punch. "South Coast G and E said that our perp canceled his utility service ages ago on Felspar Street and closed the account."

"Well he must have electric service."

"Not in his name."

Al pondered for a moment. "How about Pacific Tel?"

"Same story. Closed the account a long time ago, and never requested they transfer phone service."

"He doesn't have a fucking telephone either?"

"Apparently not. What did the DMV tell you?"

Al gave the captain an update. "I'm on my way to Benson Ford now. Maybe his real address will show up somewhere in the paperwork."

"Check his credit report. Those fuckers know what you ate for breakfast."

"Good idea, boss."

"Keep me posted, Al."

After Al hung up, he pulled copies of Simon's driver's license and parking permit application out of his shirt pocket. The home telephone number listed on the application was 619-555-7288. What did he have to lose? Al dialed the number. After four rings Al heard the recording: "The cellular telephone you are trying to reach has been turned off by the customer. Please try again later."

So, Al thought, the bastard has a cellular. Al guessed there were at least a dozen cellular providers in Southern California. Maybe more. Time to enlist the services of his colleagues. He called Davidson.

"Do me a favor, captain. Our perp has a cellular telephone. If we can find out who's providing his service, they might have his address."

"I'll have someone get right on it."

"While they're at it, have them check with the *San Diego Chronicle* and Southwestern Communications. Maybe the son-of-a-bitch reads the newspaper or watches cable TV."

"Good idea, Al. Anything else?"

"See if he has any relatives anywhere in the country. Can't be too many unrelated Kwosokowski's."

౿

Quite to Sami's surprise, Angelina fell asleep in front of the television. She turned off the TV, carefully lifted her daughter, carried her to the bed, and lay her down. Angelina's timing couldn't be more perfect. She kissed her warm cheek and covered her with a blanket. Still hungry and fighting nausea, Sami ate a sesame bagel with a dab of cream cheese and raspberry preserves, hoping it would absorb the acid churning in her stomach. Just as she swallowed the last mouthful, Simon returned. What she really wanted was a warm shower.

"If you're eating, I can come back," Simon said.

"Just finished." She hadn't heard his tone this friendly since before he drugged her. Maybe playing the role as a woman seeking a spiritual awakening was a viable strategy, she thought.

Instead of sitting on the bed, risking that Angelina would awaken, Sami sat on a small love seat in the play area. Simon sat next to her, closer than she expected him to.

He showed her the Bible, holding it with obvious reverence, pointing to the cover. It was as if he were caressing a priceless figurine. "This is the New Believer's Bible. Its translations are written in a more contemporary manner. Much easier to follow." He handed it to Sami.

She fanned through the pages, stopping every so often and glancing at a page. "Where do we begin?"

For over thirty minutes Simon read various passages about God and Jesus and Satan and salvation. Sami asked questions and Simon answered all of them with the precision and passion of a renowned theologian. That the man sitting next to Sami was the same person who slaughtered four, possibly five innocent women seemed hard to grasp. How could he read the word of

God with complete devotion and then commit such unspeakable acts of violence? She feared him now more than ever.

Somewhere along the way, some thing or some one affected Simon in a profound way, twisted his perspective on good and evil. Sami knew a little about sociopaths. Many were physically and emotionally abused as children. But she never encountered a religious fanatic. This was new territory for her, and she didn't have time for on-the-job training. The man sitting only inches away from her was a cold-blooded murderer, yet he preached God's word like a distinguished pastor.

"Did your parents teach you the word of God, Simon?"

"My father abandoned us when I was very young."

"So your mother was your religious mentor?"

His eye switched. "You could say that."

"Does she live in San Diego?"

"She—" His angst was obvious. "—died about ten years ago."

"I'm sorry."

"For what?"

"That your mother died. You must miss her terribly."

"She's not dead, she just doesn't live an Earthly life."

"Does she ever talk to you, Simon?"

He stared at her. "What are you fishing for, detective?"

"It's called intimate conversation."

He thought about her answer for a moment. "She's warned me about you."

Sami sat upright, her spinal column feeling as rigid as titanium. "She knows me?"

"Better than you could possibly imagine."

"What has she told you about me?"

"She said that you want to seduce me. Make me a sinner like you."

"Do you believe that, Simon?"

"I didn't expect that you accepted my dinner invitation merely because you were hungry for food."

"Have I acted inappropriately?"

"You didn't have a chance to."

"So you expected that I would tear off your clothes after we had dessert?"

"Something like that."

The conversation was not heading in the right direction. "Simon, explain to me why crucifying women does not break the fifth commandment."

"It's complicated."

"God has appointed you to cleanse souls?"

"Indirectly."

"How?"

Simon didn't answer. He tugged on his collar as if it were too tight.

"Does God talk to you through your mother?"

"I know what you're thinking, detective. But you're way off base."

Again Sami hit a wall. "You told me that crucifixion cleanses the soul and ensures salvation, right?"

"It does."

"Are you the only one in the world appointed to perform God's will?"

"I have no idea. God doesn't consult me before making decisions."

"The Bible claims that anyone can be saved, correct?"

"Jesus is the only path to heaven."

"I'm confused, Simon."

"About what?"

"If any mortal can be saved by accepting Jesus into their hearts, then why must you crucify them?"

The question seemed to stump him. "Do you expect me to defy God's will?"

"No. But if people can be saved without dying, I don't understand why God would wish to impose such pain and misery on the families of those crucified."

"You're questioning God's wisdom?"

"Only suggesting that people can be saved without dying." Sami tried to rationalize with an irrational man. She didn't feel as though she were making progress, but pressed on. "Couldn't you save me, Simon, without crucifying me?"

"Not without disobeying God."

"So you really believe that it is God's will for my daughter to be an orphan?"

"Not at all."

"But I'm her only living parent."

With wide-open eyes, Simon glared at Sami. He grinned like a child who just found an unopened package of Oreo's. "Not to worry, Sami. I am quite fond of Angelina."

Suddenly, Sami's heart was racing. "What are you talking about?"

"I can't think of anyone who would be a better spiritual advisor." His face contorted, almost like a monster. "When I'm finished with you, I'm going to adopt Angelina."

All sense of reason vanished. Sami's blood pounded in her temples. "Are you out of your fucking mind?"

∽

Simon stood and headed for the door. Sami charged after him. He turned and doubled-up his fists. She took a hardy swing, aiming for his throat, but Simon blocked it with his forearm, latched onto her wrist and twisted her arm. Sami fell to her knees. Still gripping her wrist, Simon grabbed a handful of hair with his free hand and yanked her head back.

Bonnie Jean Oliver.

He could feel the rage boiling in his gut. Like a slowly-closing curtain, a sheet of blackness fell in front of his eyes. He'd been to this place before, a world out of control. In a few seconds, another self would take over and Simon would be a puppet, his actions manipulated by a demonic force. He knew that Sami's life would abruptly end and he would never have the opportunity to follow the word of God. He couldn't let that happen. Desperate and frantic he appealed to his mentor.

Help me, Mother!

Close your eyes, son. Ask the Almighty to strike down Satan's grip.

Simon squeezed his eyes shut.

Dear God, banish this demon from within. Come into my soul and free me from this evil force.

In the past, he had not been able to summon God's help. Never had he overcome the other self. But today seemed different. Just enough reason remained for him to appeal to his Master.

∽

Sami could feel his grip loosening. Kneeling on the cold concrete floor, she saw his contorted face slowly untwist. Agape mouth, she watched him in stunned silence. An eerie calmness reflected in his eyes, a dramatic contrast from the maniac she observed only seconds before. As if a hypnotist had just snapped his fingers, Simon came out of his trance and looked afresh, like he'd just come back from a brisk walk.

"Such a silly girl. Do you really think you're clever enough to get into my head and outwit me?" He tightened his grip on her hair again. Sami moaned. Tears filled her eyes. "Our foolish conversations are over, Detective Rizzo. I have indulged your fruitless attempts to analyze me long enough. Your low opinion of my intellect insults me. Let me tell you where we go from here, detective. Tonight, at precisely six p.m., I'm going to walk through that door with two four-by-fours, and you're going to watch me assemble a crucifix. Then, you're going to lie on top of it, and by the word of God I'm going to drive inch-thick spikes through your wrists and feet. You're going to scream, Sami, scream like never before. But they will be good screams. Cleansing screams." He licked his lips and his eyes were wild. "In that hole in the concrete"— he pointed to the dirt-filled hole Sami had noticed earlier—"I'm going to erect the crucifix upright, sit by the base, and read you Psalms from the Bible. I will be with you all the way as you journey toward salvation. Jesus will come into your heart, sinner. As you struggle to draw your last earthly breath, the Almighty will cleanse your tarnished soul and purify your heart."

He let go of Sami's hair and wrist and she collapsed, her face pressed against the cold concrete floor. Gasping for air, she lay on her stomach with her eyes closed. She heard him slam the door, and struggled to stand, feeling drunk, disoriented. From the corner of her eye, Sami saw Angelina sitting up, rubbing her eyes.

"Can we go home now, Mommy?"

Sami couldn't find her voice.

TWENTY-TWO

"What an ungodly mess," Al whispered, tightening his grip on the steering wheel.

Such a bizarre phenomenon that Friday traffic in San Diego—for no apparent reason—moved more slowly than any other day.

Where the hell is everyone going at three p.m.?

Frustrated and panicky, he got off the freeway at Seaworld Drive, headed east, and turned right on Morena toward Freeway 8. Benson Ford was located on Auto Circle, an area in Mission Valley where a dozen car dealers sat side-by-side. In an effort to preserve precious minutes, Al thought for an instant about calling the dealer, but how could he prove that he actually was a homicide detective? They wouldn't divulge confidential information about a customer over the telephone. By the time he finished arguing with the sales manager and exercising his Latin temper he'd be pulling into the dealership's driveway.

As Al negotiated his way toward the dealership, weaving from lane to lane, occasionally flashing the beacon and sounding the siren, he was struck by a haunting feeling that he'd forgotten something, as if he just left a supermarket with a cart full of groceries, knowing an item on the shopping list never made it to the cart. An idea ricocheted inside his head, like a bee trapped in a jar, but he couldn't stop it long enough to get a glimpse of what it was. Surely someone knew where Simon lived.

His cell phone rang. He hoped the captain had good news.

"What did you find out, captain?"

"*Amigo?*" Lorenzo's voice bellowed in Al's ear. An image of Rita, Lorenzo's teenage plaything, flashed through Al's mind. He could see her standing in front of Lorenzo, smiling at him while he . . .

"How are you, my friend?" Al said.

"I am doing well."

Al almost asked about Rita, but had no time for idle conversation. He didn't want to offend his dear friend by brushing him off, but couldn't really deal with the distraction right now. "Have you learned anything about Tommy DiSalvo?"

"Just like I told you, trying to compete with Flavio Ramirez was not good for the *gringo*. I knew that the *bandejos* in Tijuana did not kill him."

"How reliable are your sources?"

"*Amigo.* Believe what I tell you. Ramirez cut his balls off. This is how he does business."

"I appreciate your help, my friend."

"When will I see you, again?"

"Not sure, Lorenzo."

"You are always welcome in my home."

"Behave yourself."

"Maybe in my next life."

Al turned onto Auto Circle and could see the Benson Ford sign. "*Adios*, Lorenzo. Take care."

Taking two spaces, Al parked the Chevy in an area designated for customers only. For a moment he sat in the car, staring at a pack of hungry salesman gawking at him through the tinted showroom window as if he were a fresh kill. Sucking in labored breaths, a feeling of great anxiety gripped him. He wanted so desperately to tell Sami that she was in no way responsible for Tommy DiSalvo's death. If only he could give her just a sliver of relief. He could never remember feeling such utter exasperation. It felt as if a priceless antique vase were tumbling to the floor, just out of his reach. No matter how hard he tried, he couldn't quite rescue it before it smashed into a million pieces. At this particular moment, a grim premonition assaulted Alberto Diaz.

I'm never going to see Sami again.

Today, he hated his intuition, and prayed that his instincts were wrong.

His cellular rang again.

This time Al knew he'd hear Captain Davison's voice.

"This is Diaz."

"We struck out, Al. The fucker doesn't have any living relatives, and he doesn't subscribe to the newspaper or cable. Sorry."

"Did you find his cellular provider?"

"He has an account with Sprint, but like everybody else on this fucking planet they have the Felspar address."

Al felt as if he were an over-inflated beach ball that was just punctured. "With all of our goddamn resources we can't find this bastard?"

"We'll find him."

"How, captain? I'm running out of ideas."

"Where are you?"

"About to turn a car dealership upside down."

"Keep your cool, Al. Without a warrant they can tell you to go shit in your hat, so you better find a diplomatic way to approach them."

"One way or the other, I'm going to get my hands on the paperwork, even if I have to walk in the dealer's office and hold a gun to his head."

"Don't do anything stupid, Al. I'm warning you."

He didn't have time to debate. "I'll call you in a little while."

"Al—"

"Gotta go, captain."

The door barely closed behind Al and a salesman cheerfully greeted him. "Welcome to Benson Ford. My name is Bob Daily. Are you looking for a new or used vehicle?"

Crafty, Al thought. The squatty salesman had been trained never to ask a yes-no question. As he'd done so many times this morning, Al showed the smiling salesman his police I.D. "I need to speak to your manager."

Daily led Al to a platform overlooking the show-room. Two well-dressed men stood like sentries watching Al with obvious curiosity. Perhaps they were wondering how much profit they were going to make on yet another naïve car buyer?

"What can I do for you?" the taller of the two asked. The round-shouldered man looked about thirteen months' pregnant. The other man listened passively.

Al explained what he wanted without offering too much detail.

The man shook his head. "Can't let you rifle through a customer's deal folder without the general manager's approval."

"How long will that take?"

"Afraid he's at a convention in Vegas."

"Then let me speak with Mr. Benson."

The man laughed. "He's in Vegas too."

"Then who the fuck is in charge?"

The other man held up his palms as if to say, "whoa." "No need for foul language, detective."

Al glanced at his watch. "Here's the deal, guys: you've got exactly five minutes to produce Simon Kwosokowski's deal folder. If it's not in my hot little hands at precisely three-ten, I promise that in less than twenty-four hours a DMV inspector is going to crawl up your asses and audit every sales transaction for the last fucking decade. How do you think Mr. Benson would feel about that?"

Without saying a word, the portly manager double-timed his hefty body to the main office. He returned with the deal folder in less than three minutes, cheer-fully escorted Al to an unoccupied salesman's office, and welcomed him to take as much time as he needed.

Al closed the door and dumped the contents of the folder on the desk. He could not believe the quantity of papers. It looked more like Simon had bought a home than a car. He examined the buyer's order, DMV forms, mileage affidavits for both the traded and purchased ve-hicle—every form showed the Felspar address. Finally, near the bottom of the pile he found the Experian credit report. He couldn't bear to look at it. As Al pain-fully suspected, not even the credit bureau knew his cur-rent address.

Simon's a goddamn ghost!

He may have been a sociopath, Al thought as he studied the credit report, but the son-of-a-bitch had stel-lar credit—a seven-fifty credit score, which put him in an elite class. Next Al searched for a mortgage lender. Assuming of course that Simon owned a home. For all Al knew, Simon might live in a broken-down barn in East Bumfuck!

Line by line he studied the printout. Three Visa cards: all paid accounts. A Sears card: zero balance. American Express: paid in full. Nowhere on the credit report did Al see a mortgage lender, which meant that either Simon still rented a place or he'd paid cash for his house. Shit.

Now Al looked at the credit application, which pro-filed Simon's vital statistics. Banks required this infor-mation before approving an auto loan or lease contract.

Much of the information was incidental: name, address, employment, income. Al paid particular attention to the area near the bottom of the application that asked for nearest relative. The only thing written was a bold N/A. Below this area Al noticed a section entitled, PERSONAL REFERENCES. Blank.

He returned the deal folder to the men on the platform. "Can either of you tell me why his credit application is incomplete?"

Having learned their lesson, neither manager dared harass Detective Diaz any further. The well-dressed manager huffed and gave Al an evil look. He pawed through the folder and scanned the credit application. "Normally we require completed apps, but when a guy with golden credit pays cash for a thirty-thousand dollar vehicle, we try not to hassle him."

"He paid cash?"

"Not cash-cash. He wrote a check."

"Do you still have the check?"

"Already been deposited."

Al asked them what had happened to the vehicle Simon traded in. The portly manager promptly made a telephone call and informed Al that the Ford Supercab sat in the reconditioning shop. He gave Al directions and he dashed out the door.

∽

As Al approached the detail area where mechanically reconditioned cars were washed, waxed, vacuumed and made "front-line-ready" for the used car lot, he spotted the black Supercab sitting in the last stall. Because unfriendly weather rarely befell San Diego, the long building had only three sides and a corrugated roof, but the front was completely open. A short Hispanic man busily vacuumed the interior of the truck. Al prayed that he hadn't yet cleaned out the glove compartment. After his futile attempt to communicate with Rita and Lorenzo in Spanish, he hoped the man spoke English. How embarrassing to have been born and raised in Mexico, and struggle with his native tongue.

The man gave Al a quick glance but kept busy. Al tapped him on the shoulder. The man flipped the switch on the deafening vacuum cleaner, and stood in front of Al fidgeting like a man with a hornet in his underwear. A broad smile seemed to be frozen on his face.

"*Habla Ingles?*"

The man rocked his head from side to side. "Little bit."

Al identified himself, told the man he needed to check out the truck, and suggested he take a quick coffee break. Without question, the man vigorously retreated a few steps away. Al hopped in the truck and immediately popped open the glove box. Brand-new clean. He flipped open the center console. Empty. Sitting behind the wheel where Simon had sat innumerable times gave Al an eerie feeling. Actually, he felt repulsed. Masked by the perfume of chemicals used to make the interior smell showroom-new, Al could still smell evil. He could feel cold blood seeping through his veins. In spite of the sun-drenched day, he felt chilled from the inside out.

Al spotted the Hispanic man leaning against a bench, puffing heavily on a cigarette, still grinning like a stoned orangutan. Al had seen wiry little Mexicans like him before. They had two speeds: hyper and warp. American companies loved hiring energetic Latinos. They worked their butts off for much less money than Americans, never complained, and unless they were deathly ill, were as dependable as a Maytag washing machine.

He summoned the man with a wave. The man couldn't get there quickly enough. Al glanced at the nametag embossed above the pocket of the man's light blue shirt. "Arturo, were there any papers in the glove box or console?" Al didn't know why, but pantomimed as if he were communicating with a deaf man.

Still grinning, he nodded.

"What did you do with them?"

He pointed to a rusty, overfull barrel the size of a garbage can with a Quaker State motor oil logo on its side.

The last thing Al wanted was to dig through a trash container. Not with his ornery stomach. "Are the papers on top?"

Arturo shrugged.

Not wanting to overlook even the most insignificant remnant from Simon's truck, Al rolled up his sleeves and examined the contents of the barrel one item at a time. Most of what he found was generic pieces of paper and trash, nothing that indicted it once occupied

Simon's glove compartment. Al dug deeper and discovered a receipt for a lawn mower repair. East County Lawn and Garden was located in El Cajon, a community about twenty miles east of San Diego. Al saw Simon's name scribbled across the top, but he'd left the designated address area below blank. Al stuffed the receipt in his back pocket. More junk. The remains of a Big Mac. Coffee cups. A myriad of debris. An oily rag. Wet, smelly rubbish.

He spotted a colorful brochure. The cover looked like a Théodore Rousseau painting. Snowcapped mountains. A blue sky. A crystal-clear pond. Windmills? It had been distributed by a company called Blue Mountain Energy. Al leafed through the pamphlet.

Then it hit him.

A few years ago California lawmakers deregulated the utility industry, crushing South Coast Gas and Electric's hundred year stronghold on the market. This consumer-driven legislation allowed independent utility providers to compete for a piece of the billion-dollar industry. Blue Mountain, an environmentally conscientious company, claimed to offer all-natural energy at a lower cost.

Of course. That's where the son-of-a-bitch is getting his electricity. Perhaps not from Blue Mountain, but from somebody. And whatever company provides his energy, most certainly knows Simon's address.

For the first time since sitting opposite Josephine Rizzo, staring at her sullen face, listening to her terrifying story, Al felt just a thimble-full of relief. He needed to dig further, to search for other treasures, but once again he had to enlist the services of the department. He wiped his hands on the front of his jeans and called Captain Davison. As Al expected, Davison was equally as dumbfounded that neither of them had thought of this angle. In fact, the entire detective squad had overlooked this significant lead.

Davison's voice resonated with energy. "I'll get back to you within the hour with the fucker's address."

Al spent another fifteen minutes playing the role as Trash-Can-Annie, but found nothing else worthwhile. Until he heard back from Davison, he could do nothing but wait. His body was not accepting its reunion with alcohol favorably. His temples throbbed unmercifully and his stomach felt ablaze. As unappealing as the thought was, he had to force some food into his body if he had any hope of counteracting the residual effects of the alcohol.

TWENTY-THREE

Still fuming and injured from her confrontation with Simon, Sami stepped into the shower stall and let the warm water soothe her skin. So inflamed with anger, she grit her teeth fiercely. The mere fact that she stood naked washing her hair and body as nonchalantly as she might at home, completely disregarding the distinct possibility that Simon could wander in at any minute, proved beyond a reasonable doubt that her rational mind was nowhere to be found! Was she as mad as he?

As Sami showered, she kept one eye on Angelina's blurry image through the cloudy glass doors, occasionally sliding the door open and asking if Angelina was okay. Her daughter sat on the bathroom floor playing with Legos. A quick shower was all she needed. Just enough to clear the cobwebs and tend to her injury.

The muscles in her lower back, which had been feeling fine, were again tight and tender. When Simon twisted her wrist and forced her to the floor, she felt a twinge in her pelvis. The twinge subsided, but not before the muscles twisted into a knot. If she wasn't careful, the knotted muscles would spasm and bring her to her knees. She could not afford to be physically impaired. In the past, pulsing hot water loosened the taut muscles. She hoped that once again her home therapy would be successful.

If ever she needed to rouse instincts for self-preservation and tap her sense of reason and logic, it was now. She had lost control, and that posed great danger. To survive, Sami had to tame these incensed emotions and proceed logically. The mere thought of Simon "adopting" Angelina infuriated her beyond any rage she'd ever felt. He had now signed a declaration of war, and Sami wasn't going to surrender without a fight. Her motherly instincts shifted into a no-holds-barred frame of mind, but she had to harness these emotions and focus her energy on a strategic plan.

As she turned in lazy circles, she couldn't help but marvel at the quality and craftsmanship Simon had employed when designing this . . . she didn't know what to call a self-contained studio in the basement of a madman's home. To her it represented a prison. Why would he spend so much money on a facility whose only purpose was to accommodate "sinners" awaiting execution? Further proof that the depths of his insanity had no boundaries. Then again, perhaps it was Simon's way of compensating for his deep-rooted guilt. Could it be that he actually had a conscience?

Not a chance.

The psychotherapy was over. Sami would now engage in a bare-knuckles fight.

She already learned a bitter lesson: trying to outwit Simon and beat him at a game of chess proved futile.

He was too shrewd for an easy checkmate. This battle would indeed be won by the most fit gladiator; a clash to the death. As much as she abhorred the thought, her only chance of survival—unless Al and a posse of detectives showed up with a battering ram and rescued her—would be to physically defend herself, even if that meant fatally injuring Simon. Somewhere in this prison she had to find something she could use as a weapon.

Under the circumstances, the act of violence itself did not bother Sami. She had been placed in a life-threatening situation, and any measure of self-defense, no matter how brutal, would never be questioned. It wasn't in her nature to harm another human, but when she thought about the women Simon had crucified, about the children who were left motherless, about the irrevocable damage to which Angelina had already been exposed, her blood ran cold. Yes, Samantha Rizzo could indeed kill this vile monster. In fact, part of her derived great excitement anticipating how it might feel to strangle the bastard with her bare hands! She was no longer a detective governed by rules of conduct. She now assumed the role of hostage and potential victim. And any measures she employed to defend herself would never assault her conscience.

She once crippled a man; a cold-blooded murderer who tried to kill her. When she fired her weapon she had hoped to hit him in the leg. Instead, the bullet tore into his spinal column, causing irreparable damage. She'd received a commendation for confining a man to a wheelchair. Four years had passed since the incident, and at times, a pang of regret plagued Sami. But Simon and the current situation were different. She could not foresee even a morsel of regret.

There was, however, another alarming issue flashing through Sami's thoughts: how could Sami protect Angelina from witnessing such a heinous act of violence? She could not predict how events would unfold. As of yet she didn't even have a plan. In her mind's eye Sami saw an image of herself bludgeoning Simon to death like a wild woman, while Angelina stood to the side watching in horror. How could a young impressionable mind ever erase such a horrific image? Sami had no choice. She didn't know how, but she would find a way to insulate Angelina from watching her mother batter another human. If she could not, she'd face the consequences later.

Simon didn't know how extensively Sami had been trained in self-defense. She knew exactly where to hit an assailant to incapacitate him. Her earlier exhibition had been driven by anger instead of logic, and the first commandment of self-defense was to remain calm and clear-minded. The second, equally important, was to wait for your opponent to attack first. To maintain her composure and suppress a flood of out-of-control emotions would prove to be a monumental task.

When Sami stepped out of the shower, she dried herself with a thick bath towel, then wrapped it around her body and dried her hair with a smaller towel. Nexxus shampoo and conditioner. Dove soap. Lush towels. As wacko as Simon was, somewhere in his twisted brain lived a repressed man with class.

Such a mystery.

Sami cringed at the thought of wearing her dirty underwear. As she slipped them over her feet her face puckered like she just bit into a lemon. She couldn't pull them past her knees. Disgusting, she thought. With the towel still draped around her, she went to the sink, scrubbed them with soap, rinsed them out, and hung them over the shower doors. For now, she'd have to do without panties. After quietly dressing in front of Angelina, who still occupied herself with the Legos, Sami found a hair dryer in the vanity and dried her hair.

How totally bizarre.

In less than three hours, Simon would walk through the steel door with intentions of crucifying Sami, and here she stood like a teenager getting ready for a prom.

"Are you hungry, sweetheart?"

Angelina vigorously nodded. "Really, really hungry, Mommy."

"Want lunch?"

"Can we go to McDonald's?"

"Maybe tomorrow, honey. How about some chicken noodle soup?"

Angelina wrinkled her nose. "Okay."

After lunch, Sami planned to check every square inch of this prison. Six p.m. drew near. Somewhere in the confines of these soundproof walls were a weapon and a plan.

∞

Al forced two bites of the grilled ham and cheese sandwich down his throat, dropped it on the plate, then nibbled on cold French-fries. Of all the terrific places to eat in Mission Valley, he'd chosen Nikolos' Diner, a fast-food restaurant heavy on the grease and light on the quality. Al would be willing to wager a hefty bank-roll that the chewy ham had once belonged to a pig old enough to collect Social Security. Sometimes he wondered if he purposely punished himself.

With the innumerable resources available to the police department, Al could not fathom how Simon's home address remained a mystery. The lunatic had to live somewhere! It was possible that Simon lived with a roommate. And if his roommate was the primary resident, Simon's name might not appear on anything. Based on what Al had learned about sociopaths, it seemed unlikely that a man as antisocial as he could tolerate a roommate. Then again, who could figure out the pretzel-logic of a serial killer?

Even more than trying to locate Simon's mysterious residence, the possibility that Simon held Sami and Angelina in some remote cabin or abandoned barn, miles away from civilization, troubled Al even more. If Davison called back with good news, it did not guarantee that Sami and Angelina were held captive in Simon's home. Al gripped the seat cushion and dug his nails into the vinyl. He could feel the veins pulsing in his neck.

The waitress, a mid-twenties woman who looked like she could star in an MTV video, streaked-pink hair and all, topped off his coffee cup for the third time in ten minutes. Her flirtatious smiles and constant doting were less than inconspicuous.

She stopped chomping on a wad of bubble gum long enough to speak, and pointed to his sandwich. "Anything wrong with your lunch?"

"It's a culinary triumph."

She set the coffee pot on the corner of the table and planted her hands on her hips. "You're not a regular, are ya?"

"Not hardly."

She glanced over both shoulders checking to see if anyone stood within earshot. "The food really sucks here, doesn't it?" She bent forward and spoke softly. "I get my meals for free but bring a sandwich from home. Can you believe that this joint's been in business since the early sixties?" She shook her head. "Amazing what crap people'll put in their bodies."

Al found her candor amusing.

"Bet you can't guess who ate here yesterday."

"A critic from Food and Wine?"

She giggled. "Carlos Valdez." He was the all-star second baseman for the San Diego Padres. "Right where you're sitting. In this exact booth."

"What did he eat?"

"Apple pie à la mode." She whispered again. "The desserts are good cuz they're from Leo's Bakery."

"I'll keep that in mind."

"Know what? He left me a fifty-dollar tip."

"I'm afraid twenty percent is the best I can do."

"Oh, don't get me wrong. I wasn't hinting that you—"

"Can I have the check, please?"

She licked her ruby-painted lips. "Sure thing." She tore it off the pad. "Um . . . I get off work at six. Can I buy you a beer?"

"I don't drink."

"How about a cappuccino?"

He glanced at her name tag. "I'd love to, Lisa, but I've got other plans."

"Married?"

He shook his head.

"Got a main-squeeze?"

He shook his head again.

"You're not that kind of guy?"

"Precisely. I'm gay."

It took Lisa less than ten seconds to drop the guest check on the table and beeline for the kitchen.

❧

Al sat in his car, staring at the cellular telephone. *Ring, you useless piece of shit, ring!* Totally dumbfounded, he watched droves of people flocking in and out of Nikolos' Diner as if they were dining at the Ritz.

Al's instincts were again warning him of the unthinkable: the possibility that neither technology nor desire could rescue Sami and Angelina. He felt the helpless desperation quietly eroding away at the little remaining optimism. He neared the crucible, a point of no return, a time at which the glass would be half-empty instead of half-full. If Davison's call didn't prove positive, Al would slip into an abyss of total hopelessness.

The cell phone rang and Al snatched it and flipped it open in a heartbeat.

"This is Diaz."

"We came up with a goose egg, Al," Captain Davison said.

These were not the words Al wanted to hear. "You're shitting me, captain. Tell me that this is some kind of perverse-fucking-joke."

"I wish the hell it were. I've had a powwow in my office for the last thirty minutes, trying to brainstorm how to find this slime-ball. Even got the FBI involved." There was a long pause. "We're lost, Al. I don't know where to go from here."

Al could feel a cold dagger twisting in his heart. From his back pocket, he removed the receipt he'd found in the trash barrel at Benson Ford. He stared at it blankly. East County Lawn and Garden in El Cajon was about a twenty-minute ride. If someone there didn't know where Simon Kwosokowski lived . . .

"Al?"

"Yeah."

"I'm . . . sorry."

The captain's voice reeked of resignation. Al wanted to curl up in the fetal position and wither away. But he had to pull himself together and drive to El Cajon. He told Captain Davison about the lawn and garden receipt.

"Have you sent someone to watch her house for any activity, captain?"

"Around the clock."

"And you've got someone calling her home, cell phone and mother's house regularly?"

"On the half-hour."

A long silence.

Davison breathed heavily into the phone. "If you need anything, call me immediately."

❦

Sami lifted Angelina onto her lap. "Would you like to play Hide and Seek?"

Angelina's face lit up. "Yes, Mommy."

Sami wasn't completely comfortable with her plan, but at least she had one. She'd learned through her martial arts training that a rational person had a definite advantage over an opponent driven by anger. And although size did play a role, a clever David could almost always overcome a crazed Goliath. If she could incense Simon to a point at which he'd be consumed with blind rage, she'd have the upper hand. She needed to provoke him beyond reason. A dangerous strategy, especially considering his strength. When he grabbed her wrist and twisted her body to the floor, she felt his power. But she did not have the luxury of options.

"Do you remember how to play, honey?"

Angelina pressed her index finger against her lips. "Shh. You have to be really, really quiet." She thought for a moment. "And hide in a really, really dark place."

"That's right, sweetheart. And if you hear a lot of noise and screaming, what do you do?"

"Don't be afraid?"

"Very good."

Although Sami's lower back still felt tight and could easily worsen, she had to risk injuring it further and paying the painful price. To support her ailing back muscles, Sami tore the bed sheets into several wide strips, wrapped them around the small of her back, and tightly tied them at her waist. The makeshift brace would not offer as much support as the elastic back brace she'd purchased from her chiropractor, but at least it might help.

Careful to use her leg muscles and upper body strength, Sami pushed the love seat across the concrete floor. Her back retaliated with a knife-like jab. She took a breath, bit her lower lip, and barricaded the love seat snugly against the steel door. She realized that the barrier served merely as a temporary safety net, and that Simon would find a way to break down the door even if she wedged the Rock of Gibraltar against it. By postponing Simon's entry though, she hoped to buy enough time to get Angelina settled inside the tall broom closet in the kitchen, and of course to infuriate him.

Sitting on the mattress, Angelina curiously watched her mother moving furniture. "What you doing, Mommy?"

How could she possibly explain her strange behavior to a two-year-old? "When I'm finished, I'll tell you, honey."

Next, Sami dragged the armchair across the floor and tipped the back forward so it leaned against the love seat. Standing upright, holding her lower back, she looked around the room.

∾

Selectively using the siren, Al raced east on Freeway 8 at breakneck speed. Staying in the left passing lane, he occasionally encountered a driver actually observing the speed limit, which in Southern California seemed as rare as July rain. With a quick blast of his siren, panicky drivers couldn't get out of his way fast enough. He exited on El Cajon Boulevard and pulled into the first service station he spotted. The young attendant told Al to drive three blocks, turn left, and continue for about five miles. East County Lawn and Garden would be on the right.

Al could not avoid using the siren and flashing beacon. The boulevard was thick with traffic, and at every intersection the signal lights were forever-red. Once he weaved his way through six lanes of congestion and turned on Redfield Road, he switched off the police accouterments.

Expecting the facility to look like a country Home Depot, Al almost drove past East County Lawn and Garden. The place looked no bigger than a shanty. He turned into the dirt parking lot and a cloud of dust whirled around the car. In front of the small structure were maybe a dozen used lawn mowers and an assortment of various garden-related products, each with a hand-printed sign displaying the discounted price. Al grabbed the receipt and copy of Simon's driver's license and headed for the open front door. The hunched-over man seated behind the counter, repairing a weed-whacker with trembling hands, turned his head and glanced at Al over his reading glasses. The man looked like he'd missed an appointment with the Grim Reaper a decade ago.

"Howdy." His voice sounded gravely, thick with a southern drawl. Strange, Al thought. Thirty miles west of the ocean and it looked and felt like the outskirts of Amarillo, Texas. Al expected tumbleweed to roll across the parking lot at any minute.

Al didn't think it necessary to flash his ID. He laid the papers side-by-side on the glass-top counter. "I'm trying to locate a gentleman who lives in this area."

It took the man awhile to stand. His face twisted with pain. Briefly, he examined the documents. "Yep. That's my receipt all right."

Al pointed to the photocopied picture. "Do you remember this man?"

He lifted a shoulder. "Lots of folks come in here. Hard to remember 'em all."

"This is really important. Please take a closer look."

He poked at his glasses, pushing them up his nose, and scratched his unruly beard. "If my memory ain't playing tricks, he's a big fella." He held his hand about a foot over his head. "Six-six. Maybe taller."

"Do you know where he lives?"

"He ain't a regular, so I can't say fur sure."

"Do you remember if he paid for the repair with a credit card?"

As if overcome with a sudden feeling of pride, the man stood as tall as his twisted bones would allow and pointed to a handwritten sign over his head. "Don't take no checks or those damn charge cards."

"You have no idea where he lives?" Al could feel his throat tightening.

"'Fraid not."

Al stared at the man for several minutes, feeling a compulsion to grab him by the shoulders and shake him silly. He knew nothing about this broken-down old man, but wanted to wring his neck. That he could not tell Al where Simon lived was not the geezer's fault, but Al was beyond proceeding logically. He stuck his police ID under the man's nose and let him get a long look. He picked up the photocopied driver's license and poked his index finger against Simon's picture. "This man is a murderer. He's kidnapping young women and fucking crucifying them! Do you know what crucifixion is, old man?"

The old man wobbled a bit, then groped for the chair just behind him. He sat and ran ten fingers across his almost-bald head. His lower lip was shaking.

"If I don't find the son-of-a-bitch soon, he's going to kill my partner."

"Geez. Wish I could help. Honest. But I just don't know where the guy lives."

∾

Sami barricaded every piece of furniture—including the mattress and box spring—against the door. With her arms folded, she paced barefooted across the cold concrete floor, while Angelina occupied herself sitting cross-legged on the small area rug watching television. Sami licked her lips and whispered to herself, "I'd pay a king's ransom for a Corona right now." Four-fifteen. The hour drew near. With each passing moment, Sami's fear and angst intensified.

Sami amazed at how well Angelina had behaved. The last thing she needed was a whiny, nagging kid. For a child to be incarcerated in this hellhole without having an apoplectic fit was extraordinary. She hoped that her daughter maintained her even-tempered demeanor just a little longer. Angelina had been known to throw a tantrum now and then, and Sami had never been able to foresee these rampages. There had never been a recognizable "trigger," or particular event that preceded these episodes. The last thing Sami needed was for Angelina to go berserk.

Strictly speculating, she guessed that Simon did not crucify his victims in front of the children. Perhaps he escorted them upstairs and either bound or sedated them. She remembered the interviews with the victims' children. None remembered seeing their mothers harmed. It was entirely possible that such a traumatic experience would remain repressed in a child's mind indefinitely. However, if the four children had witnessed the crucifixions, Sami could not fathom that none could remember even sketchy details.

Unable to find anything she could use as a weapon, Sami grew frantic. She rifled through every drawer and cupboard, but nothing would suffice. Exasperated, she glanced at the box spring leaning against the door. The frame—covered with a translucent cloth—was constructed of one-by-four wooded slats. Although the slats were not heavy, if she could pile-drive the butt end of one into the base of Simon's neck as soon as he walked through the door, she might be able to incapacitate him just long enough to retrieve Angelina from the broom closet and escape.

Conscious of her tender lower back muscles, Sami lay the box spring on the concrete floor, face down. She tore away the cloth covering and began twisting the wood slats at the corners where they were held together with thick staples. Surprisingly, she dismantled the frame with little effort. Part of her success, of course, could be contributed to her surging adrenalin. Her muscles were swelled with blood and her heart thumped against her ribs.

Her first inclination had been to remove the power cord from the television. When Simon finally broke through she could stand to the side allowing the swinging-open door to hide her long enough to wrap the wire around Simon's neck and strangle him to the point of unconsciousness. But she feared—particularly because of her ailing lower back—that his sheer strength might be too much for her to handle. Besides, whacking him with a blunt object seemed less intimate than strangling him. Keeping a safe distance made sense.

For her plan to work, Sami had to rile Simon to a point beyond reason. No matter how strong or resourceful, by the time he fought his way past the barricade, she suspected that he'd be exhausted and violently angry. All she needed was a split second, a moment when Simon stood frozen. If he charged into the room like a madman and she concealed herself behind the opened door for just an instant, she could ram the back of his head with the butt end of the slat as if it were a battering ram.

As soon as she dismantled the box spring, Sami recognized that an individual slat would not be effective. Who was she kidding? How could she expect to render a six-foot-six hulk unconscious with a seven-foot one-by-four? It would be like trying to knock out a rhino with a broomstick.

Brainstorm!

Tearing the already-ruined bed sheets into long narrow strips, Sami bound three slats together at both ends and in the center, so her makeshift weapon would have more punch. Surely a seven-foot three-by-four would carry enough wallop to put his lights out. In a little while, she'd know for certain.

TWENTY-FOUR

Al left the lawn and garden shop in a daze. Inundated by a feeling of utter despair, he drove without direction or an intended destination. He felt like a sailboat without sails in the middle of the Pacific, aimlessly adrift. When he looked up and saw the entrance ramp for Freeway 8, he had no idea how he got there. About to turn onto the freeway, he instead pulled to the side of the road, blocked the flow of traffic, and switched on his hazard lights. A motorist behind Al immediately blasted his horn, reminding Al of his discourteous gesture. Al paid no mind. After a caravan of cars joined in the protest, Al continued along El Cajon Boulevard and turned into a small strip plaza. He felt lightheaded and disoriented, as if gripped by a severe case of influenza.

In the corner of the small shopping center Al noticed Jose's Bar & Grill. He parked his car and trudged toward the bar as if walking through mud. Few people patronized the rundown establishment. Good, he thought. Quiet is what he needed right now. A young couple sat at the far end of the bar nursing a giant margarita with two straws. Another man downed a shot glass of tequila with a shaky hand. No more than three tables were occupied with people finishing a mid-afternoon lunch.

Al sat at the bar as far away from the other patrons as possible. Flipping through the channels on a nineteen-inch TV mounted above the bar, the bartender tuned in The Jerry Springer Show and set down the remote.

Great, Al thought. Just what he needed to hear: the sordid details of misfits playing true confessions with their lovers on national television. He tried to tune it out, but couldn't ignore the ranting bleached-blond with the leopard stretch pants and abundant breasts barely covered by a bra-like top. She admitted to her husband in a most animated fashion that she'd been having an affair with another woman. After the outraged husband's carefully censored tirade, the "other woman" traipsed on stage and locked lips with the busty blond while her husband had to be restrained by three stagehands. In the background the audience chanted, "Jer-ree! Jer-ree! Jer-ree!" Al thought he would surely puke.

Standing in front of Al, the bartender slapped his palms on the bar and smiled. "What can I get ya?" The man's teeth were tobacco-stained and his greasy hair hung in stuck-together strands in front of his deep-set eyes.

No Dewar's today. Only top shelf would suffice. "Johnny Walker Black. On the rocks."

The bartender delivered the drink, resumed his position on a stool behind the bar, and watched television. Al sipped the Scotch whiskey and felt it burn a slow trail to his queasy stomach.

∽

The Springer circus had now been replaced by another mindless talk show. During a station break, Al half-listened to a local news brief: "Rancho Santa Fe," the newscaster said proudly, "was just named the most desirable place to live in the country. It was voted even more prestigious than Beverly Hills, which ranked second."

The bartender chuckled. "Shit man." He directed his comment toward Al. "I'd be lucky to pay the property taxes on a pad in Rancho Santa Fe."

Al sat upright in the barstool. "What did you say?"

The bartender folded his arms across his chest. "Said I couldn't scrape up enough money to pay the taxes on one of those uppity estates."

Property taxes? Al fumbled through his pockets and dropped a crumpled twenty-dollar bill on the bar. As he stumbled toward the door, he heard the bartender yell, "Hey, Bud, don't you want your change?"

Al waved his hand as he shoved his way out the door.

The sun warmed his face and the air felt slightly oppressive. Thirty miles from the coast, El Cajon had a reputation for sultry days. He tried to take deep breaths, but the air was too thick. A little woozy, Al tried to focus on rational thoughts. He eased his way into the front seat of his car. He had to clear his head.

On his cellular, Al thumbed in Davison's private number. After four rings, he got the Captain's recorded message.

Where the hell are you!

Al slammed his fist on the dashboard.

A woman walking by his car gawked at him and shook her head.

When he heard the beep, Al said, "Captain, this is Diaz. Call me immediately."

After leaving the message, Al called the precinct's main number. He recognized the administrative secretary's voice immediately. "Gloria, have you seen Captain Davison?"

"And good afternoon to you, too, Detective Diaz."

"Look, I'm in no mood. Where the hell is Davison?"

"I don't see him in his office. Hang on for just . . . a . . . minute. No. He hasn't signed out, so he must be here."

"Where?"

"I don't know, detective. Maybe he's in the bathroom."

"Gloria. This is"—his tongue could barely form words—"a life and death situation. I don't give a rat's ass what you have to do, just find Davison and have him call me at once. Understand?"

"Um . . . yes, detective."

❦

At first when Sami heard the footsteps above her, she panicked and thought Simon was stomping down the cellar stairs. She almost grabbed Angelina and whisked her into the closet, but decided to wait until he actually tried to open the door. It was almost five, and she didn't think he'd be coming quite yet. Of course, she hadn't written the script. Simon was director, producer and leading man. He had liberal creative license to play this out however his twisted mind saw fit. She felt reasonably secure though that he could not possibly break through the barricade in less time than it would take her to safely hide Angelina and position herself beside the door with her lance-like weapon. Then again, when dealing with a man as complicated and unpredictable as Simon, she could not take anything for granted. He might twist the handle a few times, and in a fit of raving lunacy pump enough adrenalin through his powerful legs to kick the steel door open with a few wild thrusts.

The sounds of heavy footsteps persisted, and they annoyed the hell out of Sami. She wondered what Simon was doing. What do murderers do to pass the time while waiting to kill another victim? How do serial killers occupy their leisure time? Maybe they torture stray cats? What kinds of magazines do they read? Guns and Ammo perhaps? What television programs do they like? Probably not Cops or PBS. And what thoughts do they think when fleeting moments of reason prickle their conscience and force them to recognize that their ruthless behavior isn't as honorable as they'd like to believe?

Sami had a lot of questions for Simon. If by the grace of God and a twist of fate she survived this ordeal and didn't lose all sense of self control and civilized conduct by repeatedly pulverizing Simon's head with her weapon, she intended to sit across from his shackled ass, look deep into his eyes, and badger him until she got the answers she needed.

Her emotions continued to vacillate. One minute she felt terrified, the next enraged. Waiting for the inevitable—whatever that might be—was perhaps the most profound torture. Over the last six years, she'd apprehended three murderers who were now serving life sentences. One rapist-murderer waited on death row. In an abstract way Sami more clearly understood just how punishing a lifetime behind bars truly was. All one could do was eat, sleep and think about their miserable existence.

As a detective, Sami had heard all the pro and con arguments regarding the death penalty. Most people involved in law enforcement believed that capital punishment should be a mandatory sentence for violent crimes. Sami had always agreed with this viewpoint, but now she wasn't sure that death by lethal injection or electric shock was indeed as punishing as life in prison. The mental anguish resulting from lifelong incarceration now seemed a more fitting sentence for murderers. She hadn't been in this cage twenty-four hours and as each minute crept by her anxiety grew more unbearable. A vivid image of Simon rotting in a jail cell brought a smile to her taut lips. She longed to be sitting in the courtroom when the judge issued the sentence. To look into his hopeless eyes would surely thrill her to hysteria.

Now Sami heard pounding above her.
Maybe Simon is building the crucifix?

∽

While waiting for Davison to return his call, Al spotted a Starbucks in the strip plaza. Caffeine. That's what he needed. Lots of it. He managed to totter over to the coffee shop, order a gigantic cup of Colombian, and find his way back to the car before his cell phone rang.

"This is Diaz."

"Tell me you have good news, Al."

Al started his car and turned on the air conditioning. "It's a long shot."

"I'm listening."

"If our perp owns a home in San Diego County, he pays property taxes, right?"

"Unless he owns a church, he does."

"Then his name and real address have to be recorded on the trust deed."

It took a moment for Al's theory to sink in. "You may be cooking with oil, Al."

Al filled his mouth with the hot coffee and swallowed. "Do we have an in with the assessor's office?"

"Don't need one. It's public record."

"So I can call the county, give them our perp's name, and get his address?"

"If he owns property in the county you can."

"I'll keep you posted, captain."

"If you find this guy, let's not overreact and storm the fort like a one-man wrecking crew. Call me before you do anything."

Al couldn't hang up quickly enough. He dialed 411 and got the number for the County Assessor's Office. Still dizzy, nerves ablaze, he fumbled with the keypad.

One ring.

Two rings.

"Assessor's office, this is Jodie speaking."

"This is Detective Alberto Diaz calling. I'm trying to locate a piece of property owned by, Simon"—he spelled the last name—"K-W-O-S-O-K-O-W-S-K-I."

She repeated the spelling to be sure she'd written it correctly. "Give me your telephone number, detective, and I'll get back to you in the morning."

"That's not going to fly, young lady. This is a police emergency."

"I see. Um . . . let me talk to my supervisor."

"You've got thirty seconds." The alcohol did not enhance Al's ability to remain tolerant.

By the sound of the garbled conversation, Al guessed she covered the mouthpiece with her hand so she could tell the supervisor that some asshole detective with a bad attitude was trying to rough her up.

"Well, detective, I guess I can help you. But you'll have to be patient for a few minutes while I access our database. It's an old system and sometimes—"

"I don't need an explanation. Just do it as quickly as possible."

Helpless, Al waited. He sat in his car overwhelmed with anxiety, sipping the hot coffee as quickly as he could without burning his mouth. In spite of the cool air fanning his skin, beads of sweat dotted his forehead. With moist hands he tightly grasped the steering wheel. The stubborn alcohol wasn't quite ready to release its grip on his thoughts or motor skills. He felt shaky.

"Hurry," he whispered.

In the solitude of Al's car, the world no longer existed. Only Sami and himself. He couldn't feel the sun reflecting through the windshield, nor could he hear the traffic and activity churning around him. He couldn't smell the lemon-scented deodorizer hanging from the brake release. The taste of Scotch whiskey no longer lingered in the back of his throat. He lived in a world of self-recrimination.

During these quiet moments of waiting, Al again felt overpowered with a feeling of regret for never revealing his love to Sami. Why had he acted like a teenager? How many times in a man's life does he truly fall in love? He worked in a volatile environment; never knowing when he awoke in the morning if this would be the day a criminal's bullet might snuff his life. He'd always lived a somewhat fatalistic life, never believing in saving for the future or planning for his golden years. In almost every aspect of Alberto Diaz's life, he subscribed to the Carpe Diem theory. But not with his hopeless love for Sami. With this, he had tucked it away in a secure corner of his heart, foolishly thinking that one day when the timing was perfect he would offer it to Sami like a gift. The day never came.

Now it seemed that it never would.

Jodie's voice thundered in his ear. "Could you please spell the last name again."

Al could barely contain himself. "K-W-O-S-O-K-O-W-S-K-I."

"Just another minute."

Unless the air conditioning had been designed to make a body drip with cold sweat, it wasn't doing its job. Al's shirt was almost wringing wet. The knot at the base of his neck felt as hard as a golf ball.

"I may have something for you, detective. According to my records, Simon Kwosokowski owns a single family home in Alpine. Eighty-seven-fifty-one, Clearwater Road."

The air slowly escaped from Al's lungs. "And that's the only listing you have?"

"Yes, sir."

"Thank you, Jodie. Sorry if I was . . . a little pushy."

"Don't mention it." Her voice was like ice.

⚭

Al checked his weapon for the second time today to be sure he had a full clip. His hands were shaking, his mouth dry as sand. He grabbed the Thomas guide from the back seat—a required accessory for a man "who couldn't find his ass with a road map," as Sami so often said. Al struggled reading the map. Not having his glasses didn't help the cause. Alpine was about twenty miles away. Other than heading east on Freeway 8, Al wasn't quite sure how to find Clearwater Road. He made a U-turn in the parking lot, chirped a tire turning into the street, and barreled for the freeway ramp.

Once on the freeway, again taking control of the left lane, testing the resolve of the Chevy five-liter engine, Al telephoned Captain Davison and gave him an update.

"Wait until I can send some backup, Al."

"Send all the troops you want, but I'm not waiting, captain."

"I'm not giving you the choice. That's an order."

"That lunatic could be nailing Sami to a fucking cross as we speak, I'm not going to sit here with my thumb up my ass while—"

"What's your plan, Al? You going to knock on the front door? Bust it open with your shoulder? Break into a window? It's broad daylight. Don't you think our perp is wise enough to be on the lookout for unwanted visitors?"

Al thought about that for a minute.

"I know what you're going through, Al, but if he spots you, Sami doesn't stand a chance. You can't tackle this thing half-cocked. You're too emotionally involved."

And a little drunk. "Do whatever you want, captain, but I'm not waiting."

"He's methodical, Al. He's waited at least three days before murdering the last four victims. Sami's got some time."

"How long did he wait to rape them, captain? How many times did he rape them? How long does it take to crucify someone? How long before they die?"

The captain had no retort. "Okay, Al, go with your gut. But I want you to think about this: if Sami dies because of your reckless heroics, are you prepared to deal with the guilt?"

"That's not something I can think about right now."

"I'll contact the El Cajon and Alpine police departments. Backup is on the way."

∽

Simon hadn't eaten anything all day. He'd paced the floors. Tried to read the Bible. Took a long hot shower. Nothing eased his frayed nerves. Something gnawed at his subconscious. He didn't feel the same exciting anticipation. In the past, when the final hours whittled away, his body erupted with fever. All he felt now were doubts and apprehension. He knew that he made a mistake by indulging Sami's futile attempts to get into his head. At the time he found it entertaining, but hadn't realized how insidious its residual effect.

You're such a pathetic fool.

"Please don't taunt me, Mother."

You are so weak, my son.

"I have done everything you've asked."

Ah, but this one troubles you.

"It doesn't feel the same."

The longer you wait, the more difficult it will become.

408

"I don't know what to do."

Do it now, my son, before Satan's grip on your soul forces you to defy God's will. Redeem yourself, Simon.

∽

In less than twenty minutes Al reached the Alpine exit on the freeway, but not without first scaring a few years off the lives of at least six motorists. Slowing down, approaching a stop sign at the exit ramp, Al spotted a convenient store half a block south. Rather than waste valuable time flipping the Thomas Guide every which way trying to find the quickest route to Clearwater Road, it made more sense to ask a local for directions. Al left the motor running while he jogged inside the store. Behind the counter stood an emaciated teenage girl, a modern-day Twiggy wearing more makeup than a circus clown. Her strawberry-colored hair was overdosed with gel, and she looked like a poster girl for anorexia nervosa.

Al prepared himself for the defiant attitude so prevalent in teenagers with that "don't-fuck-with-me" look. Despite her appearance, she cheerfully obliged. In fact, with articulate prose, sprinkled with a few lofty adjectives, she tried her hardest to elicit a conversation with Al, but he dashed out the door with a quick wave.

The Scotch was losing its grip, gradually surrendering to the clear-minded authority of adrenalin. As Al hopped into the car, he could feel his heart hammering against his rib cage. His racing heart didn't need more caffeine, but the rest of his body did, so he emptied the tall cup and tossed it on the floor. Clearwater Road—the teenage girl had said—was less than a ten-minute drive. He glanced at the directions she'd written, took a deep breath, and headed south.

After driving five miles, Al saw the street sign for Clearwater Road on the left. When he turned onto the road he drove slowly so he could read the address on the first mailbox. Twenty-one-twelve. Simon lived at eighty-seven-fifty-one. Al didn't expect the sequence of numbers in a rural area to increase gradually like they did in heavily populated urban areas. The houses were separated by acres of land. He guessed that addresses would ascend by hundreds rather than tens. Sure enough, the next mailbox he passed had twenty-eight-twenty printed in bold box letters. Next to the mailbox he observed a man wearing brown overalls and a badly soiled John Deere baseball cap, sorting through a fistful of mail. The man robustly waved at Al as if they were dear friends. If Al were driving past a home in the city, gawking in the same fashion, the only wave he'd get would be a raised middle finger. Country folk sure were friendly.

Al continued driving just fast enough to read the addresses on the passing mailboxes. In less than five minutes, he saw Simon's house. Just looking at the home sent chills through his body. He didn't stop the car. Instead, he drove slowly past while absorbing as much as he could. The unremarkable home looked much like the other century-old structures in the area, most of which hadn't seen fresh paint or a face lift in decades.

The original clapboard siding was severely weathered and the paint peeling. The windows were trimmed with sun bleached black shutters, and the front door, painted red, was badly faded. There were mature shade trees scattered around the property. Cedars. Cypresses. Elms.

The lawn was overrun with weeds and dandelions, their yellow flowers standing tall.

In the gravel-covered driveway, Al spotted a white Explorer without license plates. He could see the temporary registration scotch-taped to the windshield. He didn't need to compare the vehicle identification number to the one he'd gotten from the DMV to be certain the vehicle belonged to Simon.

This was no doubt the house.

Al continued driving for another half mile. He made a U-turn and parked on the shoulder of the road. What now? How would he get in? Was Sami even inside?

TWENTY-FIVE

The moment Sami heard the key turn in the dead bolt lock, she charged over to Angelina, grabbed her hand, and almost yanked the little girl to her feet.

"Ready to play Hide and Seek, honey?" She was almost panting.

Angelina didn't take her eyes off the television. "Not now, Mommy. Babe is gonna fight with the bad dog." Angelina had watched, *Babe: Pig in the City,* a dozen times, but never grew bored with the movie.

"You can finish watching it later. You don't want Simon to find you, do you?" Her plea was desperate.

Sami heard pounding on the door.

Angelina shook her head. "No, Mommy. Then I would be it! I don't wanna be it."

"Then you better hide."

Without further protest, Angelina crawled into the broom closet and sat as far back as possible.

"Remember what I told you, honey. No matter how much yelling or noise you hear, don't come out of the closet. Okay?"

The pounding got louder and Sami could hear Simon screaming, but she could not make out his words. With trembling hands she picked up the makeshift weapon and assumed her position beside the door. Her heart felt as if it were trying to leap out of her chest.

∽

Totally dumbstruck, Simon stood in front of the steel door shaking his head. That the naïve detective believed she could save herself by barricading the door insulted him beyond words! He leaned against the door with his shoulder and shoved for the third time, but the door opened only slightly. He held his face close to the crack so Sami could hear his warning. "If you don't open this door right now, Sami, I promise you, Angelina will feel my wrath."

No answer.

Simon picked up the longer of the two four-by-fours, held it like a harpoon and rammed it into the center of the door. With an echoing thud, the steel buckled slightly and the painted surface cracked and split. But the door yielded only an inch. Simon's face felt as if it were on fire. His eyes were out of focus. Again he used the lumber like a pile driver and slammed it into the door.

It opened another inch.

A curtain of blackness fell in front of Simon's eyes; an event more frequent of late. He moved only by instinct, as if he were a machine programmed by a mad professor. He did not think about God or his mother or the Bible or his sacred mission. All he could think about was pounding his fists against Sami's face. He wanted to teach her a lesson.

Bonnie Jean Oliver.

You're going to pay for this!

He spoke into the slightly open door. "This is your last chance, wench. If you don't open this fucking door right now, I'm going to cut your daughter's heart out and stuff it down your throat!"

༄

Sami held her ground and remained quiet. All she could hope for was a clean shot the moment he burst through the door. Her barricade had worked well, but soon he'd break through. One shot to the base of his skull. That's all she needed. No second chance if her aim wasn't perfect. To knock him out the impact had to be pinpointed with near precision and the force extreme. The blow could kill him. But Sami had to thrust forward and focus all her weight against the weapon. The time had come to abandon second thoughts or regret.

From the sound of his wild voice, she felt certain Simon boiled with rage. Good. That's what she'd hoped for. Sami knew that if he lost control and all sense of reason, her plan might work. One instant of disorientation, a split second of hesitation is all she needed. But Sami had other concerns. How could she stop her hands from shaking? What if Angelina wandered out of the closet? Suppose Simon didn't give her a clean shot?

༄

Al thought it through carefully, considered every possible scenario, then, reluctantly, he decided to knock on Simon's front door. Any other less-direct approach would most certainly raise suspicions. If Simon spotted him poking around the house, he would surely conclude that Al was either a cop or thief. Either way, the perp would be spooked and take precautionary measures. If Al simply knocked on the door, he could be anyone: a man soliciting magazine subscriptions, taking a survey, or selling Girl Scout cookies for his daughter. Maybe, just maybe, Simon would be foolish enough to open the door. If not, Al would have no choice but to break in and hope for the best.

Another issue perplexed Al, one he had thought about earlier. He couldn't know for certain that Simon held Sami and Angelina captives in this house. Having his Explorer parked in the driveway was a good sign, but still, Simon might own another vehicle and Sami and Angelina could be hidden away in some remote cabin miles from here. Al tried not to think about this dis-heartening twist, but could not deny that it was a viable possibility.

He parked behind the Explorer, quickly checked his weapon one last time, and briskly walked toward the front door. He heard a dog barking and it sounded like the yelps were coming from behind the closed ga-rage door. Almost to the front steps, Al noticed small windows built into the cinderblock foundation. He knew little about construction, but recognized that the windows meant the house had a basement, or at least a crawl space below ground level. It made sense for Simon to keep his victims in a basement. Perhaps in a sound-proof room? Considering that only a handful of homes in Southern California even had basements—most were built on concrete slabs—it seemed appropriate that a murderer who kidnapped his victims and held them hostage before crucifying them would buy a home with a basement.

Al lifted the heavy brass knocker and tapped it against the door three times.

⤫

After repeated blows to the center of the steel door, it yielded enough for Simon to stick his head through the open space. He twisted it from side to side but could not see Sami or Angelina. The furniture piled against the door obstructed part of his view.

"Angelina is dead meat, Sami. You're going to watch me cut her heart out."

⤫

Frantic, Sami could not steady her hands. Suddenly, she realized that her plan was ridiculous. Not only would Simon murder her, but now she had placed Angelina's life in jeopardy. But at this point, it was too late to abort or alter her plan

⤫

Two more thrusts with the butt end of the four-by-four, and the steel door opened wide enough for Simon to squeeze through.

༄

Al knocked more aggressively this time, pounding the doorknocker repeatedly.

༄

Sami caught a glimpse of Simon's face as he tried to wedge his body through the small opening. She held her weapon in its ready position. Two more steps.

༄

The front door was solid wood, so Al could not force it open without making a great deal of noise. But if he chose to enter the house by crawling through a window, Simon might see him and take retaliatory measures. Al would be vulnerable. He had no choice but to burst through the front door. The element of surprise was always an advantage. The compelling question: who would surprise whom? He removed his Glock 9mm from its holster and clicked off the safety. Standing back about three feet, he raised his right foot and kicked the door just below the doorknob.

༄

Simon couldn't quite fit his body through the opened door, so he leaned against it one last time and pushed with his shoulder. As he stumbled into the room, his eyes scanned from left to right looking for Sami and Angelina.

෬

Unable to get a clean shot to the base of Simon's skull, Sami's only option was to drive the weapon hard into the side of his head. She planted her feet, took aim, and with all her might thrust forward.

෬

With his peripheral vision, movement flickered in Simon's right eye. He turned his head quickly and felt something smash into his face.

෬

Sami aimed for his temple, hoping a severe blow would knock him unconscious. When the wood smashed into his lips, his forehead snapped forward and his chin lay against his chest. Blood immediately spurted from his mouth and his arms flailed like a giant eagle unable to fly. Simon's eyes rolled back as his body wobbled. During this harried moment, Sami, realizing that one blow wasn't enough, cocked her weapon and prepared to strike him again.

෬

The door stood strong. It took Al five hefty kicks before the door jam ruptured and the oak door swung open. Holding his weapon with his arms extended in front of him, gripping it tightly with two hands, he slowly moved into the living room, careful of blind corners, resting his index finger on the trigger. He listened for signs that the house was occupied, but heard nothing but the muffled sound of the barking dog. He crept from room to room until he reached a closed door. Carefully, he twisted the doorknob and pushed open the door.

What Al saw when the door swung open sucked the air from his lungs. In the center of the room stood a six-foot tall statue of the Sacred Heart of Jesus, mounted atop a marble pedestal. Lit candles—a dozen or so—three inches in diameter and over a foot tall surrounded the base of the statue. In front of the statue was a small crescent-shaped table covered with a red velvet cloth. On the table were four large restaurant-size glass jars that looked like pickle or mayonnaise containers.

Al walked toward the table to get a better look. Inside each jar an unusual-shaped object floated in some kind of clear liquid, but Al couldn't quite make out what they were. Six steps into the room, Al stood stone-still.

Inside the three jars, floating in formaldehyde, were the perfectly preserved hearts of Jessica Connelly, Linda Cassidy, Molly Singer, and Peggy McDonald. The hearts Simon had cut from their chests and offered to Jesus as tokens of his good deeds.

Al charged out of the room, knowing beyond a doubt that Simon was the serial killer.

Mortified and drenched with sweat, Al tiptoed into the kitchen and discovered an open door with steps leading to the basement. Before easing down the stairs, he listened carefully, and heard something, but did not know what. Musty air enveloped his face. The old stairs creaked with each step down and Al grimaced with anxiety. When he reached the bottom of the steps, he stopped and tuned his ears toward the sound.

༆

Simon blinked the tears from his eyes and saw Sami standing eight feet away, holding a long piece of wood. All he could think about was charging toward her and tearing her throat out with his bare hands. Rage gushed through his body, yet he still maintained control. His mouth, filled with warm blood, dripped off his chin and soaked the front of his white shirt. Simon's temples pounded without mercy. He fixed his eyes on Sami's face and moved toward her.

༆

Sami vaulted forward with her weapon and tried to jam the butt end square into Simon's nose. But Simon, more agile than she thought, and not nearly as incapacitated, reacted swiftly. With a quick Bruce-Lee-like defensive action, he blocked the blow with his forearm, hitting the side of the makeshift weapon with a circular motion, then snatched it with his hand. Sami tried to tighten her grip, but Simon yanked it out of her hands.

Simon grinned broadly and his teeth were as red as V-8 juice. He took a step toward her.

"Where's Angelina?"

Sami backed against the wall.

"I'll find her Sami. And when I do, you can watch me tear her rib cage open and cut her little fucking heart out."

With the grace and speed of a big cat, Simon leaped toward Sami and drove the wooden weapon into her stomach. With the wind knocked out of her, she doubled over and fell on the floor, unable to breathe.

"Ange-leena. Come out, come out wherever you are." Simon inched toward the kitchen.

Al heard a man's voice coming from the other side of the basement. He rushed across the concrete floor and found the partially opened door. He held his head near the opening and listened.

"Ange-leena, it's time to come out. Your Mommy has a present for you."

For a moment, Al froze. He pressed his palm against the center of the door and gave it a slight push. Something prevented it from opening further. He could squeeze through the opening, but not without a little effort and a slight delay. If Simon had a gun, he could easily pump a few rounds in Al's face before he could even begin to defend himself. He listened for Sami's voice, but heard nothing.

❧

Sami couldn't move. Gulps of air came sporadically. Simon had not merely knocked the wind out of her, he had further injured her back. She felt almost paralyzed lying on the floor. Pain shot from her lower back, across her butt, and settled behind her right thigh. Her toes tingled. The makeshift back brace offered no relief. Simon approached the kitchen, dangerously close to where Angelina hid. Sami prayed that Angelina stayed put until she could figure out what to do. But what could she do? With every ounce of strength left in her beaten body, fiercely biting her lower lip, Sami tried to get up. On one knee, as if she were genuflecting, she planted her foot and attempted to stand, but her legs went numb and she fell to the floor.

"Simon, I beg you, please don't hurt my daughter!"

With wild eyes and a demonic grin, he laughed out loud.

ᔆ

Al didn't know exactly what was happening on the other side of the door, but knew he had no choice but to squeeze through the small opening and take his chances. He took two quick breaths, exhaled to make his body as lean as possible, and eased through the door. He saw Simon walking away; his back facing Al. Sami lay on the floor to Al's right. He knew she'd been injured, but to what extent he wasn't sure. That she lay on the floor alive filled him with a wave of relief.

Thank God.

Their eyes met, and Al could see Sami's painful grimace erased by a thankful smile. He gave her a thumbs-up.

Closing one eye and aiming his weapon at Simon, Al shouted, "Put your hands over your head and freeze!"

With grace and a fluid motion, Simon pivoted and fixed his stare on Al. "Congratulations, detective."

Al waved the pistol. "You've got five seconds to lock your fingers together and put your hands behind your head."

Simon grinned hideously, blood still seeping from the corner of his mouth.

From out of nowhere, Angelina appeared. She looked at Al, glanced at her Mother—now sitting on the floor—and froze. She stood inches from Simon, partially hidden behind him. Al took his eyes off Simon for a split second and Simon took full advantage. He crouched down and with one quick motion, grabbed Angelina's arm and yanked her in front of him. He locked his arms around her waist and stood. Angelina now strategically shielded Simon's face and torso.

"It seems we have a standoff, detective." Simon gently stroked Angelina's hair. She didn't seem to mind.

"Put her down," Al ordered.

"Angelina and I are going to play a little game." Simon cupped his hand around the side of her neck, inching his fingers toward her throat.

Angelina began to fidget.

"There, there," Simon said, "everything's going to be just fine."

"In less than ten minutes," Al said, "a dozen cops are going to storm through that door."

"Great. They can join the festivities."

⌒೨

Still in excruciating pain, Sami found enough strength to stand. She extended her arms toward Angelina. "Come to Mommy."

Simon tightened his grip on the squirmy two-year-old. "Angelina's staying with Simon. Right, my little princess?"

Angelina twisted like a worm on a fishhook and started to moan.

Sami no longer operated with all of her faculties or a rational mind. Her actions were motivated by sheer primal instincts. Risky? Extremely. Insane? Perhaps. She was driven by the purest form of survival. With little effort Simon could snap her neck in an instant, but Sami knew that Angelina hated to be restrained, and no matter how powerful Simon might be, when Angelina threw a temper tantrum, she was a handful. Maybe Angelina could distract Simon just long enough for Al to get a clean shot. "Come to Mommy," Sami repeated.

Angelina, now screaming, flailed her arms and legs. Simon was losing his grip. With one quick motion, Angelina's body stiffened, she arched her back, straightened her legs, and the back of her head smacked Simon square in the nose. She slipped out of his arms, and like a little gymnast landed square on her feet, then charged toward her mother with outstretched arms.

Simon covered his face with both hands, moaning in agony. Blood dripped from both nostrils. Al moved toward him and pressed the gun against his temple.

"On the floor."

Without protest, Simon lay face down on the cold concrete and Al secured his wrists with handcuffs. Sami and Angelina were locked in an embrace. Angelina still whimpered, but no longer cried with purpose. Sami let go of Angelina and leaned against the wall.

Her eyes welled with tears, Sami could barely speak. "You're . . . my hero . . . Al."

"All in a day's work." His eyes were misty. "You all right?"

"I need a back transplant, but other than that, I think I'm okay." Sami stepped toward Al and stood only inches away.

Al had his arms around her in an instant, completely forgetting about Sami's back.

"Easy there, cowboy."

Feeling the contours of her body firmly pressed against him, Al closed his eyes and savored the moment. His heart thumped erratically. He tried to say something clever, but the words hung in his throat. He wanted to hold Sami for the rest of his life.

"Have you been drinking, Al?"

Busted. "I guess we need to talk about that."

"Yeah we do."

They stood silent for a few minutes.

Now tears were streaming down Sami's cheeks. She whispered in his ear. "Thank you, partner."

Al let go of Sami and they stood face to face. It seemed as if they stared speechlessly at each other for an eternity, forgetting about Simon and Angelina. He moved toward Sami, and she inched toward him. He saw an invitation in her eyes, a sparkle he'd never seen before.

Angelina tugged on Sami's skirt. "I don't like this place, Mommy. Can we go to grandma's for dinner?"

"Sure, Sweetheart."

Al felt his heart sink.

Sami glanced at Simon, still lying on the concrete floor. Again the anger welled in her gut. "Take Angelina upstairs and call my mom. Tell her we're okay."

"And leave you here with—"

"I'll be fine. I just need a minute."

He handed her his weapon. "Just in case."

৩৩

Reluctantly, Al grabbed Angelina's hand and disappeared behind the steel door. Sami gave them enough time to get upstairs. She limped toward Simon and carefully squatted next to him. He lay on his stomach, watching her, a defiant grin plastered on his sweaty face.

"This is far from being over, little lady."

"Indeed. It's just beginning." She grabbed a handful of his thick hair and yanked his head back. "I want you to know that I'll be in that fucking courtroom every glorious day. Heckling your sorry ass. And when the jury reads the verdict, 'guilty as charged,' I'm going to jump up in the air, hooting and hollering."

"God will protect me, sinner."

"Seems to me that he's already abandoned you."

"What do you mean?"

"You're lying on your belly like the snake you are, and in a few minutes a whole bunch of cops are going to haul your ass to jail."

"The Lord will free me."

"Free you? Ha! You're going to spend the rest of your life in a ten by ten cage. Living like an animal. And you know what else, Simon? Even hardened criminals have a code of ethics, and they don't like rapists or men who hurt children. They're going to get your sorry ass. There's no place to hide in that concrete hell. And one day soon, I can only hope that some seven-foot, three-hundred pound inmate with a real appreciation for boys like you, falls in love with your tight, white ass!"

He lay silent. The defiant grin replaced by grim eyes.

"Hope you rot in hell, you son-of-a-bitch!"

TWENTY-SIX

Captain Davison insisted that Sami take enough time off work to both physically and mentally recuperate. She didn't argue. For three days she could barely get out of bed. She hadn't shared her fierce internal struggle with the captain. During her hiatus she carefully considered whether or not to resign. This decision posed much anguish for Sami. Money, of course, was a primary concern. How would she live? Obligation to her father's dying wish was another issue. Quite to Sami's relief, Josephine Rizzo not only supported Sami, but also suggested that she sell her home and move in with her so Sami could go back to school. If there was some truth to the cliché that good can come from evil, Sami's life-threatening ordeal paved a new roadway to her mother's heart. Things were not the way they should be between mother and daughter; at least not the way Sami envisioned it. However, something positive was happening and for the first time in her life, Sami actually enjoyed spending time with Josephine Rizzo.

After six visits with Doctor Alvarez, chiropractor-extraordinaire, Sami began to feel like a human again. He gave her a series of home exercises and instructed her to perform them religiously. She didn't know if her back would ever be one hundred percent, but at least she had resumed normal activities without feeling gut-wrenching pain.

The nightmares hadn't yet stopped; the horrific image of lying on a wooden cross and feeling Simon drive spikes through her wrists persisted. She didn't expect that pleasant dreams would replace them soon. She thought seriously about seeking therapy. Al, in his own lovable fashion, told her, "People who go to shrinks ought to have their heads examined." But after they stopped laughing, he lobbied hard for her to seek counseling. "Just to clear the cobwebs," he'd said.

Two weeks after Al's heroic rescue, Sami was sitting in her living room watching TV when she heard the doorbell. Expecting it to be Al, who had stopped by to see her every day, she opened the door without first looking through the security lens.

"Are you Samantha Rizzo?" The well-dressed young man smiled warmly. He wore a stylish gray suit and carried a brown leather briefcase. His white shirt was crisply pressed and stark white. Sami guessed that either he wished to sell her something or was a Jehovah Witness looking for converts.

Skeptically, Sami asked, "Can I help you?"

He handed her a business card. "May I come in?"

She studied the card. "I'm really not interested in life insurance."

"I'm not here to sell you any."

Still wary from her ordeal, Sami was not about to let in a total stranger, no matter how innocent he looked. "What's this all about?"

"You're not going to let me come inside?"

"With all due respect—no."

"Were you aware, Ms. Rizzo, that you are named beneficiary to a life insurance policy?"

"Pardon me?"

He squatted, set his briefcase on the step, and flipped it open. After fumbling through a stack of papers, he handed her an official-looking form. "Just sign your name where indicated and you should receive a check in about ten days."

"I think you're mistaken."

"You were married to a Thomas DiSalvo, right?"

Tommy? Al had told her about his covert investigation into Tommy's death. She wasn't shocked when she learned that the supposed gambling debt had been a ploy to exploit money from her. That Tommy had been murdered by a drug dealer did not erase all her guilt or angst, but it served to alleviate much of it.

"I was," Sami whispered.

"Well, Mr. DiSalvo belonged to the Laborer's Union and all members are entitled to life insurance. It's part of their overall benefits' package."

"But Tommy and I have been divorced for years."

"Makes no difference. You're named as sole beneficiary."

Sami gawked at the young man. "This is unbelievable."

431

He handed her a pen. "Would you mind signing the release forms?"

Now Sami felt like a paranoid idiot refusing to let the young man into her home. She stepped to the side and motioned with her arm. "Why don't you have a seat in the living room."

He picked up his briefcase, stepped inside, and sat on the sofa. He handed the release forms to Sami.

Sami read the fine print and stopped cold at paragraph nine. "Two-hundred-fifty-thousand dollars?"

"That's correct, Ms. Rizzo."

༄

The check arrived certified mail five days after the pleasant young man from North Pacific Life Insurance informed Sami of her windfall. In a way, Sami felt uneasy profiting from Tommy's death, but the money would also benefit her daughter. Not that it would make up for Tommy's gross incompetence as a father, but Sami had already spoken to a financial advisor and arranged for a chunk of money to be invested in a trust fund for Angelina.

༄

Except for Al, Sami had not seen any of her fellow detectives or support people from the precinct. When she walked in the front door unannounced, she felt like a movie star. After thirty minutes of goodwill and lots of tears, Sami wandered into Captain Davison's office. Davison wouldn't stand if the mayor walked in, but the moment Sami stepped over the threshold, he sprang off the chair and his arms were around her in an instant.

"Are you ready to go back to work, Detective Rizzo?"

She opened her purse and handed Davison her weapon and badge along with a sealed envelop. "I can't do this anymore, captain."

Davidson tore open the envelope and read it. He fixed his stare on her. "You've been through hell, Sami. It's natural you'd have doubts about your career."

"I no longer have doubts. I want no part of law enforcement."

He looked at her over his reading glasses. "What's your plan?"

"Going back to school to get a degree in social work."

The captain's eyes were misty. "Why don't you take another week or two—"

"That's not necessary."

He sat behind his desk and tapped a cigarette out of the fresh pack. "If you ever change your mind, you know where to reach me."

"Thanks, captain."

He lit the cigarette. "Have you told Diaz?"

"Not yet."

"You're gonna ruin his day."

"If you see him before I do, please don't say anything. I'd like him to hear it from me."

"No problem. I never enjoyed being the bearer of bad news." Davison glanced at the front page of the newspaper sitting on his desk. "Have you heard the latest twist in the case?"

"I haven't looked at the newspaper or watched the news since . . ."

"A panel of psychiatrists has determined that our perp is a bona fide nut-case, but he refuses to let his lawyer use an insanity defense. The jury's gonna fry his nuts."

Sami didn't flinch. What happened to Simon was inconsequential. She just wanted to move forward with her life.

The captain handed Sami a sealed envelope.

"What's this?"

"Betty in Missing Persons said you were trying to track down a couple of people?"

∾

On Christmas Day, just before noon, Sami and Al were on their way to Katie's Kitchen.

"I must be out of my mind," Al mumbled.

"I know a good shrink," Sami replied. "Maybe we can get a group discount."

"How did I let you talk me into this?"

"Don't be such a pain in the ass. It'll be fun."

"If serving chow to a bunch of smelly homeless people is what you call fun, then you need to get a life, my dear."

"You're just pissed cause you had to get up early this morning."

"I'm pissed because Davison wants me to partner-up with Zimmer. The guy's a goddamn relic."

"Look at the bright side." Sami couldn't keep a straight face. "At least you won't have to put up with my PMS-tantrums once a month."

"That's a valid point."

At Sami's insistence, Al had become involved with AA again. He hadn't touched a drop of alcohol since the day he'd rescued Sami.

Sami pulled into the driveway and turned off the ignition. "Are you going to behave yourself, or should I cuff you to the steering wheel?"

"You're not a cop anymore. Remember?"

"Civilians can still buy handcuffs."

"Never guessed you were the kinky type."

"There are lots of tidbits you don't know about me, Al."

Sami hopped up the front steps and Al trailed behind. Surprisingly, the dining room looked only a quarter full. She spotted the man sitting in the far corner. She pointed to the kitchen. "That's where the working folk congregate. I'll catch up with you in a few minutes."

Al shook his head. "Are you going to bond with the homeless people?"

"Something like that."

Sami walked up behind the man and tapped him on the shoulder. He turned and did a double-take.

"By golly, is that you, Detective Rizzo?" He almost knocked over the chair when he stood.

She felt no need to get into a windy explanation about her resignation. "How are you, J.T.?"

"Didn't think I'd ever see you again."

"Me neither."

"I read in the paper what happened. Geez. I'm glad you're okay. The guy who gave me the shoes really was a loony, huh?"

"Indeed." Sami opened her purse and removed an envelope. "I'm afraid I can't return the shoes. Evidence, you know. But I think this will make up for them." She handed the envelope to Williamson.

"Is this a summons to appear in court?"

"Take a look."

Williamson wiped his mouth on the paper napkin and carefully tore the end of the envelope. He unfolded a single piece of paper and squinted it into focus. With his mouth agape and eyes almost bulging, he grasped Sami's hand and vigorously pumped her arm. "Well I'll be damned. I must confess, detective, I never really thought you'd follow through." His face flushed and his eyes filled with tears. "You really found my wife and kid?" Tears seeped from the corners of his eyes. "You've made this a very . . . special . . . Christmas."

Sami removed another envelope from her opened purse and gave it to Williamson.

After he looked at the contents, he almost fell back into the chair. "A plane ticket and five-hundred dollars?"

"Merry Christmas, J.T."

∽

"Now that wasn't so bad, was it, Al?"

"I haven't had that much fun since Doctor Martin checked my prostate. You owe me, Sami, and you owe me big-time."

She glanced at her watch. "My mother won't have dinner ready for another hour. Why don't we grab a cup of Starbucks and walk on the beach?"

"You buying?"

"Absolutely."

∽

Christmas was the only day of the year when Pacific Beach was all but deserted. Al and Sami sat on the sand sipping coffee and watching a handful of diehard surfers. The ocean air felt chilly and the sky was overcast, but Al didn't mind. He snuggled next to Sami, and for the moment his life had meaning.

"Thank you, Al."

"For what?"

"For everything."

"My pleasure."

Sami gulped a mouthful of coffee. "I've got something on my mind."

He turned and looked at her. "I would guess you've got lots on your mind."

"I do. But this has to do with you."

"Am I in trouble?"

"Maybe."

"Should I call my attorney?"

Sami smiled. "Let's be serious for just a minute."

Al listened.

"After you rescued me and restrained Simon, you gave me a hug. Remember?"

How could he forget? "Vaguely."

"When we stopped hugging, I felt certain you were . . . "

Al could feel the blood rushing to his face. "What?"

"Were you going to . . . kiss me?"

Their eyes met and Al was certain Sami could see right through him.

"Well . . . I . . . um . . . guess I kind of thought about it. Um . . . Jesus. I was happy you were alive."

"I see."

They sat silently for a minute.

"So I shouldn't read between the lines and make more of that moment than it was? You were just happy I was alive?"

Al's hands were dripping wet. It felt as if his tongue were three times its size. "Sami, I . . ."

"What?"

I must be out of my mind. She opened the door and I'm slamming it in her face. This is your chance, Al!

A flock of seagulls squawked relentlessly while an old woman tossed bits of bread in the air. A young woman walked past holding a bundled-up infant in her arms. An elderly couple strolled barefoot across the sand.

Al kissed Sami on the cheek.

Their eyes met.

"What was that for?"

Al moved closer. "About that kiss?"

Made in the USA